# THE
# SEVENTH
# STONE

### A THRILLER

## PAMELA HEGARTY

### Sky Castle Publishing

*If you have built castles in the air, your work need not
be lost; that is where they should be.
Now put the foundations under them.
- Henry David Thoreau*

This book is a work of fiction. The author doesn't actually know any maniacal pharmaceutical titans set on creating a new religion even if it means purging millions of lives. Although unsung heroes are no doubt saving the real world as you read this, the characters in this book are imaginary. Much of the history, including the Biblical references to the Breastplate of Aaron, is real.

ISBN 978-0-9630791-3-8

Library of Congress Control Number: 2011917818

Cover Image: Cat's eye emerald superimposed on photo of the Helix "Eye of God" Nebula. Helix nebula image credit: NASA/JPL-Caltech/Harvard-Smithsonian CfA.

*"You shall make the Breastplate of judgment.*
*Artistically woven according to the workmanship of the*
*ephod you shall make it: of gold, blue, purple, and scarlet*
*thread, and fine woven linen...*

*And you shall put settings of stones in it,*
*four rows of stones:*
*The first row shall be a sardius, a topaz, and an Emerald;*
*this shall be the first row;*
*the second row shall be*
*a Turquoise, a sapphire, and a diamond;*
*the third row, a jacinth, an agate, and an amethyst;*
*and the fourth row, a beryl, an onyx, and a jasper.*
*They shall be set in gold settings..."*

-    Exodus 28:30

# DAY 1

## CHAPTER 1
### NAVAJO RESERVATION, ARIZONA

Christa Devlin slammed on the jeep's brakes. He appeared out of the darkness like an apparition. With his wizened face, salt and pepper braid and colorful striped blanket wrapped around his shoulders, he had to be Joseph, the Navajo shaman whom her father had sent her to meet. And she was going to run him down, in the middle of a moonless night about as far from civilization as possible in the lower forty-eight. He stood still as she careened towards him, the tires slewing through the desert sand. He held up his hand. She rammed hers on the horn. The jeep stopped with a jolt, as if the old shaman had stared it down.

This was the man who was going to help her save the world, according to her father. Joseph knew the secret of the Turquoise. The sacred Turquoise. The one stolen from an artifact that had sent armies to war and men to the executioner, the most powerful artifact ever lost to humankind. The ancient ones had squirreled away the Turquoise stone in this canyon five hundred years ago. Hardly bigger than an acorn, she had to find it. In less than twenty-four hours. Before the others who would kill to possess it. She was glad Joseph was on her side.

She drew in a deep breath and shut off the engine. The silence was unnerving. She turned off the headlights. The darkness was complete until her eyes adjusted. Then she could make out objects a good ten feet into the pitch dark. Great. She creaked open the jeep door and jumped down, her hiking boots landing softly in the sand. A river babbled nearby. Insects chirped. The hoot of a lone owl underscored the stillness. She almost longed for the familiar annoyances of a barking dog or fighting lovers, until she looked up. The night sky was alive with stars that most people could only take on faith, framed by the black silhouettes of the canyon walls.

Joseph nodded to her. "It's cold tonight," he said. "Come to the fire." He turned and walked towards a cottonwood grove. He had to be one of Dad's friends, all right, cloaked in mystery with a hint of danger.

She reached to the passenger seat and grabbed her new lucky pack, picked up at the local trading post. When she had dragged her old lucky pack out of the closet for this trip, it stank of mildew. A bad omen. She stretched the elastic band of her new headlamp over her forehead and flicked it on.

Joseph's campfire was in a small clearing beyond the patch of cottonwood trees. He crouched and stirred a log deeper into the coals. Sparks spiraled up into the wisps of pungent smoke. He sat down, tugging his blanket in tighter.

She sat opposite him. "My father sounded desperate last night," Christa said, "when he called from Morocco." More than desperate, he had sounded scared. Dad didn't get scared.

"You've had a long journey," Joseph said. "You should rest. We face a difficult climb in the morning, and we must rise with the sun."

A long journey didn't begin to describe what brought her to this remote corner of the desert on this dark December night. She had all but abandoned her cluttered office back at Princeton, the stacks of final essays to grade for her first History of Exploration class as an assistant professor, and probably any hope of a career at the university. Just like she had abandoned Dad. Not this time. "If that turquoise is out there," she said, "I'm damn well going to find it."

"The future depends on it," he said.

"You believe in the power of the Breastplate."

"Not believe," he squinted into the darkness beyond her, "I know."

The Breastplate of Aaron.  It was a golden shield emblazoned with twelve sacred gemstones, including the Turquoise.  God designed the Breastplate, commanding man to create it, as written in the Book of Exodus, if you believed in that sort of thing.

Aaron, brother of Moses, was the first of the high priests to wear it.  He wore it in the Inner Sanctum, the Holy of Holies, as he stood alone in front of the Breastplate's companion piece, the Ark of the Covenant.  The Breastplate's gems would flash with brilliance and open a portal to Heaven.  The one who wore it could speak directly with God.  He could actually hear God's voice.  Dad was obsessed with finding it and the seven of its gemstones which were stolen from it in the 16th century and concealed around the world.

A sudden flutter of wings and the alarm call of a quail disturbed the cottonwood grove behind her.  She twisted around, but couldn't see further than the firelight's dance on the tangle of tumbleweed.  Nobody could be out there.  Without Joseph's local knowledge, they couldn't possibly have honed in on this stretch of valley so fast.  "But both the Breastplate and the Ark of the Covenant haven't been seen since 586 years before Christ was born," she said, still trying to see into the shadows, "when the Babylonians sacked the Temple of Solomon.  How could the Turquoise stone from the Breastplate have ended up here in Arizona?"

This could be another of Dad's crazy ideas spawned from his fixation on finding the Breastplate.  *Those bastards who are racing after the stones will kill others,* Dad had said last night before the phone line went dead, *just like they killed Mom.  It will kill me, Christa, if we let them win.  The Breastplate will prove that life exists beyond death.  Don't you want to reach Mom?  Don't you want to know that her love for us didn't just end?*

Joseph flung away his blanket and stood, his eyes wide, peering into the cottonwoods.  Christa grabbed the nearest weapon, the burning log.

An old man stumbled into the clearing. His chest was shiny with blood.  His hand clenched a knife. He collapsed face first towards the red Sonoran dust, near the glowing coals of the campfire. Joseph caught him and eased him to the ground. "Samuel," Joseph said.

Joseph reached for his bedroll, then eased up the man's head, and rested it on the makeshift pillow.  Samuel looked and smelled like he'd been wandering the desert for decades, and neither he, nor his matted white beard, had seen civilization, never mind running water, for weeks. He might have appropriated his baggy, threadbare Levis from the skeleton of an unlucky forty-niner. He had tied a prospector's gold pan to his belt. The stink of his sweat and blood made her gag. She stepped back and jammed the log back into the fire. Flames flared up from the coals.

Joseph loosened Samuel's grimy neckerchief and unbuttoned the ragged plaid shirt. The wound in the chest was bad, near the heart. It was circular, as if drilled with a bullet, not stabbed with a knife.

Samuel's eyes snapped open. The knife rolled from his hand. The blade wasn't metal. It was black, obsidian, its jagged edge a telltale sign of being sharpened with flint. Its handle was carved into a crouching jaguar and decorated with turquoise mosaic. She had researched knives like this. It looked pre-Columbian. Most likely Mayan. Possibly sacrificial. What the hell was it doing on a Navajo Reservation?

Samuel grabbed Joseph's shoulder, snatching the flannel like a drowning man clutches a lifeline. "I found it!" he said. He shuddered and coughed. He closed his free hand into a fist, fighting for a breath. "I found the path to the lost cliff dwelling."

Christa drew in closer. The lost cliff dwelling. So the cliff dwelling, at least, could be real. Her father had told her that, five hundred years ago, a sandstorm had buried the remote village inhabited by a mysterious cult of Anasazi Indians. Two days ago, a second once-in-a-millennium windstorm exposed it.

"Samuel, who did this to you?" Joseph asked. Samuel grasped at something tucked into his hip pocket. Joseph eased it out. A dented, stainless steel flask. Joseph unscrewed the top and helped his friend take a sip. She switched on her headlamp and directed it at the cottonwood grove. Nothing.

Samuel swallowed, wheezed and sputtered out a cough that intensified into an incapacitating spasm. He stabbed the darkness from where he came, towards the babble of the river. "All these years, I must of walked beneath it a thousand times. Right above me. I knew it was there, even if I couldn't see it. I knew it." He coughed violently. Blood gurgled onto his beard. "Damn double-crosser. He hired me to guide him, then figured he was going to kill old Samuel, in my desert." Samuel narrowed his eyes at his chest and grimaced. "Reckon he did kill me." He waved a finger at

Joseph. "But not before old Samuel done unto him what he done unto me. Stabbed him with this here knife the ancient ones left behind. I watched him drop right over the edge of that cliff dwelling plateau. Heard him snap when he hit dirt."

"We've got a jeep here, Samuel," Christa said. Whoever did this to him could still be out there, no matter what Samuel believed he'd done. Years travelling with her father had taught her that bad guys were tenacious. "We'll get you to the hospital."

Samuel yanked Joseph closer with surprising strength. "Like hell you will. The bastards are after it, Joseph. They're as close as I am to kingdom come, maybe closer." He sucked in a rattle of a breath. "You're the only one who can beat them. When you get to the body of that scum who killed me, start climbing." He released his grip on Joseph's shirt. "It's an old toe and hand path up the cliff face. It ain't easy, but it's there." His burst of strength played out, Samuel sank back down.

Joseph closed up Samuel's shirt and crossed his hands over his chest. "Goodbye, old friend," he said. He stood and looked towards the river. "We have little time."

She pointed at Samuel. "He has even less, if we don't help him."

"We can only help him by doing what he asks."

Blood oozed rhythmically from Samuel's chest wound. With a rattling cough, he battled every few seconds for a breath. "Joseph, I want to get to that cliff dwelling more than you do," she said, "but I am not leaving him here. Help me get him into the jeep."

"He won't make it," Joseph said. "It takes forty-five minutes to reach the nearest paved road. Two hours from there to the hospital."

"No damn hospital!" Samuel groaned. He raised his hand, as if grasping at the stars. "I am gonna die here, in my desert. And I don't want my spirit to hang around here and haunt you, so you better not let them that killed me win. Now leave an old man alone."

Joseph turned and headed into the cottonwood grove, out of the feeble circle of light cast by the dying campfire.

"Joseph, wait." Damn it. It went against every fiber in her being to leave a man to die. What if it was Dad, lying hurt, with nobody to help him? She grabbed her lucky pack. She swooped up the Mayan knife, the blood on it repulsive and sticky. "Hang on, Samuel," she said. "I swear to you, I won't let them win." Samuel's lips, oddly youthful beneath the white wilds of his beard, cracked into a smile.

## CHAPTER 2

### ONE HUNDRED NAUTICAL MILES
### OFF THE COAST OF MOROCCO

Ahmed Battar did not sweat, until today. He bore the blood of generations of Arab desert tribesmen, which flowed cool in the heat of the sun and true to the values of loyalty. And yet again he had to wipe the perspiration from his brow. He stood on the upper deck of the *Aquila*, anchored one hundred miles west of his homeland and a world away from his beloved wife and daughter. Beneath the surface, a school of silvery pilot fish gathered in the shadow cast by the hull of the *Aquila*. Ahmed watched as their instinct, or a divine plan, guided them to the deception of shelter, just as it coaxed them to school together, in a mass, the weak with the strong. A tiger shark swam into view, its eyes glassy, without emotion. The shark's jaws snapped up one, two, and then three fish as the school circled. As a single mass, the fish darted into the sunlit waters. Only escape, not a shadow of a shelter, could save them. The school survived. The shark, satisfied, slid back into the deep.

On the surface, men toiled in the heat, lashing crates and coiling lines. No breeze stirred the heat, as if Allah had lowered a bell jar over them, to watch and wait. Today, the men were happy. The *Aquila* was a treasure hunter, and they had found their treasure.

Ahmed slipped his hand through the slit in his djellaba, the traditional tunic of his people, and toyed with the tiny device in the pocket of his khakis. He didn't press the button, not yet.

With his other hand, he fingered the photo of his wife, Leila, and their daughter, Ambar. The photo, snapped when Ambar proudly walked her first steps, was creased and faded from the salt air, heat and touch. She was six years old now, could write her own name in flowing if hesitant Arabic, and insisted on the best of manners and sweets at her frequent tea parties. But the photo was still his favorite. He saw in it her innocence, her future, and, most importantly, hope. They had not destroyed her innocence, had not stolen her life, not yet. He had to press the button, but he couldn't.

He eyed the men on the foredeck below him, the men whose lives he would soon put in grave danger. They were securing the last crates under the disciplined but kind direction of Captain Bertoni. Ahmed noticed that the captain's trademark white cotton shirt with red epaulets was damp with sweat. At this morning's briefing, it had been, as always, pristine and starched. The captain doffed his navy cap, looked up to Ahmed and saluted him.

"The captain likes you, kid." The voice startled Ahmed. It was Stubb, the elder statesmen of their crew, with the mind and know-how of an historian and the physique of a longshoreman. He had been with Bertoni for years.

"I admire the captain," said Ahmed, "the way he keeps his ship and crew on an even keel, in calm, or stormy, times."

"It's because he chooses his crew wisely," said Stubb. He pulled out his trademark pipe from his pocket. He no longer smoked it, just chewed on its black nib. "Like when he hired you as translator six months ago. I thought you were a bit too eager to get the job. He said that you reminded him of himself, when he was your age."

The words, meant as a compliment, stung Ahmed like the bitterest insult. He had thought himself clever to secure a position that would allow him to fulfill his vow to Thaddeus Devlin. Now the manipulations needed to retain this job shamed him, but he had no choice. "I knew Captain Bertoni would succeed," he said.

"He had to," said Stubb. "This treasure will buy back his father."

Ahmed couldn't hide his surprise. "The captain has never spoken of this." He thought of his wife, his child. Had the pirates also threatened Bertoni's father?

Stubb clenched his pipe. "His father disowned him," he said. "Dear old Papa got tired of ticking off the years and hundreds of thousands of dollars. Told the captain that a delusional fool could be no son of Antonio Bertoni."

"Then the captain is hunting for more than treasure," Ahmed said, his voice soft.

Stubb pointed his pipe at him. "He is seeking redemption."

"The most elusive quarry," said Ahmed.

"Spoken like someone who seeks it."

Stubb was fishing. Ahmed couldn't take the bait.

"Captain Bertoni almost gave up hope," said Stubb. "I'd watch him, in the wee hours of the morning, his long, vacant stares across the open sea. I thought he might step over the side. Be one with his treasure like Ahab with his whale. He thinks he has found what he was seeking, but I don't believe he has."

"Without belief," Ahmed said, "redemption is hollow."

Stubb slapped Ahmed on the back. "Enough of that. We found the bloody ship, the *San Salvador*, sunk in a storm in this very spot 429 years ago. We've got the conquistador's treasure now. After all these centuries, it will be Captain Bertoni who returns in triumph to Europe with the New World's bounty."

Ahmed could almost believe it. He could almost picture Captain Bertoni returning to his father, opening wide the strongbox brimming with gold, silver, Emeralds and Turquoise. But he knew Mishad and his bloodthirsty pirates were out there, just beyond sight, waiting greedily to rip his captain's dream from his grasp.

Ahmed couldn't fathom how Mishad had learned the secret of the Emerald. When Ahmed was deep inside the medina on their last supply run, he had been pulled aside by the pirate. The cat's eye Emerald, Mishad had said in his hiss of a voice, was of special interest to his "patron." When the Emerald had been recovered, Ahmed was to press this button, signaling them to attack. Mishad, with his dirty hand, shook Ambar's favorite doll. *It was so easy to get it*, he had hissed, *just as it would be to get her if you don't do as I command.*

Stubb bounded down the stairs to the deck, jovially greeting the men. He tightened the lashing on one of the crates.

Ahmed had devised a plan. He had pictured himself saving his family, the men of the *Aquila*, and, most daring of all, the Tear of the Moon Emerald. But now that it was time to take action, an almost incapacitating dread crept over him. The risks were great. His plan could save them, or lead them all into a bloody, painful death. All this, like a poison vine sprouting from a single seed, a gemstone which was better left nascent on the bottom of the Atlantic.

Time had run out. Ahmed saw in his mind's eye little Ambar's smile when she invited him to tea. He felt the silk of Leila's black hair, smelled her lavender perfume. Ahmed fingered the device in his pocket. He flipped it open. He pressed the button.

# CHAPTER 3

Christa pawed around for the next notch that the ancient ones carved out of this vertical slab of a sandstone cliff 1,000 years ago. They called this a toe and hand trail; each notch was only big enough to fit the toe of her hiking boot and the tips of her fingers. Back in their heyday, the Anasazi, or ancient ones, had climbed down to the river valley every morning to hunt and gather. Every evening, they had climbed back up so they wouldn't be hunted and gathered.

After centuries of erosion, the notches were more like dares. Climbing in the middle of the night was crazy. She and Joseph had no choice. Using only the feeble beams of their two headlamps, Joseph had followed Samuel's blood trail from their camp to the river, and then picked it up again after they forded the frigid waters. At the base of the cliff, they didn't find a body, only the crushed creosote bush where Samuel's assailant had fallen. A trail of blood and broken branches led upriver, most likely to his back-up. The tenacious bastard wouldn't be coming back to haunt them. He'd be coming back to kill them. She and Joseph had to reach that cliff dwelling first or all would be lost.

Every loose rock looked like a notch in the shadows cast by her headlamp. She relied more on touch than sight. They had to be about ninety feet above the valley floor, but it was so dark below that it looked bottomless. About ten feet above her, she could just make out the lip of the plateau.

The bang of a rifle split the night. The bullet drilled into the rock three feet above and to the right of her. She snapped back her hand. Slipped. Scrabbled to regain a foothold. Oh God, she was going to fall. She pancaked herself against the cliff. Her heart hammered.

"Headlights," Joseph said. "Opposite rim of the canyon. Quarter mile." He turned off his headlamp.

Her hands shook.  She fumbled with trembling fingers for her headlamp switch and turned it off.

"Hurry," he said.  As if being shot at wasn't motivation enough. Joseph scrambled upwards, as sure-footed as a mountain goat.

Christa was no mountain goat.  The only time her footing was sure was on the fencing strip with a foil in hand.  She had fenced blindfolded once, a coaching strategy.  It hadn't gone well.  She looked back.  Alongside the headlights, a glow rimmed the high canyon wall.  The moon was rising.  She and Joseph wouldn't have the cover of dark for long.  The headlights swung around, towards the dirt road that zigzagged down into the valley.

"He's coming into closer range," Joseph said.

"He can't get a bead on us in the dark," she said, based more on desperate hope than experience.  The barking howl of a coyote punctuated the drone of a car engine.  She felt for the next notch, clamped on and heaved herself up.

Joseph's moccasin disappeared over the rim.

She clambered up behind him, rolling onto the flat, dusty plateau.  The moon breached the horizon.  It was full and bright.  Its light flooded the cave in a timeless silver.  She crouched, too stunned to be sensible and run for the nearest cover.  The cliff dwelling was magnificent.  It wasn't in ruins, but its architecture perfectly preserved from being buried in sand for five hundred years.

Joseph grabbed her hand. Keeping low, they ran away from the edge of the plateau and deeper into the eyebrow-shaped cave.  The cave had to be at least seventy feet wide and thirty feet high, eroded out of the sandstone cliff eons ago.  The pueblos clawed into the recesses of the cave, crammed into its shelter like a child's jumble of building blocks, crafted from crude stone bricks and plastered together with adobe clay.  Many didn't have doorways, and only few had windows; the ancient ones accessed their pueblos via ladders through the ceiling.

Joseph pulled her behind the ruin of the outermost wall.  He was breathing hard.  Sweat beaded around the faded red bandana tied around his forehead beneath his headlamp.  He corralled his salt and pepper braid back over his shoulder.  "This place is not right," he said.

"I agree.  No potsherds.  Not even the charred remains of a cooking fire." She fished the Mayan knife out of her pack.  "But

Samuel said he found this knife here. Did you ever know Samuel to carry a knife like this?"

"As he told us, the ancient ones, the Anasazi, left it for him, here in this cliff dwelling."

"Samuel was dying, possibly delirious. How could the ancient ones foresee a catastrophic sandstorm burying the dwelling in their time, and then, in the future, another windstorm revealing their dwelling, but choose to leave behind only one mysterious knife?"

He turned his dark eyes on her. "It is a useful perspective, to see what waits beyond that which is visible."

"If you're alluding to the Breastplate, that's not why I'm here," she said. "I'm no longer a believer, like my father."

"You will be."

"I don't need the Breastplate to know trouble's coming." She peered over the wall. The headlights bounced jaggedly, halfway down the opposite side of the canyon. "The Breastplate is Dad's Holy Grail, not mine. Or, as I like to think of it, his Moby Dick."

"We seek a piece of the Breastplate, once worn by Aaron, brother of Moses," he said. "Its power destroyed entire villages. It is not to be taken lightly."

"And it's dragging my father to his death," she said. "Throughout history, people have sacrificed their lives for quests for religious artifacts, thinking some divine power will create a happy ending, when it only leads to disaster and ruin." Like in her recurring dream. In it, she held the sacred Breastplate, its gold heavy and warm, sparkling with twelve precious gemstones. The diamond, ruby, Emerald, and sapphire engulfed her in a prism of brilliant, seductive light. But the more she tightened her grasp, the faster the Breastplate disintegrated, falling to her feet as black ash. Somehow, that black ash was Dad.

She pointed to a round building, the size of a large silo. "That could be the kiva," she said. Like the ones she'd studied at other cliff dwellings, a kind of temple, a place for men to sweat and pray. Early kivas were dug out of the ground, a dark respite to the desert sun. Later, the Anasazi built them on the surface, which was less atmospheric, but more elaborate; some were even keyhole shaped. "Let's go."

"That is not the kiva," Joseph said. He scrutinized the dwelling, his eyes squinting with eager fear. "Keep low." He crept along the wall.   His moccasin clad feet barely made a whisper as he approached the circular structure.  Christa followed, each footfall of her heavy tread hiking boot sounding like thunder awaking echoes in the dead, muted air of the cave.  He traced his fingers across the lintel topping the T-shaped portal.  Sweat trickled down the back of his neck to the collar of his plaid flannel shirt.  His hands trembled.  "The ancients who lived here practiced the witchery way," he said.

Cursed.  Dad's kind of place.  "You really think the Turquoise is hidden inside?"  She peered inside the circular chamber.  It was dark, and felt like a trap.

"The Turquoise is close.  I can sense it," said Joseph.  "One of the seven gemstones taken from the Breastplate."

"Right," she said, "by a priest in the sixteenth century, Dad's favorite bedtime story."

"A conquistador found the Breastplate.  He brought it to the new world to begin a new empire with its divine power."   Joseph gestured to the night sky, as if recounting the tale around the campfire.  "A priest saw that the conquistador had used its power for evil.  The priest ripped away seven of the twelve sacred stones from the Breastplate and scattered them around the world.  No man could ever again use its power for evil."

"And the gems and Breastplate were lost to history and humankind," she said, trying to tame her skepticism.  "Listen, I've searched for years for historical evidence to support this story.  Didn't find anything."  *We will find it, Christa,* Dad would say.  *We will write the ending to this story.*  She should know by now.  There are no happy endings.  Only last chances.

An eerie call wafted up to them from below.  It began softly, almost like a hungry infant's pitiful keen.  It quickly intensified in pitch and volume.  A monstrous, primeval howl pierced the night air.  Christa peered over the wall towards the plateau rim.  A sudden breeze sliced through the stubborn scrub that crept between the rocks and scratched cool fingers down the back of her neck.  "What the hell is that?" she whispered.  The yowl spiraled around them.  It was close, very close.  And it wasn't a lone coyote.

Joseph fingered the cowhide pouch strung around his neck, his medicine bag.  "The yee naaldlooshii," he said.  "Protectors of what we seek.  We have awoken them.  They will not sleep again until they kill."

# CHAPTER 4

## VISCILLUS RUINS,
## SOUTHERN COAST OF MOROCCO

Thaddeus Devlin twisted off his neckerchief and rubbed the fine red sand from his Sig Sauer pistol. It had been a long, cold night, waiting, hidden behind the ruins of the Roman wall. He had watched the full moon rise and set while he listened to the waves beat relentlessly against the shore. His back ached, pressed against the rough granite block. He could feel it, like the damp sea air, seeping into his bones. They were coming for the letter. He might have to kill them. He might be damned either way.

"I tell you, Professor Thaddeus," Muktar whispered, "no bad men come. Nothing is here. Nothing for them." Muktar's stomach growled. He tossed the long tail of his turban over his shoulder. Muktar was a good head digger, but too trusting.

"That worker who deserted last night," said Thaddeus, "he overheard my phone call to my daughter about the ancient cliff dwelling revealed in America." The connection had been terrible. The entire nearby village could have heard him shout over the static through the still desert air. "He was a spy."

"Not a spy. Lazy." Muktar spat with disgust.

"Nobody quits a dig as remote as this one in the middle of the night," Thaddeus said, "unless he has a very good reason." Like a lot more money than an archeologist could pay. The location wasn't just isolated. It was forgotten, a rocky patch of Atlantic coastline in southernmost Morocco. Even the locals abandoned it, only leaving behind foundation stones too cumbersome to steal, a ragged reminder of arrogant Roman city planning.

He stretched his right leg to pre-empt the threatening cramp. He couldn't abide these tedious aches and pains. His dimming eyesight was the worst of it. It might affect his aim, especially in low light. He wasn't ready to be old.

Three long years had passed since he had explored this isolated coast, dragging Christa along with him, hoping to mend their father-daughter bond. Christa was so much like Angeline, beautiful, smart and feisty. God, he missed her. He had conducted a cursory search, and found nothing. It wasn't the time. But the events of the past two days couldn't be coincidence. In Arizona, a windstorm revealed the lost cliff dwelling that he was sure concealed the Turquoise. One hundred miles west in the Atlantic, they had found the wreck of the *San Salvador*. By now, they may even have salvaged the Tear of the Moon Emerald. These two of the seven sacred stones stolen from the Breastplate of Aaron had resurfaced against seemingly impossible odds.

"Your loyal friend, Ahmed Battar." Muktar pointed to the vast Atlantic, its eternal waves clawing the gravelly sand down the slope from their perch. "He is close to treasure. Out there, from the wreck of the ship. Not here. No gold and Emerald from across the ocean is here. If this deserter was a spy, then what secret does he know?"

"That it is all happening now," Thaddeus said. "It took me years, Muktar, and miles of searching, but I finally found the clue to Salvatierra's fate buried deep in the Vatican archives. It was nothing more than a soldier's log entry, filed away since the sixteenth century. I could have overlooked it, but the page fell to the floor, as if it is destiny." He was certainly no prophet, but these signs didn't take a prophet to interpret.

Salvatierra had known the enormity of his responsibility, that the power of the Breastplate spanned time. In 1586, Pope Sixtus V sent Salvatierra to the new world to recover the Breastplate of Aaron and stop the conquistador who brought it there to create a new empire with its power. Even then, Salvatierra knew that the Vatican's command was not his destiny, but his story had been lost to time, unless he recorded it in his letter. "That soldier's log entry leads to this place, Muktar. Salvatierra died here, in these ruins. He must have left something behind. I must find the letter he had hoped would reach his brother in the Vatican."

Shouts pierced the silence. Thaddeus yanked Muktar down. The marauders attacked from the east, the rising sun at their backs. "Stealth clearly isn't their strong suit." Thaddeus kept his voice low.

"Which means they're ready to kill." He glanced around the side of the wall. They were hungry and lean in faded sweatshirts and dirty cutoffs,. They headed straight for the huddle of three tents in the old Roman plaza. He leaned in close to Muktar. "Only three of them. One machete. Two with pistols."

They ran into the tents, weapons first, shouting. A camp stool flew out of Thaddeus's tent. A prayer rug was tossed out of Muktar's. They came out again, wide-eyed, scanning the ruins. They had clearly expected to have the advantage of surprise, attacking a presumably sleeping camp at sunrise. They thought it was going to be easy.

Thaddeus put his fingers to his lips and blew. His sharp whistle was the signal. The diggers revealed themselves from their hiding places behind the Roman ruins. Thaddeus and Muktar were positioned on one side of the plaza. The four diggers stood opposite them. Thaddeus had given pistols to four of them, including Muktar, along with a quick lesson in how to shoot them. They had flanked their attackers, but left them a way to retreat. With any luck, the outgunned attackers would simply turn back the way they came. This was a strictly pay for hire operation. This attack was supposed to secure the camp until the trained operatives had time to get here.

The guy in the sunbleached University of Southern California sweatshirt strafed the diggers with his gaze, not bullets. But Thaddeus knew his type. He was calculating odds, forming a plan, figuring out how many diggers he could take down and which of his men it would cost him.

The ruins took on a sudden, unnatural stillness. Above the clawing of the waves, Thaddeus could just make out the soft singing. He picked up the scent of the fresh baked bread. Damn it, it was Ambar, Ahmed's mother. He hadn't warned her. He had been too obsessed with protecting the letter, the letter he hadn't even found yet. She came every morning from the village with fresh baked bread for the camp. She came for any news about Ahmed and to scowl at him for sending her son to work on a boat instead of at home with his wife and her granddaughter.

The guy in the USC shirt swiveled to target her. He'd found his advantage.

Thaddeus swung himself over the Roman wall, landing hard on his stiff legs. Ambar clutched her bundle of loaves closer to her flowing kaftan. He raced towards her. She dropped the loaves to the ground, raised her hands to her mouth in fear. She screamed.

Thaddeus leapt towards her. He spread his arms to create as large a human shield as possible. A force struck him from behind, propelling him forward. A burning pain seared into his shoulder. He reached towards her, shoving her behind the toppled discs of a Roman column.

He toppled to the packed earth, his cheek smacking a Roman paving stone. The air exploded with bangs, screams and guttural shouts. Then silence and the smell of gunpowder blanketed the ruins. A hand pressed against his uninjured shoulder. Then more hands eased him around, onto his back. He peered up to the cloudless sky, vibrant in the sunrise.

"Professor Thaddeus." It was Muktar, leaning over him. "The bad men, they are dead. My diggers killed them. We will dump their worthless bodies into the sea." He spoke with a tinge of pride, but his eyes were wide with fear, and his voice breathless.

"Ambar?" Thaddeus asked. Even the exertion of saying that one word hurt.

"I am here." She was kneeling next to him, her face wizened from years in the sun, but her expression no longer as hard as the cracked earth.

"I'm sorry," he said. "I almost got you killed."

"You save me," she said. She frowned at his wound. "Now, I save you."

But he knew, just as Salvatierra knew when he was dying in these very ruins five hundred years ago, only one thing could save him now. The letter.

## CHAPTER 5

### VICEROYALTY OF NEW GRANADA, SOUTH AMERICA, FEBRUARY 1586

Juan de Salvatierra saw this Godforsaken jungle for what it was, not the genesis of a new world, but the end of the old one. He held a sprig of mint leaves to his nose. The stench of death permeated the air even here, a full day's march from the last village of the dead. The sun's heat held no mercy. Neither could Salvatierra's heart. Like the jungle with its impenetrable canopy, he cloaked himself in the perpetual twilight of despair. He had come here to retrieve the most powerful artifact known to mankind, the Breastplate of Aaron, thought lost for thousands of years. But he had to destroy it, even if it cost his life, even if it risked his immortal soul.

"You must not destroy the Breastplate, Padre," young Elias pleaded with him. The captain and thirteen soldiers behind him glowered in agreement. Their swords and long-shafted halberds clanked as they marched. "The pope commanded you to return it to Rome."

"God has commanded me to destroy it," Salvatierra said. He refused to reveal his doubt that this command could have come from a fevered delirium, not a divine dream. He swiped at a mosquito sucking the blood from the back of his neck. His sandaled foot tripped on a root, stabbing pain into his many sores, rending another tear through his tattered brown robe. He had been a young, hopeful missionary when he left Spain three months ago on the trade wind of hope for the new world. Now his skin was pallid and wrinkled with the relentless damp, aging him to his very core. "I must right what is wrong."

"Forgive me, Padre, but that village back there." Elias nearly jogged to keep up with Salvatierra's long strides. "You saw the evil.

That old man had bashed in the heads of six women," he swallowed, "with a rock." The boy looked at his hand with a perplexed expression as if trying to imagine what could drive a man to do such a thing. Salvatierra slowed as the boy leaned in closer. "That young mother," he said, his voice quiet. Salvatierra understood the boy's fear that such words might beckon the devil. "Her fingers were still clutching the throat of her dead infant."

The innocent killed by the hands of his mother, a young, lithe woman whose own face was beaten beyond recognition until death. That was the image which had galvanized Salvatierra's terrifying decision. She had gone mad, like the others, and murdered the child or, even more heartrending, she had killed her baby to save him from a worse brutality. As Salvatierra and the men followed the muddy river deeper into the jungle, their hearts darkened seeing village after village of savages who had gone mad, then murdered each other brutally before dying themselves. "Do you want to see that in our own country, Elias?" he spat back. "In our own families? That is what the almighty power of the Breastplate can do in the hands of evil men. I must stop it."

He bristled at the muttered curses of the men tramping behind him, a discontented cadence to the spiteful chatter of birds, the menacing growl of a jaguar, the endless buzz of millions of insects. These were feared, ruthless men, but the taste for the fight that lay ahead had soured in their mouths. They knew it would be a fight to the death, with fellow countrymen this time, not savages.

Captain Diaz was a battle-hardened leader and fortune seeker, but it was clear from his expression that he saw their trepidation. He straightened his shoulders and spoke loudly over the howl of a red monkey. "Our reward is nearly within our grasp," he said, clenching the air with his fist. "Isn't that right, Padre Salvatierra?"

"I seek no earthly reward," he said. The men laughed. He was a constant amusement to them, a means for them to bolster their bravado.

"And we will be victorious," said the captain, "for God is on our side."

"If He is not," Salvatierra said, "then we are doomed." This time, the men did not laugh.

"You have your mission, Salvatierra. I have mine. Our Majesty, the King, assigned me this task," the captain boasted.

"Return the traitor, Alvaro Contreras, to Spain in chains. Kill his men and leave them to rot in unconsecrated ground. Contreras did not seek El Dorado. He had the savages bring their gold to him. And we will get a conqueror's share of his treasure. Gold, Emeralds, it waits there, men, just ahead of us. Do what you will with your Breastplate, Padre." He pointed into the dark, dense jungle and breathed in deeply. "I can smell a traitor's blood."

The men penetrated deeper into the heart of darkness. The volcano on the horizon shuddered and rumbled, belching out a hellish, sulfuric smoke. Only young Elias's eyes were still wide with wonder. "The Breastplate, Padre," Elias said. "The others in our Circle of Seven believe it is a weapon of unmatched power."

His inquisitiveness was insatiable, but that's what drew Salvatierra to the boy. Elias was one of five sailors Salvatierra had taught to read using the Bible during their ocean crossing. A sixth man joined their group to teach science and astronomy. He was an aristocrat, hardly more than a boy, who was sent by his father so he would grow iron in his hand and take over the family's business rather than flit about with intellectuals. They named themselves the Circle of Seven. The others in the Circle waited back on their ship, guarding her. Salvatierra now understood the Lord's hand in this. Without the loyalty of the Circle of Seven, his plan would never work.

"Its power is unmatched, as it is the Lord's," Salvatierra said, "but it was never meant to be a weapon, of that I am sure. You have read the passage in Exodus. God commanded man to create the Breastplate. He commanded Aaron, brother of Moses, to wear this very Breastplate to determine God's will for His people, not to destroy them."

"Is it true that the Breastplate allows the wearer to talk to God?" asked Elias. He looked to the heavens with an expression of fright and awe. "That the inquisitors can use it to decide the guilt of a man?"

*The inquisitors need no device to condemn*, thought Salvatierra, *and their thirst is not slaked by burnings at the stake.* He shuddered to think what they would do to him. "In ancient times, the high priest donned the Breastplate to judge the guilt of the accused," he said.

"And we must bring the savages to understand the power of God," said Elias, "but they are terrified of the twelve stones of the Breastplate.  This savage told you."  He gestured towards the shaman guiding them.  "They fear especially the Emerald, the Tear of the Moon."  The brown-skinned shaman was wrinkled and thin, wearing only a loincloth and a necklace strung with a finely wrought, golden pendant.  It was an eagle clutching a figurine of a man in its talons.  Nobody dared steal it.  He carried a blowgun and, incredibly, wore no coverings on his feet.  Though his stature was short, Salvatierra sensed that his heart held more courage than all of the thirteen soldiers who tramped behind him combined.

"I have learned much in this new world," he said.  "Most importantly, to believe what is true to your soul."

"With the Breastplate, the Vatican will have the power," said Elias, "and the divine right, to save and rule over all the souls. Imagine, Padre," he pressed.  "With this Breastplate, we can talk with God.  We will hear His voice, as in the time of Moses."

The words clutched at Salvatierra's heart.  His whole life, he had sought to be closer to the Lord.  Now he might destroy his only chance to be one with Him while still on His Earth.  He could be wrong.  Perhaps he should don the Breastplate, just once.  The ground beneath them trembled.

"Silence," Captain Diaz hissed.  The men halted.  They clutched their weapons tighter.  The heat was stifling, heavy with silence. Salvatierra listened.  A low, keening wail wafted through the forest ahead of them.

The shaman spoke in his melodic, staccato language.  Salvatierra translated.  "He says that wailing we hear is the men from the tribe. They wait for us ahead.  They grieve.  He says the man we hunt is very near."

"And the temple?" Diaz asked, his hand on the hilt of his sword, his expression a fight between dread and lust.  "The treasure?  He shoved aside the shaman and quickened his pace.  The men pushed by to stay on the captain's heels.  Salvatierra hurried to keep up.  He followed as they burst into a clearing.  The men stopped, their bravado sucked out of them like water through a reed straw. Salvatierra could only see above them, to a giant rock outcropping that towered above the trees.

He stretched onto his toes to peer over the soldiers. Savages crowded the perimeter of the circular clearing. Red markings on their naked brown skin mimicked bloodied skeletons. Their posture was unyielding, their eyes black with hate. Three of them gripped Spanish swords, red with blood, at their side. A preternatural silence enveloped the clearing. God had silenced and stilled even the birds and insects. The only movement was the drip of Spanish blood from the tip of a Spaniard's sword.

# CHAPTER 6

Christa spun around as the bloodcurdling yelps and howls shrieked through the haunted walls of the cliff dwelling. The recent drought made prey scarce and predators more aggressive, more territorial. But these howls sounded more vicious than those of ordinary predators. "Those wolves sound crazed, bloodthirsty," she said. *Oh God, those animals could have found Samuel.*

"They are not wolves," he said. "The Skinwalkers are hunting us."

"Skinwalkers." She couldn't hide the skepticism in her tone. "You mean Navajos who have trained in the witchery way," she said. A homicide by Skinwalker monopolized this morning's local headlines. Investigators had found a stick across the victim's throat and a clump of grave grass near her pickup. Skinwalkers had been a part of Navajo culture for years, but the history of these paranormal beasts was scanty. Skinwalker stories might have originated to scare off the white man's western expansion or evolved from when men wore animal pelts for the buffalo hunt. But whatever was howling out there definitely was not human.

"Evil men," said Joseph. "They have the power to shift shapes and the soul of a killer."

"Wolves don't need to shift shapes," she said. "They are born killers." Her only weapon was the Mayan knife. Their only defense might be their position. The ancient ones had built these cliff dwellings in inaccessible caves for protection from predators. The fact that the Anasazi had all mysteriously disappeared centuries ago was not reassuring.

Joseph's expression of dread inspired even less optimism. "You try to understand what you do not believe," said Joseph. "You must believe to understand."

"I believe any creature who howls like that won't settle for a jackrabbit."

"It is human prey they stalk," he said. "Skinwalkers are shapeshifters. They can become a crow, an owl, a wolf." He fingered his medicine pouch like a hunter might judge his load for his shotgun.

"So you're saying they could fly to this cliff dwelling as crows, and attack us as wolves," she said.

"They were human once. Yee naaldlooshii are evil men who have embraced the witchery way. To fully realize the power of Skinwalker, a witch must kill a member of his immediate family."

"Gives a whole new meaning to sibling rivalry."

"They are on the scent of the potential power of evil," he said, "of the sacred stone we seek. They are gathering in the dark. We must leave here. Now."

Joseph was a brave man. That's what frightened her. "I can't leave," she said, "not without that Turquoise."

"Now you believe."

"Not believe, I know. I made a promise to Samuel, and to my father. If there is any chance the Turquoise is here, I'm taking the risk." She stretched on tiptoes to peer down into the canyon. The headlights were barely visible, weaving through the cottonwoods at the foot of the cliff across the river. "Those men chasing us, they won't let wild animals stop them from finding the Turquoise." Dad would never give up, not when that pride of lions stalked their campsite in the Serengeti. Not now. She still had nightmares about it, but had survived. She'd survive this. If only she could stop her fingers from shaking. "This may be our only chance." Slipping sideways through the narrow portal, she crossed the threshold into the circular structure of the cliff dwelling.

It was pitch black. She switched on her headlamp. The room was round, about twelve feet in diameter. Ragged blood stains splotched the pounded earth floor. Samuel must have been shot here, and stabbed his killer.

The howls pierced through the portal, swirling around her like a whirlwind. A scuffling at the doorway. Joseph. He didn't abandon her. She wanted to hug him. Instead, she crouched, looked up. The stone ceiling formed a stepped pyramid, twenty feet above their heads. "A pyramid?" she said, her whisper of a voice like thunder in the small room. "Not exactly typical Anasazi architecture."

Joseph flicked on his headlamp. "This was not a typical Anasazi village." His beam and hers joined in a macabre waltz, twisting and weaving across the stone walls.

"The walls are more Incan than Anasazi," she said. "The sandstone blocks are precisely hewn and fitted together, without mortar." The beasts' howls grew more strident, a bone-chilling chorus of yelps and wails. All she needed was one speck of evidence, one clue to the location of the Turquoise, to know that this was worth the risk, to take that last leap of faith. The chamber was eerily beautiful, and utterly empty.

Dad would have found it, an archaeological anomaly, an unnaturally shaped stone, *a bump in the wall*. Her beam tripped over it, on the stone abutting the entrance, no more than a flicker of a shadow. She drew closer and ran her fingertips over a rough brick of stone. It was eye level, a perfect, 15-inch square. In its center, it had an indentation nearly obscured by centuries of dust. She directed her light and blew on the stone. A billow of fine, silvery sand danced in the beam of her light. This was no stonecutter's slip. It was a symbol. Joseph came beside her. The symbol had four cardinal points, like a compass, each point marked with four lines, like rays.

"The Navajo symbol for sun," said Joseph. He wiped his sleeve across his sweaty upper lip. "For life, growth, and all that is good."

"Of course, I recognize it now." She brushed off the stone's squared edges with the flat of her hand. "This stone with the symbol isn't flush like the others. It sticks out a little. It could hide a secret niche. The Turquoise could be right here, behind this stone." The beasts yowled. "Come on, help me get it out." She hooked her fingertips on the edge of the stone and shimmied it. Dust and gravel rained down on them from the pyramid roof above them. The whole chamber shook and trembled. A massive brick cracked out of the ceiling. It slammed to the floor so close that its concussion puffed away the dust at her feet. Stupid. She knew better. It wasn't the first trap that had almost killed her. "A booby trap," she said. "Remove the wrong brick, the ceiling collapses on top of us."

"Jenga," said Joseph.

"Navajo for we're screwed?"

"My grandson's favorite game as a boy," he said. "Small, rectangular wooden blocks, assembled criss-crossed on top of one another to make a tower. The trick is to remove a block low down on the tower without knocking over the whole thing. It's all about balance, and choosing the right brick."

"My father and I played a game like that, with river rocks at the digs." They were too busy traipsing over the world to buy her any mass manufactured toys. "Of course, it didn't involve being crushed to death, most of the time."

"The tribe that lived here centered their lives on protecting the Turquoise. When the Spaniard brought it to them, they picked this cliff because of its inaccessibility. They built this chamber before the cataclysmic sandstorm hit, to hide the clue to the Turquoise so that no outsider could attain it."

"Until us," she said. "I haven't seen a single potsherd. People that meticulous had a reason for carving this symbol and leaving it behind. Maybe they thought their descendants would return, and retrieve the Turquoise. They wouldn't want them killed for their trouble. So they left them a sign."

Joseph directed his headlamp around the room, landing on another eye level stone that protruded from the west wall. He hurried to it, blew away the dust. "The morning star," he said. The carving looked like a blend between a cross and a diamond, "honored by the people of the Plains as a symbol for courage and purity of spirit."

"So it's a pattern." She crossed to the wall opposite him. Brushed it off. "A circular symbol," she said. "A complex maze, with a stick man above it."

"The man in the maze," said Joseph, "signifying life and choice. Choose wisely, and you will find harmony with all things, although the road may be long and difficult."

"Choice is highly over-rated," she said, "especially with malicious beasts breathing down our necks, not to mention whatever is howling all the way to hell out there."

They moved to the north side of the round chamber, opposite the entrance. A fourth protruding stone. A fourth symbol. Joseph blew off the dust.

He frowned. "Square with rounded edges, border of zigzag patterns surrounding a simple face with closed eyes," he said. "I do not recognize it."

Outside, the howls intensified. At least three large animals shrieked like demons in a chorus of murderous intent. "It's Mayan," she said. "It is Pakal, the glyph for shield."

She recognized it, all right, but hadn't seen a carving like this since her research trip to the Yucatan for her doctoral thesis on the conquistadors. "A Mayan glyph, hundreds of miles from Mexico," she said. "The conquistadors searched this area for Cibola, the legendary lost city of gold, but they didn't give a rat's ass about Mayan culture. I think our odds of finding the actual Breastplate Turquoise just went up." She fished the Mayan knife out of her pack. "The Spaniard who brought the Turquoise here, he must have brought this knife along, too. It's Mayan. I'm sure of that now."

Joseph played his fingers over the shield glyph. "The clue to the Turquoise is hidden behind one of these symbols. Four possibilities, one answer."

"And three potential death traps, if removing the wrong one makes that ceiling collapse."

The howling stopped with the unexpected abruptness of a trap door slamming shut. She listened for the stealthy pad of clawed paws. She sniffed to detect a musky smell through the lingering wisps of fine sand. Joseph unsheathed his hunting knife, its blade glinting in the beam of his headlamp. "The predator grows silent when it smells its prey," he said.

"I don't suppose that means those animals are closing in on the bad guys with guns."

"The beasts awoke to protect the Turquoise. They are very close."

"This Mayan knife was used for sacrifices, not defense." She frowned at the pathetic blade.

"Only a bullet dipped in white ash will kill a Skinwalker," said Joseph. He wasn't joking. He faced her. "Which symbol do we look behind?"

She stepped back. "How would I know?"

"You know."

And the weird thing was, she did know. She could almost feel it, a tingling coming from behind one of the four symbols. "The

Pakal," she said. "We have to look behind the Mayan Pakal symbol."

Joseph stabbed the blade into the seam around the carved block, wedging it into the crevice. The ceiling peppered them with dust and grit.

"Wait," she said, "I'll do this. You stand guard at the portal. Keep watch for those beasts." This was absurd. Her "tingling" could crush them both.

Joseph's blade scraped against the rock, clawing at the silence. It was more unnerving than the howls. But at least the ceiling wasn't collapsing, yet. He jimmied the stone outwards, striving for every millimeter. "The Turquoise stone is called the Yikaisidahi. It is Navajo for It Waits for Dawn, the name of a constellation. And, truly, the Yikaisidahi is of the heavens."

"I had a hunch, not divine guidance, in choosing the Pakal block," she said. And she was headed to hell, not heaven, if her hunch killed this kind, old man. "I'm doing this for my father. You don't owe him. I do."

He wedged his knife deeper into the seam, levered it back and forth. "I am the guardian, my destiny inherited from my father, and his father before him. Since my son was killed in the war, my grandson was to become the next guardian. I have sworn my life to protect it." The chamber trembled. "I cannot let the Yikaisidahi Turquoise fall into the hands of the evil ones. The Yikaisidahi can destroy," he said. "Or it can heal."

Now he was sounding like her father. "The destroying part I get," she said. "The jury is still out on the healing."

He grunted with exertion and pulled his knife back. "It isn't moving."

"The stones are meticulously fitted together. Maybe it's locked in place somehow, with a mechanism." She looked closer and rubbed the dust from the face of Pakal. "Pakal's mouth," she said. "It's not just a carving. It goes deeper than that." She held the Mayan knife close to it. "Looks like the blade is a perfect fit. But that can't be right, not if it means defacing Pakal. The Mayan chief would behead me for sacrilege, after he sliced out my beating heart with this knife. It might trigger the ceiling to collapse."

"You know what you must do," Joseph said. "You are not here by accident, Christa. You are the chosen one."

"You mean the sucker," she said.

His eyes turned to hers. "Are you ready to cross that line, between reality and faith?"

She wiped the sweat stinging her eye and looked away. Joseph couldn't possibly know. Her father never spoke of it, not even with his closest friends. She had reached the brink before, but was too frightened to step over that precipice between reality and faith. Even to reach Mom. "I'm here to find an historical artifact," she said, "not religion."

Joseph slipped his knife back into its sheath. "You must find one to find the other."

She wasn't going to find anything but a shallow grave if she didn't hurry up. She drew in a deep breath and plunged the Mayan knife into the stone. The tip of the blade hit something solid, hesitated, and plunged in deeper. A clunking sound. The chamber trembled. She was wrong. The chamber was collapsing. "Get out of here," she yelled. "I'll pull out the knife. Try to reset the mechanism." She yanked. It didn't budge. The knife was stuck. Pakal scowled. She pulled again. The sandstone block shifted. The crack exhaled a cold draft, emitting the dry breath of an ancient time.

She pressed her foot against the wall for leverage and yanked back the Mayan knife. It worked. The full weight of the stone block slid out. They sprang back as it fell with a thud to the ground and cleaved in two. The Mayan knife dropped to the floor. The chamber quaked. Christa grabbed Joseph's hand as they fought to stay balanced. Then the chamber became utterly still.

A chorus of howls rent the air. She spun around, throwing up her arm in defense. They sounded that close. She directed her headlamp beam through the narrow opening into the night. The dark was alive with guttural, savage voices. A black shadow skulked across the open portal, then another. The beasts cut off their only escape.

# CHAPTER 7

The *Aquila* took on a festive air as the men stowed the lines and began preparations to hoist the anchor. Ahmed could delay no longer. His breaths came short and shallow as his chest tightened. He looked to the sky. *Allah forgive me.* He had pressed the button.

Nothing happened. No sound beeping. No light flashing. Yet everything aboard the treasure hunter *Aquila* had changed. The cool sea breeze that had fluttered his djebella teasingly across his breast just moments ago now felt like fingers of death clawing at him before snatching him down, down, to the deep, dark ocean bottom. The sun, once welcomed, even celebrated, now promised the burn of the Christian hell. The laugh of the albatross that had been circling the *Aquila* all morning now sounded like the cry of a child who has lost his father at sea.

"Ahmed! Ahmed!" Captain Bertoni clanged up the metal stairs to the flying bridge, laughing aloud as he reached Ahmed's side. He clapped him on the back and, for the fifth time that morning, tugged the velvet pouch from his pocket.

The velvet pouch was new. Ahmed had bought it in the medina and presented it to Bertoni before they left port. "It contains a prayer," he had told his captain, "that we find the treasure we seek." Ahmed's prayer had been answered, but his soul was damned.

Like a starving dog eyes the bone in the hands of his master, Ahmed watched Bertoni ease apart the drawstrings of the velvet pouch. He watched the pouch's contents tumble onto his captain's open palm. The sun glinted on the stunning Emerald, a deep green gem the size of a walnut.

"A cat's eye Emerald," Bertoni said, "extremely rare."

"Unique," said Ahmed, glad to tell the truth, at least in this, "in all the world." He fought the compulsion to reach out and snatch away the gemstone, to close this eye of the all-seeing God.

"The Muisca Indians called Emeralds the tears of the moon," Bertoni said. He blinked away his own unwanted tear. Bertoni was an emotional man.

But even Ahmed could feel the palpable energy that the gem emitted. It hadn't been found in *San Salvador's* main strongbox, which held the lion's share of Emeralds, Turquoise, gold and silver. At the time, Ahmed was afraid, and hoped, that this cat's eye Emerald would never be recovered. Then, on the last day, they found the smaller strongbox on one, final submersible dive.

Bertoni cradled the Emerald between his thumb and calloused forefinger. He held it to the heavens, letting the sun play through the green, as if looking for an answer. Ahmed ached to tell him that he wouldn't be the first to seek answers from heaven through the power of the stone. "Do you wonder, Ahmed, why this Emerald was in its own strongbox, kept with a book of some sort?"

Ahmed witnessed the opening of the strongbox. Bertoni had fished the Emerald from a glop of pulp that was once cherished pages. "A Bible," said Ahmed.

Bertoni raised a bushy white eyebrow.

"Conquistadors weren't known to bring books with them on their voyages," said Ahmed. "But if a missionary came along, then he would have a Bible."

"You rascal," said Bertoni, a glimmer of green in his eye. "You think a missionary spirited this away, hidden in the pages of his Bible."

"Only for the greater good," said Ahmed, intoning a joke when he could not have been more serious. He looked east across the blue abyss. Thaddeus Devlin searched there, in the ruins near his village, for the letter the missionary wrote. Ahmed struggled to keep his thoughts from history and home. His expression might reveal his darkest secrets. Yesterday, when he saw the Tear of the Moon Emerald, he felt the hand of Juan de Salvatierra, the *San Salvador's* sole survivor, tearing through the fabric of the centuries to grab hold of him.

In last night's dark hours, as his crewmates snored, he reviewed his daring plan. This Emerald was, indeed, the seventh stone.

Without it, the power of the other six sacred stones was toothless. For five centuries it had rested at the bottom of the ocean, where God had sent it. Now His will was once again undone by man. Thaddeus Devlin had told him the gems and the Breastplate possessed a power that could bring catastrophe upon the Earth. He could not let the Emerald fall into the hands of someone like Mishad and his mysterious patron.

"I heard chatter on the radio last night while the others slept," Ahmed began, taking that first step on the path to either salvation or damnation.

Bertoni smiled crookedly. "You mean while the others were passed out from drinking," he said. "There is much to admire about your Muslim religion, that you refrain from alcohol."

"I couldn't make out the words, but the signal was strong," pressed Ahmed, realizing he was talking too fast, too loud. "The pirates are close." Ahmed said.

Bertoni frowned. "I have no doubt they are."

"You should arm your crew, now."

"I don't know when, or even if, the pirates will attack," said Bertoni. "My men are mariners, treasure hunters. They can't do their jobs effectively if they must also be constant soldiers."

"You've said you could never defend against a surprise attack," said Ahmed, "but, I tell you, the pirates will attack at any moment. They see we are preparing to hoist anchor. That is the way they work in these waters."

"Then we are lost."

"The Aquila is well armed," said Ahmed, "and your men loyal and brave." And Mishad's men rangy and backstabbing.

"It's true that I could not ask for a better crew," said Bertoni, "but our armory is spare."

"But I saw it, racks of machine guns, several RPGs." More than enough to deflect Mishad towards easier prey.

"Almost all sold," said Bertoni, "at our last supply stop. What good are guns, without food? I needed the funds for this last search. And it paid off, Ahmed. I had almost given up hope."

A vice tightened around Ahmed's chest. He sucked in quick, shallow breaths. "How many guns did you keep?"

Bertoni clasped his fingers around the Emerald. "Barely enough to fight off a hungry shark." It was as if he knew what was coming, the way he looked to the east. He sensed the gunboats approach, as surely as when Ahmed had seen him prepare for a sudden, violent squall before the black cloud even appeared on the horizon. But this time precautions against impending disaster would not save them. His eyes met Ahmed's. Could he sense Ahmed's guilt as well? Did he know that he had been betrayed by the man whom he had called friend, this servant whom he had treated like a brother?

The roar of distant speedboat engines skimmed over the waves, the sound reverberating off the *Aquila* broadside. Bertoni snapped up his trademark binoculars. Mathew Joy, who had been known to fix his beloved vessel's engine cooling system with an empty can of Guinness and a strip of duct tape, called them Bertoni's x-ray vision glasses. The machinist joked that Bertoni's penchant for using them for gazing over the empty sea was his way of looking for sunken treasure. These were the men Ahmed had betrayed.

"God help us," Bertoni said, "eight pirates, all armed with semi-automatics, probably sidearms as well. Two runabouts, outsized outboards." He dropped the binoculars to his chest. "One of them is shouldering an RPG launcher."

"Pirates!" Thomas shouted from the pilot house, finally spotting the runabouts. The *Aquila*'s klaxon blasted the air, shooting spears of fear into the men on the deck below. For a moment, it was as if time had stopped, the men frozen in place. Then, as one, they raised their faces towards Bertoni.

The captain squared his shoulders. He gestured towards the four men who had been assigned sidearms this morning. "Owen, Charles, take positions on port side. Barzillai, Benjamin, starboard!" He yanked a set of keys from his pocket and tossed them down to Isaac. "Get the rifles, on the double. Fedellah, Obed, Pollard, go with him. Bring every last bit of ammunition. We'll need it." He twisted back towards the pilot house. "Thomas, shut off that damn alarm!"

The buzz of the pirates' outboards roared into a crescendo. The scrappy runabouts approached rapidly, hulls bashing over the waves, the pirates standing on the deck as if nailed to it, their knees absorbing the shocks.

Bertoni let the Emerald drop off his palm, back into its velvet pouch, and tightened the silk ties. He reached for Ahmed's hand. The captain pressed the soft velvet into Ahmed's palm and cupped his calloused hands over it. "Take the Emerald," he said. "Go to the engine room, to the hiding place that I showed you, the one used by the smugglers who once owned this ship. Hide in there."

"I will not hide," countered Ahmed. "I will fight, with you. You need every man."

"I need you to keep this Emerald. Do not let the pirates have it. Promise me, Ahmed."

"I promise," he said. "I will never let this Emerald fall into their hands. To do that, I must fight."

"To do that, you must live."

"They know I am on board."

"I will tell them that you were killed and fell overboard. If anything should happen to me, take the Emerald to my father, in Milan, Antonio Bertoni, in the Villa Bertoni, north of the city. Ask any Milanese. They will know him." Ahmed felt the desperate press of his captain's hands. "My father must know that I made real my dream. This is proof. Promise me, Ahmed."

"I promise you that your father will know his son is a good man, a great man."

"Go now, before it's too late."

Bertoni released him and clambered up the stairs to the pilot house. Ahmed called after him, but he had quickly ducked into the pilothouse. Ahmed could see Thomas shouting maydays into the radio microphone. Help would never arrive in time. He clutched the Emerald in its pouch, the velvet soft, the Emerald hard, in his hand. He had no time to think. Bertoni gestured sternly at him through the pilothouse window. "Engine room," he yelled. "Now!"

Bullets ripped through the conning tower's port windows. Shards of glass exploded across the gangway. A force smacked Ahmed in the thigh. He cried out in agony as his leg collapsed beneath him. He fell to the deck, blood seeping from his thigh.

## CHAPTER 8

Thaddeus woke with a start. Pain stabbed his back. It came back to him in a flash. The camp had been attacked at dawn. He had raced to save Ambar and took a slug in his back. He rubbed his eyes to clear his vision. Muktar stooped over him, his expression grave, his gray and white striped kaftan splattered with blood. Thaddeus grabbed Muktar's wrist. "How long have I been out?" he asked, his voice hoarse. He had to shake off the dizziness. He had to find that letter and clear out before more people were hurt because of it.

Muktar braced his arm beneath Thaddeus's shoulders. "Less than one hour," he said. He held a terra cotta vessel to his lips. "Drink this. Just one little drink."

The cool water felt like life on his parched throat. "Where am I?"

"Ambar's home," said Muktar. "In Ahmed's bed. My friend, we send for the doctor. An American doctor. A doctor without a border. He is five hours away only."

Thaddeus looked around at the whitewashed adobe walls. The sun slanted through the open window onto the handcarved wooden table next to the bed. "Patch me up, a quick fix until I get to the doctor. I must find that letter. More bad men, better armed and better trained, are coming."

Ambar entered the room. Her dark eyes bore into Thaddeus. He couldn't blame her. She'd almost been killed this morning. His presence had triggered the attack on her peaceful, isolated village. Muktar rose from the crude wooden chair at his bedside. She sat stiffly on it. She smoothed her skirt over her knees, and placed a parcel on her lap. It was wrapped in a blanket, an intricate Moorish weave of reds, browns and yellows faded with age.

Without a word, Ambar carefully unfolded the blanket. A musky odor, no stronger than a tease, emanated from the folds. Within lay a gold embossed leather folio, burgundy in color, about the size used in Morocco's finer restaurants to hold menus. It was tied shut with a leather cord. Ambar took the utmost care in untying the knot, but the cord deteriorated in her fingers and a piece of it fell to the pounded earth floor. The folio was old, that was clear, but by the way Ambar handled it, age was the least of its value.

Thaddeus squeezed Muktar's wrist. "Help me up," he said, restraining a groan of pain as he raised his shoulders. Muktar grabbed an embroidered pillow from the head of the bed and propped it under him.

Ambar opened the folio's cover. Inside was a paper, pressed stiff and brown with age. "I see this paper only one time before," she said, in Arabic, her voice hushed. Muktar translated. Thaddeus's Arabic was passable, but he wanted to understand every nuance. "It is passed down through generations of my family. My ancestor wished it. It is only to be given to a Christian who is worthy." She frowned, hesitating, her eyes searching his. "For five hundred years, no Christian is worthy."

He stopped himself from snatching it from her. "You've had this paper all this time," he said. "All this time that I've been searching." He had interviewed all the villagers and asked them for any local history about a marooned missionary. "I asked you, Ambar," he said. "You said nothing."

Her expression was unyielding, her voice steady. "My ancestor wished it to go only to a Christian who saves the life of a Muslim," she said. She spoke further, but Muktar hesitated in his translation. "To make good, to make equal," he held his two hands out, raising one while lowering the other, "the past."

"To restore balance," Thaddeus said. Muktar nodded.

She held the paper towards him, and placed it on his open palm. The paper quivered. He was trembling. He tilted the paper towards the daylight fighting through the dust motes from the open window. The writing was faded but legible, with the smudges and scratches of quill dipped in indigo. The flowing artistry of penmanship was from a time when people cherished letters, the only form of communication between distances. "Latin," he mouthed the word, his throat too parched to speak. He blinked and squinted, struggling to focus as he read the date, "14 February, 1586." His gaze rushed to the signature at the bottom. "Juan de Salvatierra," he read.

"It is the letter you seek," Muktar said. "Truly, it is destiny, as you say."

He couldn't think straight. The sinuous Latin script swam across the page. "Ambar," he said, "where did you get this?"

"The priest who wrote this," she said, "was called Juan de Salvatierra. He washed upon the shore here, after the wreck of his ship, the *San Salvador*, five hundred years ago. He asked my ancestor to be his messenger. He asked Abd al-Aziz, which means servant of the strong. Abd al-Aziz made a vow to the priest to deliver his letter. The holy man was dying. He could not deny him." She unwrapped another layer of the woven blanket from the parcel on her lap and removed an object from its folds. She narrowed her eyes. "The priest made him take this, as payment, to keep his promise. This, he did not need to do. We do not profit from the death of one we take into our care."

By God, it was the crucifix. Ambar dangled it from its golden chain. It glinted in the morning sun. He handed Salvatierra's letter to Muktar and reached towards her. "May I?" he whispered, his throat dry. Ambar let the crucifix and its gold chain fall onto his palm. His hand dipped with the weight of it.

The crucifix was magnificent, about two inches high by one wide of solid gold. Each of its cross bars was tipped with three tiny pearls. The Christ figure hung in such a way as to make the arms look upraised in victory, rather than weak with death. His face was pained, His expression sad but accepting. Below His feet was an uncommon skull and crossbones crafted out of ivory. Above His head, the typical inscription, INRI, was engraved on a golden scroll. INRI was the Latin acronym for Jesus of Nazareth, King of the Jews, the banner written in Hebrew, Latin and Greek which Pilate ordered placed on Christ's cross to show his "crime."

Thaddeus turned over the crucifix. Its back was enameled with primary blues, reds and greens, clearly an Iberian influence. He could make out what looked like a spear, and the words "Lux et Veritas." "Light and Truth," he translated from the Latin.

"My ancestor try his best to keep his vow," Ambar said. "He travel to Rome and to the Vatican. He is an Arab, and he fight many bandits and hateful people on the way. The Swiss Guards do not let him pass through the gate. They threaten him. He show the Guards the crucifix and the letter. They yell and point to him their swords. They accuse Abd al-Aziz of stealing the letter and crucifix from the priest. One guard go to kill him. Abd al-Aziz fight them. He escapes."

"Your ancestor was the one in the Vatican guard's report I found about an Arab with a stolen crucifix and a letter," Thaddeus said. "So I was right. He returned here."

Ambar nodded. "For many years, the letter and crucifix is the burden of my family. We wait all the time for one worthy. Professor Thaddeus, you are that man. The letter and the crucifix are yours now."

The room spun dizzily around him. "I've got to get these to safety or your ancestor's courage will have been for nothing." He pushed up on his elbows, only to collapse onto the bed.

Ambar's hand gripped his shoulder, her craggy fingers surprisingly strong. "I will do it," she said in English. "I will keep my family vow to Salvatierra to deliver his dying message. Where?"

Blackness flooded towards him. Like Salvatierra, his mission could not end, even if he should die here, alone, so far from home and family. "To my daughter," he said, "before it's too late."

# CHAPTER 9

Salvatierra made a quick sign of the cross. They would now reap what they had sown in this new world. It was a world not full of gold, but abundant in a native people that the Spaniards, not the jungle, had forged into savages. These savages formed the human chain ringing the perimeter of the clearing. They tensed when they saw him, crouching, strengthening the links. Each began stomping his bare, calloused feet on the pounded earth in a slow, threatening rhythm, injecting an unholy life into the skeletons marked in blood on their bare, brown skin. But still, he could not keep his gaze from wandering beyond this threat of brutal death, or worse.

For there he saw what he had suffered through days and death to find. A magnificent temple towered above the far side of the clearing. The temple filled the canyon pass, fifty feet wide and one hundred feet high. It was buttressed against the steep canyon walls, its central roof a series of pyramidal steppes. On either side of the temple, trees and vines clung upon a cliff that extended deep into the jungle to his right and left, like a fortress wall built by God. The man they sought, and the Breastplate, waited within that temple.

Young Elias crept to his side. He gripped the blunderbuss, careful to keep it aimed towards the ground. "Is it true, Father Salvatierra, what the stories say, that beyond this temple is the Garden of Eden? Perhaps the Breastplate will show us the way to paradise."

"I fear it is not a portal to Eden," he said, "but the gates of hell." The temple completely blocked the pass to the valley beyond. The only entrance into the pyramid was a tapered opening into a narrow, dark tunnel. The two geometric carvings above and to each side of the stone lintel that topped the entrance were stylized eyes, threatening all who would be bold or impudent enough to enter. The entrance was the icon's mouth. From the look of the worn, wet rock, it had once poured forth the life-giving waters of a small river from the hidden canyon that lay beyond. Now, no more than a trickle dribbled through the mouth to moisten the clearing. The river bed, winding into the jungle to their right, had dwindled into a muddy waste. Somewhere, deep inside the temple, the river had been dammed. Above the front of the temple, the rocky outcroppings on either side of the pass were rounded smooth and bare of vegetation. "The temple is the face of a demon," he said, "and those rocky outcroppings the shoulders of its wings."

"Demon's wings," Elias whispered. Truly, it looked like the shoulders of Satan lording over the jungle below.

Captain Diaz unsheathed his sword. "Stay alert, men." With his left hand, he snatched his knife from its scabbard.

One of the tribesmen shouted with an anger as sharp as the bloodied Spanish sword he jabbed into the air. He wore the grand, red-feathered headdress of their chief. Salvatierra translated his words. "We followed the demon to defend his new empire. We waited to hear from the Almighty God of his golden Breastplate and the Tear of the Moon Emerald. The demon Contreras promised the elixir for our families to cure them when they became sickened with the madness. He, like all Spaniards, only speaks the lies of a snake. He has killed our hearts."

Diaz grabbed the shaman who had guided them here. He pressed the point of his sword against the shaman's throat. "Tell them I will kill their holy man if they attack us."

The chief gestured toward the entrance, his expression grim. Salvatierra's throat grew dry as he translated. "Enter the temple of the demon's empire," he said. "Find your tribe in the demon's belly."

The shaman spoke, his voice calm, unequivocal.

"The tribesmen will not attack," Salvatierra translated. "They want us to take the devil, Contreras, from their midst. If they kill the Spanish demon here, his spirit will lay ruin to their land." The shaman's gaze turned to Salvatierra. "But we must not take the golden Breastplate. They will never let its power destroy others as it has destroyed them."

Diaz turned and advanced toward the entrance into the pyramid, pulling the shaman with him.

Salvatierra crouched as he entered the dark, dank tunnel behind Diaz's men. His shoulders brushed against the rough, stone walls. The men were swallowed into the belly of a beast which emitted an unholy odor that reeked like the breath of Satan.

"I smell blood," Diaz called back, recognizing the coppery stink. "Act quickly to kill all but Contreras. They think they have us at a disadvantage, forcing us to enter single file. We will show them how men fight."

The earth shook them with a sudden lurch. Salvatierra fell to one knee. He foolishly covered his head with his arm. The weight of the temple above him would surely crush him if it collapsed. The men rushed forward. They funneled into an inner chamber, their battle cries wrenching the space as they attacked. But, as Salvatierra emerged into the chamber, he saw that the battle had already been waged.

Salvatierra covered his mouth with his hand but the stench of stone dust and death lay thick in his throat. Contreras's men, all, were beheaded. Their dismembered bodies bristled with dozens of poison blow darts. They lay strewn about like flotsam. Their decapitated heads, with eyes pried open wide with terror, lay piled in a ghastly pyramid, an echo of the stone temple which had become not their treasure house, but their tomb.

Contreras stood before them, arms outstretched. A shaft of sunlight speared him from a hole carved from the ceiling, as if God had thrust down his judgment. It shone upon a man red with other men's blood smeared upon his body. It shone upon a face mad with evil. It shone upon the magnificent golden Breastplate.

Salvatierra fell to his knees. Blinded by the Breastplate's brilliance, he could not look away. "Lord, come to me in this den of evil," he prayed. "Speak to me through the stones for I fear what I must do."

The twelve sacred gemstones emblazoned the Breastplate, three across, four down. The sapphire, once worn by Saint Edward, encompassed the totality of blue in the heavens. Babur's Diamond sparkled with the brilliance of all the stars that shine on a cloudless night. The red of the ruby known as Urim was the sunset, the golden topaz of its partner Thummim, the dawn. In the center, it was as if the eye of God watched through the green cat's eye Emerald the natives named the Tear of the Moon. The Turquoise nearly sang of

Turkish armies vanquished long ago. The jacinth glowed as if it imprisoned the flames of hell. The agate, amethyst, beryl, onyx and jasper—all magnificent, radiant.

Even as Salvatierra was sickened, elation seized him at seeing the Breastplate. This was indeed the sacred Breastplate of Aaron, thought lost long ago in the fall of the Temple of Solomon. The power to communicate with God lay within his grasp.

"In God's name, Captain Diaz," said Salvatierra. "Do your duty." The yearning to hold the Breastplate was unbearable.

"In the name of His Majesty King Phillip the second," said Diaz, the words strong but his voice dry and weak. "I arrest you, Alvaro Contreras, for treason. You will surrender all bounty and you will return to Spain in chains aboard the *Espiritu Santo* to stand trial for treason." The crew's eyes revealed their desire to seize the traitor, but their revulsion held them in check.

Contreras raised his bloodstained hand. It held his Bible. He pointed it to a dark recess of the chamber and the entrance of a passageway carved through the canyon wall. Salvatierra could see the wink of gold, silver and Emeralds in the torchlit cavity at its end. The chamber they were in, but for this side tunnel to the treasure room and the passage back to the clearing, was a dead end. If the temple had been a portal to a Garden of Eden and a river of life, or to a hell beyond imagining, a wall now blocked them from it.

The men, giddy with the thought of treasure, or simply desperate to escape this horrid tomb, raced down the stone passageway to the treasure. Salvatierra could hear their cheers, and the captain's voice. "We are rich, men," his voice echoed. "This bounty will fill the coffers of the *San Salvador.*" It was his flagship, sister ship to the *Espiritu Santo*.

Only Elias and the shaman stayed behind with Salvatierra, Contreras, and the corpses. "Remove the Breastplate," Salvatierra said to Contreras, "and give it to me." Even he dared not approach the madman.

Contreras merely smiled.

Elias targeted him with his blunderbuss. "Do what the Father says."

Contreras removed the Breastplate. He flung it away. It landed on the pile of lifeless heads with a sickening clank, toppling over the topmost head, sending it tumbling to the dirt floor. Contreras laughed.

Salvatierra raced to the Breastplate, holding back the bile as he lifted it, the metal warmed from the sunbeam and heavy in his hands. The wonder of the stones chased away earthly sickness. They were magnificent, but more. God forgive his unworthiness, he could feel their power.

Contreras's cackle faded and he spoke. "Go ahead, priest," he said. "Put it on. Wear the Breastplate of Aaron and become one with the Lord."

His heart pounded, his lungs felt as though they were being crushed. He focused on his dream, a message sent from the Lord. "I must destroy it," he said. Hot tears stung his eyes. A sharp buzzing pierced his ears.

"Destroy it? You would not dare commit such heresy!" Contreras advanced, pointing his Bible at Salvatierra like a deadly weapon. "The Breastplate is the work of God! With it, we can do more than save the souls of this savage land. We can save the world."

"I saw the villages." Salvatierra could not take his eyes off of the Breastplate, but in his mind he conjured the image of the young mother murdering her baby. "In the hands of man, it can annihilate the world."

"As after the great flood, the world will be born again," Contreras said. "The gems of the Breastplate reveal the secret to my domination." He pointed to the vast stone wall before him. "Don the Breastplate. Stand upon this platform. Call God's light to shine upon you. You will hold the powers of the Heavens in the palm of your hand."

The stream of sunlight piercing the chamber had shifted as the sun traversed the sky above. Its outer edge shone now on the grisly pile of disembodied heads, glinting on the gold earring of one man, and in the vacant blue eye of another. "I know the will of God."

"Heretic! I have worn the Breastplate. I have spoken to God. He told me you were coming. I know you made a promise to the pope. You vowed to return the Breastplate of Aaron to a Christian land, to the Vatican."

"Murderer, you cannot tell me of priestly vows."

"The inquisitors will flail you alive if you defy the Vatican and destroy the Breastplate."

Salvatierra snatched a knife from the scabbard of the headless body next to him. He could feel his will weakening. He had to act now. He pried the sardius, known as Urim, and the topaz, known as Thummim, from the Breastplate and stuffed the gems into his satchel.

Contreras moved to attack. Elias snapped up the Blunderbuss, aimed it at Contreras's chest. "I will stand by you, Padre Salvatierra," Elias said. "I swear it."

Contreras clenched his hands into fists. "You fool. You can only see today," he said. "But I know the future. This will not end here. This world is young and my destiny will be fulfilled. It is a matter of time. If not me, then my heirs will rule the world and bring all to God's light."

Salvatierra found renewed strength in having removed the first stones. His plan crystallized in his mind. He pried out the Tear of the Moon Emerald, stowing it in his pack. He pried away at the gold settings and removed the second row of stones, the Turquoise, sapphire and diamond. He did not dare succumb to the seduction of admiring the stones, but went directly to work on the third row.

Contreras grabbed an abandoned halberd from his headless soldier. Elias raised his weapon. Salvatierra held up his hand to stop the boy. With a deafening blast, Elias fired a warning shot above Contreras's head, carving a hollow into the stone ceiling. The earth trembled. A mighty quaking began, as if God in fury was shaking His globe in His almighty hands. Small rocks tumbled from the rough hewn walls. Granite boulders crashed from above. The men shot out of the treasure chamber hallway, heaving burlap sacks heavy with gold and silver. Captain Diaz, almost as an afterthought, grabbed hold of Contreras and dragged him from the chamber into the tunnel towards the clearing.

With unequalled desperation, Salvatierra struggled to pry out the last stone, the flame-colored jacinth. He had removed seven of the twelve stones, the vision he had seen in his dream. Elias crouched by him. "We must go, Father," he begged. Rocks pounded down around them. One smashed upon Salvatierra's shoulder, crushing it. "Leave the Breastplate here. It will be buried, lost again to the ages." Even in his dizzying pain, and holding his quickening breath against the stench, Salvatierra forced down his bile and clawed through the pile of heads, their skin slippery with blood. He shoved the Breastplate deep within them, and buried it beneath the faces of those men who would wield its power only to be struck down by it.

He fled for the tunnel, Elias on his heels. The savages wailed and chanted as Salvatierra dashed across the clearing into the edges of the forest, leaving the shaman at the mouth of the tunnel. Behind him on the horizon, the volcano roared, spewing smoke and thunder like a furious demon.

"Go ahead of me, Padre," Elias yelled over the din. "I will protect you."

"You will indeed be a guardian, along with our Circle of Seven," Salvatierra called back. The energy emitted to his very soul by the stones in his satchel terrified and emboldened him. "We will carry these seven stones to the far corners of God's Earth, and never shall they be together. The power of the Breastplate in the hands of evil will pitch mankind into hell, and no one will be able to save us."

CHAPTER **10**

Christa flicked off her headlamp. Her eyes adjusted. The full moon cast an eerie glow over the ancient cliff dwelling homes outside the chamber. It seeped through the open doorway, bringing with it the musky, primeval odor of the predators pacing just outside the open doorway. The padded thuds of paws crunched the gravel. Dark shapes crossed in front of the entrance, glimpses of sinewy muscle, rangy black fur, red, soulless eyes, a gray tongue licking jagged teeth. She swiped the sweat from her hands across her khaki shorts and snatched up the Mayan knife.

Joseph shifted behind her. For a man who didn't make a sound walking, he was creating a downright ruckus. As if that made a difference. The wolves, beasts, whatever they were, knew they had trapped their human prey in the chamber.

"The Skinwalkers will not cross the threshold into this human habitation," Joseph said.

"Except this place hasn't seen a human in five hundred years." Her heart hammered like a klaxon calling the beasts to dinner. "Until us."

"Turn away from the beasts. Just because you face what frightens you doesn't mean you can stop it."

"At least I'll see it coming. I'd like a little warning so I can see my life flashing before my eyes before my throat is torn out of my neck," she said.

"Then you'll want to see this first."

Reluctantly, she took her eyes off the open doorway. Joseph directed his headlamp beam into the niche that the Pakal stone had hidden.

She drew in closer. "It can't be," she said.

"What is it?" Joseph asked.

"An armillary sphere." Saying it out loud did not make it feel more real. "It's a model, of the heavens. European. Sixteenth century."

"Like the man who brought it here." Joseph shifted in closer.

It was an armillary sphere, all right, its brass armature reflecting the headlamp beams through a silky weave of ancient cobwebs. "About six inches in diameter, twelve inches high, including the base," she said. "Looks authentic."

"Take it out. Hurry."

She reached in, swiped away the sticky cobwebs. "Could be another booby trap."

"Risk it."

She grabbed the metal rings of the sphere. "Damn it," she said, jerking her fingers away. "It's tingling." This was crazy. The nearest electricity was miles away. She grasped it again, tighter, and lifted it. "Heavier than it looks." She reached in her other hand, cradled the pedestal base and drew the sphere out of the niche.

She blew off the fine covering of dust and swiped away the more stubborn cobwebs. The armillary sphere was shaped like a globe that an old-fashioned elementary school teacher might have in her class room, but the globe was only skeletal, formed with sequentially larger, interlocking brass rings, orbiting a small metal orb. A wide band circled the orb's "equator." An ornamental finial topped the "north pole." The south pole of the rings perched on the tip of the center pole of a brass tripod, its three legs gracefully arched. Each leg was bolted to the corners of a black, six-sided marble base. Each of the base's bottom six corners had a miniature golden clawed foot.

Joseph focused his beam on it. "Have you seen these spheres before?"

"Only in museum display cases and Renaissance portraits, usually clamped in the hands of some notable scientist. The armillary sphere symbolized the epitome of wisdom and knowledge." She squinted to make out the numbers and symbols engraved on the rings. "I'd date it to the last half of the sixteenth century, post Copernicus. You see here." She pointed to the small solid orb at the core of the sphere, in the center of the concentric rings. "This is the sun. Before Copernicus, astronomers considered the Earth the center of the universe."

"Was it used for navigation?"

"More as a model for teaching." She traced her fingertip around the cool brass rings which formed the skeleton of the sphere. "This ring represents the planets, this one the constellations of the Zodiac." Her touch released the tangy aroma of metal. "Turning the rings shows the relationships between the movements of celestial bodies. The European telescope hadn't been invented yet. Before they could see that some stars were actually planets, they studied, and thought." This was real. She felt it. She could see the rub marks made by the Spaniard's fingers, so many centuries ago, caressing this one object that connected him to home. "This is it, Joseph, the container for the Yikaisidahi Turquoise."

"It does not hold the Yikaisidahi," he said. "The Yikaisidahi remains hidden."

"But you told me Yikaisidahi is the name of a Navajo constellation, It Waits for Dawn," she said. "The armillary sphere is a model of the heavens. And it's been buried here for five hundred years. You said yourself that the Spaniard must have brought it here."

He gestured for her to hand the sphere to him. He turned it, scrutinized it from different angles. "The base looks like it was carved from one piece of stone," he said. "It is heavy. It feels solid."

She cringed as he tested the strength of the tripod, tugging at the lip of the pedestal. "A 16th century armillary sphere in mint condition is worth a fortune," she said, "but if one of those rings gets dinged, you can knock a couple zeroes off that price."

"Its fortune lays only in its value as a clue to the location of the Yikaisidahi," said Joseph. "That is why the Spaniard left it here, for whoever unlocked the secret of the Pakal to find the Turquoise. But why an armillary sphere?"

"His native tongue was Old Spanish," she said. "He no doubt became fluent in the language of the Anasazi cult who lived here. But he needed something that transcended language, and time. He needed to use the timeless, international language of science."

"Or of faith in the heavens," he said. He handed the sphere to her. "We need to get this to your father."

"We're so close," she said, "to finding the Turquoise. This sphere must hold the clue to its location. This may be our only chance. Just give me five minutes." She turned the elliptical ring

representing the Zodiac, forcing it a bit.  It was stubborn with age.
"The Spaniard who hid the sphere used a Mayan symbol.  Mayans
were advanced astronomers.  Maybe it has something to do with the
alignment of stars," she looked up, "or with the pyramid roof."

"Those beasts will not give us even one minute more.  And the
others who are chasing us will not find the Turquoise without the
sphere."

"You go.  I'm not leaving this cliff dwelling without the
Turquoise."

"And I'm not leaving you here to die."  He grabbed the sphere
and strode quickly across the chamber.  "Stay behind me."  He
advanced to the portal, posture low, leading with his hunting knife.
"And do not look into the eyes of a Skinwalker.  If you do, they can
rip out your soul."

"I'm more worried about our throats," Christa called after him in
a loud whisper, but he was already through the open doorway.

Just outside the chamber's entrance, Joseph nodded to her to
follow.  She stepped across the threshold.  She crouched, scanning
the plateau.  Nothing.  The beasts had drawn back out of sight.  It
was preternaturally still.  But she could smell a dank, musky odor.
The moon edged the rim of the plateau in silver.  The top of the steep
toe and hand trail and their only way down was fifty feet, but could
be a lifetime, away.  A snarl, menacing, guttural, to their left.  She
swung to face it.  Then another snarl, to their right.  Dark shapes
skulked towards them, one on each side.  A third beast loped in front
of them, cutting them off from the plateau rim.

She could see them fully now.  They looked more powerful than
wolves, their fur rangy and black, thick around their sinewy
haunches, like an unkempt lion's mane.  Their ears were pointed,
their eyes red, shining with cunning, not the vacant look of a hungry
predator.  And, most alarming of all, each beast's face was unique.
One had a shorter nose, the other, larger, rounder eyes.  The lead
beast snarled, exposing his long, sharp canines.  He paced, crushing
the sparse scrub weeds that had managed to grow in the cracks of the
plateau rim.

"We can make it," she said.  Her voice, hardly more than a
breath, reverberated through the cliff dwelling.  "Go for the edge of
the cliff and the toe and hand trail.  I'm right behind you.  Get the

sphere to my father." She'd distract the beasts, give Joseph a head start to make sure he made it safely over the edge.

"There is another way," Joseph said. "My grandfather told me the story of the tunnels that lead back into the mountain from the lost city of the Yikaisidahi. We will search deeper into the dwelling, find the tunnel, and move downwards, always downwards. It will bring us to the canyon floor and the river."

Tunnels, the word alone twisted her gut. "Legend," she asked, "or truth?" She looked behind them. They were a good fifty feet from the nearest room entrance. The beasts had waited to flank them halfway between the safety of the cliff dwelling and the plateau rim. Clever. "Could be a dead end, if you know what I mean."

"For my grandfather, legend was truth." He stepped back. The beast to their left loped around behind them, cutting them off from the rooms. It clawed hungrily at the loose gravel.

She quickly scanned for a way up from the cliff dwelling to the top of the plateau. Not a chance. It was an overhang, worse than vertical. "Just how many tons of rock are pressing down on these ancient tunnels?" she asked.

Joseph dropped to one knee. "Give me your pack," he said. She slipped it off her shoulder and handed it to him. "The Skinwalkers are after the armillary sphere," he said. He stuffed the sphere into her pack.

"Those beasts are after dinner. I say we go for the plateau rim." Anything but those tunnels. "You first."

"You must take it, back in the tunnels, to safety, to your father. Tell him. The Abraxas is with the Black Magic Woman, in San Francisco. He will know what to do."

"Abraxas? Black Magic Woman? No, don't even explain that." It wasn't what Joseph said, but how he said it, like he wasn't ever going to get the chance to tell her father that crazy message himself. "We are getting out of this," she said, "together."

He pulled the jeep keys from his jeans pocket, dropped them into her pack and shoved the pack at her. He pivoted and ran for the plateau rim. The dwelling exploded in sharp, staccato barks. The beasts rocketed out of the darkness. Powerful front quarters propelled them forward, their claws spitting out gravel behind.

Joseph teetered on the rim, his silhouette dark against the sky. The beasts closed in around him. "Leave me, Christa," he called to her.

"Not a chance," she said.   She started towards the beasts, yanking the sphere from her pack.  She thrust it up in the air.  She waved her arms.  "Over here!" she yelled, determined to redirect the beasts.  "You want this?"  This was crazy, rationalizing with wild animals.

"Christa, you must run!  Back into the tunnels!  Now!"  A light flashed on the opposite rim of the canyon.  The bang of the rifle split the night.  Joseph spun around.  She thrust her hand towards him, reaching across space, desperate to stop time.  He teetered, flailing his arms in a frantic struggle to regain balance.   He twisted backwards over the precipice.

# CHAPTER 11

The marauding pirates closed in on the *Aquila*. Ahmed clutched at the searing pain in his thigh. The bullet had pierced through the fleshy part of his muscle. He scrambled to the starboard cabin door, pulling himself across the decking, tracing a stark red trail of blood. Gunfire blasted from belowdecks as the crew returned fire. The acrid scent of gunsmoke fouled the sea air. A man screamed in agony. Ahmed stole a look over the railing to see Stubb writhing on the deck, clutching his belly as his blood formed a slick puddle beneath him, his massive strength stolen away in a moment by a small piece of lead.

The speedboats bulleted toward them, now less than one hundred meters away. Two pirates manned the deck-mounted machine guns, spitting out bullets in sickening spurts. Another pirate pressed a rocket launcher to his shoulder, barely holding it steady as their speedboat bucked over the waves. Ahead of them, their bullets found their marks. Isaac went down with a thud, a deceivingly small hole through his left temple.

"Arm yourselves!" Bertoni yelled. "Get the guns of those who have fallen!" Thomas, hardly more than a boy, dashed out of the pilothouse and bounded down the stairs. He grabbed Isaac's semi-automatic rifle and started firing blindly to starboard, the recoil of the gun making him dance as if dangling from puppet strings.

Ahmed pulled his gaze away. He would keep his promise to Thaddeus Devlin, to his captain, and to himself. He bellycrawled across the flying deck, used the railing to heave himself up, and hobbled down the starboard stairs, his leg in a flame of pain. He had to make it to the engine room, two decks down. He glanced out the porthole to see the pirates clambering on board.

Owen, wide-eyed with terror, shoved him aside on the inner stairway, fled through the door and dove overboard. What did he hope to do, swim to safety? Ahmed slammed shut the engine room door behind him and nearly slid down the final, steep set of stairs. He staggered around the pistons and spark plugs, dragging his injured leg behind him like an anchor, thrusting himself across the last few feet. His hands hammered into the cold steel of the circuitry cabinet that held the engine's thermostat system. He quickly loosed the hidden latches at the top of the circuitry panel and pushed, then pulled. The whole panel came forward, revealing a space behind, dark, empty, barely large enough to hold even Ahmed's slight frame.

Reluctance hit him like a rogue wave. What if the *Aquila* sank? He'd be trapped, with no escape from the cold ocean water that would fill his lungs with a few last, tortured gasps. Or worse, what if the pirates found him inside? Mishad would show no mercy for a man who disobeyed him. His torture would prove worse than the pangs of drowning, but, ultimately, be just as deadly.

Rapid thunks of boots on metal reverberated from above. The pirates were on board. Ahmed squeezed into the compartment, bringing his knees to his chin. He twisted to grab the circuit board with his fingertips, its metal edges sharp. He pulled it into place. It got stuck. On an angle. This was insane. Of course Mishad would find him. Pirates knew of smugglers' hiding places. Mishad would never believe that Ahmed had gone overboard.

Running, pounding footsteps clanged all around him. Bertoni, yelling, he couldn't make out the words. He snatched at the circuit board, its razor-sharp edges slicing his fingertips. He pushed, then pulled, only to wedge the cockeyed board tighter. Blood dripped from his fingers. Gunfire. In just moments, the pirates would be scurrying belowdecks like rats. They'd see him. He could kick out the circuit board, dash for the side. Yes, he'd most likely drown or be shot, but the Emerald would be safe again, at the bottom of the sea. Perhaps that's where the accursed stone belonged. But Bertoni had given him the chance to live, to keep his promises. If Allah was willing, he would survive, like the missionary survived the shipwreck five hundred years earlier. Ahmed twisted as much as he could in the confined space, raised his heels, and prepared to kick with all his might if the pirates found him.

He could see nothing but darkness, but the noises proved more terrifying than any vision. He could hear more shouts than gunfire now. He heard calls of surrender, Bertoni pleading for the lives of the survivors, a spatter of gunfire, then, most horrifying of all, laughter. After that, silence.

Ahmed clutched his knees tighter to his chest in a vain attempt to stop trembling. Part of him wanted to run, try his luck overboard like the fool earlier, anything but wait in darkness for the ruthless killers to find him.

At the clang of the engine room door being kicked open, he tucked in tighter. Footsteps. A metallic smashing sound as the engineer's rolling desk chair was shoved aside. The adrenaline-pumped boasts of two men speaking Arabic. They were searching the engineer's desk. Then more footsteps descending the steel stairs to the engine room. Two, quick shots, followed closely by two thuds. Bodies falling to the floor.

"Check them. One of them could have found the Emerald." The man was speaking English, American English.

"You just had to shoot them, didn't you? Couldn't just ask. I was beginning to like these guys. A pirate's life for me." Muffled sounds, coughing, then banging of metal being tossed and turned onto the metal floor. "The Emerald's not in their pockets, and I'm not doing a body search on a corpse."

"You'll cut open their innards if The Prophet tells you to."

"Hold on. Check out this blood trail."

Ahmed stopped breathing. They knew. His leg throbbed. The blood from his wound. He had been a fool. He had led them right to him.

The rumbling start of an oversized outboard motor. A speedboat starting up.

"Damn. That's got to be Mishad. He's getting away."

The footsteps retreated up the stairs. Ahmed realized he wasn't breathing. He sucked in oxygen. More gunshots rang out from somewhere on deck.

A deafening blast concussed through the ship, pounding into his head and chest. The *Aquila* lurched perilously on its side, then lolled back upright. Ahmed pressed his palms against his ears to steady his dizziness. Mishad must have hit the *Aquila* with a rocket. Through the ringing, he could barely make out another sound, even more terrifying than the blast, rushing water. The cold fingers of the Atlantic reached into his hiding place. No more time. He had to hope that the Americans were killed by the rocket blast.

Ahmed twisted and kicked out the circuit board. The lights were out, but a stream of daylight tumbled down the metal stairs, along with a powerful cascade of ocean water. The frothy water swirled and eddied across the engine room floor. Already it had nearly covered the corpses of the two pirates and lifted them into a macabre float. Ahmed slogged past them. The ship listed at an alarming rate.

He strained to hear voices from the deck above, but he could hear only the ringing in his ears and the horrifying sound of ocean gushing into the Aquila. He grabbed the handrail, barely able to pull himself against the force of the water cascading furiously down the stairs. Water sprayed onto his face, the salty brine fingering his lips like a murderer lusting after his horrific death.

Ahmed yanked himself onto the foredeck, then up the last set of stairs to daylight. He rushed across the threshold, and tripped, stumbling over something wet and soft. A body. Bertoni. Ahmed's stomach lurched. The captain's grimace of death was very nearly a smile. He raced, limping, dragging his leg, across the deck. Quickly, he ducked. The two Americans hadn't been killed. They were dressed as Mishad's pirates in ragged khakis and cast-off t-shirts and were hurriedly lowering themselves into the remaining speedboat. They shoved off and started after the other speedboat, now some 150 meters away.

Another explosion. A rocket ripped through the Americans' speedboat and into the *Aquila*, sending body parts and metal shards screaming into the sea and sky. The concussion knocked Ahmed backwards. If not for Bertoni's body, Ahmed's head would have been cracked against the steel door. His ears rang. He could no longer hear the water, but could feel its power coursing over the railings. Ahmed gasped for breath, toppled and rolled across the deck, splashing into the water, the cold ocean slapping him into focus as he fell below the surface.

For a moment, all was muted and slow-moving beneath the chaos above the surface. But the stab of the salt on his wound nearly knocked him unconscious. He kicked towards the sunlight, but was held back. The jagged metal from the blast hole in the hull hooked the hem of his djellaba. A fingerless forearm floated towards him from the ship's hull. Frantically, he ripped his clothing free and surfaced. He swam as hard and fast as he could. He turned to see the bow of the *Aquila* slip into the sea, then huge air bubbles rising and bursting, creating a boiling stew of bodies and flotsam.

Ahmed was utterly alone in the vast ocean. The image of the missionary haunted him, the sole survivor five hundred years earlier, bound mercilessly to a flotsam of decking as his caravel sank before his eyes, not able to choose life nor death. His God had saved him, for what? So that Ahmed could bear witness to more brutal death? That's when he saw it, the pirate's speedboat, bobbing in the waves not one hundred meters distant, its motor silent.

Ahmed swam for it. The salt water knifed his leg wound. He ignored it. He thought of the shark he had seen earlier. He hoped, revoltingly, that the shark would feed on his dead shipmates before him.

As he neared the speedboat, he could see the pirate, slumped over the wheel. His back was red with blood, but was he dead? Ahmed approached cautiously, every splash deafening the ringing in his ear. The pirate remained still. He could see now, it was Mishad. He called to him, "Mishad!" As far as Mishad knew, Ahmed had completed his mission, pushed the button that alerted him to attack. No answer.

With great difficulty and the last of his strength, Ahmed hoisted himself over the gunwale. He crawled to Mishad and pulled him back. His face had been obliterated. Ahmed gagged. His stomach heaved. He summoned will from deep within, and heaved and shoved Mishad over the side. The body floated for a moment, then sunk with the weight of his sidearm, still holstered.

Ahmed sat in the bloodied seat. He turned the key. The engine stuttered then started with a roar. He dared to realize that he had been saved. He yanked the velvet pouch containing the Emerald from his pocket. He held it over the side, ready to drop it back into the depths where no man would find it. His grasp remained tight. He knew he couldn't let go. It was as if Allah told him that the power behind the attack, the master of both Mishad and the Americans who killed him, would cause more death and destruction. Ahmed knew, like his ancestor five centuries before him who had passed down the missionary's letter through generations of his family, that he was destined to help stop that evil power. He knew he had to get the Tear of the Moon Emerald to safety, to the only person who could protect its power from being unleashed, to its guardian. He had made a promise, and he would not break it.

Ahmed pushed the throttle forward. He didn't look back. His fate lay not in the past, but in the future, and he had to do what he could to change it.

# CHAPTER 12

Christa stared towards the dark abyss where Joseph had fallen. The beasts sniffed the rim of the plateau. One of them howled. Joseph had wanted to leave sooner. That kind, brave grandfather was dead, because of her. She had come here to do the right thing. How had it gone so wrong?

A light flashed from the opposite canyon rim. A second bang blasted through the darkness. The beast to the right yelped as it was bodily lifted, and thrown down in a heap. Its paws kicked pathetically. It whimpered, and wobbled back up to all fours. Slowly, with clear menace, the beast to the left with the long snout swiveled its massive jaws towards her. Its eyes flashed red, and it wasn't the reflection of her headlamp beam.

The beast bared its sharp canines. It emitted a guttural growl. The animal with the gray-tipped mane turned towards her. The two of them stalked closer, their haunches down, their lips stretched back against their teeth.

She snatched up her pack and the sphere, pivoted, dug in her toes and ran. The monsters brayed angrily. Thirty feet to the nearest doorway. Paws slapped at the gravel at her heels. Five feet. A claw tore at the back of her calf. She dove through the open portal, landing hard on the packed earth floor.

The lead beast skidded to a stop at the doorway. He lurched his massive head through the narrow space, his teeth bared in a snarl. A drip of saliva coursed from the point of his canine to the pounded earth floor, landing with a soft fizz. Joseph had said that Skinwalkers could not enter human habitation.

The beast lifted its clawed forepaw, its powerful muscles rippling beneath its ragged black fur. It stepped across the threshold.

The beast stalked towards her. Its breath stank of rotting flesh. But those red eyes, they weren't the soulless shark eyes of an animal. They were intelligent, scheming. Smart enough to know that she had one option--the open doorway about ten feet behind her, leading back into the cliff dwelling. It would come down to speed, and the animal with four legs would probably win. She spun and sprinted for it. The beast sprang at her.

She ran through and raced towards the far wall, her headlamp beam jagging crazily. The light hit on another opening, darker, narrower, hardly more than a foot wide. It could be a storage room, a dead end. The air smelled old, stale. She's never fit through. She had to try.

The beast crept into the room, stalking, patient. The armillary sphere, she could heave it at the thing, maybe daze it, or at least distract it. Sacrifice it for a sliver of time to escape through that doorway. She recoiled her arm. "Damn you," she screamed at it. "Damn you to hell." She couldn't let Samuel's murderers win. She couldn't let the bastards who shot Joseph grab the prize. She couldn't let her father down. "You want this? Never!" She pitched the sphere through the narrow portal. She yanked off her pack and threw it in after the sphere, then turned sideways, and squeezed herself into the doorway.

The other two beasts loped into the room. One more foot and she'd be free. Not good. This wasn't a doorway, it was a stone vise. And it was crushing her. She couldn't move. The three beasts crouched in a stalking position, haunches tense. The lead beast growled.

This was absurd. She was dead meat. Why weren't they attacking? She pressed her palms against the coarse sandstone, not caring that it scraped the skin raw. She kicked out with her foot. The lead beast snapped at it. A feint. Did they know that she was between them and the armillary sphere?

A voice seeped through the cool air. *Calm down.* She sensed it, didn't hear it. Mom's voice. This was crazy. It's not like Mom was helping her from the other side. There was no other side. Her heart hammered. Each breath wedged her in tighter. She couldn't die like this, through the very act of breathing to stay alive. She couldn't fail Dad again.

She breathed out, emptying her lungs, collapsing her chest. With one last thrust, she pushed through the opening, landing with a hip-bruising thud. The lead beast sprang at the portal. Its claws scraped the stone. It jabbed in its head, snarling, snapping its teeth. Its hoary breath blew hot on her ankles. But its massive haunches couldn't fit through the opening.

The beasts hunkered down at the threshold of the portal, and began digging with the vicious determination of a bloodhound on the scent. Damn it. They were creating a tunnel of their own, to get to her. She speared her headlamp beam into the darkness. It didn't reflect back. This wasn't a storage room. It was the mouth of a tunnel. Joseph's tunnel.

She leaned into the tunnel, straining to see, struggling to breathe. The air was thin and heavy at the same time. *You can do this, Christa. This mesa is not going to collapse on top of you.* She jammed the sphere into her pack and ran. The tunnel narrowed. She ducked to protect her skull from bashing into the rock. The weight of the sphere shifted wildly in her pack. But this tunnel went uphill, not down.

Up to the top of the plateau, or back down into the valley. It didn't matter. Anywhere but in the black throat of the cliff and its suffocating darkness. Her elbows scraped against the stone walls. It was getting darker. No, the headlamp was dying. It was a rookie mistake, not checking the batteries when she picked it up along with her new "lucky" pack at the trading post. She couldn't die here, not in this black loneliness, her desiccated corpse left behind for some future and better prepared explorer to find and place on exhibit. Like they'd find Joseph, his body twisted and abandoned in a tangle of creosote bush. *Hold it together, Christa.*

The blackness engulfed her. This was death. Black. Empty. Hopeless. It gripped her with cold, spindly fingers. Her father had never sounded so desperate, so weak when he called last night. She knew he'd been hurt, though he would never admit it. Her father was dying. That was why he had sent her to find the Turquoise. That was why he hadn't come himself to hunt down a vital piece of his ultimate treasure. She would never see him again. Never be embraced by his love. Never prove herself worthy of his pride.

She ran on. Her hand scraped against the rough rock sides of the tunnel. Her footsteps rasped against the gravel, violating the utter silence. The headlamp died.

She stopped. Her hand was poised in front of her face. She couldn't see it. Total darkness. She had to turn back. At least that was a way out. She crept backwards. The tunnel was too narrow to turn around. But the retreat would get wider, easier, and lead her out. To what? A cruel, meaningless death, her flesh eaten away? Even that was easier then plunging forward into the black unknown.

Her father wouldn't turn back. He wouldn't surrender to fear. She stopped again. She stretched her arm ahead of her as a guide. She stepped forward.

It seemed an eternity before she felt the split in the tunnel, but it was probably only a few yards. She pawed around. The path on the right sloped downhill. It could be a dead end. The top of the plateau was closer than the valley floor. Joseph had said to head downhill. She had to risk he was right, that history was right. She crept downwards.

Another brief eternity, another split in the tunnel. This time both paths headed downhill. It was too loud, the thunder of her heart, the whooshing of her breath through the utter silence. The air smelled old. She couldn't think. Just choose. Stay right, always right. Her father taught her that, at the dig in the catacombs. If she had to retrace her steps and choose another route, she could. *Never give up*, he said. She hated when he said that, but it kept him alive. The path plunged downward, a steep drop. Her boots slid on the slick rock.

Then, in the still air, a hint, no, a definite wisp of fresh, river-cooled air. She crawled towards it, the distant splash of water over rock, and the sweet fragrance of the cottonwood trees.

A light at the end of the tunnel, ahead, a brightening, a gray, not black. Heaven wouldn't have looked as glorious. Oh God, Dad was right. Never give up. She still had time to save him. Moonlight wove its way through a rough tumble of sage overgrowing the small opening, no more than three feet across and high. She yanked at the sage branches, snapping pieces away, releasing a distinctive herbal scent. She bulldozed her way through the last layer of brush. The spindly branches scratched and scraped her arms and legs. The pain felt like life.

Joseph was right. She had arrived at the bottom of the canyon, a dry, sandy area about twenty yards from a sharp bend in the river, a hundred yards downstream from where she and Joseph had climbed up to the cliff dwelling. Joseph could be back there, somehow miraculously survived the fall. Samuel's assailant had. Joseph needed help, fast.

She snugged her pack straps tight, raced upriver along the rock wall, careening around the bend in the canyon. She stopped short, her clunky hiking boots clattering the loose rock, and ducked back behind the angle of the canyon. Like they hadn't seen her, two of them. The bad guys. She plastered herself against the cliff, a sage brush poking at her bare thighs. The river ran fast and shallow here, as it angled down the valley. She strained to hear above the noise of its water splashing and coursing over the polished boulders. No shouts of alarm, but definite voices, coming this way, in a hurry.

Run or retreat. A cavalry riding to her rescue would be nice right now, but that only happened in old westerns with happy endings. The jeep, and any chance of returning with outside help, was parked across the river. Midstream was completely in the open. Easy target, especially slowed down by those slippery rocks.

She pivoted and retreated, racing across the short open ground between the river and the opening to the tunnel back into the cliff. Three gunshots blasted the sand in front of her feet. That stopped her. That meant they didn't want her dead, not yet. A second chance. One day her optimism was going to get her killed.

"You will not find escape in retreat," the voice was nasal, just loud enough to be heard above the rushing water.

If he thought fortune cookie philosophy was going to creep her out, he was right. What kind of man shoots first, plays word games later? She raised her hands and pivoted towards him, first taking in the beefy guy on the right with the smoking gun barrel protruding from his meaty paws. He wore a badly tailored black suit. He looked like he'd just buried a bullet-riddled body in a shallow grave. He was six-two, massive enough to make linebacker, but no doubt suspended from school too often to get a football scholarship, opting instead for a PhD from the school of hard knocks. White shirt, no tie, even the silvery moonlight couldn't soften his jagged features.

A stout man came up beside him. This shorter guy shook his wet, clinging pant cuff with each step, but that's where any resemblance to a puppy ended. He wore a pristine khaki safari shirt and pants and an orange neckerchief. His Tilley hat brim cast a moonshadow upon a face that was as pale and smooth as moonlight on river-polished granite, marred with eyes like black pinpricks. His cheeks were flaccid, his chin, weak. He had the look of a man who was teased and lonely as a boy who had spent his formative years trying to prove himself worthy. His arrogant smile implied he'd been defiant, or ruthless, enough to succeed.

Their vehicle was equally dark and built to overpower. A hundred yards up and across the river, a four-wheel drive, oversized SUV, its black exterior dusted with red sand, was parked next to Joseph's beat-up Jeep Wrangler. The SUV's headlights blasted the cottonwoods with light.

The stout man tipped the brim of his hat with gloved fingers. "I am the Prophet," he said. Just the kind of nutcase her father's eternal quest for the Breastplate attracted. "Perhaps you've seen my website. I have thousands of loyal followers," he spread out his arms, "worldwide."

Reality check time. Christa glanced around. Still in the desert wilderness, bad guy pointing a gun at her, mysterious armillary sphere feeling really heavy in her pack, poking into her shoulder blades. Who was this internet prophet? "A friend of mine," she dared to point upriver, "he may be hurt. I think he fell from the cliff."

The Prophet clasped his hands. "The Navajo shaman," he said. "He's fine, a tad bruised mind you, shoulder wound, but he didn't fall far before catching onto a ledge and climbing down. My man is with him."

"Thank God," Christa said, but the fact this guy had shot at her didn't inspire relief.

The Prophet laughed, soft, a kitten laugh. "Yes, well put, thank God," he said. "It is my life's goal, to save people." He nodded to the man on his right, who raised his pistol level with her heart. "I need what you have found."

The easy thing to do would be to tug that armillary sphere out of her pack and toss it to him. But the easy thing never came easy to her. And they had Joseph. "I need to see my friend first," she said. Her voice actually cracked in fear. She swallowed, hard. Allow the predator to smell fear, and the prey was doomed.

He nodded approvingly. "I knew you'd be worthy," he said. "You and I are here together for a reason. My new religion will bring peace to the people. You can be a part of it. The artifact you found will lead me to the catalyst my followers are waiting for."

He still hadn't said armillary sphere, nor Turquoise, nor Breastplate. He didn't know what they'd found. Like most prophets, he spoke with authority in order to deceive with ignorance. As much as she wanted to believe Joseph was alive, belief was not reality. "Where's Joseph?" she said. She could still try for the tunnel. Once inside, that thug was too big to pursue her. But he could shoot her.

"It all comes down to that," he said, "what and whom you believe."

He must have sold patent medicines in a former life.

"I know you've lost a loved one," he said. "I, too, lost a parent to violence. I want redemption, like you. And we shall find redemption, working together."

Lost a parent? Redemption? Her legs trembled. Her knees turned to rubber. He couldn't possibly know how her mother died. Nobody knew. "You killed Joseph," she said. She wanted to run. She wanted to fight. She wanted to kill this guy.

He clapped his hands twice. A man appeared from around the bend, dragging Joseph with him. The bad guy was massive. The old shaman looked frail. He had a gash on his left temple that looked like it was caused by a pistol butt and not a scrape against the cliff. Blood seeped through a slash in the shoulder of his plaid flannel shirt.

Joseph struggled to free himself. Christa reached towards him. He freed a hand, reached towards hers. "Run, Christa, now," he said. "Get the artifact to your father!" He yanked back his elbow and thrust it into the thug's gut. The thug collapsed to his knees, gripping his stomach.

The man with the pistol pivoted, aimed at Joseph. A shot rang out.

The gun flung away, splashing into the river. The thug screamed in pain and grabbed his forearm. "FBI!" a man's voice called from across the river. The cottonwood grove. The moon glinted on the barrel of a pistol, the man holding it barely visible behind a tree. "Toss your weapon into the river!" A stand-off. Nobody moved.

"Tell your men to disarm, Prophet" the voice called, "or you're next."

The Prophet hesitated, a calculating look narrowing his eyes, and nodded. The thug tossed his pistol. It landed with a splash. The FBI shooter emerged, pistol first, right arm straight out in front of him, forearm steadied with his left hand. He wore a black t-shirt, brown leather holster across his shoulder, faded jeans and black, army style, heavy tread boots. The moonlight accentuated his features, his chiseled face, military cut hair, sharp eyes, and muscular build.

He waded across the river with surprisingly steady footing. He circled round to the bank upriver of them.

"Agent Braydon Fox," the Prophet said, with venom in his voice. "Your presence here is disturbingly unexpected."

"You don't know what I'd do," said Fox. "Sticks in your craw, doesn't it?"

"You can't arrest me," said the Prophet. "I haven't committed any crime here."

"That's one. Title 18, United States Code, Section 1001, lying to a federal agent." This agent, Fox, his eyes kept glancing at her. "And kidnapping."

"Kidnapping?" said the Prophet. "This is an historical expedition," he gestured toward Joseph, "with my faithful Indian guide." The Prophet waved his hand dismissively. "Be a good lone ranger and ride back into the wilderness before you do something you'd regret."

"Haven't saved the damsel in distress yet," Fox said.

"A criminal case would involve hours of questions," he looked pointedly at Christa, "and confiscation of evidence. Nobody wants that."

Her pack grew heavier under the weight of Fox's probing gaze. The Prophet had a point. She and Joseph had risked their lives to secure the armillary sphere. She couldn't let it be squirreled away in some evidence locker for months. She needed time now to unlock its secret. But she couldn't let Samuel's killers get away, either.

"He's lying," she said. She pointed at Joseph. "They shot him."

The Prophet shrugged. "A hunting accident."

Joseph remained silent.

"They killed a man," she said, "an old prospector. He's back at our campsite. You can see for yourself."

"I have no idea what this young woman is talking about," the Prophet said.

Joseph said nothing.

Fox gestured towards the Prophet's men with a flick of his gun. "Get going, into the river. And keep your hands up." He nodded his head towards the Prophet. "You, too. Get to the middle of the river, and stay there."

The Prophet hunched his shoulders. If he were a cobra, this is when he'd strike. He waded into the river.

Fox backed away, his gun still targeting the Prophet as the man splashed deeper into the cool waters. "Get to that jeep," he said, nodding towards Christa and Joseph.

The Prophet swore as he slipped on a stone. "My friends at the Bureau will not be pleased, Fox." A look of pure disdain darkened his face. "I'll see that you're fired this time."

"You can't let them get away," Christa said. Joseph grabbed her hand, pulled her towards the river. Fine, she'd show Fox Samuel's body. Then he'd believe her.

She pushed through the frigid water. They scrambled out to the opposite bank, and hurried to the jeep. Their fire glowed weakly with the last of the embers. Moonlight splashed across their campsite. No Samuel. "He was here," she said, "the old prospector. He was dying. They killed him. He couldn't have just gotten up and walked into the night." The sand had been stirred around, erasing their footprints and any telltale blood stains.

"Hard enough to prove a homicide out here," Fox said. "Nearly impossible without a body. You don't know the Prophet like I do."

"Samuel was here," she said. "I swear it."

"The Prophet has two guys out there," Fox said, "maybe more. We have the advantage, but not for long. They got plenty of desert to hide three more bodies."

"I can't let them win," she said.

"You won't," said Joseph. "The only way to keep your promise to Samuel is to leave him behind." He swayed dizzily.

Damn it. She couldn't abandon Samuel again, but this Prophet knew about the cliff dwelling. He might know about Dad in Morocco, which meant Dad was definitely in trouble. She had to warn him.  She fished the keys from her pack and helped Joseph climb into the back.  Blood streamed down from his temple to his chin and dripped onto his plaid shirt.

"Drive," Fox said.  He slid into the passenger seat.

She climbed in behind the wheel, hoisted her pack onto the floor behind Fox's seat, and jammed the key into the ignition.  The engine stuttered.  It roared to life, sending a confused quail scampering for the low undergrowth.  She threw the jeep into gear.  Fox thrust his gun out the window, training it on the men standing in the middle of the river, their arms upraised.

As the jeep backed away, the Prophet advanced down the river, parting the tumbling waters at an angry pace.  The other men dispersed.  They plunged their hands into the shallows, searching for the pistol.  Christa swerved the jeep around to head back upriver from where they entered the valley just a few short hours ago.  A cloud of dust and gravel propelled out behind them.  In the rearview mirror, the thug ran to the Prophet's side.

"Get down!" she screamed.  "He's got the gun!"  She floored the accelerator.  The jeep bucked forward.  She twisted back to see.  The Prophet snatched the gun from the thug.  The jeep made an easy target, but he didn't shoot. He didn't try to kill them, or even stop them.  He dropped the gun to his side, and smiled.

# DAY 2

## CHAPTER 13

Christa tamped the brake and shifted her VW Beetle into third gear. She had to slow down. A kid could be outside playing, bundled up against this bitter cold, unseasonable even for Princeton in December. A little kid. The older ones would be in school. God, please let Lucia and Liam be in school. Priority number one—make sure they were safe.

One more block to Windsor Street. One hand gripped the steering wheel. The other clamped her cell phone to her ear. She checked the rear view mirror, again. No federal agents. No cheaply dressed thugs with guns. What she didn't see was damn scary, worse than the nightmare that kept her from getting any sleep last night on the red-eye from Phoenix. The armillary sphere bulged against the sides of her lucky pack, heavy enough on the passenger seat to cause the seat belt reminder light to flash as if she were transporting an invisible menace.

Gabriella's landline still wasn't working. On her cell, her answering machine picked up, again.

"Gabriella," Christa said, swerving around a parked minivan. "Forget about me needing to reach Dad. Just let me know you're okay."

She was an idiot. She should have jumped at the chance for Braydon Fox's help, instead of ditching him at the hospital where they brought Joseph. The minute they'd gotten out of the shooting range of the Prophet, Fox had snatched her pack and yanked out the armillary sphere and demanded to know why it was worth killing for. She wouldn't tell him why, even if she knew. Joseph had risked his life to keep the secret of the Turquoise. She didn't trust Agent Braydon Fox with it, any more than he trusted her. He refused to identify the name of the Prophet. For her own safety, he said. She didn't give a damn about her own safety right now.

At the Phoenix airport, she had googled Prophet and Breastplate of Aaron. The most likely website was NewWorldersforPeace.com. It featured the logo of a beast with a head of a lion, the body of a man holding a whip, and serpents as feet. It was called the Abraxas and figured heavily in the beliefs of the Gnostics. *The Abraxas is with the Black Magic Woman in San Francisco*, Joseph had told her, whatever that meant. The Prophet never revealed his true name to his followers, who lived in a dozen countries around the world and remained fanatically loyal despite his anonymous rants. The power to build a following through the Internet was terrifying.

If this was the "Prophet" who tried to kill her in the desert, he was a nut, but a really well-connected, powerful nut. He knew about the cliff dwelling, that she and Joseph had found something. He insinuated that he knew how Mom died. He could know about Gabriella, Percival, little Lucia and Liam. He hadn't shot at Joseph's jeep and hadn't stopped her as she took off with the sphere. The Prophet had smiled, like a poker player with an inside straight.

She slowed as she caught sight of the dollhouse-cute lavender fishscale shingles and flaking yellow trim of Gabriella's Victorian. A black Lincoln Town Car crawled by it, the kind the car services used to ferry people to the airport. Storm clouds, swirling east from the direction of the Princeton campus, reflected in the Town Car's blackened rear window. The silhouette of the driver craned to assess the house. He wore a cap.

The Town Car pulled away. It could be nothing, a neighbor having just arrived for a family holiday. But snakes slithered in her stomach.

She eased to a stop. The wind lashed the barren maple tree branches to the point of snapping. In contrast, the house looked eerily quiet and still. Dead oak leaves skittered around and clawed at the red and yellow plastic playhouse. A string of Christmas lights, cold and unlit, clung precariously from the peeling wood gutter,

chattering in the frigid gusts. The wind toppled the gaudy fiber optic
tree on the porch, bullying it against the rocking chair. Gabriella,
biologist and expert botanist, hadn't been able to deny Lucia's pleas
for the *most shiny, pinky tree in the world*. She had bought their
traditional living tree for Liam as well.

Christa gathered up her pack. She ot out of the car and followed
the fieldstone walk that sliced through the pachysandra and vinca
blanketing the front yard. Man, it was bitter cold. She clasped her
leather jacket closer to her, the funky one she bought from that street
vendor in Madrid, not exactly made for winter, or, frankly, any other
weather. She should have indulged in that overpriced I LUV NY
sweatshirt at the airport instead of changing in the restroom into her
last clean outfit from her suitcase. The short denim skirt, the
embroidered blouse from Mexico that could be washed in a hotel
sink and looked good wrinkled, the brown dress boots, it was
supposed to be a celebration outfit, a last stab at ridiculous optimism,
thinking that her father would meet her in Arizona and she would
hand him the Turquoise over mojitos.

A man's voice shouted from inside the house. Three quick
blasts. Gunfire? The squeal of tires. The Town Car careened
around the corner, speeding back towards the house. Gabriella's
front door flung open. A linebacker of a man bowled through,
clutching a book in the crook of one arm, a pistol in his other hand.
Christa pivoted to leap out of the way. The man crashed into her, the
full force of his weight lifting her off her feet. With surprising
agility he swung her around, dropping to the fieldstones beneath her
to cushion her fall. She landed on top of him, but the momentum
flung her to the side. Her temple slammed the edge of the walk.

A popping sound. A sting in her forearm. The man scrambled to
his feet. He had a black turtleneck, a crescent scar on his right
cheek, and a smoking barrel on his twenty-two. He was the thug
from the desert! He reached for her, as if to help. The Town Car's
horn blasted. He shoved himself up. He swiped his hands through
the dense pachysandra leaves, searching. For the book. He must
have dropped it. The Town Car's tires screeched. It was pulling
away, in a hurry. The man raced for the car. He yanked open the
back door and dove in. The Town Car sped away.

Acrid smoke lingered from the gunshot. Her head throbbed
worse than her arm. She pushed up on all fours, and rocked back

onto her heels. She closed her throat to stop from puking. A hole had punched through the sleeve of her leather jacket. A bloody slash creased across her arm, halfway between her wrist and elbow.

Percival stumbled out the front door and down the stairs. He wore red and blue plaid pajamas with matching bathrobe cinched at the waist and leather slide slippers. His slender fingers clasped the butt of Dad's Smith and Wesson pistol, the one he kept locked up. He rushed to her. The Town Car screeched around the corner. He knelt by her, grasped her arm. "By God, Christa, you've been shot."

Stars floated in her eyes. It was the adrenaline; she'd soldiered through a lot worse injuries than the bullet graze. And Percy holding a gun was more dizzying than the bash on the head. "The kids, Percy. Where's Lucia and Liam?"

"In school, of course," he said. "Helen took them. That is, Lucia is in school. Liam wasn't feeling well. Helen took him to the campus clinic. They've been with her since yesterday. I just don't understand, Christa. I mean, what is this all about? Your father calls, insists our children have to go to your sister's, for their safety, he said, and it's a good thing he did, mind you."

"Percy," she said, too loudly. It hurt. "Where is Gabriella?"

"Colombia. I've been trying to reach her. She's left for the jungle, where she was last summer, searching for medicinal plants. I couldn't fathom why it couldn't wait until after the holidays. She insisted that her research was at a crucial stage, that she absolutely had to track down a new specimen. I've never seen her so anxious."

"Gabby's in Colombia? No, scratch that. Dad called?"

"He alerted me to a package coming for you, here. It arrived this morning. He's in Morocco. Did you know that?"

"Package?"

"That thug was after it," he said, looking again down the street, then up the street. "He tried to shoot me. I promised your father. Nobody was to have that package but you. I had to protect it with my life, he said. I am not your father, Christa."

No, he wasn't. Percival was a wonderful man, intelligent, kind, a loving, dedicated husband and father, but adventure to him was riding the Pirates of the Caribbean at Disneyworld twice. "You did fine, Percy. Where's the package?"

"That brute took it," he said. "I tried to stop him."

"He didn't take it." She stood on rubber legs. "He dropped it, somewhere in the pachysandra." Fighting off the dizziness, she scanned the tangle of low green leaves. Percival slid the gun into his bathrobe pocket. He swam his hands and waded his slippered feet through the dense groundcover.

He swooped up the book and raised it above his head in triumph. "I've got it."

She stepped back. She swallowed a new threat of nausea. He held a worn, stained, leather notebook, held together with a leather strap that she had braided on Father's Day when she was ten. "Not a book," she said. "Dad's journal." Dad's Bible, the three sisters called it, with both respect and disdain. He kept all his notes, ideas, and inspirations on the Breastplate of Aaron in it. "The one we burned in effigy last Christmas." Long after Percy and the kids were asleep in bed. She and Gabby were drunk. Dad hadn't shown up for the holiday, again.

Percy looked at the journal as if it were diseased. "This is the book you always talk about? It can't be. Gabby said that your father would sooner cut off his right hand than part with this."

She reached out her open palm. He balanced the journal on it. It was Dad's soul, in her hands.

Percival stepped back, scanning the ground. "The letter," he said. "He sent a letter with it, an old letter. It was here, with the journal."

"There!" Christa said. The paper was skimming along the top of the pachysandra, lifted by the breeze.

Percy chased after it. He scooped it up as it swerved onto the sidewalk. A corner of the yellowed paper broke off and flew away in a gust. "It's written in Latin," he said. "Your father said it was the key. The key to what, Christa? No, don't tell me. I don't like my family being brought into this."

"Too late," she said. As they hurried back to the house, she recapped what had happened at the cliff dwelling. His face grew paler with each description, but he didn't once show disbelief, not of Samuel's dying words, the shapeshifters, the creepy Prophet. She'd show him the sphere later. Right now, she needed to focus on that letter.

"Christa, your father didn't sound like himself when he called. He sounded," he rubbed his chin and cast his gaze down, "weak."

"Injured?" she asked.

"He said he was fine."

Which meant he must be badly hurt.

"Christa, I love your father, you know that, but if he has put my family in danger–"

"I'm sure that wasn't his intention," she said. It never was. He always claimed his work was vital to keeping his family safe, whatever that meant. "Call the school," she said. "Tell them that Lucia needs to be picked up early. I'll call Helen."

She punched in her sister's cell number.

"Christa," Helen answered, her voice sharp. "Thank God."

Helen often thanked God, but never before for Christa. "Helen, what's the matter?"

"I've been trying to reach Percival," she said. Christa could hear children crying in the background. "His phone isn't working. Gabriella is in Colombia, although why she'd leave her family six days before Christmas is beyond me. And I thought you flew off to Arizona." It was more an accusation than a question.

"Just got back. I'm at Gabby's house now." She hurried up the front steps. "Percival wants Lucia picked up early from school."

"I can't leave here," Helen shot back. "We're still at the doctor's office. The place is like a madhouse today. I had to turn off my cell phone. Were you trying to reach me?"

"You're still at the clinic?"

"Doctor Templeton still can't figure out what's wrong with Liam. The doctor says it's just a bad headache, although he's scratching his head over Liam's rash. I know it's something more serious. I know it is." Helen was never one to accept an optimistic diagnosis. Gabriella, the eldest, could find a positive side to moldy bread. The middle sister, Helen, could find black in a rainbow. Helen had become an ardent Christian because she saw eternal damnation in every sunset. "You know Liam. He never complains. If he says he has a headache, it must be bad. Something's going around. There's a pack of sick kids here. Moms don't look too good, either."

"Percival is worried," said Christa. "Me, too."

"Worried?" she shot back. "We all agree? Then it truly is God's will."

Christa cringed. Helen wouldn't butter her toast in the morning unless she felt God wanted her to. "What about Peter?" Helen and Peter loved those kids like their own, if they could have one or six.

"Peter's due back today, but his flight is delayed," she said. "I called the kids' school; let them know what's going on. I'm telling you. It's an epidemic, worse than swine flu. I'm already planning to pick up Lucia before she is exposed. Someone has to take care of these kids. And that means me. Got to go. The doctor's finally calling us in." With that, she hung up.

As Percival made his phone calls, she ducked into the powder room and washed her wound. It wasn't bad, just a graze. She'd gotten worse bruises fencing. She plastered it with Barbie bandages. That was twice in twenty-four hours she'd been shot at. Good thing she didn't believe bad things came in threes. Six, seven, maybe. This was far from over.

She headed for the library. Despite its dark walnut paneling, glum oxblood draperies and overall gloomy visage, this was her favorite room in Gabby's home. More importantly, it was the repository for the arcane texts their parents had collected. Gabriella hadn't so much inherited them as accepted their guardianship.

She crossed to the massive partners desk that came with the house because it was too heavy to move. Behind it, the painting of the hunting dogs framed in gold protruded like an open door from the wall. It hid the wall safe. They all made fun of that painting, it also came with the house, but Gabriella did use the safe for one thing, to lock Dad's old gun away from the kids. For Liam, the hidden safe had been the main reason for them to buy the house. He had spent many afternoons exploring the old Victorian for secret passages, and when none appeared, built them in his imagination.

She shrugged off her lucky pack and righted the wooden desk chair from where it had toppled to the floor. She rolled it in close to the desk. Dad's journal, here, in her hands. Those hungry lions in the Serengeti and the frigid waves swamping their canoe in the Tasman Sea were nothing compared to the terror of opening this small book. It was like admitting Dad was dead, or close to it. He'd laugh at her trepidation. *Haven't I always taught you that the greatest fear is that of the unknown?*

She sucked in a deep breath and opened the cover. But she'd seen most of this before. Dad constantly reviewed these pages with her. Most of them she could have written herself on their crazy expeditions to unearth long lost clues. The last pages were new, notes of his dig in the Roman ruins along the Moroccan coast, following up the lead of that old Vatican guard he'd stumbled across. Then, in weaker script, a note,

*To Christa: I made a promise to your mother. It has fallen upon you to fulfill it. I've found it, Salvatierra's letter, the man who started all this. It's time you learned about the Circle of Seven. You, Christa, are the new guardian of the Tear of the Moon Emerald, like your mother before you. It was her dying wish, and may be mine. Write the ending to our story, Christa. Millions of lives may depend on it. Never give up. Your loving father, Thaddeus.*

*Dying wish. Millions of lives.* Dad certainly hadn't lost his sense of melodrama. And she hadn't lost her need for denial, or burden of guilt, or, for that matter, her stubborn determination to make things right.

Salvatierra's letter. Dad had actually found the letter she had argued couldn't possibly exist. It had been the breaking point that made her abandon Dad and his quest. And here it was in her trembling hands. The date, February 14, 1586. The flowing script written with quill and ink, true to the period. The language, Latin. The yellowed parchment was splotched with red that looked like blood.

Percival entered the room. He laid her cell phone on the corner of the desk. With two fingers, he removed the pistol from his bathrobe pocket like the gun was infected and set it next to the cell phone.

The letter's script was shaky but beautifully crafted Latin. A few old Spanish words, derived from the spoken Latin, stood out. And now, the signature. "Juan Jaramillo de Salvatierra," she said aloud, her voice dry. She leaned back and swallowed hard.

Percival leaned in closer. "It's the letter," he said, "the one your father had been searching for. I didn't believe it really existed."

"Neither did I," Christa said. "Dad sent this here? From Morocco?"

"It arrived this morning."

"I'll need Dad's Latin-English dictionary, third shelf down, the Cassell's not the Oxford."

He crossed to the bookcases and ran his finger along the spines. "Gabriella should not have gone to Colombia. I need her."

"And she needs you." She moved aside a scattering of Gabriella's botanical sketches to make room for the laptop.

"You're right, of course," he said. "It's infuriating. I love her so I was desperate to stop her, but couldn't stop her because I love her." He heaved the heavy tome from the shelf, and manhandled it to the corner of the desk. He tore the glasses from his face and pointed them at her. "You know I will do anything to save my family, and my family includes you and your exasperating father."

Percival was downright rugged beneath his mathematics nerd veneer, with a strong chin and brilliant blue eyes. He had the build of a welterweight boxer, all muscle and bone. It was scary how much he resembled her father at a younger age. "As will I," she said. She bent over the letter and began keying in the translation with a heading. *Letter, written by Juan Jaramillo de Salvatierra to his brother, Pedro Alonso de Salvatierra, Vatican City. Vissilus Ruins, Morocco, February 14, 1586.*

From the first line, this was going to challenge her courage more than her translation skills. "Juan Salvatierra writes that he was dying," she said. "This is his last missive, maybe his last confession." A confession was a sacrosanct vow, between priest and confessor, and, in this case, between brothers, but that wasn't the worst part. This letter was the compass that her father had sacrificed years to find. "Dad would never have let this out of his hands unless he was desperate." Unless he was, like Salvatierra wrote in his opening paragraph, near death.

CHAPTER **14**

Braydon Fox had little time and less patience. The Prophet was after Christa Devlin and that armillary sphere she found in the desert. It had to be a clue. To something big, very big. That the Prophet was willing to risk an accessory to murder charge for. He had to puzzle this one out. Lives depended on it.

He pressed his back against the swinging door of the banquet hall to push it open, two steaming mugs in his hands. He pivoted, nearly knocking over a busboy who shouldered a service tray as round as he was tall. The boy skirted a cloth-covered banquet table like the Titanic bearing away from an iceberg. He listed to starboard. The phalanx of champagne glasses slid, clinked, wobbled. The kid let out a startled gasp of fear, overcompensated, shot up his hand to steady the glasses. Braydon's reflexes kicked in. In one move, he slid his two mugs onto the nearest table, caught the rim of the tray before it toppled and eased it onto another table. If only he could steady his concerns about Christa Devlin that expertly.

The kid laughed in relief as the last glass teetered to a stop. He made a quick sign of the cross and kissed the crucifix hanging around his neck. "Gracias," he said. "Thank you. If I break glasses, I pay."

"De nada," Braydon said. He'd bussed his share of tables, saving up for the Academy. His father wasn't about to pay his way to joining the Bureau. He gathered his two mugs and wove his way around tables and chairs, across the expanse of the banquet hall.

It was one of New York's finest venues in one of the city's finest hotels, the Platinum Room at the Waldorf Astoria. An army of busboys laid out china and more silverware at each place setting than Braydon had in his entire kitchen drawer. Buckets of flowers waited deployment from rolling trays in the corner. The clank of silver, china and crystal filled the room, along with the melodic fussing of the event manager, a gay guy who dressed in purple but could whip any man or woman into shape with a flit of his hand. The guy knew his stuff, and Braydon appreciated that he didn't argue when each of the waitstaff had to be vetted for security.

Braydon's boss was standing by the stage at the far end of the room, clipboard in hand, smartly dressed in a bold red suit that she somehow pulled off on her petite frame. Emerson Kim had been in the Bureau for decades, but didn't look a day over forty. She had scratched her way up to the top New York position by being brilliant and hard-working, although rumor had it that she first earned her bones spiriting crucial, disaster-averting intel out of North Korea when she was barely out of the Academy. She knew what it was like to be in the field, and never forgot it. Her email to him this morning was concise and to the point. *Meet me at the Waldorf by ten or turn in your resignation.*

"Special Agent Fox," she said as he drew near. "Your security plan for the presentation tonight is impeccable, as always, which is the only reason I am not firing your ass right now."

"That," said Braydon, "and the hot chocolate." Emerson was in a minority, not just as a Korean. She hated the taste of coffee. She did, however, fully appreciate the need for caffeine. Braydon was prepared with a packet of the rare caffeinated hot cocoa. He handed her the mug he had snapped up in the kitchen to add flair to his presentation, even added a dollop of whipped cream. She couldn't be bribed. He simply liked her and appreciated her integrity.

She accepted the mug, saluted him with it. "Saving the damsel in distress, again."

"Bad habit."

"What more do you know about Christa Devlin?"

"Only what I sent you in the email from the airport," said Braydon, sipping on his own coffee, black. "She is an assistant history professor at Princeton. No priors. Her brother-in-law is a Princeton mathematics professor. He's never even had a parking ticket. Her father is a bit of a mystery. Archaeologist. Travels to some edgy places. But the kicker is her sister, Gabriella Devlin Hunter. She's that botanist for NewWorld Pharmaceuticals, owned by Baltasar Contreras. I interviewed her four months ago, but she seemed clean." He slid the folded printout from his pocket and snapped it open. It was a photo of Gabriella Devlin Hunter and her two kids at a company picnic from the NewWorld website. "She was on that NewWorld expedition to Colombia for Contreras last summer. And she flew back to Colombia yesterday. Bought her ticket at the airport."

"You're playing with fire, Fox. I told you to lay off Contreras. He's given enough money in campaign contributions to buy every Congressman a penthouse suite. And his pharmaceutical empire has offices in more countries than most people have on their bucket list."

"Ironic," he said, "that his company works to cure the world's ills. That guy's a cancer." As a special agent on the FBI's Jewelry and Gem, JAG, team, Braydon was accustomed to the intricate web of high end thievery in the art and gem world, but this felt something more like, he hated the word, a conspiracy.

"Bold diagnosis, doctor," she said, "but where is the evidence?"

"I'm working on it."

"Not according to the Bureau," she said. "That case in San Francisco is as cold as the stone that was stolen. Right now, you're coordinating security for the presentation of the Lux et Veritas sword, in this banquet hall, tonight."

"Which is why I'm keeping a close tail on Contreras." The Lux et Veritas sword was a bejeweled trophy piece commissioned by an anonymous donor to commemorate the G-20 summit on world peace. Britain's United Nations ambassador had been instrumental in coordinating each of the twenty nations to contribute a gemstone for the sword's hilt, a diplomatic tour de force. Braydon was well aware of the implications should a terrorist attack or a thief disrupt its presentation.

Kim finished off the whipped cream with a slurp that she would have restrained with anyone else besides Braydon. "So what were you doing in the Arizona desert last night?"

"The question is, what was Baltasar Contreras doing in Arizona last night?"

"Haven't you heard?" She pursed her lips. "Contreras wasn't there. He was dining with none other than the New York Chief of Homeland Security Rambitskov, going over the details of tonight's sword presentation, like you should have been. Contreras is making you look like a fool, Fox."

"Impossible," Braydon said, unless Rambitskov was in on the faked alibi.

"Don't say what you're thinking," said Kim. "You implicate Chief Rambitskov and the President, himself, will fire you."

"Contreras has a private jet. He could still have gotten to the desert after this alleged dinner."

"Contreras is a charming, uber-successful businessman who is funding this banquet tonight. You've been on his back, how long?"

"Nine months," Braydon said. "Since the theft from the San Francisco Museum of Culture and History."

"You figured the perpetrator was Adlai Stonington, that high-end jewel thief that you've been building a case against."

"I'm sure of it." Within hours of the discovery of the theft, Braydon had boots on the ground. By the next day, when it was discovered that all that the thief had snatched was a set of four stones, called the Abraxas collection, leaving behind a Faberge egg, a Rembrandt sketch and other pricey booty, his team was speedily reassigned to a high profile art theft from the Boston Museum of Fine Arts. "Contreras met with Stonington in San Francisco the day after the Abraxas theft," he said.

"As I recall, our illustrious FBI Director personally kicked you off that case."

"We both know that the Director is positioning himself for the Secretary of State." Braydon had figured Contreras for a collector who could afford any whim for stolen art or cultural gems, and a man who was used to getting what he wanted. The millions he filtered into high stakes political campaigns didn't hurt. He no doubt promised the FBI Director to throw some of his weight his way.

"The Director didn't want to listen to any nutty ideas about Contreras being tight with a suspected thief like Stonington."

Which is why Braydon had cashed in his personal chits, and got his off-the-grid guy, Torrino, to go in deep undercover. He had taken a bullet for Torrino, saved his life, and, more importantly, killed the bad guys before they could kill his pregnant wife.

It proved remarkably easy for Torrino to get close to Contreras, thanks to Contreras's odd preference for beefy men and the alarming attrition rate of his "enforcers." Torrino had become Contreras's go-to guy for anything that required his ample brawn, apparently unshakeable loyalty, and bulldog persistence. Torrino had slipped

Braydon evidence that Contreras was a nut who fancied himself a Prophet, a megalomaniac who had designs on starting a new religion, which was terrifying, but not against the law. In fact, if Braydon tried to stop him, then he'd be the criminal.

"It was a bunch of old stones that was stolen," said Kim, finishing off the last of her hot chocolate, "not the Crown Jewels."

"Exactly why I think there's something else going on," said Braydon, "something big. Or Contreras wouldn't waste his time."

"Neither should you. These Abraxas stones aren't worth it. Even the museum curator admitted the value of the Abraxas stones was more historical than material. So what if Contreras met with a jewel thief. It won't be the first time some billionaire maneuvers to buy something that's not for sale."

"True, and the second time was last night, in the Arizona desert."

Kim pointed the clipboard at him. "I took a big chance, Special Agent Fox, trusting you when you begged me to take on the security of the Lux et Veritas sword. I know you did it because Contreras is hosting the banquet tonight. I figured a suspicious agent would be more diligent than an ass-kissing one, but a paranoid agent could kill both our careers."

"It's not our careers that concerns me."

Kim shook her head. "It's about her, isn't it? Christa Devlin," she said. "Just like Iraq. You were sent over to track down the gems looted from the museum. Instead, you defied orders and risked your life for your informant, an Iraqi, no less, who got himself caught by the bad guys. Or taking that bullet for an expendable snatch and grab snitch. You're falling into the same trap with Devlin. You can't save everyone who dives in over their heads. Use them, then lose them. You've got courage and you're a damned good investigator, but rogues don't last long under my watch, Agent Fox."

"Neither will Christa Devlin," he said, "if I don't get to her, now."

"I saw her photo on the Princeton's history department's website," she said. "I'm telling you this as a friend, Braydon, not the boss. Don't do this, not for the wrong reasons."

Of course Emerson would have checked the website, and seen the resemblance to his partner in work, and he had hoped, in life. But nothing was going to bring her back. Nothing was ever going to settle the score. "I'm doing this because it's my job," he said. It was all he had left.

CHAPTER **15**

Baltasar Contreras cracked open the lobster claw with a satisfying snap.  He relished the day when he'd do the same to Torrino's neck.  For now, he had to twist only his manhood, to find out if his failure was idiocy, or destiny.

"Percival Hunter shot at me." Torrino paced as he spoke, his beefy Italian arms gesticulating wildly. "What the hell was he doing with a gun? I had the journal in my hand. I had to get out of there, or kill him.  And you told me not to kill him."

"Failure is weakness," said Contreras, as his own father had taught him, "and weakness is unacceptable." It was the cornerstone of the family's pharmaceutical fortune.  It had built this estate, this leafy orangery where Contreras enjoyed taking his lunch on Princeton's wintery days.   As a boy, this garden was his Eden. Father had even introduced a variety of highly poisonous dart frogs to the garden, to teach his son a lesson in fear, and to remind him of his family's destiny. "It is a good maxim, don't you agree, Mister Torrino?"

"I was expecting a math geek," said Torrino, "not a marksman."

Contreras smiled crookedly at Torrino's stab at wit.  Part of him liked Torrino.  He could not deny it.  He breathed in the invigorating aroma of citrus from the nearby lemon tree and the fertile scent of the wet, dark earth from which it grew.  So much more promising than the arid Arizona desert of last night.  Upon arriving home, he had washed away his fury along with the pervasive red sand.  He told himself to remain calm, especially now.  He tamped down the ember of anger that threatened to flare inside him.

"Percival Hunter is the weak link," said Contreras.  "All you had to do was pilfer his wife's journal.  Then you were to wait to see if

Christa Devlin showed up with the Turquoise and take that from her."

He laid the nutcracker on the glass topped, wrought iron table and extricated a juicy bite of lobster from its crusher claw. As his greasy lips circled the meat, a drip of juice fell from his chin onto his custom-tailored lapel. He didn't bother dabbing the spot with his linen napkin. The suit was now imperfect, ruined. He gestured to his butler. "Get Mister Lee out here from Manhattan," he said. "I need to replace this suit." He squeezed his thumb into the waistline of his slacks to ease the binding tightness. "Tell him he is off in his measurements. I will not tolerate it." Fool. Didn't Lee understand that in religion image is everything?

Contreras made sure Torrino understood. He charmed this disenchanted former altar boy with a power that towered above earthly laws. Contreras caught his own reflection in the glass table top. His thinning hairline and soft belly just made him all the more resistible. It showed Torrino that if a man like him could rule others, then he could rule him, and, oh, how Torrino wanted to be ruled.

Like all the men who followed him. Deliberately, Contreras had stayed the course set by his father, and his father before him, hiring only those who would fear him completely. Surely his father would see that he had succeeded in that, at least. "You know, Mister Torrino, what God did to those who failed Him at Sodom and Gomorrah."

Torrino swallowed. "Destroyed them with fire and brimstone."

"That was the work of the true God, the Old Testament God, before mankind in their hubris corrupted the divine power into something more earthly, more human, more," and he laughed when he thought about it, "loving." They needed a teacher, these pretenders to the heavenly throne. The time had come to put himself fully into the service of God. "You know why they have named me the Prophet," he said.

"Because you will know God's true command," said Torrino.

Contreras nodded. "So I have taught you." He took another sip of his espresso, the aroma almost as strong as the liquid was hot on his tongue. "God wants me to have the sacred stones," he said. "Percival Hunter risked his life for the journal. Perhaps he knows something after all."

"He didn't know nothing," Torrino stammered, his eyes darting between the two men on either side of him. Their hands, as if synchronized, eased inside their sport coats to rest on their pistol butts.

Torrino should be shot for his bad grammar alone. But Contreras needed men like him, beefy, ruthless men, the T Rex's of their business. "So he must know something."

A perplexed look crossed Torrino's face. "Listen. He's in the library, standing by the side window, squinting at some old letter, all weird-like. I'm telling you. It was dark. The guy doesn't have the sense to turn on the light. As if light's going to come through that side window. It was like night out there on the side of that house."

Contreras tented his fingers. Curious. Why was this letter important? "And yet, perhaps, he had seen the light," he muttered. Others might overlook this detail, shrug it off as a misguided diversion. Others did not have his genius to weave these thousands of details into a master plan. Others were meant to be ruled, not to rule.

"He didn't see the light," said Torrino. "He saw me, and the minute he did, his eyes shoot over to the book on the table next to him. It was old, leather, no title. I figured it had to be that plant lady's journal you wanted. Hunter would make a lousy quarterback."

"Describe the letter."

"The letter was old, yellowed, like it had been around awhile," he said. "That's when your driver panicked and texted me. I grab my cell from my pocket. 'Bug out,' it says. Hunter is looking across the room. The wall safe is open, couple boxes of ammo in it. He's eyeing the twenty-two pistol on the desk."

Contreras leaned forward. "Hunter had removed his gun from the safe. He was anticipating an immediate threat." This could mean nothing, or everything. How much had his wife told him? Had Christa Devlin reached him? His landline was down, Contreras had made sure of that, but the cell phone was not so easily controlled.

"Then all hell breaks loose."

"Not all of it," said Contreras, "not yet."

Torrino lunged forward, his fists clenched. "Hunter goes for the gun on the desk. I shove him aside and snatch the journal. I figured that letter could be important, so I grab that, too. I take off, and Hunter starts shooting at me."

Contreras's gaze swerved up to meet Torrino's. The sight of the big man's eyes widening with fear filled him with a warm satisfaction.

Torrino's eyes darted away. He hunched his shoulders. The man was hiding something. Torrino chanced a sidelong glance to the body guard to his right. The guard maintained his granite edifice. Contreras had trained him well. "I'm not going to let no crazy man shoot me," Torrino said.

"No," Contreras replied. "That should be left to a sane man."

Torrino pointed at him, then withdrew the gesture and shoved his hands into his pockets. "It was the girl, from the desert. She was coming up the front walkway."

"So Christa Devlin arrived, as I suspected she would," Contreras said. He wasn't about to let Braydon Fox's gambit in the desert delay him. Within minutes of the unfortunate encounter, Contreras had called in a helicopter using his satellite phone. His private jet had been fueled and ready for wheels up. He'd been back in his Princeton estate for hours, analyzing Christa Devlin's next move. He smiled. As he had hoped, Fox's annoying charms hadn't won her over. She had gone racing straight to Gabriella, except her sister wasn't there. The woman had gone missing, and he hadn't disappeared her. It was infuriating.

Torrino nodded. "She looked different than in the desert, wore this short skirt, tall boots. In the daylight, I could see those amazing green eyes. Who knew a history professor could be so hot. Man, I wished I'd gone to Princeton."

Not many statements left Contreras speechless. This one did. He leaned forward. "And Devlin's pack, the one she had in Arizona?"

"Yeah, she had it."

"And yet you returned here without the journal, nor this mysterious letter, nor Devlin's pack, Mister Torrino." He said it more as a threat, than a question.

"When I crashed into Devlin, the journal fell into the damn bushes. Letter, too." Torrino dared to point at him, then thought better of it. "Your driver panicked," he said. "He must have seen Hunter come out, with that gun, because he starts driving off, leaving me there. I figured I'd better clear out. If Hunter didn't shoot me, then that FBI guy might show up. And you said I shouldn't let them take me alive."

"That's what the cyanide is for, dear Torrino."

Torrino jabbed his trigger finger in Contreras's direction. "Not that I'd talk, Mr. Contreras. I'd never tell them nothing."

"Your double negatives are not reassuring." Contreras smacked the lobster juice from his lips, then dabbed them with his linen napkin.

Contreras signaled for his butler to clear the lunch dishes, but placed his hand over the nutcracker so it would be left on the table. Christa Devlin. In his mind, his fingers picked up her strings, toyed with them a bit. She would be desperately alone, with her father and sister unreachable. And yet she hadn't given in to Agent Fox. That took courage, and loyalty to her father. Contreras smiled. It was time to twist tight the tragedy of her mother's murder, to spin her destiny in a new direction, like his destiny had been. He almost hated doing it, but she'd thank him in the end.

The butler placed a generous slice of lemon meringue pie and a chilled dessert fork on the table. Contreras carved out a bite and waved it at Torrino. "You shoot with your right hand, don't you, Mister Torrino?"

Torrino stepped back. The bodyguard on his right gripped his elbow to hold him in place.

Contreras filled his mouth with the bite of pie. The meringue fairly melted on his tongue and the lemon had just enough punch to invigorate his cheeks. He put down the dessert fork and picked up the nutcracker. "Left hand, then," he said, beckoning to Torrino.

"I did everything you told me to," said Torrino

Contreras pursed his lips impatiently. The bodyguard on Torrino's left pulled his pistol from his shoulder holster. Torrino hesitated, then leaned forward, stretching his left hand over the glass table towards Contreras. It trembled gratifyingly. Contreras grasped it gently, such strong fingers, rough and calloused, but so very warm. He did not want to hurt this man. He wanted to save him, to save humankind. Why was he forced to always prove his power? He folded Torrino's hand closed, but tugged out the man's beefy pinky finger, pulling it straight. He encircled the finger with the nutcracker, pressed, and he twisted until the bone snapped.

Torrino's cry, give him credit, was loud, but brief. Torrino cradled his pinky with his other hand and pulled it close to his chest, grimacing at the sight of the finger, its middle bone bent grotesquely at a right angle, pointing accusingly at his own ring finger.

Contreras tried another bite of pie, moaning in delight at the blend of flavors and textures. "Fenton," he addressed his butler, "tell Pierre that he has truly outdone himself. The meringue is exquisite." He leaned back in his chair. "Mister Torrino, what exactly did Percival Hunter say?"

Torrino unclenched his mouth. "Nothing. He didn't tell me nothing."

Contreras leaned forward, tenting his fingers, catching Torrino's reddened eyes in his razor sharp gaze. "Surely, amongst all this gunplay, he must have said something."

"Just crazy talk," Torrino answered.

Contreras reached for the nutcracker. "My patience is limited."

Torrino cradled his injured hand closer to his chest. "He was chasing me. He thought I was getting away with the goods. He said Devlins never give up."

Contreras smiled. "Oh they will, dear Torrino, they will."

## CHAPTER 16

Christa keyed in the last tweak to her translation of Salvatierra's letter. Now she had to figure out how, or if, it would lead her to the seven sacred stones that could restore the Breastplate of Aaron. She drew in a deep breath and pressed print. With a rhythmic whir, the printer churned out a five hundred year old letter that challenged the conventions of New World history, and dug into the very roots of Judeo-Christian beliefs. Not to mention her relationship with her father. A desperate man. Desperate enough to forge a letter that so conveniently proved witness to his story.

Percival entered the room. She hadn't noticed he left. He had shaved and changed from his pajamas into navy slacks, worn at the hem, and a wrinkled oxford shirt.

"This letter tells quite a tale," she said. "It certainly looks and reads authentic, but it can't be real." Even if she wanted it to be. Even if she clung onto that last thread of belief.

"I believe it is," he said. Percival was not a religious man, not by a long shot. He constantly argued with Helen, their family's token fanatic, about the Bible passages that were mathematically impossible. And he only tolerated Dad's obsession with the Breastplate because he loved Gabriella. He crossed to the open Fed Ex box on the table by the window, pawed through the Styrofoam curls, and extracted what looked like a faded blue-bordered scarf tied into a small bundle. "This came in the package with the letter and your father's journal." He placed it on her open palm.

The cloth was soft with wear, faded by the sun, the border an intricate geometric weave of blues on white. Whatever it held had heft to it, weight and substance for such a small package. As she untied the ends that knotted the bundle, a familiar scent escaped. It was the earthy hint of the desert, the red sands of Morocco, and the salty tease of a far-away ocean coast.

Percival leaned in closer. "Even with my rudimentary Latin," he said. "I recognized the word."

Swallowing her trepidation, she spread open the scarf. "Crucifix," she said aloud. But not just any crucifix. The gold gleamed even in the dim light of the library. The Christ figure was intricately detailed, His expression one of pained acceptance. Beneath His feet, the unusual skull and crossbones, carved from ivory, grinned at her ominously. She turned over the cross. The bright red, blue and golden enamel, indicating 16th century Iberian roots, was inscribed in gold with two words, Lux et Veritas. Latin for Light and Truth. "Juan Jaramillo de Salvatierra's crucifix," she said. He had embarked to the new world with little more than this crucifix and his faith. His crucifix was evidence that the letter was authentic. "All this time, Dad was right."

Percival frowned, adjusted his glasses. "I don't know if I'd say that," he said. He took the crucifix from her and clasped the chain at the back of her neck. "But it's clear he wanted you to have this."

"This is the proof," she said, "that I've been searching for all these years. The 1755 Lisbon earthquake and resulting tsunami and fire destroyed the city. I thought, maybe, the historical record of this expedition could have been lost. But to find no reports, no passing references, no captain's entries about the Breastplate in any other cities, nor libraries, nor texts. Even a leap of faith didn't account for that."

"Leap of faith," he echoed. He twisted his wedding band, a nervous habit. "As I said, my Latin is a tad rusty, but before that intruder grabbed the letter from me, I saw a name, in darker ink, bold-faced in today's vernacular. Contreras."

"The name Dad has been searching for, Alvaro Contreras," she said, pointing to the name in the letter, "the conquistador. He was the one who brought the Breastplate to the new world."

"The villain, so to speak."

"Returned to Spain in chains," she said, "according to Salvatierra's letter."

"The head of NewWorld Pharmaceuticals," his eyes met hers, "his name is Baltasar Contreras."

"NewWorld Pharmaceuticals," she repeated. "Gabriella's company. Gabriella's boss is named Contreras?"

"I was computing the odds whilst I was upstairs shaving," he said, "and, well, it simply cannot be a familial connection. It's just a peculiar coincidence. Baltasar Contreras is no villain."

"What does he look like? Stout, pale skin, pudgy face, contrived wardrobe, like wearing a safari suit into the remote Arizona desert?"

"I wouldn't know."

Percival had plenty of smarts to puzzle out fifty-page mathematical proofs, and none for social skills. "You don't know what Gabriella's boss looks like?"

"He's a recluse," he said. "Won't even allow a photo of him online on their website. Gabriella and the children met him once, at last summer's company picnic. Bit of a miracle that he showed up at all. Rich people are eccentric, you know, not crazy."

Crazy, like a self-proclaimed prophet. It would explain how that thug this morning found out so quickly where Gabriella lived. "Lucia and Liam met him?" Panic clawed into her gut. She handed him the phone and fished out her cell. "Call the school. See if Helen's picked up Lucia. I'll try Helen's cell."

No answer. She left a message, trying to restrain the desperation in her voice.

"I spoke to the principal," Percival said. He replaced the handset in its cradle. "Lucia is fine, just finished rehearsing for her part of angel in the school play. She's out at recess."

It still didn't feel right. "I couldn't reach Helen. And she never turns off her cell phone."

"She'd have to turn it off at the clinic. Liam receives excellent care there, you know. The campus clinic is state of the art, thanks to Baltasar Contreras. He's quite the philanthropist. And he's done well by Gabby. Her holiday bonus was generous, to say the least. He even sent a gift for the children." His face paled.

"Percy, what is it?"

"His gift to the children," he said. "It was a Trojan Horse."

She handed him the printout. "Read this," she said. "We both need to get up to speed, fast. I'm going to pick up Lucia."

# CHAPTER 17

*Letter, written by Juan Jaramillo de Salvatierra to his brother, Pedro Alonso de Salvatierra, Vatican City. Vissilus Ruins, Morocco, February 14, 1586.*

My dear Pedro Alonso,

Pray for me, brother, that I have earned everlasting peace, for my death is nigh, and I go to my grave in a heathen land, without the benefit of last rites. Yet it is oddly fitting. I lay in a remote village, Muslim tents erected in the old, forgotten Roman ruins of Viscillus. God's breath blows through the abandoned streets this night, beating upon the tent walls, reminding that when man aspires to rule the world, then his empires surely will crumble.

I pray that you have received the missive I sent to you via our sister ship, the *Espiritu Santo*. It is a faster vessel, and its captain determined to return his prisoner in great haste, without making further stops. You know by now that I could not complete the mission for our Holy Father Sixtus V which carried me to the New World and, ultimately, my earthly end, but I believe, with all my soul, that our Supreme Creator, in His wisdom, called me to the path I followed. I ask your forgiveness, and pray that you believe, after you read this final missive, that I have acted only by God's hand, in service to Him and no other.

I was not without doubt, especially when Our Lord sent a mighty storm to wrack the *San Salvador* even as we neared home, safety and victory. I could have endured this storm with less anguish if my life alone had been in danger, not only because I know that I owe my life to the Supreme Creator, but also because deep in the jungle I had seen death only a hair's breadth away. What caused me infinite grief and anxiety was the thought that after our Lord had deigned to enlighten me with faith and certainty in this enterprise and had crowned it with victory, abashing our nemesis and sending him back to Spain in chains, his Divine Majesty should now seek to hinder this with my death—a fate that I could have borne more easily had it not also threatened the people on board with me, who sought only treasure, with no aspiration to our sacred enterprise.

By the third day of this ravenous storm, all men aboard had made our vows to the Supreme Creator, no longer relying on lots cast by the officers. Every crewman, from Captain to Able Seaman, swore to make pilgrimage, barefoot, to the first shrine of the Virgin that they might encounter if saved by our Lord from the wrath of the seas. Yet the storm grew more violent. I, for my own part, clutched my crucifix to my breast and created my own secret pact with the Lord, that if He should save me, I would then tell you of our enterprise, and what had come to pass. If I should drown, then my secret would be buried with me in my watery grave.

This vow, I humbly propose, is what saved me from being swallowed by the sea that so did open its gaping maw and gulp down our caravel *San Salvador* and all souls aboard save one, being myself. For even as the storm raged, the men's cries of fear and anger barely audible above the din of the crashing waves and angry wind, Our Lord's hand reached down from above, pushing a mighty wave across the gunwales of the ship, cracking the mast like a stick, and wrapping a line around my torso like the fearsome snakes of the New World jungle. The sea water coursed over me and I knew at that moment I should be drowned even though I lay lashed tight to the deck of the *San Salvador* and not thrashing in the ocean. Yet then, Our Lord's hand came down once more. A wave, even mightier, ripped the decking I lay lashed to clear from the *San Salvador*. I know not what happened next, but when I awoke, I and my small plank of decking was all that was left of the *San Salvador*, the ship and all its souls gone.

The storm abated, but the sun, equally harsh, burned me like a demon's tongue. I lay trapped, lashed as securely as any treasure barrel, to the planking that I feared would only prolong my death, not save my life. I could not sink. I could not swim. I could choose neither life, nor death. And yet, the Supreme Creator saw it fitting to save me. His wave carried me to the shore of this heathen land. I now pen this missive to you, for my physical body, the earthly vessel of God's will, lays crushed and broken in this foreign land. I can only surmise that Our Divine Majesty offered these last days to me so that I may keep my vow and share with you the outcome of my mission.

It is with this urgency that I stave off death. The heathens have sent to me a man who speaks a rudimentary Spanish. I have requested that he deliver this missive to you at the Vatican, and have given him my cherished crucifix as payment in good faith. It pained me to proffer such intimate and holy treasure to a Muslim, especially with my being so close to God's judgment at my death, yet I pray that the gold and jewels of the crucifix will be his reward. The information I am sending in this letter is of utmost importance. It is God's will.

In one part, I have accomplished the mission which you, under the auspices of the Vatican, assigned to me. Alvaro Contreras is in chains, returned to Spain on the *Espiritu Santo* to stand trial for treason. He will most certainly be damned. But I swear to you, brother, I shall not be damned.

As for the golden Breastplate that my earthly words so inadequately described in my last missive, I could not, as a man of God, follow the order of the Vatican. The Lord opened my eyes to bear witness to the destruction that the Breastplate could cause in the possession of an evil man. God's hand brushed the stench of death through the jungle lest I forget. If you had been with me, brother, you would know. Whole villages were destroyed, every savage dead. A mother had strangled her infant child. An old man had bashed in the heads of young women. Contreras had promised to give them an elixir to cure their madness, but he broke that promise.

Through this hell, the Lord led me to the clearing lorded over by Demon's Wings, the rock outcropping that towered above the trees. Demon's Wings watched over the pyramid temple that Contreras enslaved the locals to defend, blocking access to the Oculto Canyon. The temple's eyes, above and to each side of the stone lintel, gave warning to all who dared enter. But the temple's mouth, which had once poured forth life-giving water, Alvaro Contreras had strangled dry.

In its inner sanctum, the very heart of Satan, the Lord pierced it with a beam of sunlight, sending His true wisdom. I saw the golden Breastplate with the twelve sacred stones, worn by Aaron, brother of Moses, that God designed and built by man's craft. The Breastplate truly is a conduit between the Lord and His Earth, for it was our Supreme Creator who commanded, *Salvatierra, destroy the Breastplate!*

Contreras tempted me. *"The gems of the Breastplate reveal the secret to my domination."* He enticed me. *"Don the Breastplate. Stand upon this platform. Call God's light to shine upon you. You will hold the powers of the Heavens in the palm of your hand."*

I refused to submit.

My heart pounds. Each breath is a stab of pain. I lay close to death. I had prayed to tell you in person the end of my adventure, for I dared not risk anyone learning of His divine plan, but this missive shall be my testament. After I wrenched the seven stones from the Breastplate, as the boulders rained down around me, I buried the Breastplate deep beneath the heads of those who had once claimed dominion over its power, knowing the Indians will not touch it. Escaping the temple, our ragged crew returned through the jungle to our ships. At the port before we disembarked from the New World, I learned that natives had ruled Contreras's pyramid to be kept strictly secret and forbidden.

As for the seven sacred stones, God showed me clearly His divine plan in a dream. I compelled my most trusted allies, our Circle of Seven, to each become a guardian of a sacred stone. I bade each one to embark on a voyage of opposing directions, to the far corners of God's Earth. My hands were steadied only by the will of God as I entrusted to our noble astronomer and my dearest friend, Tristan de Luna, the Turquoise, to carry north into the desert wilderness. The Sapphire headed east to England, Babur's Diamond west to Asia. The Urim and Thummim, and the jacinth, secreted to distant lands. My Circle of Seven risk execution for desertion, and can never again return to their homeland. They are the first generation of guardians, but can not be the last.

I, for my part, took custody of the Tear of the Moon, locking it away in my strongbox with my Bible. Both sacred stone and sacred words now lay at the bottom of the sea with the *San Salvador* and all her souls. God has relegated the power of the Emerald to a place that no mortal may reach. If it is God's will, then the other stones have met a similar fate.

I now seal this letter and my fate. I kiss my crucifix and my life goodbye. I pray that Our Lord and His Holiness will judge that I have served well.  And I pray with my last breath that this heathen will deliver this missive to you and fulfill my destiny.

May the Lord have mercy on my soul, Juan Jaramillo de Salvatierra

CHAPTER **18**

Christa slowed as she passed the statue of the Virgin Mary whose open hands and perpetual calm welcomed all comers to Rose Hawthorne Catholic School. *Just let me get Lucia home safely. And I will believe. Really.* After all, Mary was the miracle maker, not the least of which was that Gabby sent Lucia and Liam here. Ever since she returned from Colombia last summer, Gabby had grown more spiritual, more afraid that she wasn't raising her children with some kind of religious foundation. *If I don't, they might never meet Mom, after, you know,* she admitted late one night.

Christa knew, all right. That's what this was all about. What her life was all about. The letter was the evidence she'd searched for. The letter answered so many questions, and raised so many more. It named several of the seven sacred stones that Salvatierra removed from the Breastplate. The Urim and Thummim were pivotal in ancient Judaism, and were used to translate the Book of Mormon. Babur's Diamond, now known as the Kohinoor, and Edward's Sapphire, were two of most famous gems in world history. Real enough. She'd seen them in the British Crown Jewels. Was it possible that they went missing for a gap of time, in the mid-1500s, secretly placed in their original mounts on the Breastplate?

The letter told of Luna, the astronomer and Salvatierra's friend. He had to be the one who left behind the armillary sphere as a clue to the location of the Turquoise. It even recounted what Salvatierra had done with the Breastplate. He'd buried it beneath the heads of those who tried to claim its power, whatever that meant, in the New World jungle. Most significantly, Salvatierra named the conquistador who had possessed the Breastplate, Alvaro Contreras.

The kids were out for recess. She parked in the nearest spot to the playground, its primary reds, blues and yellows inviting and happy. The children ran, swung and slid. They didn't care about the storm clouds darkening the sky. They shouldn't have to. Maybe she was being paranoid. She shouldn't drag Lucia away from this innocence. She might scare her, for nothing. She had no proof that the Prophet was Baltasar Contreras. Sharing a last name with a long dead conquistador and a propensity to give educational toys shouldn't condemn him. Like Percival said, the man was a scion of the community, a well-known, if little seen, philanthropist. None of that alleviated the vise tightening around her heart.

She got out of her car, hugging her arms across her chest to fend off the biting chill and hide the hole the bullet had sliced through the sleeve of her leather jacket. The blood, thankfully, hadn't seeped through. She scanned the swings first, Lucia's favorite activity. Not there. She looked to the monkey bars, the slides. She tried to fix on each child's face as they raced in every direction, in their plaid uniforms, screaming with delight. Nothing. A growing panic gripped her. "Lucia!" she called, stooping to peer in the "hut" beneath the slide.

"Professor Devlin," a voice called from behind her. Sister Mary Therese approached, the breeze swirling her white novitiate veil around her wizened face. Like Lucia, she was new to the school, a widow on a fresh path. She had taken Lucia under her wing, and for that Christa was grateful, and she tried to tamp down the spark of suspicion lit by anyone who was both friendly and committed to the church. "It's amazing how children can hide in plain sight," she said, as always with the uncanny ability to tune into the needs of people around her. "We'll find her." Together, they walked towards the grove of evergreens to the far side of the playground.

A mom's hand caught Christa's shoulder from behind. "Lucia's gone already."

Christa spun to face her. It was Yvonne, Courtney's mom, dressed to the nines in skinny jeans, fur-trimmed leather coat and Ugg boots. She had met her many times when picking up Lucia and Liam after school every other Wednesday, which she and the kids had proclaimed "Wacky Wednesday with Crazy Aunt Christa." "Gone?"

"Her uncle picked her up," she answered. "Such a nice man. Arrived in a black Rolls Royce Phantom. All the children were very excited. You never told me that Lucia has a rich uncle. That poor

girl. I'm glad she has someone with some substance in her life."
Her tone of voice underscored her opinion of parents who'd rather
spend money on books than boots.

Christa's heart raced. "You let her go with him? What did he
look like?"

Yvonne frowned. "He wore a Gucci suit. Custom-made, not off
the rack." She bent closer and softened her voice. "Gucci doesn't
do short and stout off the rack."

"Did the man say anything?" Sister Mary asked Yvonne.

"He was taking her for ice cream, and shopping for a Christmas
gift for her," said Yvonne. "I suggested the Nordstrom's at the
mall." Yvonne pouted, picking up on Christa's distress. "I called
the principal's office," she said, holding up her smart phone as
evidence in her defense. "They told me that Percival had called to
say Lucia was being taken home early. And Lucia's Uncle Peter is
on the approved list of people who can pick her up. He is your
sister's husband, isn't he? He assured me he'd sign her out before
leaving school property."

"Peter's been out of town," Christa said. "Due back today."

"Well that explains it, then," Yvonne said, corralling a wisp of
windblown hair. "The Rolls was an airport car service. It's the
holiday travel season, after all. Not beyond them to fill in with their
status cars."

Sister Mary placed a hand on Christa's forearm, on her wound.
It hurt. She didn't care. "Christa, do you have Peter's number?" the
nun said in a soft tone that could calm any tantrum.

Christa jerked the cell phone from her pocket. She wanted to
believe it more than anything. She dialed Peter's cell. A recording
answered. This time she was calling the cops. Before she could
punch nine, the phone chimed. She pressed it to her ear. "Peter?"

A laugh answered her. "I do so enjoy optimism, Christa Devlin,"
a man's voice said. A nasal, arrogant voice. The Prophet. "By all
means, confirm to your friends that I am Uncle Peter. Lucia's life
depends on it."

CHAPTER **19**

Baltasar Contreras was delighted with the little girl, with her mop of curly strawberry blond hair and infectious laugh. She had taken off her pink, faux suede jacket trimmed with fluffy pink fur at the wrists, hem and around the hood and laid it neatly next to her. She hadn't wanted ice cream to drip on it. She had told Baltasar that it was Barbie's jacket, and laughed when he asked why Barbie had given it to her. Barbie, he learned, was a doll. Lucia would be his doll, to manipulate to make his dream come true.

She hated her starched navy and green plaid school uniform, and confided that she didn't care at all if ice cream got on that. She toyed with the drop-leaf table in the back of the limo, raising it, latching it, lowering it, while his chauffeur, Simon, went inside Jimmies to get the ice cream cones. Baltasar had been tempted to go in, himself. He'd never been in a "family restaurant." His research into the Hunter family had revealed this quaint spot as a favorite of the little girl. She had ordered one scoop of cookie dough, and one scoop of chocolate, on a sugar, not a cake, cone, with rainbow sprinkles. She knew what she wanted. So did he.

She licked her cone on one side then the next, sprinkles dropping on the napkins that Baltasar had spread over her lap, despite his own distaste for the plaid uniform. Even he had ordered a cone, pistachio, amazed that he found joy in such a pedestrian act. He hadn't had an ice cream cone since he was a child and that was a vanilla gelato in Cairo. He wanted a second cone. His mother, ever indulgent in her love, went back into the shop to get it for him. That's when the bomb blew the shop and his mother to bits.

"Now, Professor Devlin," he spoke into his cell phone, "I will wait while you assure that nun and the woman wearing the peculiar sheepskin boots that I am Lucia's uncle and I've picked up little

Lucia from the school. You're quick enough to deduce that I do have someone watching you. If you do not do as I say, you will not hear from me nor Lucia again."

She hesitated. Baltasar expected that, but then heard her forced laugh and stumbled reassurances that Lucia was fine. He listened. He could hear footsteps on pavement, her quick, short breaths and a car door opening and shutting.

After his mother died, his father equated ice cream with poison and indulgent love with punishment. He turned to Lucia. "If I had children," he said, "I'd make it a rule to have ice cream in my house year round. I'd hire a nanny just to play with you and a tutor to make sure you rose above your peers." If only he could have had his own children, then it might not have fallen on him to fulfill his family's destiny. It would not be him who would cause all those deaths, who must take the crown upon his head. He dabbed a drip of chocolate from Lucia's dimpled chin. It was a tragedy that she might be one of the first to die.

"Where's Lucia?" Christa Devlin asked finally, her voice surprisingly strong.

"She is right here with me, naturellement. We're having ice cream. Aren't we Lucia?"

"I want to talk to her."

"Quite understandable. I will put you on speaker."

"Lucia, honey? It's Aunt Christa. Where are you?"

"Aunt Christa!" Lucia smiled widely. "I'm in a Rolls Royce Phantom!"

"Yes, I know, in a Rolls Royce Phantom. Heading home?"

Baltasar smiled. Christa Devlin was smart, thinking on her feet, hoping to eke out information. More importantly, she was struggling to remain calm so as not to scare the little girl. She didn't want her to suffer. Baltasar was pleased he was able to take full advantage of the fluctuating circumstances. Like a chess master, he could visualize every possible move, counterattack and response, all while keeping fixed on the final goal, to topple a king. He licked his pistachio.

"Mr. Profit bought me ice cream. He got me two scoops! Aunt Helen never lets me get two scoops. And rainbow sprinkles!"

"Mr. Profit?"

"He's Mommy's funny friend." Lucia laughed. "I had to tell him who Barbie was. He said he'd get me Princess Holiday Barbie for Christmas."

"Where did you go?" The strong voice weakened, began to tremble. "Jimmies?"

Baltasar pressed the speaker off and brought the phone to his ear. "Jimmies is simply charming," he said. "Of course, we're not there now." He chewed a pistachio from the ice cream. Delightful.

"It won't take the cops long to find a Rolls Royce Phantom."

"In which case, Lucia would not have long to live."

"Don't hurt her." The voice leaped back. A hesitation. "She's just a little girl."

"That's entirely up to you, Professor Devlin."

"I know who you are, Contreras."

She was a quick study. "You don't know who I am," he said, "but you will."

"What do you want?"

He had her hooked. There was no need to prolong her suffering. It was time to reel her in. "It's not what I want from you. It's what you can get from me. Despite your impudence in the desert, I still offer you a wonderful opportunity, Professor Devlin. You could be instrumental in changing the world, in making sure that little girls like Lucia no longer have to suffer."

"Percival will give you whatever you want to get Lucia back."

"The question is, Professor Devlin, will you? Beginning, of course, with the Yikaisidahi Turquoise and the Tear of the Moon Emerald."

"I don't have the Turquoise. And as far as I know, that Emerald is at the bottom of the Atlantic. But you know that, too, I'm sure."

"Do not try to deceive me!" He slammed his ice cream cone, scoop first, into the ashtray. "It is my destiny to complete my ancestor's mission. It is my destiny to bring peace to the world. Hate killed my mother, just as it killed yours!"

His tirade was answered with silence from Christa's end of the phone. Lucia looked at him. Her tiny lip trembled, her ice cream forgotten. He forced a smile and a wink, and drew in a deep, calming breath. "Meet me at that charming playground, the one on Whitscomb Street. Lucia loves the swings, but you know that. You have three minutes."

He flipped the phone closed and laid his hand gently on Lucia's knee. An unfamiliar feeling crept through his insides. Compassion. He swallowed it down like bile rising at an awkward moment. "I apologize for shouting," he said. He couldn't have the child carrying on. It might draw attention. "Now, how would you like to play on the swings while we wait for Aunt Christa to meet us here? After, you can come to my home for a visit and I'll have Simon stop and get you the toy store's most beautiful Barbie on the way."

"The one with the sparkly hair?" Lucia asked. She did not wipe the tear from her cheek. "The Princess Holiday Barbie?"

"The very one," Baltasar said. "Now finish up that ice cream."

Lucia nodded, but let the chocolate ice cream melt over her fingers.

# CHAPTER 20

Christa's tires slewed through the fallen leaves as she pulled in behind the black Rolls Royce Phantom in front of the Whitscomb Street playground. There she was! Lucia was on the swing, safe, unharmed, but not singing like usual. Her face looked grim and cold. She was the only child here. The older kids were still in school, the other parents too sensible to take their toddlers out on this blustery day and risk catching a cold before the holidays. These were the dangers they worried about. Not some crazy nut calling himself the Prophet. She had to get Lucia away from him.

He sat at the picnic table. He wore a tan overcoat that looked like expensive cashmere even from a distance. What the hell was he doing? Setting up chess pieces on a board? One of the thugs from the desert was here, too, dressed in a black suit, arms crossed, oblivious to the chill. He was not the one who invaded Percy's house this morning.

She hovered her finger over her cell phone again. Three numbers, 911. It shouldn't be that hard. But the Prophet had given her three minutes, just enough time to make it to the playground and no more. He had planned this precisely. He knew things about Mom and about Lucia's school. He'd know if she called the cops.

She got out of the car.

"Aunt Christa!" Lucia called. She smiled broadly. "It isn't it fun to fly up to the sky," she sang. Christa had taught her that song, like Mom had taught her. *Mom, if you're out there, help me. Help Lucia.* It was a prayer of desperation. A nonbeliever's prayer.

Christa crossed to the picnic table. The Prophet gestured for her to sit opposite him. She could leap across the table, grab the perfectly fringed ends of his Burberry scarf and choke him, buying a few minutes for Lucia to run away. Too risky. Lucia might run towards her or be too terrified to act at all.

She sat down, her eyes glued to the black and white squares of the chess board. She couldn't let him see her fear. His fat, gloved fingers played over the pieces waiting deployment from the molded foam hollows in the box. It was an unusual set. One side was conquistadors, in white Breastplates and gold pointed helmets. Their opposing pieces were Aztecs, with pale blue tunics and bright, feathered headdresses. Macaws served as the Aztec's knights, with tall stepped pyramids for their rooks. The chess board was bordered in geometric Aztec patterns of orange, red, blue and white.

"Does this disturb you?" the Prophet asked, without looking up. "My playing a strategy game in which, historically speaking, one culture decimated another?"

"On the contrary," Christa said, fighting to keep her voice steady, "this chess game could be the only victory a Mesoamerican culture could win over the Spaniards." The real Spaniards had allied themselves with Montezuma's enemies. That's what brought them victory. She needed an ally. Braydon Fox came to mind. "You've got me where you want me. Let Lucia go."

He had selected four chess pieces to place on the board, the two "kings," a white Conquistador pawn, and an Aztec rook. He straightened his ring, a gold band embedded with a pear cut diamond, which he wore over his gloves. The movement was contrived. He wanted her to notice the ring. "Are you familiar with the Saavedra endgame, Professor Devlin?"

"I don't like playing games."

"But you do," he said. "You're an A-level fencer. Fencing and chess, they're very much alike. You must assess your opponent, create a strategy, and adjust, constantly fine-tune, to win the bout."

If only she had a weapon in her hand right now. Maybe a feint would knock him off-balance. "I know who you are, Prophet. You're Baltasar Contreras, head of NewWorld Pharmaceuticals. Gabriella's boss. Her husband knows, too. You can't get away with this."

"The Saavedra is a classic problem" he said. "After many moves, white against black, these final pieces remain on the board on these particular squares. Pawns have been sacrificed. Rooks, knights and bishops have attacked with corresponding strategies, all with one purpose in mind, to topple the enemy king. Now it is the endgame, with only one acceptable solution out of dozens of possible moves. At first, it was seen to be no more than a draw. But with cunning, strategy and prudence, white can move and win."

So he was Baltasar Contreras. At least he hadn't denied it. "You kidnapped my niece. Witnesses saw you pick her up from school." She leaned forward. "End this, before it's too late."

He swiveled his face up to her. His lips, as thin as his jowls were fat, bent into a tight grin. His eyes were sharp and as dark as a rat's. A whiff of expensive aftershave wafted from the folds of his scarf. "The key to victory in the Saavedra endgame is underpromotion. When a pawn reaches the end of the board, its player would normally trade for a queen, the most powerful piece in chess. Saavedra, he was a priest no less, realized he had to underpromote his white pawn, trading it for a rook, not a queen. Then white would attain checkmate."

"Got it. Underpromotion. Now let me take Lucia home."

His grin managed to creep into an outright smile. It looked uncomfortable on his face. "You, Christa Devlin, are my rook."

"I am not your anything," she said.

He pointed his finger like a gun. "That's where you're wrong," he said, his eyes no more than a slit. "This isn't about a little girl. She is merely a pawn. It's the Breastplate of Aaron I'm after. You're going to help me restore the Breastplate to its Divine mission. We will write a new ending to this story."

She stood, paced away from him and returned, both repulsed and drawn in. Who was this bastard? Her father's evil twin? How was he in on what had been history's deepest secret? "The only ending I want is to get Lucia home safe."

His gaze dropped to the chess board. He slid the white king one square closer to the black king cowering in the corner. "For that to happen, I need three things from you, beginning with the Turquoise."

She felt Lucia's life being torn from her grasp. "I don't have it," she said. "I didn't find the Turquoise."

He moved the black rook, tracking the white king for check. "You have the Spaniard's armillary sphere. It must be a clue to its location. You'll figure it out, retrieve the stone, and bring it to me."

How did he know about the sphere? Had he learned about it that night? Maybe his sniper saw it through his scope. "I wouldn't even know where to start," she said.

"You're a historian. Start in the past." He studied the board, as if still strategizing his next move. "Second, you need to bring me the seventh stone, the Tear of the Moon Emerald."

The words clenched her gut. "Impossible. That Emerald is at the bottom of the Atlantic. If you believed in all this crap, then you'd know that it was irretrievable. That's why the Breastplate of Aaron could never be restored, even if it did exist. That's why they call the Emerald, the Seventh Stone."

"I have reason to believe that the Emerald will soon come into your possession," he said. "This is the endgame, Professor Devlin, but you need not lose. Many pieces will fall, pawns, knights, bishops, even heads of state." He picked up the black king and tumbled it deftly through his pudgy, gloved fingers. "I am offering you and your loved ones a reprieve."

"A reprieve? You tried to kill me in the desert."

"I don't try," he said. "I do." He pointed the black king at her. "And you are alive."

"You kidnapped Lucia."

"I simply treated her to her favorite ice cream. I needed you to see your position clearly." Contreras raised his eyes to hers. "I am doing this for the good of the world," he said. "You have known the keen loss of a loved one by those who claim to want to change the world. I will create a world in which that will not happen again."

If this prophet didn't see the illogic in that, she wasn't about to point it out to him. "So you will not hurt Lucia."

"That's where your third task comes in." He slid the white pawn to the last row, removed it from the board and placed a rook in its square. "It's simple, really. Bring me your sister's journal. Once I have that, you'll realize that I am the only one who can use the power of the Emerald and Turquoise to save thousands of lives."

"Gabriella's journal? Her research notes?" But the thug this morning had tried to steal Dad's journal, not Gabby's.

Contreras slammed his fist on the table. The chess pieces jumped. "I paid for that research. My company sent her to Colombia last summer to find new botanicals for potential cures. Hiding her results is nothing less than theft."

What was he talking about? Yes, Gabriella had gone to the Colombia rainforest last summer to talk to the Muisca shamans and retrieve plants as potential medicines. She was the only one who could speak the local dialect. Dad had taught it to her. It was one of the far flung places he had explored searching for clues to the Breastplate. "So why did you send her down there again?"

"Down there?" He pursed his lips, and smiled. "Of course, she's returned to Colombia," he said. "She thinks she can find the specimens. She thinks she can stop me."

That bad feeling in Christa's gut burned with a vengeance. Contreras hadn't sent Gabriella to Colombia this time. He'd been hunting for her. And Christa had just pointed him in her direction. "Gabriella has no connection to the Breastplate," she said. Or so she had believed.

"Strange what people fear," he said. "Airlines force passengers to remove their shoes, in a lame attempt to appease unfounded paranoia, when what people should fear is something simple, something they depend on every day, something that is in every home around the world. Every one of us is connected by it, right here in Princeton, for example, or even all the souls in the city of New York." Contreras slipped his hand into his coat pocket, removed a brass flask. He unscrewed the cap that also served as a shot cup and poured a finger of the flask's contents into it. "Drink this," he said. the l'eau de vie."

She stepped back. "No way."

"If you do not drink this, you will be of no use to me, and neither will your niece," he said. "It's for your own protection." He nodded to the bodyguard on the right, who wrapped his fingers around the butt of his gun.

The guard made a move to yank the gun from its holster. Lucia could get hurt. Christa snatched the cap from Contreras and drank. It tasted like plain water, with a sweet aftertaste lingering on her tongue. She handed the cap back and waited for an effect, but her mind was reeling so fast she could have drunk pure opium and not felt it.

"The poison intensifies the most primal emotions hidden deep in the human brain, violence, paranoia, delusions. It causes death in seven days," he said. "If the world was created in that time, then surely it can be saved in that time."

"Was that poison?" She felt sick.

"I'm here to save you, Christa." Contreras screwed the cap onto the flask, let it drop into his pocket. "Lucia will stay with me for the afternoon. I will call you at six tonight. Give me what I want, and your niece will be home in time for dinner." He beckoned to Lucia.

Lucia skipped over to the table. She stopped to pick up a knight that had fallen on the cold, hard ground. She searched for its spot in the wooden box and placed it in, turning it sideways to fit properly. She looked up at Christa. "Can you take me home now? I'm cold." She hugged herself and shivered in an exaggerated way that would have been comical in other circumstances.

Contreras bent down, leaning his hand on his thighs, his face close to the child's. It was sickening. "But I promised to buy you that special Barbie doll," he said. "Don't you want to come with me?"

Lucia pouted thoughtfully, look up at Christa. "Can I, Aunt Christa?"

Grab her and run. This might be her best, her only, chance. The thug slipped his hand pointedly inside his jacket. She knelt on one knee and hugged her, tight. Lucia's soft curls brushed her cheek. "I love you, Lucia."

"Love you, too, Aunt Christa. Can I get the Barbie now?"

Contreras reached for Lucia's tiny fingers with his gloved hand. He coaxed her from Christa's embrace. He stood and walked towards the Rolls Royce, Lucia skipping beside him. He helped her into the back seat, then followed and drew the door closed with a sickening thud. The thug got in the passenger seat. The Rolls Royce crawled off, crushing the dead leaves beneath its tires. Lucia's empty swing teetered in the chilling gust.

CHAPTER **21**

Percival clutched Christa's translation of the letter in his hands. God commanded Salvatierra to destroy the Breastplate. Absurd. God sent a storm to maroon him, keeping him alive just long enough to tell the tale of the seven sacred gemstones scattered around the world. All to usurp the power of the golden Breastplate designed by God, according to the Bible, a book fraught with mathematical impossibilities. A man attacked his house this morning, for this? Thaddeus had no right to ask him to protect this letter and tattered journal "with his life." What if the children had been here? He had to distance his family from this mad situation before one of them got hurt.

First, he had to warn Gabriella to return home immediately. He tried her satellite phone again. Still no answer. It could be the tree canopy. Satellite coverage in the Colombian rainforest was spotty at best. Is that why Contreras had sent her on this last-minute expedition? To ensure that she wouldn't be here to receive the package from her father? But even if Contreras was somehow connected to this quest for the Breastplate gems, how would he know the letter and journal was arriving this morning? The man wasn't some James Bond villain with a worldwide network of spies.

Contreras's life goal was to find medicinal cures from rainforest plants, granted for financial more than altruistic motives. That's all. Gabriella wasn't in danger. He couldn't fathom the idea. Truth be told, it was a miracle that a beautiful, intelligent woman like Gabriella had married him. It still felt like a dream when he woke up next to her. He could feel the weight of that other shoe suspended above him. When it dropped, it would crush him. He closed his eyes and felt her soft curls in his fingers. In his mind, he breathed in the beguiling scent of exotic blooms that always shanghaied his focus when she walked into the room.

He shook his head. He had to stay focused. If Contreras was the "prophet" who accosted Christa in the desert, then he was the one who sent his thug here this morning to appropriate the Turquoise. A man like Contreras didn't rule his pharmaceutical empire by giving up. That thug could return at any moment. It was time to call the authorities. Working outside the law was the Devlins' way, not his. But there would be an investigation, questions asked, the letter and journal perhaps confiscated as evidence. That could end any chance of saving Thaddeus. Gabriella would never forgive him. .

He heard the front door slam open. What an idiot! He hadn't locked it. He grabbed the gun. Footsteps, running toward the library. He crouched behind the desk. Christa skidded across the threshold.

"Percival!" she shouted.

"Good God, Christa." He stood. His hand holding the gun was trembling. He laid the pistol on the corner of the desk and stepped away from it. "I could have shot you."

"It's Contreras, Baltasar Contreras." She crossed to the desk, turned on the laptop. "He's the Prophet. He took Lucia."

"Slow down, Christa. What's this about Lucia? She's not with you?"

"We've got to contact Gabriella."

"I tried her satellite phone. No luck."

"I blew it. I told Contreras she went to Colombia."

"But he knows that. He sent her there, thinks she's on the verge of finding a botanical cure for cancer or something. Where's Lucia?"

Christa pawed through the papers on the desktop. "Contreras took her. I'll tell you everything, but we've got to find out what Gabriella was up to."

"Took her?" His throat tightened so quickly he could barely speak. "What are you saying?"

She crossed over to him and grabbed him by the wrists, her grip surprisingly strong. "Lucia is safe, for now."

His knees buckled. A sharp buzz zinged through his brain. He had to hold it together. He had to be strong, for Lucia. He grabbed the gun. "I'm going after her. If he hurts her, I'll kill him." This couldn't be him talking. He'd never even shot a gun before this morning. He put down the gun, snatched up the phone. "I'm calling the cops."

She grabbed the phone from his hand. He almost slapped her. His impulse for violence was frightening, and enticingly empowering. "We can't call the police, Percy," she said, holding her eyes steady on his. "Contreras will know. He has connections."

Think. Christa was right. It could put Lucia in more danger. "That FBI agent, the one who rescued you in the desert. The Bureau handles kidnappings."

"Fox," she said. "Agent Fox. I thought about that, all the way back here. But Fox didn't arrest Contreras in Arizona, probably because he couldn't prove anything, but I don't know for sure. Contreras and Fox have a history. I just don't know if we should trust him."

Christa with intense mixed emotions about a man was never a good sign. She hadn't said what this Fox looked like, but it wouldn't be the first time a dashing man had blindsided her brilliance. Christa had rappelled into a sea cave, camped with lions in the Serengeti and could list the Egyptian dynasties in order, but, like Gabriella, relationships were one foreign territory she hadn't had much chance to visit. "Then whom can we trust?"

"Gabriella. Contreras didn't know that Gabriella went to Colombia. It may be our only advantage. We've got to reach her before Contreras does. Damn it. No new emails from either Gabby or Dad."

Of course, this all came back to Thaddeus and his damn obsession. "I don't give a fig about the Breastplate, or, frankly, your father, at this point."

"You've got to," she said. "Contreras wants the Turquoise and Tear of the Moon Emerald from the Breastplate. He thinks I can get them."

"The Turquoise and Emerald! The Breastplate of Aaron!" He was shouting. He didn't care. "Those damn stones are more legend than truth." He paced away, then back. "From an artifact that your father has spent years trying to find. Lucia's life depends on that?" He reached for the gun. "That's impossible. I'm going after her before your father's damn obsession destroys us all."

"Percy, wait." She grabbed his arm. "It may be the only thing that can save us."

He shook her off. "I thought you'd finally come to your senses, Christa, when you left your father and started your career here in Princeton. You can't believe all this nonsense."

"I can't deny what I've found." She reached for her daypack and shoved it to him. "Go ahead. For Lucia's sake. See what we found in Arizona, in a cliff dwelling that's been buried for five centuries."

He grabbed the pack and unzipped it. It smelled like sand and metal. He yanked out the metal object. What the hell? "You found this, in Arizona," he said, "an armillary sphere." Early astronomers had used them, mathematically inspired models of the known universe. This had no place in an ancient Native American village.

"Copernican, mid to late sixteenth century," she said. She gestured towards the translation. "Luna, the Spanish astronomer from Salvatierra's letter. He brought it into the desert. Joseph believes it's a clue to where Luna hid the Turquoise. Contreras wants us to puzzle it out. That Turquoise could help save Lucia's life."

"I'm a mathematician, not an astronomer," said Percival. He scrutinized the symbols, the structure and mechanics of the brass spheres. All he could see was Lucia, alone and afraid. He resisted the impulse to dash the damn sphere through the window. "Gabriella has nothing to do with the Breastplate. She swore off helping your father in his obsessive quest years ago. She knew it was destroying him and that it might destroy us."

"Contreras took off with Lucia the minute I let slip that Gabriella was in Colombia. It's not the Emerald nor the Turquoise that topped his demands. You know what Contreras's priority was? Gabriella's journal," Christa said. "He was furious that Gabriella had kept her findings from him. We've got to figure out why and what the hell it has to do with the Breastplate. Lucia's life depends on it."

# CHAPTER 22

Christa sensed, rather than saw, the being just beyond the library window. A shadow emerged from the decayed, fetid leaves beneath the trees in the side yard. She crouched and squinted. It was there all right, but it wasn't exactly corporeal. It looked more like the wind had pinched the black from the storm cloud and stretched it into a specter-like being. A faint scent, sickly sweet yet ashen, the smell of death masqueraded, seeped in through the drafty panes. The specter could be a hallucination, a side effect of whatever Contreras gave her to drink. She was an idiot to have left Lucia in the hands of that mad man. She had to focus, find Gabriella's journal to buy Lucia precious time.

A pounding thundered on Percival's front door. "Hunter," a man's voice bellowed.

She yanked aside the heavy velvet drapes. The specter spun away. Its whirlwind cracked off a barren maple branch and hurled it to the earth. Keep it together. Specters weren't real. Beyond, no cars were parked on the street.

"It's Donohue," Percy said, his voice quick with relief. Donohue was the retired Colonel from next door, Army, Special Forces. He could kill with his thumb. The man refused to call Percival by his given name, even after she pointed out that his namesake was a courageous knight of the round table. "Gabriella told me to trust him and call on him in case of emergency. This is damn well an emergency."

"I've got a message," Donohue called, "about Gabriella."

Percival practically sprinted towards the front door.

"Percival, wait," she called. Percy must have misunderstood. Gabriella would never trust the military. Dad had drilled that into them. She quickly swiped the pistol into the desk drawer and shoved the sphere in between the Greek vase and Zimbabwe stone carving, hiding it in plain sight.

Colonel Donohue rumbled into the library like a Sherman tank through the gates of a ravaged French village. He was a big man, powerful and dark in his trench coat. His eyes strafed the room. When Percival had first moved in with Gabby and the kids, the Colonel was downright intimidating, grumbling like distant artillery when the kids' ball rolled into his disciplined platoon of boxwoods. His wife, Eleanor needed rest, he'd bark. Eleanor was a recluse, with a self-imposed sentence in solitary after their only son was killed in Iraq. She gazed out the window, in her disheveled bedclothes, at the kids as they played, too pitiful to be creepy. Then, as weeks passed, Donohue began dropping by with little toys and books. *From Eleanor,* he told them, barely managing a stiff lip, *those kids, they're getting her out and about again.*

Churchill, his poodle, skittered around his master's feet, sporting a red and green striped doggie sweater, one of a plethora that Eleanor had knit in her confinement. Churchill yapped in excited anticipation.

So did Percival. "This very morning, a giant of a man, dark suit, barged right in, I had to scare him off, he forced me to shoot, but, no, he wasn't hurt, ran into Christa right out on the front walk, she was shot, in the arm, flesh wound."

"Colonel, you said you had a message," Christa interrupted, before Percival could tell him about Lucia. Donohue was a bulldozer. They needed to rescue a flower. And did Percy really say *flesh wound?* "About Gabriella."

Donohue targeted his sites on her. "Before she left for Colombia, Gabriella asked me to check with my connections in the Pentagon."

"Gabriella asked you," Christa confirmed.

"I told her intel is keeping tabs on a new group of commandoes trawling the Muisca's rainforest."

"Drug runners," Christa said. So that's why Gabriella had brought in Donohue. Drug runners were spreading like a cancer down there and they were as potentially deadly.

"Not drug runners," Donohue said. "Mercenaries. Maybe hired by the local drug lord to take down his competition. Maybe not." Churchill whimpered. He tugged on his leash, hoping to sniff out the kids. They loved that poodle. "Now we know. Our local contact learned that the commandoes are heading towards Gabriella's camp."

"Colonel, what are you saying?" Percy said. "Is Gabriella in danger?" He grabbed Donohue's arm.

The Colonel recoiled, repressing the reflex that would judo flip Percy to the ground. His stare alone shoved Percy back two steps. Churchill yapped, sensing the sudden tension. Donohue gathered up the little dog in his powerful arms. "I can have boots on the ground in Colombia in forty-eight hours," he said. "Retired military. Good men. They can retrieve anything or anybody, and won't ask questions."

"When did these commandoes go on the move?" Christa asked. She had pointed Contreras in Gabby's direction and suddenly commandoes go into action. That couldn't be good.

"Ten minutes ago," Donohue said. "Locals, but an elite group, ten of them, armed with rapid fire weapons."

"What did Gabriella tell you?" Christa asked. She would never have told him about the Breastplate, so why, beyond being a good neighbor, was Donohue risking his reputation, and, possibly, his life for this? "Why did she suddenly return to Colombia?"

Donohue frowned and narrowed his eyes. "Classified," he said, "a matter of national security."

Percival clamped his fists and drew in closer. "My wife is in danger," he said. "My child is in danger." Churchill growled, fierce for a poodle.

"Your child?" Donohue let Churchill leap to the carpet.

"Lucia," said Percival, "she's been kidnapped. The kidnapper met with Christa, just a few minutes ago. It's Baltasar Contreras, the head of NewWorld Pharmaceuticals, Gabriella's boss."

Christa wanted to punch Percival. She had to salvage this, fast, before the Colonel's commandoes went into action and Lucia was killed in the crossfire. "We've got this under control," she said. "All he wants right now is Gabriella's journal."

"Baltasar Contreras," Donohue said. He crossed to the library window. He squared his shoulders as if expecting the wind-bullied oaks to snap to attention. No sign of her imaginary specter. Was she even thinking clearly?

"That's not all he wants, Christa," said Percival. "He wants the impossible, those two gems from the Breastplate of Aaron."

Donohue released his grip on Churchill's leash. The dog, sensing his master's tension escalate, didn't scamper around the room, but cowered at his feet. "The Breastplate of Aaron," Donohue said, "brother of Moses. As written in the Book of Exodus."

Percival raised his eyebrows. "That's right," he said, "in the Old Testament. Designed by God, so it says, to be some kind of direct line to Heaven. Used in the Inner Sanctum of the Temple of Solomon. Thaddeus Devlin has spent his life trying to find those stones. He thinks it's going to resolve mystery of life after death or some such nonsense. Now Baltasar Contreras expects us to find the sacred Turquoise and Emerald within hours. You've got to help us, Colonel. We've got to rescue Lucia."

"Life after death," Donohue echoed. The man's gaze grew distant.

Percival cringed. "You're a military man. You can't possibly put any credence in that."

"I have held the hands of men as they die," he said. "I remember each one. Command number one I tell my team before a special op. Do not fear death. Death is not the end of life."

Her head throbbed. Dad's obsession with the Breastplate spawned from a death, Mom's. She rubbed the scar on her forehead. It still hurt, after seven years, her grief, the alarm and bitter regret in Mom's eyes on that mountain road in Peru, before the bullet hit Christa and it all went black. Two weeks later, she woke up in a California hospital. Mom was already buried. "It's close enough," Christa said. "And I will never let that happen to Lucia."

She paced across the room. Percy should never have told Donohue about the Breastplate. And to make it worse, Donohue didn't react with skepticism, but with astonishment. Nothing was more dangerous than drawing an unknown element into the secret of the Breastplate. Dad had hammered in that the repercussions could be catastrophic. Right now, any distraction from finding Gabriella's journal and figuring out why it was so important could get Lucia killed.

Percy jammed his finger at her. "I know what you're thinking, Christa," he said, "that I spilled your father's precious secret. But

Gabriella told me to trust Colonel Donohue. Now our daughter's life depends on it."

"Colonel Donohue," she said, "if you expect us to trust you, then you have to trust us. Gabriella had to have a good reason for going to you for intelligence reports on Colombia. Why? And don't say it's a matter of national security."

Donohue pursed his lips and narrowed his eyes. "This information goes no further than this room," he said. "Homeland Security hired NewWorld Pharmaceuticals as a private contractor. Research only, to determine the potential threat of a terrorist attack using bioweapons, botanically based. Poisons. Antidotes. On the WMD level. Gabriella was gathering evidence. NewWorld is a pharmaceutical titan, with offices around the world. She believed that Contreras had the means and the motivation to produce a weapon of mass destruction involving a poison from a rare rainforest plant. A poison that has an antidote so elusive that even she couldn't find it. Whoever controls that antidote could hold the world hostage."

CHAPTER **23**

Braydon Fox eased over to the curb two houses away from Hunter's. He checked his watch. It had been forty-five minutes since he received the text from Torrino. He read it again. *Im back in NJ. Prophet plan kidnap Hunter girl*, then *Im hurt, at clinic. Sign says turn off cell.* As soon as he had read it, Braydon had rushed out of the Waldorf's banquet hall, his boss fuming in his wake. "*When? Where?*" He texted as he ran through the lobby. No answer. Damn the man, why pick now to follow the rules, and clinic rules at that?

Braydon broke any number of laws as he sped out of Manhattan to get to this bucolic neighborhood in Princeton, New Jersey, weaving in and out of traffic, using every lesson of his agency-honed driver training to avoid the loss of life or limb for himself and those around him. His thoughts raced equally fast, repeatedly dissecting his operative's text message. Had Contreras already kidnapped the little girl, or would he wait for Torrino to return from the clinic before moving in on her? Torrino couldn't have been badly hurt, since he was able to send a text, but that was the first he'd heard from him since he saw him last night in the desert.

Braydon raised his camera, zoomed in on the plate on the purple Volkswagen bug. It was Christa Devlin's, not exactly indistinctive. Devlin might be infuriating, but probably a decent woman caught up in something she didn't understand, even if she did ditch him at that hospital in Arizona. He lowered the camera and scanned Hunter's house. A mom in a minivan drove past it. The mother glanced over to the home, its gingerbread eaves dripping with holiday lights, the glittery pink tree on the porch a sure sign of little ones waiting eagerly for St. Nick. The mom smiled with the sadly mistaken reassurance of peace on earth. But a darker truth gathered like the storm clouds above the house. Gabriella Devlin Hunter, loving wife and mom, had suddenly left the country for Colombia. Now her little girl was in mortal danger from her boss, Baltasar Contreras, but why?

A light illuminated what looked like a library through the large mullioned window facing the street. Christa came into view. She paced in front of the window. He focused the camera on her, clicked off a few shots. She'd changed into a leather jacket, short skirt, tall boots. She'd let down her hair which now fell in long, brown waves. The way Julia used to, as soon as she got home from work. But Christa Devlin was definitely her own woman, fiercely independent, and on the wrong side of the law. That meant trouble. She was gesticulating wildly, clearly upset, probably arguing.

Hunter came up behind her. He looked just like his photo on the Princeton mathematics department webpage. A geek, complete with plastic frame glasses and loose-fitting button down shirt and khakis, except he was taller and better built than expected. They looked like they were arguing.

Hold on. A third player. Male. Sixties. Buzz cut. In better physical condition than most men half his age. Didn't need a uniform to know the guy was military. Probably a command position. Had a dog with him. Poodle, with a red and green sweater. So the guy was likely retired military. Maybe a neighbor. Braydon clicked off several shots. It wouldn't be hard to identify him. But if this was Christa and Percival Hunter's idea of calling in the cavalry, they clearly didn't know who they were up against.

He scanned for that armillary sphere spirited out of the Navajo Reservation. Contreras wanted it, and it wasn't just to model the known universe of the sixteenth century. But why not just overpower them and take it? Two college professors were no match for Contreras's thugs. Unless that sphere wasn't what Contreras wanted. It could be a clue to the location of something more valuable, and Contreras needed the professors to figure it out for him. That was more the "Prophet's" style. Or it could be connected to Gabriella Devlin Hunter and her sudden trip to Colombia. If a new plant-based drug she had found could cure cancer, or give people a new, organic high, it could make Contreras one of the richest and most powerful men in the world. That would be something to kidnap and kill for.

Then there was the Lux et Veritas sword. Contreras knew Braydon was overseeing its security, and figured, correctly, that now that Braydon had saved Christa's life, he felt responsible for her. Contreras might be using the kidnapping as a diversion, to draw him away from the sword.

Braydon fished out his cell phone and punched in the number for the prepaid cell he had handed Jared Sadler when he arrived in the States. As Britain's Crown Jeweler, Jared was entrusted by the Queen, personally, to transport the ceremonial sword to the banquet. Braydon had practically held the man's hand to escort him through the airport. Jared had been excessively nervous, and his overdressed young wife overtly flirtatious.

Jared answered on the first ring. "Agent Fox, is something amiss?" Jared sounded more nervous than before, when he should be safely ensconced in the hotel room for the duration.

"Where are you?" Braydon asked.

"In my room at the Waldorf," he answered. "No visitors, no phone calls but from you, as you instructed."

"The sword?"

"With me. I'll not let it out of my sight."

"Good," said Braydon. "I'll be back as soon as I can. Just stay put." He flipped the phone closed.

Contreras had an obsession for ceremonial gems. He could be after the sword, the real reason behind his generous hosting of tonight's G-20 banquet, rather than an blatant attempt to grease the insides of the politicians and diplomats so he could more easily peddle his drugs in their countries. It seemed a ridiculously high price to pay for an item whose value was more honorary than monetary, but, then, the same held true for the set of Abraxas stones stolen in San Francisco. Both items were unique. Neither could be bought, legitimately. Acquired as ransom, a definite possibility. Lucia Hunter was now the priority. Contreras had set his sights on the little girl, and, like a bunny being hunted by a hawk, she had precious little time.

# CHAPTER 24

Christa sank into the desk chair. Percival stopped in mid-step, too stunned to move. Gabriella had been working on an antidote for a poison that could be used as a weapon of mass destruction. She suspected that Baltasar Contreras had plans to deploy the weaponized poison, once he had control of the only antidote. The antidote that Gabby probably hadn't identified yet. And Lucia's life hung in the balance. Along with potentially thousands of other lives. That's why Contreras was willing to kidnap and murder for Gabriella's journal.

"My God," Percival said, "the letter. People going mad. Villages destroyed. A promised elixir." He swept up her translation of Salvatierra's letter and thrust it at Donohue. "Thaddeus Devlin found this letter in Morocco. It was written by a missionary named Salvatierra in 1586. Salvatierra was the last man to see the Breastplate intact. It was deep in the Colombian rainforest."

Christa yanked opened the top desk drawer and rummaged through it, panic swelling in her gut. She no longer cared if Donohue knew the secret of the Breastplate. Percival was right. They needed him. Contreras had to be stopped. "Gabriella's journal has to be here somewhere," she said. "She's too smart to risk taking it to Colombia." She only found Lucia's crayon drawings of rainbows and Liam's scribbles that passed as smiley faced trains. She slammed it shut.

Percival spilled out an executive summary of Salvatierra's letter as Donohue scrutinized it and Christa continued searching the desk. She bent down to force open the sticky file drawer. The old scar on the back of her shoulder pinched. She'd gotten it protecting Lucia. She'd been hiking with Lucia on a family vacation in the Smoky Mountains two years earlier. Lucia got between a mother bear and her cub. Christa quickly got between the bear and Lucia. She could understand a bear protecting her young, but a man like Baltasar Contreras, how could she fight him?

Donohue pursed his lips and narrowed his eyes. "Does Contreras know about this letter?"

"He sent that man here this morning to steal it," Percival said, "along with Thaddeus's journal."

"Not for Dad's journal," said Christa. "Contreras can't possibly know about that letter. He was after Gabriella's journal. He thinks she's found the antidote and is keeping it from him."

"This letter identifies the conquistador who brought the Breastplate of Aaron to the new world," said Donohue, "as Alvaro Contreras."

"Yes," Percival said. "Baltasar's ancestor, no doubt about that now."

"Baltasar Contreras is out to finish his family mission," Christa said. His crazy tirade at the playground was beginning to make sense. "Salvatierra was a priest. The Vatican sent him to stop Alvaro Contreras. Salvatierra destroyed the Breastplate. He ripped out seven of its twelve stones and scattered them around the world. Baltasar Contreras thinks I can get two of them, the Turquoise and the Emerald."

She pulled the laptop closer and tapped in a website address. She turned the computer screen towards Donohue. "This is an artist's drawing of the Breastplate, based on the Bible passage." It depicted a painting of a man dressed in robes, wearing a golden, bejeweled Breastplate. The old, bearded man raised his arms in supplication, his expression of adoration heavenward. "The Emerald ended up on the bottom of the Atlantic when Salvatierra's caravel sank in a storm. My father has a man aboard the treasure hunter ship that's trying to locate the wreck. His name is Ahmed Battar."

Donohue crossed his arms. "Sounds like an Arab Muslim," he said.

"Ahmed is a friend," said Christa, "and our only chance of getting the Emerald that might save Lucia's life."

Donohue grunted. "What about the Turquoise?" he said. "Do you know where that is?"

"Cibola," she said.

"The legendary lost city of gold," Donohue said.

All right, that he knew that was impressive, very impressive. But he didn't know the whole story. "Back in the sixteenth century, Fray Marcos, a missionary, explored the area. He returned to New Spain with stories of the seven cities of gold and of Cibola, which alone held more gold than all of the Incas. Coronado was sent out, with hundreds of conquistadors, Indian mercenaries and slaves, leaving death and destruction in their wake, almost starving themselves, only to find a rather ordinary pueblo, and no gold. Marcos was spared death at the hands of the enraged conquistadors, but returned to New Spain in disgrace."

"That's why they call Cibola a *legendary* lost city," Donohue said. He was losing patience.

"All legend is based on some truth," she said. "There was, indeed, a lost treasure, of incalculable value. The Turquoise."

"You want me to believe that this Fray Marcos," said Donohue, "really wanted a Spaniard to find not a golden city, but the Turquoise, one stone."

"The Yikaisidahi Turquoise. The real goal of Coronado's quest was a well-kept secret. You won't find it in any history books," she said. "A Navajo shaman told me that his ancestors guarded the secret, that the Spaniard brought Yikaisidahi to the people of that pueblo. He warned them to hide the stone away, in the innermost heart of the cliff dwelling. He warned them that the Turquoise held the power to destroy the world. They believed him. The tribe formed a cult, centered on keeping the Turquoise hidden."

Percival crossed to the bookcase where she had placed the armillary sphere. He grabbed the sphere and held it towards Donohue. "Christa found this in the abandoned cliff dwelling in Arizona. It's an armillary sphere, an early model of the universe, probably Spanish in origin, sixteenth century. It may be a clue to the location of the Turquoise."

Donohue narrowed his eyes at it and frowned. "I don't care if it can align the stars," he said. "A five hundred year old clue is not going to help. Our country's security, and your daughter's safety, is at risk. We need to take action." Donohue reached into his trench coat, extracted a folded paper from its inner pocket. He opened it and flattened it on the desk. "When Gabriella came to me with her suspicions, I took the liberty of attaining a satellite photo of the Contreras estate. I've worked up three attack scenarios."

This was moving way too fast. Christa knew Donohue's type, over-confident, hero complex compulsion to save others, recovering adrenaline junkie perpetually on the edge of a relapse. She was one, too. "We don't need a battle plan," she said. "We need the ransom."

"You got your sister's findings on the poison?" Donohue asked.

She had no answer for that. "We have until six before he calls," she said.

"Wait. Gabby's botanical sketches," Percival said. He flipped up the corner of the satellite photo. "From last summer's expedition." He gestured towards the sketches on the desk. "She left her work scattered about. That's not like her. I thought it was because she thinks she found a new species. But even then she acted more frightened than excited. She must have left them here on purpose, for me to find." He picked them up and searched through them. He pulled one out. "In case something went wrong."

He handed the sketch to Christa. The plant had a central stem, with oval, pointed, deeply veined leaves, an occasional green tendril and delicate, white flowers with four petals. Most distinctive, however, was the cut-away drawing of the underside of the leaf. It was colored a deep purple. The sketch was labeled in Gabriella's neat print. *Plant X, South American adaptation of Atropa belladonna? How/When introduced? Possibly indigenous?*

"Belladonna," Christa said. She looked up from the sketch, her stomach roiling at the thought of that capful of liquid Contreras made her drink at the playground. "Belladonna is a deadly poison."

Donohue gestured for her to hand him the sketch. She did. "Can this poison be weaponized?"

"It already has," she said. "Macbeth used the belladonna poison. The real Macbeth, from eleventh century Scotland, not the legend from Shakespeare's play. During a truce, he poisoned the enemy's troops. They grew so sick that they had to retreat."

Percival snapped up her translation of Salvatierra's letter. "*Whole villages were destroyed, every savage dead,*" he read. He jabbed his finger at the words. "*A mother had strangled her infant child. An old man had bashed in the heads of young women.*"

"So this form of belladonna poison drives people mad," said Donohue, "then kills them." His face flushed with barely controlled rage. "This is the ideal weapon for a terrorist."

"But it says in the letter that Alvaro Contreras had an elixir," said Percival, "the antidote, presumably. He had promised to return to the village and cure them. He lied to them of course. He was a conquistador."

Thunder rumbled in the distance. A storm cloud rolled over Gabriella's house, pitching the library into an even thicker gloom. Christa's stomach spasmed. Stress? If only that's all it was. "At the playground, Contreras had a flask in his pocket. He poured me a capful of the liquid it contained."

Percival clasped her shoulder. "You didn't drink it, did you?"

"I didn't have a choice."

"It may have been this poison."

"It wasn't Scotch," she said. She crossed to the wet bar. "Speaking of which." She reached down the bottle that Gabby kept on hand for Dad's rare appearances.

"How do you feel?" Donohue asked.

"Scared to death, not to use the term lightly," she said. "Other than that, I don't feel any reaction to the liquid at all. We've got to find Gabriella's research on this new plant species, fast."

"You need to get to a doctor," Percival said.

"No time," she said, "not until Lucia and Gabby are home safe." She poured two fingers of Scotch. "Salvatierra writes that Contreras tempted him to put on the Breastplate. *Stand upon this platform and call God's light to shine upon you and you will hold the powers of the Heavens in the palm of your hand.*" God's light. The powers of the Heavens. "He's talking about the power of life over death."

"He's talking crazy," said Percival.

"Dad would figure it out," she said, "if we could reach him. Contreras wants that Breastplate, to complete his ancestor's mission. He wants to stand on that platform, and conquer a new world." He wanted to redeem himself, for his family.

"A modern-day conquistador," Donohue said.

"And look how that ended," said Percival. "But Baltasar Contreras is only one man. He has no army at his command."

"Forty million people were killed in the new world," said Christa, "most of them not by an army, but diseases for which they had no defense. Smallpox, measles and bubonic plague, all easily spread. It was a deadly battle against an enemy they could not fight."

"Because they did not know how," Donohue said.

Christa picked up the glass of Scotch, the golden liquor swirling with the clear water. "Contreras told me that people should be afraid of something that connects all of us, every day. He used the words l'eau de vie."

"The water of life," Percival said.

"He used the examples of Princeton and New York City," she said. "It doesn't make sense. Contreras wouldn't poison me. He's gone through a lot of trouble to get me to track down what he needs." She raised the glass to her lips.

Donohue knocked it away. "He didn't give you a poison," Donohue said. "He gave you an antidote. You've already been poisoned. We all have." Donohue slammed his fist on the desk. "He's infiltrated the cities' water systems."

"Contreras said the poison intensifies primitive emotions, paranoia, violence and delusions," she said. "In one week, everyone goes stark, raving mad and murders anyone they think is out to get them."

"Like the villagers," Percival said. "They relied on the river systems of the rain forest. They still do."

"That's why Contreras is after Gabriella's findings," said Donohue. "She was working on the antidote. Contreras thinks that she found it. But she knew about Contreras's scheme. She'd never let him have the antidote and she could hold the only way to stop him."

"He doesn't want to find Gabriella's journal," said Christa. "He wants to destroy it."

"Mission priority number one," Donohue said. "Retrieve that journal. Think like her. Where would she keep it?"

"It might be at her greenhouse," Christa said, "where she conducts most of her research."

Donohue checked his watch, worn military-style, clock face on the inside of his wrist. "Christa, double time it to Gabriella's greenhouse," Donohue said. "We'll keep searching here. I'll get my contact at CDC to test the water and call in my team. Hunter and I will strategize a plan to extract Lucia. If the world was created in seven days, we can certainly save it in that time."

She didn't point out that those were the words Contreras used only a few hours ago.

# CHAPTER 25

Braydon peered out of his Impala's window at the Hunter home. His blackberry vibrated in his pocket. Percival Hunter's front door opened. Christa emerged, slung her pack over her shoulder, and hurried down the walk. The pack was the same one she had in Arizona, but it didn't bulge out. She wasn't taking the armillary sphere wherever she was going. She climbed into the Volkswagen, pulled away.

He could tail her or stick with the sphere and this new player, the ex-military guy. He pulled away from the curb and followed her. She turned the corner onto Winslow.

He glanced down at the text message. It was from Torrino. *Prophet kidnapped LH. I quit.*

Damn. He was too late. Contreras had his talons on the little girl. Braydon punched the contacts button for Torrino's phone, risking that Torrino was in a position to talk, or at least answer the call. This might be one of the few times he could catch him alone.

Torrino picked up on the first ring. "What are ya doin', calling me?" He sounded scared.

"I take it you can talk," he said. "Where are you?"

"Question is, where am I going? Answer is, outta here."

"Are you badly hurt?"

"Like you care. I told you. The Prophet, he's crazy. I'm not going back."

"What do you know about the kidnapping?"

"Nothing," he nearly shouted, then lowered his voice back to an angry whisper. "I had nothing to do with hurting no little girl. And I want nothing to do with any of it, no more."

Christa turned onto Elm Street. Did Christa know Lucia had been kidnapped? Had they been contacted? Braydon could try forcing her to pull over, insist she tell him what they know, but she was the type to clam up rather than give in. Stubborn. A loner. Like him, damn it.

Christa's bug turned onto Dickinson Street, headed right for the heart of Princeton campus. What was she up to? Had Contreras been bold enough to set up a ransom drop in his own back yard? He was practically a de facto landowner considering how much money his pharmaceutical corporation had donated to the University. NewWorld paid for most of the clinical trials at the University medical center. What better venue to try out new drugs? No doubt Contreras sent his "employees" there, as well, to keep track of their healthcare. Contreras liked control. Torrino was Lucia's best chance. He couldn't risk letting him go.

"Torrino," he barked into the phone. "You're at the University Medical Center, right?"

A hesitation, then, "Yeah, I'm here."

The bug turned right on Dickinson, away from the medical center. She wasn't headed there. Two choices, work the case from the outside or from the inside. "Just stay put, Torrino," he said. "I'll be there in five minutes." He pressed end before Torrino could answer.

He floored the accelerator; inciting an angry horn blare from the car he nearly sideswiped rounding the next corner. The Volkswagen continued straight. He slid into the drop-off only spot on the curb.

The emergency room was buzzing. Patients moaned and rocked, doubling over their stomachs. The nurses' worried chatter centered on food poisoning, but it seemed to be affecting a surprising number of people and an odd range of ages. Down the hall, a woman argued with her husband, her cheeks red, as if he had slapped her. Torrino sat in the waiting room, a *Sports Illustrated* that he wasn't looking at clutched in his beefy hands. A splint was taped to his left pinky finger.

Braydon scanned the room. Although the crowd, two dozen or so, of sick people and their companions packed into the small clinic was alarming, he saw nobody from the Contreras entourage besides Torrino. Braydon nodded at him. Torrino put down the magazine, then stood and brushed by Braydon, heading for the men's room down the hall. Braydon waited a beat and followed. In the men's room, an acne-faced teenager in torn jeans washed his hands at the sink.

Torrino shot him one glance. The kid left without bothering to dry off. Torrino turned to Braydon. "The Prophet will kill me if he sees me talking to you," he said. "Kill you, too."

"He'll do worse if we don't stop him."

"You don't know how crazy he is." He held up his injured hand. "Broke my finger for screwing up at Hunter's house. Twisted it with a nutcracker. Enjoyed it."

"So you screwed up the kidnapping."

"Not the kidnapping, I'd never do that, not for nobody. The Hunter kids were in school. Contreras sent me to get Gabriella Hunter's journal."

"A journal? What for?"

"You think the mastermind lets minions like me in on his plans?"

Contreras was after his chief botanist's journal. This could connect to some new miracle drug after all. "What about the artifact Christa Devlin found in Arizona, the armillary sphere?"

"Armillary what? That's what was in Devlin's pack?" He thrust his splinted finger at Braydon. "This is what I got for holding back with that Devlin girl and not grabbing that pack this morning. I figured she had the Turquoise, one of these *sacred* stones the Prophet says is going to change the world or something. You don't know how crazy he is."

"I do know how crazy he is," Braydon said. The Turquoise, Gabriella Hunter's journal, the Abraxas stones, the Lux et Veritas sword, he couldn't see the link, but couldn't shake the feeling that it was something utterly dangerous, potentially catastrophic. And the immediate threat was to a little girl's life. "That's why you've got to go back."

"I'm done."

"Lucia Hunter is just a year older than your little girl," he said. He didn't need to add that Torrino's daughter would never have been born if Braydon hadn't taken that bullet for him and killed the bad guys before they shot his pregnant wife, who was caught in the wrong place at the wrong time. Then Braydon gave him a chance to come clean. Torrino was a good man at heart, deeply damaged by a very bad upbringing.

"If I went back, I couldn't just stand by and let him hurt her," said Torrino. "I wouldn't care much about blowing my cover."

"Exactly why she needs you."

Torrino's phone buzzed in his sport coat pocket. He pawed it out and studied its small screen. "Text from The Prophet," he said. "He expects me back in ten minutes." He shoved the phone back into his pocket, leaned his hands on the edge of the counter. He assessed himself in the mirror, looking deep, frowning. "I'll probably get myself killed."

"You can't," Braydon said, allowing himself a sardonic smile. "It might get Lucia killed, too."

## CHAPTER 26

Daniel Dubler hated the heat, humidity and putrid fecundity of Gabriella's greenhouse. It made him nauseous, the same queasiness he felt when he was forced to attend the football match-up between Princeton and Harvard in the suffocating student section. He considered congesting spores and contact sports freaks of nature whose goal was to overtake and strangle civilization.

His cell phone chimed Beethoven's Fifth from his tweed jacket pocket. The screen read Private Caller. Those two words identified no one more acutely than Baltasar Contreras. Fine. He was ready, in a sense.

"We are out of time, Dubler," Contreras said.

"I'll find Gabriella's journal for you," he said. "Then I insist on telling Christa the truth." That sounded lame, as his students at Washington Prep would say. Besides, he shouldn't have to get approval to talk to the woman he loved.

"The truth," Contreras spit it out, as if the word repulsed him, "will reveal that you are a liar. You became friends with her sister because of a lie. You became close to her because of a lie. You've been building towards this endgame for six months. One stupid move now and you'll lose your queen."

Contreras treated the Princeton community as his fiefdom. The only reason that Gabriella's greenhouse was on the Princeton campus was because Contreras, and his generous donations to the university, waved a hand and made it so, staking out a prime if diminutive piece of property within a stone's throw of the Merick Rehabilitation Center. The greenhouse was tucked away in a sunny, quiet corner in the back, seldom visited and often overlooked. Nobody would guess that it could change history.

Daniel, too, had been seldom visited and often overlooked, and he was primed to change history. The Breastplate would be the find of the millennium. More than that, it was a direct conduit to God. He believed that. Yes, he believed that. Those fools at the seminary. They had no idea what he was capable of, given the opportunity. "This isn't a game," he said. "Not since she told me about her father's obsession with finding the Breastplate of Aaron. It took a lot for her to open up to me about that."

"That was the moment you should have thrust forward. That was the moment to lay bare her soul. To learn what she knows. Two weeks have passed since you told me this revelation. And you have done nothing with it."

"You mean I haven't continued to lie to her." He couldn't. He couldn't even talk to her. He pretended to have never heard of the Breastplate. Him, with his dual degrees in theology and history. Lame. She had to have seen right through it. He stopped calling and sending emails.

"Deception molds a relationship, not truth," said Contreras. "She didn't tell you about the Breastplate. You manipulated it out of her. Bravo, by the way. But doesn't it make you wonder, Daniel, what other truth she is hiding from you?"

For a man who only understood human nature through books, not actual experience, Contreras was a master. "Christa is afraid to trust anyone. With good reason, obviously." Daniel yanked at the right-hand desk drawer. Locked.

"Or is it because she fears that someone else will find the Breastplate and wield its power? Daniel, I did not choose you by random chance to join Hunter's Colombian expedition last summer as the historian. You are an integral part of the Lord's divine plan. You must embrace that, not fear it."

Daniel hadn't been with anyone this crazy since his days at the soup kitchen, putting in service hours as stepping stones on his path to priesthood. People had looked to him to calm down the drunks and druggies, but he was much better at theology than psychology. Now, he found a new calling. Christa Devlin. He grabbed a trowel from the shelf next to the desk and wedged it into the drawer to force the lock open. "I got in tight with Gabriella over these last months, just like you wanted."

"And you got in tight with Christa Devlin," Contreras said, "just like you wanted."

Contreras was either mocking or manipulating him. The locked drawer wouldn't budge. "I'm doing this for Christa, not me."

"Touching," he said.

"She needs a man in her life." She was so alone, like him.

"And if you are the one who is instrumental in finding the Breastplate, in bringing her father home," he said, "you won't be just a man. You will be her hero."

"All she wants is a family," he said. "I told you how her mother had been murdered." Maybe Gabriella kept the key to the drawer nearby. He hoisted the terra cotta pot holding a thorny, putrid smelling vine. Nothing but dirt beneath it. "You wouldn't understand." Love was as foreign an emotion to Contreras as the sun was to a worm.

"Understand this," Contreras said, his tone so sharp it nearly made Daniel jump. "Secrets beget secrets, revelations beget revelations. Sound familiar?"

Impossible. Nobody knew what Daniel had done. Contreras was dangling a hook. "It was tragic," Daniel said, "those very words, spray painted across the beautiful granite altar in my seminary's chapel."

"You were angry," Contreras said, his tone condescending. "So close to earning your doctorate in theology, only to be spurned by your advisor for your oral presentation. What was it he said in his review, *Not in keeping with your foundation of research.*"

"More like not in keeping with my advisor's idea of God," he countered. "Even without the doctorate, the seminary was desperate to ordain me as a priest."

"The Vatican won't even defrock child rapists," said Contreras, "as long as they are male and single."

"It's not why I left. I wasn't about to kowtow to their cultish hierarchy promoting religion by repression." Truth was, they suspected him of the vandalism, and he knew it. "The police arrested two local hoodlums for desecrating that altar."

"The rector at the seminary treated you like a triviality," said Contreras, "just as your father did. And it was, what, just two days after you were denied your PhD that your father passed from this life. Think of it. He spent his last hours knowing that his son had failed miserably, again."

Daniel dashed the potted plant to the slate floor. "Leave my father out of this."

"You not only defiled the altar with graffiti, you tore the seminary's precious collection of historic texts to shreds. I'm afraid an historian like Christa would find that unforgiveable. And, given their value, it is a federal offense."

Secrets. He could lose everything because of them. "She suspects I'm hiding something."

"Only the depth of your ignorance," said Contreras. "We are closer than ever, Daniel. Together, we will know the power of the divine artifact. The power to save souls."

To save Christa's soul. With Christa by his side, he'd find the strength to become the man he was born to be. No more demeaning himself teaching history to snotty boys. "Listen, I'll get you the journal, even though I can't imagine why you think this journal is so important. Christa is our best shot at finding that Breastplate." Contreras couldn't always be right. He had to stick to his guns, tell Christa the truth, or at least part of the truth.

"That is only proof of your lack of imagination," said Contreras. "Christa now knows that I, too, seek the Breastplate of Aaron. And she is on her way to you."

He scanned the street. "Christa is coming here, to the greenhouse?" He combed his fingers through his mop of blond hair, straightened his trademark bow tie. Dirt had streaked onto his jeans. It lent him a man of action mystique. No, this was ridiculous. Contreras thought he could control everyone, but not a woman like Christa. Never Christa.

"Play this as I directed you," Contreras said, "and you will win her."

A car skidded to a stop at the end of the greenhouse walkway, a purple Volkswagen beetle with a dent in the front fender. Brief elation at seeing her collapsed into sheer dread. "She's here," he said.

"As I told you," said Contreras. "Help me find the Breastplate. I will deliver to you Christa's soul. Now, go to work."

# CHAPTER 27

Baltasar Contreras frowned as he keyed in the finishing touch of his latest missive to his followers. He hit the send button, his words reaching around the globe instantaneously. *The plan is in motion. We are on the threshold of the New World. Be prepared. The Prophet.* For the first time, he felt trepidation.

He leaned back in the burgundy leather wing chair behind a mahogany desk so massive it dwarfed even his substantial girth. Surrounding him here in the billiards room were shelves of books and references collected for decades on strategic warfare, empire-building, and, of course, histories of religions. He had read them all, under the watchful eye of his father. Hunting trophies, from the elusive Kudu to a massive grizzly, gazed at him with a glassy-eyed awe, even though it was his father and ancestors, not him, who had conquered them. His trophy would be far greater.

The warmth of power rushed through his veins just as his message coursed through the veins of the Internet. Like a conqueror on his horse addressing the troops before the charge, he had rallied his legions with the code word, *threshold*. In twelve countries around the world, his cardinals shifted into high alert. His family had been building up to this moment for generations. He would be the one to guide their plan to its ultimate victory. He, Baltasar Contreras, was the descendent of the conquistador who had first braved the idea of ruling a new world order and the namesake of one of the three kings who visited the baby Jesus in Bethlehem. He would achieve nothing short of world peace.

And yet he had been forced to make his move. A command decision? Or an impulsive leap borne of the fear of failure? More worrisome, now that it was becoming real, he became aware of a tiny anomaly, a calcification, which could grow into a tumor of doubt.

"You disgust me." Baltasar stood suddenly. The voice alarmed him. He hadn't even seen his father, sitting stiff and straight in his wheelchair in the gloom by the window overlooking the pied a terre out back. "My son," he spat the words, "my own flesh and blood." The man's voice was both quiet and deafening, "a traitor to The Family." His craggy hand crept from beneath the plaid lap blanket and twisted the left wheel of the chair. It turned like a tank turret sighting on a hapless villager. An ashen, crumpled face of frowning lips and narrowed eyes targeted Baltasar. "I'd say you were not my son at all, but it would defame your mother."

Baltasar strode over to the crystal carafe on the wet bar. He reached down a snifter from the shelf above and poured himself two generous fingers of brandy. He breathed in the fortifying aroma. He watched the light play on the golden liquid. He would not be chastened like a schoolboy, not anymore. "I've done it, Father. I have set the wheels in motion to fulfill our family's destiny."

"You have done nothing!" The old man leaned forward in his wheelchair and tightened his arthritic fingers into pathetic, misshapen fists. "Where is my grandchild? Where is the heir that will carry on the mission of the Contreras dynasty?"

The words stabbed Baltasar like blowdarts, the poison stinging his flesh, burning through his veins to his core, clutching at his gut, squeezing the very breath from him. If only he could have begotten a child. If only that's all he had needed to do. But the mandate of glory and victory had been thrust upon him. "I am the last in the line," he said, struggling to steady his voice. "I am Baltasar. I am the one."

The old man sneered, and bent his thin mouth into a crooked smile. He parted his lips, revealing teeth yellow with age. With a gasping rattle, he cackled. "You! You are the one!" The cackle sputtered into a hacking cough that seemed almost to shake loose the desiccated flesh from his bones. Baltasar stepped forward, concerned. The old man thrust out his hand to stop him. "Your mother was pregnant when she was murdered, pregnant with the true heir. We knew, no, she knew you'd never be strong enough." He buried his face in his hands. "If only she were not killed."

Baltasar placed the snifter on the corner of the desk. He knelt by his father's chair. "And she wouldn't have been, not if we had restored the Breastplate."

Father's head snapped up. "Impossible! You know the story that has been passed down through the generations. That foolish missionary, Salvatierra, destroyed it five hundred years ago. He scattered the stones to the far corners of the Earth. God, Himself, sent the Tear of the Moon Emerald to the bottom of the sea."

Baltasar dared to place his hand on his father's. "The seventh stone," he whispered, worried that his father's thin heart might shatter like crystal to the contralto's aria of his amazing news, "the Tear of the Moon Emerald, it has been found." The old man looked at him, his glassy eyes wide. "You see, Father, this is the time. I am the one. Our network is in place. Through it, we know the Emerald is found. We are ready to pounce on all seven stones. I have arranged everything. It all hinged on the discovery of the Emerald, and now it has been found. It is my destiny."

For several long minutes, the old man did not move. His eyes were fixed at a point far beyond this realm of reality. A passerby might wonder if he had died and hunt for signs of breath, of a beating heart, of warmth in his sunken, pale cheeks. Baltasar felt his own heart quicken. What if his father died now, when he was so close to proving himself? The old man's chest heaved in a breath of air. "Show me the Emerald," he growled. "Show me the seventh stone."

Baltasar stood. He stepped back. "I do not have it, Father, not yet."

The old man narrowed his eyes. "The other six sacred stones, then."

Baltasar felt as if he were melting, shrinking back into a little boy who had been caught burning a text book in defiance of his relentless schooling. "They are within my grasp," he said. All his brilliant planning, his years of hard work and sacrifice, had he done the right thing? Father was right. He as yet had none of the stones.

"The ancient Jewish oracular stones, Urim and Thummim, you know where they are?"

"I will. Christa Devlin will lead me to them."

As Baltasar shrunk, his father seemed to grow in stature despite being confined to the wheelchair. "You fool. You don't even know

the location of the Breastplate. I suppose that Devlin will lead you
to that, too."

"Even now, Gabriella Devlin Hunter is on the path to
enlightenment."

The old man crept his chair forward, like a lion stalking his prey.
"Only the one who wears the Breastplate, complete with its stones,
has the power to communicate with God. Moses used the power of
the Breastplate to part the Red Sea. Aaron, his brother, wore it to
communicate with God to determine the fate of his people. History
thought that the Breastplate was lost when the Babylonians
destroyed the Temple of Solomon."

"But history cannot bury what God has created," said Baltasar,
pride bolstering his courage. "In 1082, our ancestor, a friend to the
great El Cid, conquered the Moorish ruler Al-Hayid, who, in utmost
secrecy, traded his life for the most powerful artifact known to man,
the Breastplate of Aaron."

The old man coughed and spat. "Al-Hayid had lost his battle,"
he said. "He thought the Breastplate powerless because it had been
desecrated. Its gemstones had been removed and distributed as
bounty in centuries past."

"He did not have the faith and foresight of a Contreras," said
Baltasar. "For four hundred years, our ancestors tracked down those
stones. Alvaro Contreras, the mighty conquistador of the sixteenth
century, acquired the last of them, the Kohinoor Diamond, and
restored the Breastplate to its God-given glory."

The old man's cheeks flushed with his passion, giving him the
semblance of renewed vigor. "He brought it to the New World and
defended from the chaos of the jungle a temple befitting the Holy of
Holies, for it is written, *You shall make the Breastplate of judgment.
Artistically woven according to the workmanship of the ephod you
shall make it: of gold, blue, purple, and scarlet thread, and fine
woven linen.*"

"Exodus 28:30," shouted Baltasar. *"And you shall put settings
of stones in it, four rows of stones: The first row shall be a sardius, a
topaz, and an Emerald; the second row shall be a Turquoise, a
sapphire, and a diamond; the third row, a jacinth, an agate, and an
amethyst; and the fourth row, a beryl, an onyx, and a jasper."*

The old man granted him a nod. "The Contreras family had the
Breastplate in our possession. We are the ones destined to start a

New World, to make right what is wrong." He jabbed a craggy finger at Baltasar. "They took him back in chains, to be hung by the neck until dead. They stole that power from us. They were afraid!"

Baltasar swallowed hard. He had heard the story hundreds of times. "The Vatican was afraid," he said. "Our ancestor, Alvaro Contreras, was jailed and sentenced to hang because the Vatican recognized his power to create peace. Mankind would be doomed, they thought, for who would need God, who would need His church, if people had nothing to fear?"

The old man snatched his son's brandy snifter from the edge of the desk. He held it high. "The quest for the Holy Grail is a fool's errand," he said.

Baltasar dared to step forward. "The Holy Grail is nothing more than a legend glorified by stories in the twelfth century. To find the grail and drink from it to gain immortality is no more than a folktale."

"A man can gain immortality only through death." His father dashed the snifter to the wide plank floor. It shattered, the sound ringing in Baltasar's ears. The brandy spewed from it like blood, splashing onto Baltasar's shoes. "And why should a man seek the Ark of the Covenant?"

"When he already knows the power of the ten commandments."

The old man sat up straighter. The tinge of life seeped through his gray pallor. "The Contreras family will not seek what other men seek."

Baltasar raised his arms heavenward. "We will only seek the word of God from God." Baltasar knelt again at his father's knee. "I will find the Breastplate of Aaron," he promised. "I will gather the seven lost stones and make it whole again. I will purge the world, and make it new."

Baltasar reached his hand to his father's. The old man recoiled. He turned away. "You are too weak," he said. "We are damned." His fingers gripped the wheels of his chair. He turned and creaked towards the billiards room door.

"Father," Baltasar called after him. "I will not fail the family. I will not fail you."

The door swung open. Baltasar's driver stopped at the threshold. He peered hesitantly into the room.

Baltasar sucked in a controlling breath. He realized he was still on his knees. He stood. "What is it, Simon?" he snapped.

"Miss Lucia is asking for you," Simon said.

Baltasar smiled, an unfamiliar warmth embracing him. She was asking. For him. Of all the years of complex planning, she was the one who was least predictable. Now an idea was forming in his brilliant mind. She could be the greatest reward of his mission. His plan was scrupulous, meticulous. His men obeyed without question. No, he could not fail. The thought of the next phase chased away his remaining doubts and curled his lips ever upward. He was like a father now. He had to take special care of the child who would change his life, a little girl named Lucia.

# CHAPTER 28

Daniel kicked the jagged bits of terra cotta from the broken pot beneath the nearest metal shelf, and swept away the thorny plant and dirt with his loafers. He slotted the books back into their places near the desk. With the flat of his hand, he cleared a circle from the steam on the greenhouse's glass wall to watch Christa. Contreras was right. If playing his part in a divine plan could save this amazing woman, then he was all in.

She skirted around the front of her purple Volkswagen, thumbing a text into her cell. She didn't even try to hold down her skirt when the frisky wind played around her long, sleek legs. She was wearing those brown leather boots, both practical and unwittingly sexy, like her, that he dreamed about before going to sleep at night. Her brown curls whipped around her face, teasing him with peeks at her sculpted cheekbones and rosy lips. He even loved that scar on her right temple from that rebel's bullet in Peru. It showed she was vulnerable.

He took one last look around the greenhouse to make sure he left no evidence of his search and opened the door. After the tropical heat of the greenhouse, the cold bit at him with sharp piranha teeth. He snugged his tweed blazer tighter and waited near the relative shelter of the greenhouse.

Christa shouted above a gust, her cell against her ear. "Percival, I've texted Helen. I didn't tell her anything, like we agreed, except that I'm here at the greenhouse. Give me a little time. That's all I ask."

She looked up, saw him, and jammed the phone into her jacket pocket. She rushed up to him and hugged him, tight. He tentatively wrapped his arms around her. Six months ago, he sowed the seeds of their relationship with more hope than promise, but, like the rainforest plants that choked the shelves of the greenhouse, he could adapt to unexpectedly fertile conditions.

"What are you doing here?" Christa asked. She stepped back and swiped her hair from her face.

"Storm's coming," he said. His answer was too abrupt. He should just tell her the truth. Truth begets truth. He poked his wire-rimmed eyeglasses tighter on his nose. "I wanted to make sure the greenhouse was secure. I heard Gabriella was out of town, so I figured I'd better come take care of her plants."

Christa grabbed his hand and drew him inside the greenhouse. Her hand felt so small in his. He flushed, not because of the cloying heat. He released her to shut the door behind them, sealing out the cold. He fought with the wobbly knob until it latched with a click. He gathered her in close again. He ached to kiss her. She pushed away. But not for much longer. Not, as Contreras said, if he played this right. "What's wrong?" he asked.

She crossed to the crude, wooden desk, started pawing through the pile of reference books on the corner. "I need Gabriella's journal, Daniel. Have you seen it?"

The damn journal. There had to be something in it after all. He came to her side and pretended to hunt through the left-side drawers, which he'd already searched twice. "Sorry I haven't called," he said. "End of semester is crazy. Busy grading essays, trying to find an excuse to make a C into an A. Parents don't pay thirty grand a year for a C." He brushed his elbow against hers.

She edged away. "Lying today doesn't help tomorrow."

She had nerve. Contreras had claimed that she was lying to him. She thought she was smarter than him. Truth was, she was smarter, way smarter. But he had something she didn't have. Faith. And inside information. "You're right," he said. He straightened up and squared his shoulders. "I pretended I didn't know anything about the Breastplate of Aaron when you told me about your father's obsession with it. Fact is, Baltasar Contreras, you know, the head of Gabriella's company, he told me about it when he hired me as historian for last summer's expedition. He asked me to keep my ear open to any local knowledge in Colombia."

That got her attention. Her eyes, those amazing Emerald eyes, met his. "And you didn't tell me."

"I figured Contreras was wacky," he said. "What would the Breastplate of Aaron be doing in Colombia? It's been lost since the sacking of the Temple of Solomon." Until, according to Contreras, his ancestor possessed it in the sixteenth century and brought it to the new world. "I was there to gather historical information on medicinal plants to produce new drugs."

She shrugged the army green pack off her shoulder and removed a paper from it. She thrust it at him. "What do you know about this?"

The drawing was definitely Gabriella's work, completed in situ, no doubt during their research trip to Colombia. "A plant?" What an idiot. He had let her veer off course. "What's this got to do with the Breastplate?"

"That's what I need to find out," she said. She began a search of the shelves of plants. The greenhouse was not large, only about fifteen by twelve feet, but Gabriella had packed a surprising variety of greenery into the space. On a sunny day, in the late afternoon, the wet smell of green and soil became suffocating, despite the oxygen the plants breathed into the air.

Daniel had always been better at reading books than people, but he knew Christa. Once she had her sights set on a goal, nothing would stop her. He had crammed in plenty of research on identifying plants so he could impress Gabriella. And it worked. She had introduced him to Christa, even had them both over to dinner until the roots of their relationship had established. The plant had better be what he thought it was. He needed to steer her back towards the journal and the Breastplate. "It's not in flower right now," he said. He gestured to Gabriella's desk. The desk was plain and rough-surfaced, adorned only with a microscope, pen and pad, and several potted plants. "Looks like Gabriella was working with it right before she left for Colombia this last time."

Christa hurried over. She planted her palms on the corner of the desk and leaned in for a closer look. The subtle, mellifluous scent of her skin drew his gaze to the gape between her blouse and breasts. She reached forward.

"Don't touch it," Daniel said, grabbing her hand. "If it is an adaptation of belladonna, like Gabriella wrote on this sketch, it could be poisonous." That fun fact should impress her. The crushingly dull conversation he'd had with the adoring, plant-loving and hopelessly single science teacher at Washington Academy to get close to Christa was paying off. Daniel had also scanned Gabriella's scant accessible notes into his brain, but he wasn't able to identify the plant on the desk, even with an extensive Google search. He recalled seeing plenty on belladonna, but when he learned it was an old world plant, he deleted it from his list to free up brain space for the copious exotic species from the South American rainforest. "But belladonna is an old world plant."

"True. It's been used as a poison since ancient Rome," she said. Of course she knew more about it than he did. "Poison is the perfect weapon to bring down a powerful man. Probably killed Alexander the Great."

"Dead at thirty-three." He could keep up with her. "Can you imagine what else he may have accomplished?"

"I'd rather imagine how many lives were saved by his death," she said. "Two Roman emperor's wives used belladonna to do in their husbands."

He dared to cup her shoulder with his hand. "Not the first nor last time that one woman has changed the course of history." Yes, one woman could change history, simply by changing him, making him the man he was meant to be.

"Maybe more than we know. Gabriella may have discovered a new species, indigenous to the new world," she said.

"If we find her journal," Daniel began.

No need to say more. Christa yanked open the sticky, center desk drawer. With a rolling rattle, a log jam of colored pencils wedged up against a stapler and a pad of paper given out at the local savings bank. She tried the desk drawer to his right, the locked one. She crouched for a closer look.

He had to distract her. She'd see the scratches where he'd tried to force it open. Damn. The trowel. He'd left it on the desk.

But Christa didn't reach for it. She crossed the greenhouse to the corner and its small, potted citrus tree. She bent over, lifted the edge of the pot and swooped a small object off the floor. It was a key. "Key lime tree," she said. "It's where I would have hidden it."

She tossed the key to Daniel. She did trust him. He unlocked the drawer. From it, he pulled out a field journal, spiral bound, recycled paper cover. A crude smiley face had been drawn in one corner, Lucia's trademark. Eureka. This was it. Gabriella's field journal. Now to convince Christa to give it to Contreras.

Not easy. Christa grabbed the journal from him. She traced her fingertips over the cover, bit her lip, then snapped opened the journal. She sat down in the creaking wooden chair and skimmed the bulleted notes on the first page, outlined under the heading *Belladonna*. "Okay, here's her notes on belladonna. Berries sweet but highly toxic." She rubbed the scar on her temple. "Eating as little as two berries can kill a child. Ingesting ten berries can kill an adult."

She turned the page. As far as Daniel knew, Gabriella's field journals were typically meticulous, her notes, in situ sketches and observations as orderly as cadets at West Point. Here, he saw a jumble of disconnected thoughts, as if those cadets were tin soldiers tossed and scattered by a mischievous schoolboy. Some words were circled, others underlined, arrows pointing from one to the other, as though Gabriella had tried in desperation an entirely different approach to analyzing the data, flinging it down like seeds to see what sprouted and discovered, like an ecosystem, all had to interconnect.

"What a mess," Daniel said. "Listen, Christa, I don't see anything about the Breastplate here, but I was with Gabriella in Colombia. I've made a study of these plants. I'll take the journal back to my office and sort it out."

"Over my dead body," she said. She turned the page and leaned back in the chair. "Which could be any time now."

A clever joke? He was never sure. "Christa, what's wrong?" She hesitated. "You can trust me," he said.

"Baltasar Contreras plans to poison the water supply," she said, "with an extract of this new belladonna species that Gabriella discovered." She looked up at him. "I thought she had found the antidote, but according to Gabriella's notes, the only antidote comes from a plant that's been extinct for five hundred years."

# CHAPTER 29

Baltasar snipped off the dead bloom on the Brassia maculata "Golden Web Weaver" orchid in the southern exposure corner of his orangery. The plant needed to be pruned, to survive and thrive. His plan was just that, a pruning. "Earth began as a garden," he said. "Animals were an indulgence. And when God created man, that's when His troubles began." Still, to kill so many.

He breathed in the citrus lacing the humid air. It calmed him. Baltasar had always felt more at home with plants than people. As a child, he'd spend hours in this orangery, learning the science of botany through observation, as da Vinci had. While others his age wasted hours in frivolous play, slithering down their pitiful slides, competing to throw a ball through a hoop, he was laying the cornerstone for the foundation of a new world. He moved to his prized hybrid rose bush, clipped a bloom so deeply red it was nearly black, and proffered it to his guest. "A rose by any other name would still smell as sweet," he said.

Bernard Rambitskov grunted. Baltasar recognized that his guest was not the type of man to accept a rose from another man. No, not at all. With his shaved head, bushy, scowling mustache and chest akin to an icebreaker, he intimidated people with his mere presence. He could have been the nicest guy in the world, but people feared him. And he certainly wasn't a nice guy, in any case. People who dared called him Rambo.

"Take it, Rambo," Baltasar said, holding the rose towards him. "You'll find its scent surprising."

Rambitskov snatched the rose. A thorn pricked his beefy forefinger. It drew a spot of blood as deep red as the petals. The man didn't flinch. He held the rose to his nose and sniffed. He didn't grimace. "You're perverted," he said.

Baltasar laughed. He had cultivated the rose himself, crossing it with a foul-smelling carrion flower from the tropics. The rose looked beautiful, but emitted a fetid stench when picked. He took the rose and threaded it into the buttonhole in Rambitskov's lapel. His fingers marveled at the silky weave of the high quality wool and the fit of the jacket over Rambitskov's linebacker frame. The man's tailor was almost as good as Baltasar's. "Your suit is rather dandy for homeland security government issue," he said. "Wouldn't want to raise eyebrows."

Rambitskov grabbed the rose from his lapel, crushed it like a grasshopper in his burly hand and dashed it to the floor. "I know what I'm doing," he growled.

Really, did the man always have to be so tough? Sure, it raised him through the ranks. The bastard son of a prostitute who was strangled by her pimp when the boy was ten, Rambitskov was barely making ends meet shaking down dopers as a beat cop in the Bronx. The vice president swings in for a photo op at a charter school opening and Rambo stops some anarchist from burning him alive with a blowtorch. He got second degree burns down both arms, and a free ticket to DC for a job in the Secret Service. Two years later he's first in command of New York's Homeland Security office. Right place. Right time. It could create, or destroy, empires.

Baltasar stepped back. Rambitskov could still flatten most takers, but arrogance had softened his middle. Arrogance, paranoia, flattery, they were all tools in Baltasar's chest, to be carefully selected for the job at hand. "I admire you," he said. "A good seed planted in bad soil must grow above the weeds to succeed."

"I rely more on getting to the point."

Baltasar laughed again. He could see Rambo as his number two, as long as he kept him pruned. "The finishing touches are complete for tonight," he said, "with New World Pharmaceuticals as proud sponsor, *naturellement*. I find it quite fitting that the G-20 is holding the premier dinner in the shadow of the United Nations, for this will truly unite them."

"More like ironic," said Rambitskov. He watched as Fenton glided silently into the orangery, balancing a sterling tray holding a cut crystal carafe and two snifters. The butler set the tray noiselessly on the glass table, then exited the room. "Considering their emergency meeting is on world peace."

"Only time will reveal the true irony of the venue," Baltasar said. He crossed to the table, popped the crystal stopper from the decanter. He poured two fingers of the bronze libation into a snifter. "And you have dispersed the vial into the water?"

"At noon today, despite the suddenly accelerated time frame."

"It was necessary." Gabriella had forced his hand. He couldn't risk being exposed. The deaths, beginning with her own children, would be on her head. He lifted the globe-shaped glass, swirled the liquid within its rims to warm it. He offered the snifter to Rambitskov. "Cognac?"

"No."

"Shame," said Baltasar. "It's a Courvoisier XO." He breathed in the silky aroma, placed the rim of the glass to his lips and drew a small draught into his mouth. He savored the sensation as the cognac caressed his taste buds. "You placed the poison into the single intake conduit?"

"Amazing how easy that was," said Rambitskov, "even if I am Homeland Security. It took less than two minutes to access that hydrant on Forty-fifth Street."

"So your department's information was spot on," said Baltasar. "The officials in Atlanta calculated it takes two minutes to insert toxins through a fire hydrant. The website is quite clear on the system's vulnerability."

"Like plastering it on the internet is going to help prevent the danger."

"Prevent? No. For *escalating* the danger, the internet has been remarkably helpful." Baltasar plucked a pressed linen cocktail napkin from the table and dabbed his lips. "It is a valuable tool," he said. "It is why I found you."

"And my department plastering guidebooks for terrorists on the internet is why I let you find me."

Baltasar pursed his lips. To think the man could consider that he played a part in his own destiny. "As per my plan," he emphasized, "New World Pharmaceuticals is generously providing the wine, beer and non-alcoholic beverages, but no water bottles."

"Greenies insisted the G-20 doesn't use any plastic water bottles," said Rambinsky. "I suppose you were behind that, too."

"Well," Baltasar said, "our poison is organic."

"Funny," said Rambitskov, his stoicism unmoved. "That vial didn't have much poison in it. They got one hundred and ninety-eight people on that guest list. That's a lot of water."

"You need not worry about its potency," he said. "Look at the website information. A typical hydrant holds up to seventeen gallons of liquid. Only one-twentieth of a quart of anthrax will contaminate one million gallons of water, and that can contaminate more than 100 miles of distribution pipe. That's tens of thousands of homes. Our poison is more toxic than anthrax."

"I'm well aware of the toxicity of anthrax," he said. "It's my job. But this poison of yours has never been proven."

"But it has," said Contreras, "by my ancestor, five hundred years ago. He nearly conquered an empire with it."

"And he came home broke and in chains," said Rambitskov, "returning only with two packs of seeds smuggled in his Bible."

"The seeds of life and the seeds of death," Baltasar said. "The seeds of a new world. An inheritance infinitely more valuable than any gold or silver."

"You've been cultivating the plants for generations, trying to duplicate the hybrids your ancestor created. How do you know the poison will work?"

"I know," Contreras said. The man had been told more than enough.

"So you say," countered Rambitskov, "but we know not everybody will be affected by the poison."

Baltasar swallowed, rankled that the tender burning of the cognac in his throat passed so quickly. "You need only to make a point once," he said. Nothing galled him more than an affront to his attention to detail. "I have told you that enough will succumb. Our demands will be met."

"Not until we prove the threat is overwhelming," he said. "That's going to take a lot more than making some halfwit world leaders sick. We have a powerful weapon. We should strike, like a snake, quick and without mercy."

Baltasar almost chuckled at the simile. "We'll be tempting them with the forbidden fruit soon. The masses are my weapon," he said, "and I will be the hand that wields it, in due time. My family has planned this for generations. I have honed every detail."

Rambo straightened his shoulders.    He leaned forward menacingly.  "We have to act now, before they catch on to what we plan to do to the G-20.  I will not fail because you're too afraid to use what we got."

"To veer from the plan is to invite catastrophe," he hissed. "My network is awaiting my command.  Then we will unleash the poison globally, at the precise moment it is needed."

Rambo met Baltasar's increasingly hostile impatience with a preternatural calm.  "U.S. policy is not to bargain with terrorists," he said.

"We are not terrorists," Baltasar snapped back.  He had to end this meeting.  It was souring the pleasure of his cognac.  "The G-20 is seeking world peace.  I am merely offering it to them."  He tried another sip, but it had more the texture of sandpaper than velvet. "Besides, government officials will only refuse to negotiate with terrorists if others' lives are at stake.  Now their lives will be threatened.  They get sick enough and they'll see the light, if not in this life, then the next."

"We might have to give the antidote to one of them to prove our bargaining position."

Baltasar searched Rambitskov's enigmatic face.  Part of him admired the man, one of the few still living who dared to challenge him.  He wondered if he suspected that Baltasar didn't have the antidote, or if he cared.  No matter.  He would have the antidote in time.  Getting it was all part of the intricate plan that he had set in motion.  History would remember him not as a villain, but a hero. "We'll have more power over their lives than God, my dear Rambo, and more determination in our purpose than Satan.  We will not have to bargain."

CHAPTER **30**

Christa turned on the desk lamp and checked her watch. It was 2:15 in the afternoon, but the greenhouse had taken on the veil of twilight. Dark clouds thickened the sky above. Thunder rumbled to the west, rattling the glass walls of the greenhouse. She had less than four hours before Contreras would call her and expect her to turn over Gabriella's research, the Emerald and the Turquoise in exchange for Lucia's life.

"Baltasar Contreras plans to poison the water supply?" Daniel said. "That's insane."

"True," she said, "which is why it makes sense." She'd given him the bare bones of her suspicions. "Contreras is desperate for Gabriella's findings. He wants to be the sole provider of the antidote that she's found." She reached over to the small cage that rested on a nearby shelf. She peered into it, opened the door and scrabbled her fingers through the paper bedding. "Daniel, where is Algernon?"

"Algernon?"

"The field mouse," she said. "He kept sneaking into the greenhouse when the weather turned cold. Gabriella put a box with bedding just outside so he wouldn't keep coming in. She was worried he'd get hurt." All three sisters had begged endlessly for a pet. They never had one, of course, not with their travelling to various digs around the world. So they adopted and promptly named everything from an injured dingo in the outback to an earthworm in the Amazon. "She told me he got sick. I got this cage for him from the biology department." She'd been too busy grading essays to be too concerned.

"He's gone," Daniel said.

"Gone? Did he get better?"

Daniel hesitated. "He died," he said. "The mouse was already in bad shape when I got here two days ago. I couldn't get him to eat or drink anything. It was like he was terrified of the food, of everything. He started convulsing, and died. I buried him under that maple." He nodded to the barren tree being bullied by a gust in the cold world outside.

Christa shivered. That did not bode well. She grabbed the journal, her eyes racing over the page. "Gabby found Algernon ten days ago, writhing on the desk. He had got hold of the belladonna, nibbled on a leaf." Christa turned the page. "She was trying to find the antidote, different extracts from different plants."

"There!" Daniel pointed to an entry underlined and followed by several exclamation points. "She found the antidote, an extract of papaver somniferum. Hold on, that's the same plant that produces opium."

"Algernon died, Daniel." And she knew why. The mouse had recovered, but only for seven days.

"At least he died happy," he said.

This would probably be the time to let him in on her meeting with Baltasar Contreras at the playground and tell him how Contreras had forced her to drink that capful of mystery liquid.

Percival's car pulled up to the curb in front of the greenhouse. He pushed open the car door against a gust, snugged in his windbreaker and hurried up the walk. Donohue wasn't with him. He practically tore the greenhouse door off its wonky hinges as he rushed in. "Did you find it?" he asked. "Did you find Gabby's journal?"

She held up the journal to show him. He rushed over and grabbed the book, pressed it against his heart. "Thank God," he said. "Donohue wanted it as a contingency. His plan is bold to say the least. I mean, he certainly talks like he knows what he's doing. He's served in three wars, after all." He stepped back, just noticing Daniel's presence. "Did Christa call you? Christa, you didn't call him, did you?"

"He was here when I arrived," she said. "Taking care of things. We found the plant specimen in the sketch, Percy. The Belladonna Conquistadorum. That's the good news." The only good news.

Percival flipped open the journal. "Here it is. Belladonna poison. Symptoms are dilated pupils, sensitivity to light, headache."

He swallowed, hard.        "Confusion," he read, "delirium, convulsions."

Christa picked up a pencil from the desk. Carefully, she used the pencil point to look closer at the bright violet underside of a leaf. What was that old maxim about red bringing dread in nature? "If this is an adaptation, then its poison may be even more potent," she said. As if delirium and convulsions weren't potent enough.

"And the antidote?" asked Percival.

"That's the bad news," she said.    "Gabriella extracted an antidote from a papaver, but it only lasts seven days.    The Colombian papaver that she believes provides the permanent antidote has been extinct for five hundred years."

"So that capful that Contreras forced you to drink," Percival began.

"Gives me seven days," said Christa, "before I go stark, raving mad." If not before, given that Contreras kidnapped Lucia and may be tracking down Gabriella.

"Capful?"    Daniel took off his tweed jacket.    His face was flushed. "When did you meet Contreras? I didn't think you even knew him."

Percival pointed an accusatory finger at Daniel, as if he were somehow to blame. "But you know him. You worked for him."

Daniel stepped back. "As an historian. I thought this was about the lost Breastplate of Aaron."

"Maybe it is," she said, "or Contreras wouldn't be so obsessed about finding and restoring it. Daniel, did Gabriella say anything about an artifact when you were with her in Colombia?"

"Nothing," Daniel said. He jabbed his fingers through his hair, yanking it off his forehead. "Well, probably nothing." Percival advanced towards him, his expression completely out of character. He looked ready to throttle Daniel.    "A canyon," Daniel said. "Gabriella had me asking the locals about some legendary temple at the mouth of a canyon. Nobody had heard about it and, frankly, that old Muisca shaman she was working with was suffering from dementia. All I got from the locals was a dirty look, like I was the loco one."

For a man who had studied to become a priest, Daniel was an ardent skeptic. It was one of his qualities she admired, usually. But she was beginning to rethink her own skepticism at this point. "Did you tell Contreras," she asked, "about this temple?"

If Daniel was flushed before, now his cheeks turned nearly as red as the underside of the belladonna leaf. "That's what he was paying me for," he said. "He said the temple couldn't be connected to the Breastplate."

Percival shook a fist at him. "And you believed him."

Daniel stood his ground. "Contreras is not a killer."

"For my daughter's sake, I pray you're right."    But he did more than pray. "Contreras kidnapped my daughter. He gave Christa his demands, impossible demands. He threatened Lucia. He threatened all of us." Daniel looked physically ill. Despite his awkwardness around anyone younger than eighteen, he loved the kids. He actually seemed to enjoy going on the swings with them. On that evening two weeks back when they were cracking open their souls, he admitted that the children had revealed an emotion in him that he had accepted he would never feel, the joy of innocence, and he liked it.

"A temple," she interrupted, before Percy could tell him about Salvatierra's letter. This was ridiculous. She should trust Daniel. He could help them, if she could give him the chance. "Gabriella wrote about it," she opened to a page covered with random notes. Salvatierra's letter had referenced a temple, too, and a canyon. Oculto Canyon. But another name on Gabriella's page was a far more promising lead. Gabby hadn't only asked Donohue for help. Christa knew just where to go next. She returned the journal to Percy. "Donohue's waiting for this," she said. "And we have no time to waste."

The door of the greenhouse burst open. A sudden frigid gust lanced into the greenhouse. It smelled of minerals, like before a snowstorm.

Helen stepped in, one hand clenched around the scruff of her brown wool coat, the other gripping Liam's mitten-encased hand. Liam was naturally skinny, but he looked as round as a snowman in his puffy jacket and clunky black snow boots. His hood was pulled tightly around his face and his cheeks seemed to reflect its bright red hue. Helen, despite the chill air, looked paler than usual. She was older than Christa and would be pretty, if she didn't downplay her looks in outfits better suited to a great aunt.

Percival rushed to Liam. He knelt awkwardly and encased him with a mighty hug. The greenhouse took on a complete if ephemeral hush. Helen swiped the handknit cabled hat from her head. "What's going on?" she commanded. Her eyes strafed the room. "Where is Lucia? And why are you at the greenhouse?"

Percival did not relinquish his hug. It was as if he was afraid Liam would melt away should he let go.

"My head hurts, Daddy," Liam said, speaking even more softly than usual.

Percival leaned back. He unsnapped Liam's hood and slipped it off with the gentle touch. He wove his fingers through the boy's scruffy brown hair and tenderly caressed his reddened cheeks. "Tell Daddy," he said.

Liam sniffled. Helen extracted a tissue from her coat pocket and blotted his nose. "I was at the clinic here on campus when I got Christa's text," she said. "I don't care if the doctor said it's just a virus. He had so many sick kids waiting, he didn't want to spend the time. Then two moms started arguing in the waiting room. I was afraid they were going to start hitting each other. I had to get out of there. It's something serious. I know it is."

A faint smile crossed Liam's lips. "The nurse gave me a smiley face sticker," he said.

Percival carefully unzipped the boy's jacket. "Is he overheated?"

"Of course not," she said. "He was feverish like this before we left home."

Liam frowned, his gaze on Gabriella's desk. "I want Mommy."

Percival tugged down the crew neck of Liam's striped knit top, revealing a smattering of tiny red bumps just below his neck. Percival's face visibly paled. "Mommy will be home soon, Liam," he said.

"Mommy is here now, Daddy." Liam pointed his puppy mitten towards the empty desk chair. "She's sitting right there."

Percival, with trepidation, swiveled his neck towards the desk. His expression looked confused, doubtful. Helen reached down and pressed her palm against Liam's forehead. "He's burning up," she said. "He's hallucinating."

"It's not the fever," he said. "Belladonna poisoning can cause hallucinations."

Liam screamed. He struggled to run past Percival. "Mommy! That monster is after Mommy! Help her, Daddy. Help her!"

Percival hugged him tighter. "It's okay, Liam." Liam's snow boots kicked wildly.

Helen knelt. Christa rushed towards them. Liam collapsed into Percy's arms, unconscious, his limp legs dangling. A look a sheer panic crossed Percival's face. He cradled Liam's head in his hand. "Liam!" he shouted.

"I'll call 911," Daniel offered, barely finding his voice.

"No," Helen said. "The clinic is two blocks away. He'll receive care faster if we take him there. They have an emergency unit."

Percival wrapped one arm around his son. Liam looked impossibly small in the arms of his father. "Give me Gabby's journal, Christa," he said. "I'll get it to Donohue. You find those stones."

# CHAPTER 31

Baltasar Contreras repressed a scream of rage. Dubler's text was short but clear. *I know about poison. G's antidote only lasts 7 days.* Damn it. She hadn't perfected the antidote yet. It would hold off the effects of the poison for seven days, then those who had ingested the poison would go mad and die as surely as those pathetic villagers in his ancestor's time. He had to remain calm. All was not lost. He had to put his plan for this contingency into play.

Little Lucia Devlin was down on her hands and knees guiding a courageous and very frilly Barbie through the green fringes of the blanket of purple-flowered Vinca in the orangery. The doll's pink glittery ball gown floated above the undergrowth. Is this what little girls dreamed of? He, too, had simple dreams at her age, to be beautiful, desirable, adventurous and, most of all, to be guided by someone else's adoring, all powerful hand. Man truly did not want free will. Since history began, men have wanted a superior being to tell them what to do. This burden fell heavily on Baltasar's shoulders, but he would soon have the means to communicate God's wishes. And for that, he needed to bend Gabriella's will. Break it, if necessary.

"She's a fairy," the little girl said, sensing Baltasar's presence above her. She held the doll up towards him and rocked her back and forth, speaking in a high-pitched Barbie voice. "I'm looking for the fairy prince. Have you seen him?"

Baltasar smiled. Delightful girl. "The prince is in the anthurium." He gestured to what he considered the most sexual of flowers with its erect spadix.

Lucia cocked her head, crinkled her nose and shrugged. She plunged the Barbie back into the Vinca jungle.

Fenton entered carrying an open laptop. "I have the video connection, sir," he said, placing the laptop on the glass-topped table. He bowed and left, taking up his position just outside the inner door, ready to enter if Baltasar needed him. Baltasar had made a study of manipulating adults' emotions, but he had found children's emotional reactions frighteningly unpredictable.

Baltasar took a moment to admire his virtually connected portal to the other side of the world. On the computer screen was the real-life version of the ecological microcosm in his orangery. He heard a symphony in the variations of green, with hundreds of hues in harmony yet distinct. Groundcovers just inches high formed the bass of the oboes and cellos, ferns the melody of the violins, towering trees the high pitches of the flutes and piccolos.

His cadre of soldiers, dressed in khakis and mud, looked as though they were morphing into the jungle, which waited for them to slumber so it could slowly digest them.

They had hacked away just enough of the jungle for three dome tents and a campfire ringed with stones. The laptop, his portal to that world, sat on one of the two crude wooden tables.

Baltasar punched up the volume key. He could hear the noisy clicks and scrapes of the thousands of insects, the cacophony of bird songs, the occasional screech and chatter of a curious monkey. A face appeared on the screen before him, a beautiful, if drawn, face. Gabriella Devlin Hunter was a stunning woman, even with mud, not makeup, accentuating her high cheek bones. Her dark blonde hair was unwashed and tied back carelessly. Her skin was tanned, her tank top revealing impressive biceps and an intriguing cleavage. She didn't only look like she could survive a week in a jungle with only a canteen and a cookpot, then shower and dress for a state dinner in the evening. Baltasar had seen her do it.

A man stood behind her, but all that was visible on the screen was his mud-stained khaki shirt and pants and his dirty fingers grasping his Uzi. Baltasar recognized him as Mendoza, by his signature ring and his missing pinky.

Baltasar sat before the laptop and leaned forward. The woman facing him pushed back, an expression of anger darkening her face as surely and swiftly as a summer squall. She grabbed the edges of the laptop as if to throw the computer, Baltasar along with it, out of her world. Mendoza's beefy hand grappled her shoulder and yanked her back, holding her petite but feisty frame firmly in check. Baltasar smiled. "Hello, Doctor Hunter," he said.

She struggled ineffectively against Mendoza's grip. Contreras watched his man slide his Uzi out of the way and bend down to position his face within the webcam's shot. "She's still not cooperating, Mister Contreras. Keeps claiming that it's not possible to find a plant that's been extinct for five centuries."

A cold bile rose in Baltasar's throat. He fought it down. He refused to believe this. If he did, all would be in vain. "What did the Muisca medicine man tell you?" he growled.

Gabriella Devlin Hunter did not answer. Mendoza's fingers closed like a vice clamping her shoulder. Baltasar could see his fingers press against her tanned flesh until it blanched. She grimaced and pressed her lips tighter.

"The medicine man said that his ancestors destroyed that species five hundred years ago," Mendoza said. "They figured that if one man who sought it brought death and devastation to their villages, then others like him might follow. No plant, no conquistador, they figured."

"A Contreras is not easily deterred," said Baltasar. "And neither should his chief botanist be. Researchers are discovering new species in the rainforest all the time. In 2009, they discovered a pitcher plant that eats rats. In the last few years, right there in Colombia, scientists continue to discover new species of frogs, including the golden dart frog of Supata, perhaps the very species that eats the insects that consume the plant for which you search. Surely, Doctor Hunter, you can find this one plant."

Hunter squirmed her shoulder out of Mendoza's grip. "Not if it doesn't exist," she said. "Colombia's rainforest is home to more than 583 species of amphibians. They have evolved and adapted to man's intrusions. The plant your ancestor used may well be extinct."

"You are well familiar with the Lazarus effect," said Baltasar. "A species of rat thought extinct for eleven million years was found on sale at a Laos meat market. Perhaps you're not looking hard enough," said Baltasar.

"Mommy?" The tiny voice came from behind him. The little girl, after a tentative moment, rushed towards him. She scrambled onto his lap. She felt so light, airy, the subtle scent of lilies in her

strawberry blond curls, like a fairy had alighted upon him. The little
girl's smile was captivating. "Mommy, where are you? Daddy's
been trying to call you."

Hunter's face paled. She leaned forward and thrust out her hands
to her daughter, as if she could grab her and pull her through the
looking glass. She mouthed her daughter's name, "Lucia." Baltasar
punched up the volume button, but it was only the mother who had
lost her voice. Mendoza stepped back, to the outside of the camera's
range, as if a sudden sense of decorum swayed him to give mother
and daughter their private space.

Lucia held her Barbie up to the camera. "Mister Profit got me a
new Barbie," she said. "It's the one I wanted for Christmas. Isn't
she beautiful?"

Hunter nodded stiffly. She smiled, although Baltasar could
detect a tremor in her lower lip. "Mister Profit?"

Lucia giggled. "You know, your boss. He remembered me from
your work picnic last summer, before you went to Colombia the last
time. You never told me he had such a funny name. He picked me
up from school and got me ice cream at Jimmies. Two scoops!"

Hunter's eyes fluttered. Baltasar found it curious to see someone
struggling so hard to hold back tears. He was surprised to see it
pained him. His own mother, he had seen her do that, hadn't he?
Hunter bit her lip. "Where are you, honey?"

"In Mister Profit's jungle," she said. She squinted at the screen.
"Hey, are you still in Colombia? We're learning about the rainforest
in school. I told the teacher all about how you went on a plant safari
in Colombia last summer."

It was all Baltasar could do not to embrace the girl, oddly proud
of her cleverness. "Go play with your Barbie," he said, nudging her
from his lap. It's the kind of thing a father would say.

The little girl slid to the ground. "When are you coming home,
Mommy?"

Gabriella Hunter visibly stiffened. For a moment, Baltasar was
afraid that she was going to shout for her daughter to run away. But
to where? Instead, the woman forced another smile. "Very soon,
Lucia," she said. "I love you more than the moon and stars. You
know that?"

Lucia shrugged, then looked up. "Wait, see what I found!" She
ran back to where she had been leading Barbie into the jungle.

Baltasar pushed back his chair so both he and Hunter could see the child. Lucia crouched. There, in the clearing, a Phyllobates terribilis, commonly known as the Golden Arrow poison dart frog, sat gleaming like a pure gold nugget against the dark soil. "It's the fairy prince," Lucia said. She lowered Barbie's face towards the tiny frog. "Isn't he beautiful? Barbie's going to kiss him."

On the computer, a look of recognition, then sheer terror, filled Hunter's face. "Don't touch it!" she screamed. She lunged towards the computer. "Lucia, get away!"

Lucia clutched her Barbie to her heart and stepped back. She looked towards the laptop, a sudden dismay flooding her eyes with tears.

Hunter lowered herself back into her chair. "I'm sorry I yelled, honey," she said, her voice still with an edge. "But that frog is very poisonous. If you touch it, you'll get sick."

Baltasar signaled for Fenton to come in. Perhaps children's emotions weren't so unpredictable. He could see Lucia was on the verge of crying. Besides, he'd made his point. "Go with Mister Fenton," he said to Lucia.

Lucia pouted. "I want to go home now."

Baltasar stiffened. "I told you to go with Mister Fenton."

Fenton stepped forward, crouched to lower himself to her level. "Chef just baked some cookies." He breathed in deeply and smiled. "Can you smell them? Chocolate chip, my daughter's favorite. Do you like them?"

Lucia hesitated, and then nodded. She looked at the computer screen. "Can I, Mommy?"

"Go with Mister Fenton," Hunter answered quickly. Baltasar sat back smugly. The woman would rather have her child with anyone than him.

Lucia eyed Baltasar. "Can you take me home then, after cookies?"

"When you go home," Baltasar said, "is entirely up to your mother." Fenton offered his hand to the girl. She took it, and he led her from the orangery.

CHAPTER **32**

The minute Christa bundled Liam in his car seat next to Percival, she rushed back to the greenhouse. *Find the stones*, Percival said. Like Dad hadn't been searching for them his entire life. And she was supposed to piece together the clues in Salvatierra's letter and find the Turquoise and Emerald within hours. But she was becoming more sure it wouldn't end there. Salvatierra was the last man to see the Breastplate of Aaron intact. His letter laid out clues to its location. Thousands of lives relied on who found it first.

Salvatierra's crucifix knocked against her chest as she ran. It was the kind of irony that only cycles in history could create, to be swooped up and dropped into Salvatierra's five-hundred year old mission to keep the power of the Breastplate out of the hands of evil, out of the hands of a Contreras. To right a deadly wrong, even if it cost her life, even if it cost her soul. "Tried it your way, Padre," she said, "but I need those seven stones together, not scattered around the world."

Daniel stayed on the sidewalk, looking in the direction of Helen's car and the clinic, as if wondering if what just happened was real or imagined. Christa shouldered her pack. She stepped out of the steamy womb of the greenhouse and met him in the cold dread of December.

He wrapped his arms around her. "I love you, Christa." She closed her eyes. What a time for him to say that. He stroked her hair. "I believe in you."

"That makes one of us."

He held her at arm's length, his eyes searching hers. "This is all coming back to the Breastplate of Aaron," he said. "We can find it. Think of it, Christa. To hear God's voice. To solve the eternal question. To know, without doubt, that death is not the end of life."

"That kind of god complex is what got us into this mess."

"Exactly. That's why we have to work with Contreras, not against him."

She pushed away. "Have you been drinking the water?"

"Think about it. Contreras is way ahead of us. You want to save Lucia? I know this man. I know how he works. He doesn't want to kill people. He wants to save them. He is the only one in the position to find and distribute the permanent antidote in time."

"He kidnapped Lucia. He is chasing after Gabriella. He poisoned our water supply, for God's sake."

"Lives are at stake," Daniel said. "Do you want to be responsible for all those people dying? Because you will be, if you can't admit Contreras is the only one who can save them."

"I'd make a deal with the devil first." She hurried across the grassy courtyard. Dead leaves skittered around her feet. She hunched her shoulders against the chill. Few people were hustling along the sidewalks that surrounded the square plaza. Most students had already left for the winter break. It felt empty. It felt like death. Could Daniel be right? Could Contreras be the only chance at salvation? The thought was sickening. A scattering of melancholy measures from a violin escaped the caprices of the wind and floated their way to the inner courtyard.

"The inviolate violinist," Daniel said, close in on her heels. They had named the elusive musician when she and Daniel met to read on the grassy squares on sunnier days.

"Mozart's Requiem," she said.

"Mass for the dead," Daniel said. "Most historians agree now that Mozart was poisoned to death, by his jealous rival, Solineri. It's a sign, Christa."

"A sign? Mozart sending a message from beyond the grave? You have been drinking the water."

"Christa," he grabbed her shoulders, "this is the Breastplate of Aaron, the greatest historical artifact of all time. Doesn't a part of you want to know what happens when we restore it?"

Of course a part of her wanted that, more than anything. It was screaming at her, the imp of the perverse, clamoring at the bars of its cell that she kept locked and hidden away. "Only if restoring the Breastplate will show us the antidote, how to find it, or how to create it. We've got to get the permanent antidote."

"You're talking about science," Daniel said. "I'm talking about solving mankind's ultimate mystery—what happens after we die."

"I'd rather not ruin the surprise," she said. More like she was terrified of the answer. It was easier to accept her mother's life had simply ended than to confront the fact that her immortal spirit blamed her for her death. She stepped up the granite stairs and battled the push of the wind to open the heavy oak door to the ivy-covered brownstone that held the history faculty offices. She stopped, blocked Daniel from entering. "I've got to do this alone," she said. If only she had the strength to believe it. "I can't work with you, Daniel. Not if that means working with Contreras."

"Contreras trusts me," he said. "We'll do it your way. I won't tell him anything." He grabbed her hand. "But I can get close to him, find out exactly what he's up to, if you bring me in on what's going on. You need to trust me, for Lucia's sake."

"Just to get this straight, I should trust you, because Contreras trusts you, so you can double cross him."

"I don't love Contreras," he said. "You are the one I want to spend my life with."

"Your timing sucks," she said. Once again, she was blowing it, kicking away anyone who she let close enough to care. But, in this case, he was right. She needed him, and damn it, she might only have days to live. She didn't want to leave this life so utterly alone. "As far as spending time together, let's see if we get through the next seven days."

They hurried down the linoleum tile hallway. The florescent lights cast a ghostly pall over Daniel's face, exaggerating his troubled expression. Most of the offices were already locked for the winter break. The air was still and heavy, with no way to escape the weight of the building pressing down on it. Laughter escaped from Professor Durham's office, and a snippet of his phone conversation about an upcoming holiday party. It sounded out of place, surreal, from a parallel world where people didn't kill and kidnap for sacred gemstones.

She shouldered open the heavy fire doors and headed down the worn marble stairs. Their footsteps echoed, populating the emptiness with the specter of ghosts. Phantom whispers teased the edges of her perception. Ghostly breath chilled the back of her neck.

The poison couldn't be driving her mad, not yet. And the object of her quest, Professor Conroy, needed no poison to know madness.

Her students referred to him as Crazy Conroy, not that they knew him. Like an historical figure in their texts, Conroy was someone they only had learned about. He had long ago been forced to retire from teaching, banished to a dusty, forgotten corner of the basement, becoming like one of the many curious relics in his collection. Christa made it a habit to visit him, at first to make sure he was still among the living, then to embrace his genius. She mined the Internet for facts, but Conroy, like a physicist with a proof to the unification theory, would interweave seemingly unconnected threads of information into a brilliant tapestry of humanity, a task still singular to the human brain.

"This professor is an old friend of my father's. He lived in the Colombian rainforest as a child with his missionary parents," she told Daniel. "That experience inspired him to become an historian." Same thing happened to her after Peru, desperate to make sense of the present by looking into the past.

Half the fluorescent lights flickered in the windowless corridor. Others had given up the ghost entirely. Dust dulled the linoleum floor. Even the custodians had abandoned this subterranean floor, presuming, correctly, that it wouldn't be noticed. The frosted glass door at the end of the hall was stenciled in black with the simple identification, Cornelius Conroy, PhD. At least the University had acknowledged that much.

Daniel pulled her back. "Crazy Conroy?" he said. "One of my student's older brothers talked about him. He's nuts."

She knocked. A confused muttering seeped through the door, as if someone suddenly awoke from a nap or was startled away from intense concentration. A shuffling of feet approached. The door opened slowly to reveal a man, who, for better or worse, could understudy for Albert Einstein with his wild hair and sharp eyes. The pungent scent of pipe smoke defied the musty air, although Conroy hadn't smoked in years. Conroy wore his signature V-neck sweater beneath his brown corduroy jacket. In any season, his basement office felt chilled and damp, reflected in his ruddy complexion. His bushy eyebrows, normally raised in delight at Christa's appearance, were knitted in concern. "It has begun," he said, "and I will show you the beginning." He grasped her upper arm and coaxed her forward. Daniel stepped in while Conroy checked the hall. Satisfied it was empty, he closed and latched the door behind them.

Conroy shifted the small stack of books teetering on the threadbare velvet chair to a vacant patch of floor, dropping them with a loud thud, rousing a swarm of dust mites. The spines were embossed with Conroy's name. He was a prolific author in his glory days. He gestured for Christa to sit and motioned Daniel to the chair's empty twin. Daniel hesitated, scrutinizing the chair. Its worn, red upholstery was framed by fanciful carved wood gilt in peeling gold leaf, lending it the look of a theatrical, if shopworn, medieval throne. "Professor Conroy rescued them from the dumpster after the University's production of King Lear some years ago," she said. *I like to treat my guests like royalty*, he had quipped.

Conroy wove his way past the bookshelf bursting with texts, papers and periodicals to the padded chair behind his desk. He wheeled his chair closer and leaned forward, clasping his hands on the blotter. "I've seen the phantoms," he said. "I was expecting you."

Daniel stood up. "This is crazy. He can't help us."

Christa grabbed Daniel's hand and coaxed him to sit down again. She looked out the grimy hopper window. It was there, all right. The dark shadow, hunkering on the barren tree branch. This wasn't a delusion. Conroy had seen it, too. "This is Daniel Dubler," she said. "He was with Gabriella in Colombia last summer. He was the expedition historian."

Conroy turned towards Daniel, his sharp eyes scanning him. "All historians are a bit crazy, Mister Dubler. It's how we stay sane."

Daniel turned away. He took a sudden interest in the glass enclosed barrister bookcases that were replete with an odd array of artifacts collected from remote areas around the world when, years earlier, Conroy was doing field research.

Christa leaned forward. She reached across the desk and opened her hand.

Conroy started hacking when he saw the crucifix. He couldn't catch his breath. She filled his glass with the pitcher of water he always kept on his desk. He reined in his coughs and drank a sip. "May I?" he asked. Before she could reply, he lifted the crucifix cautiously from her palm. Without taking his gaze from it, his free hand pawed blindly at the corner of his desk, finally landing on his reading glasses. He perched them on his nose and brought the crucifix closer.

Christa edged aside a stack of papers to lean her elbows on the desk. "It belonged to Salvatierra. Dad found it, Professor. He found Salvatierra's letter."

Conroy smiled broadly, clamped the crucifix in his fingers and slammed his fist on the desk. "By God, he did it. He never lost faith, Christa. Never." Then he frowned. He leaned back, his chair tilting with a reluctant creak. "But, then, where is he? Why send the letter to you?"

"I think Dad's hurt," she said, "could be bad."

"But he is closer than ever to finding the Breastplate."

Exactly why he might be hurt. "He's not the only one," said Christa. She took the letter from her pack, unfolded it and handed it to Conroy. "Baltasar Contreras, the head of NewWorld Pharmaceuticals. He wants to pick up where his ancestor, Alvaro, left off."

Daniel's chair groaned as his weight shifted forward. "Who is Salvatierra? And what is this letter you're talking about?"

Christa filled both of them in on the highlights as Conroy's eyes raced over her translation. "The Demon's Wings," he read, his voice hushed. "The Oculto Canyon. Yes, they are familiar, I think. My God, Salvatierra actually names the seven lost gemstones. This is fantastic news."

"I've got bad news, too. Baltasar Contreras plans to poison the water supply in Princeton and New York," she said. "Maybe he already has. He thought Gabriella found an antidote, but it only lasts seven days. She returned to Colombia two days ago. She must be hoping to find the antidote plant, if it even exists."

"Whole villages destroyed," Conroy read. He let the pages fall to the desk. He may be old, but his mind was quick. Like her father.

Daniel snapped up the printout and began reading it. He stood and paced, nearly tripping over a pile of books, but still not taking his eyes off that letter. Daniel fumbled the eyeglasses off his nose and swiped his forehead with the back of his hand. "My God," he whispered.

Conroy touched the tip of his forefinger to his nose, as in charades when the puzzle is solved. "That would be the one," he said.

Christa leaned in closer. "The Breastplate is connected, vitally connected. I don't know how, exactly, but Contreras is desperate to find the lost gemstones and restore the Breastplate, even more desperate than Dad." She rubbed the scar on her forehead. "He kidnapped Lucia, Professor Conroy. He is demanding that we deliver Gabriella's findings to him, but that's not all. He thinks I can get him the Tear of the Moon Emerald and the Yikaisidahi Turquoise."

"Which means the wreck of the San Salvador has been found," Conroy said. "Have you heard from Ahmed?"

"Not yet," she said, "but Contreras must have been watching. He seemed to know that the Emerald has been recovered."

"And the Turquoise?"

"I'm working on it, but how is the Breastplate connected? He calls himself The Prophet," she said. "Could it simply be religious fanaticism?"

"Religious fanaticism is never simple" he said. "It is the most deadly force in history." He pointed to the letter in Daniel's hands. "Alvaro Contreras answered your question, five hundred years ago, when he set in motion what might destroy or save our world."

CHAPTER **33**

A subtle breeze wafted a citrus scent through the orangery as Fenton, with Lucia clasping his hand, closed the door behind him. Baltasar edged his chair up to the laptop, his virtual window to the Colombian rainforest. Gabriella Hunter was on the other side of the world, but he had her just where he wanted her.

"Now that we can talk privately," Baltasar said.

"If you hurt her, I'll kill you," Hunter hissed through the video connection.

"No need for threats," he said, "especially unfeasible ones."

"It's not a threat. It's a promise."

Baltasar frowned. Gabriella Devlin Hunter had better not disappoint him. "And there is certainly no need for clichés," he said.

"The Muisca tribe eradicated the plant you seek generations ago, because of what your ancestor did."

He would not have this woman questioning his family's mission. "My ancestor was well on his way to creating a truly new world."

"Before he was sent back to Spain in chains and executed."

Baltasar slammed his fist on the table. "By an emissary from the Vatican. They were afraid, terrified that Alvaro Contreras would create the world that God envisioned, using His words directly, not the arcane whims of an interpretation written by fallible men." He sucked in a calming breath. The woman was infuriating, but Baltasar kept his rage in check. He had to remind her of the danger to her own family. "Lucia is a lovely girl," he said. "I have much to offer her, that is, if anything were to happen to you and your husband." Baltasar smiled wistfully. "I could be a good father to her. Teach her all she needs to know."

Hunter's face paled even more. "You need to tell me all I need to know."

"I have given you my ancestor, Alvaro's, missive. As of now, you know about the plants, the legend of the temple, the Oculto Canyon, knowledge that you did not have when you left for Colombia last summer. Yet, even then, you discovered the Belladonna Conquistadorum. Now, you have everything you need to find the Papaver Contrerasum and the temple pyramid."

"I told you. The Papaver Contrerasum, as your ancestor so egotistically named it, is now extinct. After what Alvaro did here, the Muisca Indians, the few who survived, forbade anyone from travelling to, or even speaking of, the hidden canyon. They destroyed any of the Papaver or Belladonna plants they found long ago. Papaver Contrerasum is derived from Papaver Somniferum, the poppy plant that produces opium. Colombia doesn't need another addictive drug that brings violence to their people. The only reason I found the Belladonna Conquistadorum last summer is because belladonna adapts so well. In North America, belladonna grows like a weed. A few seedlings of Conquistadorum escaped the microcosm of the Oculto Canyon."

"Then there is no reason to believe that Belladonna Conquistadorum and Papaver Contrerasum do not still thrive within the Oculto Canyon."

"That Papaver can only grow in unique conditions, high humidity, rare nutrients in the soil and a limited range of high altitude. That's why NewWorld Pharmaceuticals has only been able to propagate a hybrid of the original plant, despite your attempts at recreating the original species in microcosms around the world."

"An ineffective hybrid," said Baltasar.

"The seeds that Alvaro smuggled back to Spain in his Bible are from plants that can only grow in the Oculto Canyon."

"Which is why you need to find where the Oculto hides."

"How? I've studied Alvaro's missive. He happened upon the Oculto by chance, when he was on that disaster of an expedition with Quesada. His men were starving. In desperation, they ate a poisonous plant, the Belladonna. When he helped ease their dying spasms with water from the river that flowed through the temple, his men were cured. He realized the cure came from the plants growing along its bank. He was as surprised as anyone."

Not a surprise, but a divine revelation. "In the Oculto Canyon," he said, "Alvaro found a weapon more powerful than any arquebuss with gunpowder. He had the only cure to a deadly poison. Alvaro told El Dorado, the ruler of the natives, that the Breastplate's power could show the people the power of the Almighty God. He promised that they could be an army of conquerors, not the conquered. He could return to Europe and conquer the world with his army of savages and his deadly poison. He could put an end to a religion that condones murder by the tortures of the Inquisition and spread the true word of God."

"He committed genocide, Baltasar. He poisoned the river that flowed through the villages, only doling out the Papaver antidote to the men who came with him to defend his pyramid."

"Alvaro created his Papaver antidote to save the Muisca people. But first he had to reinforce the pyramid to protect the hidden canyon and his Papaver and Belladonna plants, just as God protected his Garden of Eden, the cradle of a new world. He planned to take the Papaver extract and return to the villages to save those women and children as he had promised the men. Then they would know his power," Baltasar said, "and his mercy."

"Shame he would have returned to find them all dead."

"Because of Salvatierra! Because of the Vatican and the King and Queen of Spain who feared his power. He was forced to stay on at the pyramid to make sure the dam on the river was complete before they found him. They would ruin everything he had planned for so many years. He was on the threshold, ready to open once again the portal, the direct link, between man and God." Baltasar's hands were shaking in rage. He willed them to stop. He breathed in deeply the calming yet invigorating scent of citrus that permeated the orangery. "As I told you. Find the pyramid, and you'll find the hidden canyon where Papaver Contrerasum thrives."

"Bring me home. The best way to find Papaver Contrerasum is to create it, to hybridize it, just like your ancestor hoped. I can do that for you. Just let my daughter go."

"You know I have great admiration for botanists," said Baltasar, "and you, no doubt, are nearly as brilliant as my ancestor, Alvaro. But we can no longer wait for more attempts at reverse hybridization. And I'm afraid I can't let Lucia go, not until you've found that pyramid."

"Impossible! The pyramid your ancestor found could have collapsed five hundred years ago. Alvaro's own missive to your family, the one he hid in his Bible, relates that he barely got out alive as the pyramid collapsed. And it has been so overgrown with jungle that even satellite images couldn't detect it."

Baltasar did not need a reminder of his frustration. "You told me that the limestone plaster the Mayans used in building their cities leached into the soil as the buildings aged, that the difference in plant life that the limestone created would show up on the satellite images."

"And it does," said Gabriella. "Just ten years ago, an archaeologist discovered Mayan cities completely overgrown and long lost by studying color differentials in infrared images from satellites. Perhaps this temple wasn't built using limestone."

"What modern technology cannot find," said Baltasar, "ancient man must teach us."

"Five hundred years ago, the Muisca Indians forbade talk of the pyramid," said Gabriella. "The medicine man does not know where it is."

"Doesn't he? Don' let your blind loyalty to your father's Circle of Seven stop you from discovering the greatest find of our lifetime."

"Circle of Seven?"

"Come, Doctor Hunter, don't be coy. I know that your father is in Morocco. And I knew it couldn't be coincidence that his trusted friend, Ahmed, just happened to secure a job on board the treasure hunter ship which was searching for the wreck of the *San Salvador*. The Circle of Seven has been a thorn in the side of the Contreras dynasty since Salvatierra began it in 1586, but they have unwittingly been leading me towards the very stones that they protect. I did not hire you by serendipity."

"Is that why you've taken my daughter? Because you think I'm some part of a secret society that's out to get you? Perhaps you've been working with belladonna too long. It can cause delusions."

"Your lovely sister, whom I had the pleasure of meeting in the Arizona desert, is no delusion." Hunter couldn't hide her shock at his news. "You will find the Papaver Contrerasum, and the pyramid that protects it."

"I cannot find what does not exist."

"The medicine man knows where it is. You are the only one he will trust, the only one on my team that can speak his dialect of Embera."

"He doesn't have to speak our language to understand that your team's intentions are evil. He is as brave as he is wise. He will not divulge information that may harm his people."

"That's a shame," Baltasar said, "since Papaver Contrerasum is the unique antidote to Belladonna Conquistadorum." Baltasar sipped his cognac thoughtfully. "What if, by chance, the water system in say, Princeton area, or New York City, were to be poisoned with the extract from Belladonna Conquistadorum? How would they get the antidote? Who would provide it?"

Her shoulders shook, as if burdened by a sudden weight. "You can't unleash that poison. I found an antidote, but it's only temporary."

"That is your fault. Not mine." He slammed his fist on the table. "It is a necessary purge, akin to the great flood, essential to a new beginning," he said. "Just as a plant must die to nourish new growth. Just as we now know that the very universe expands, only to collapse upon itself, so it can start anew."

She clenched her fists. "You're talking about people's lives."

"I'll kill if I must, but you can help me save them."

"The best way to get that antidote is for me to get back to my lab. I've been working on the solution in my greenhouse. Bring me home. Let my daughter go. And I will help you."

A spot of blood red against the orangery's gray slate floor caught Baltasar's eye. It was distorted somewhat, refracting through the beveled edge of the glass table. Baltasar narrowed his eyes. It was the rose that Rambo had crushed. Baltasar, too, could crush what displeased him. He leaned towards the computer screen. "Is the damn Circle of Seven that important, that you will still keep the location of the pyramid and hidden canyon secret? Do you think I have the seven stones, even though I tell you I do not? Are you willing to take the chance that I'm telling the truth? Or will you risk the lives of your daughter, and your son?"

"Liam?"

"Of course, you haven't heard. Your son, Liam, has fallen ill. He has a rash and delusions." Tears brimmed in her eyes. Baltasar almost pitied her. "The whole community is becoming sick, although it hasn't made it into breaking news. Not yet."

"I'll do anything," she said, "to save my children."

Perhaps he had gone too far. The woman looked broken. "You will find that pyramid and the antidote," he said, "within the next forty-eight hours. You must believe in your destiny, Doctor Hunter, as I believe in mine."

CHAPTER **34**

Christa felt the sharp edges of Salvatierra's crucifix as Conroy pressed it into her palm and closed her fingers around it. She hung the chain around her neck and tucked it beneath her blouse. Its metal was cold against her skin. Conroy breathed in as if gathering strength and stood. He sidled out from behind the desk and navigated his way past stacks of books to the dirty hopper window that squinted out onto the campus green. She had translated Salvatierra's letter, but she needed him to interpret it before she could hope to save Lucia, and the thousands who may already be poisoned.

"We must turn to the past to save the future," he said.

"Not before sorting out the present." She crossed over to him. "Gabriella had identified a new species of belladonna on her trip to Colombia last summer. Did she tell you anything about it?"

"Belladonna." He peered towards the peeling ceiling. "I had the opportunity to try it once, silly of me, really, but, I thought, to truly understand the effects." His voice trailed off.

"Professor Conroy," Christa said. No telling what else he'd tried for history's sake, hallucinogenic mushrooms, moonshine. "What about Belladonna Conquistadorum, indigenous to Colombia?"

He nodded and turned towards her. "As you know, belladonna, or as we commonly call it, deadly nightshade, has earned its infamous place in history, what with the wives of the Roman emperors Augustus and Claudius poisoning their husbands with the plant extract. But the name actually translates as *beautiful woman*," he said. "Like using the deadly botulism toxin as Botox for a beauty aid today, ladies centuries ago would use the belladonna extract in eye drops to expand their pupils. The look was considered quite attractive at the time. Unfortunately, prolonged use could cause blindness. True irony, using the belladonna drops to enhance your beauty only resulting in never being able to see yourself again."

"And the Muisca Indians," she said, "did they use Belladonna Conquistadorum?"

"I know the Muisca used poison," said Conroy. "For as long as they can remember, they have been using the poison dart frog to tip their arrows in poison. When I lived there as a child, I befriended the son of the shaman. He showed me. He held a golden frog near the fire. It sweated. He used that sweat for the arrow tip. Just a small drop was quite deadly. In fact, the tiny golden dart frog is the deadliest animal on Earth."

Christa stepped aside as Conroy bundled by her. He dug through a miscellany of items on a lower shelf. He extracted an old photo, square, its color faded. He blew off the dust and handed it to her. The photo depicted a tiny, golden frog.

Daniel craned his neck to see over her shoulder. He raised an eyebrow. "That frog is the deadliest animal on Earth?"

"And I thought that distinction belonged to man," said Christa.

"Don't let its size fool you," said Conroy, "nor its beauty. A plant that is poison to us is a staple of indigenous beetles and ants. The insects eat the plants. The frogs eat the insects. The poison from the frog on the dart kills the Muiscas' prey. Frogs raised in captivity are not poisonous, as long as they are not in an environment with poisonous plants."

"But Gabriella is looking for one particular poison plant," said Christa, "a species that has been thought to be extinct for five hundred years. She returned for a reason. She's got to think that she can find it. Professor Conroy, the Oculto Canyon, it's got to be where Gabriella is headed."

"Yes, of course," he said. "I should have thought of this before." He began scrabbling his fingers across the spines of the books jammed onto one shelf, finally landing on a particularly thick one, an ancient looking tome, *Atlas of the Americas*. He yanked it out of its spot, its weight nearly knocking him off balance. He blew off the dust and opened the book. From inside the front cover, he removed a piece of paper that was yellowed and creased with age. "Now that I've read Salvatierra's letter, I remember." He let the atlas drop with a thud to the floor, kicking up another cloud of dust. "She returned to find the hidden canyon."

"You know about the canyon?" she asked.

Conroy tilted the map towards the gloomy light of the hopper window. "I drew this as a child, when my parents were missionaries in the Colombian rainforest. My friend, Jairo Salaman, the son of the Muisca shaman, we'd adventure together. One day, we ventured a bit far, got lost, in fact. Jairo was terrified. We'd wandered into the forbidden area. He'd heard stories about an old temple there haunted by evil spirits. Didn't find anything, of course, but something found us." Conroy rubbed his shoulder as though reliving an old injury. "A jaguar."

"You were attacked?" Christa asked.

"The cat was after Jairo, actually," Conroy said. "He was a foot shorter than me, easier prey. The jaguar leaped out of a tree. We didn't see it coming, but the animal must have been stalking us. I pushed Jairo out of the way and, before I could think, I had two hundred pounds of hungry cat on my back. I was lucky that I was just a boy."

"Lucky?" Daniel echoed, finally intrigued enough to shift his attention from the letter.

"The jaguar, as I'm sure you know, kills by crushing the upper vertebrae in its jaws, or by clamping its jaws on the back of its prey's head and piercing the brain with its canines." Conroy bent his head forward and pointed to the back of his neck to demonstrate. He smiled. "I fancied myself a bit like Doctor Livingstone," he said. "I'd never venture into the jungle without wearing my metal pith helmet. The cat took one bite and ran off." He rubbed his shoulder again. "Did get a bit of a scratch on my shoulders from its claws. It serves as my barometer, always aches when a storm is coming. Brute of one on its way now."

"You saved Jairo's life," said Christa.

"And he saved mine," said Conroy. "He bound my wound with healing herbs and a pressure bandage of leaves. And he half-carried me back to my parents."

"But you remembered enough to draw a map," Daniel prompted, pointing at the letter, "to this Oculto Canyon."

"I drew it in hospital, when I was recovering. I tried to remember landmarks, but finding landmarks in the jungle is like finding trees in a forest. There are many of them, but few are unique. Still, I had a good sense of direction and distance. I did find our way home to the mission, after all." He handed the map to Christa.

"A Map of the Forbidden Territory," Christa read the heading.

"I apologize for the B-Movie title," he said. "A child's imagination trapped in a hospital room finds its escape with his memories of the outside world. When I couldn't adventure out there," he tapped his temple, "I adventured in here."

Christa held the map beneath the flat light of the overhead fluorescent panel. Drawn on parchment stationary bearing the hospital's letterhead, the map was deftly, if whimsically, illustrated. It featured a patch of green labeled the Forgotten Forest, a snake of blue that depicted the Tequendama River. The most distinctive feature was an outcropping of rock towering above the tree canopy that resembled the wings of a giant bird of prey. The words from Salvatierra's letter leaped out at her. He had written that the temple was in a clearing lorded over by a rock outcropping he named *Demon's Wings*.

"This temple," she said, "the one your Muisca friend feared. You think this may be the pyramid temple that Salvatierra referred to in his letter. It must be completely overgrown. Complete cities can be lost under centuries of forest growth. Hiram Bingham didn't discover the lost city of the Incas, Machu Picchu, until 1911, even though it was a thriving mountaintop city in the 15th century. Even with your map, it would be near impossible to find the Oculto Canyon."

"Jairo told me that the oral history claims that Demon's Wings can only be seen from this bend in the river." He pointed to the river bend on his map. "But we could not see it. Only the very top of the granite shows above the tree canopy. Most of the time even that is obscured by the low clouds. Botanists call these upper altitudes the cloud forest. Indeed, that is how the plants get their moisture."

"Still, this map could be the key to finding the temple," said Christa.

"Hold on," Daniel said, his eyes on the letter. "The temple, that's where Salvatierra buried the Breastplate." He raised his eyes. They were glossed over, as if he'd been drugged. And maybe he had.

"Alvaro Contreras realized that the temple defended the entrance to the Oculto Canyon," said Christa, "and the antidote plant."

"Brilliant," said Conroy. "It was easy for the conquistadors to bring death to the New World, but to bring life, now that would place them truly in the realm of a god. The death that Contreras brought was not a new disease. In was not infested, but ingested. He had created a poison elixir, with only one cure, a rare plant that would only grow under unique conditions, conditions that he alone controlled."

"Like a hidden canyon," said Christa. "A specific microcosm."

"Salvatierra didn't write anything about poisonous plants," said Daniel, shaking the letter. "We should focus on what he tells us about these gemstones."

"The Breastplate is only a means to an end," Christa said. "That's all its history has ever been. Alvaro Contreras dammed the river flowing through the temple. Why?"

"To control it," said Conroy.

"And defend it," said Christa. "The temple was remote, but he wasn't the first European to venture through that area. A conquistador named Quesada was searching for El Dorado near there. It was in 1569, just seventeen years before Salvatierra wrote that letter. Quesada sets out with 500 mounted soldiers, 1500 natives and hundreds of horses, cattle and pigs. He returns with four natives, 18 horses and twenty-five Spaniards. I'd bet one of them was Alvaro Contreras."

"Alvaro survives the ill-fated expedition," said Conroy. "He has found his El Dorado, the temple where he will create a new empire, using an indefensible weapon."

"A bio-weapon," Christa said, "the poison."

"But why go back," asked Daniel, "to a place where most of the men died?"

"Because some of them lived," said Christa. "The history is sketchy, but the men were starving. They ate a native plant and grew deathly ill. That must have been the belladonna. The legend says that the only cure was a river of life hidden deep in the mountains."

"The river that flows through the temple," said Conroy.

"Alvaro Contreras dams the river. He has sole control of the antidote," said Christa. "He is on the threshold of his new world order, but one man stops him."

"Salvatierra," Daniel chipped in. "A priest."

Christa nodded. "Alvaro is brought back to Spain in chains, but he's not about to give up easily."

"Alvaro is executed," said Conroy, "but not before he passes his story on to his family."

"And the rest, unfortunately, isn't history," said Christa. "It's happening, now. Baltasar Contreras is picking up where his ancestor, Alvaro, left off. And this time that poison won't wipe out whole villages. He aims to wipe out entire cities."

CHAPTER **35**

Jared Sadler had booked a modest suite in the Waldorf, much to the disgruntlement of his young wife, Zoe, who had now tried on and rejected three different frocks for her shopping trip to Neiman Marcus to buy yet another "perfect" dress for the event tonight. *Our role tonight is that of a humble servant,* he had told her. *Speak for yourself,* she had laughed. He had to admit, she was lovely when she laughed. And he would make her happy, if he could craft this afternoon's encounter as expertly as he crafted jewelry.

Jared sat in the Queen Anne wing chair by the faux hearth and watched her through the partially open door to the bedroom. It seemed she had settled on the skin tight red affair that cost a large amount of money for a small amount of fabric. She turned sideways to the full-length mirror and pressed her hand atop her tummy, assessing it. Still flat.

Although stiff with stress, he craned his neck to watch her shimmy into the bathroom and fluff her dyed blond hair in the mirror. Their suite was peppered with a plethora of gilt-framed mirrors that reflected the reproduction mahogany furnishings and paintings of European landscapes that contrived to lend the air of old world respect. He tried in vain to avoid seeing the most heinous fake of all, his own visage.

"Darling?" Zoe called, pausing to apply the ruby red lipstick that matched the hue of her dress. "You did call the bank to increase the credit limit on the card, didn't you? The coat I bought at Harrods for this trip maxed us out."

"Yes, Zoe," he answered, although it still rankled him that the fake lynx had cost more than real. She had explained patiently that she wanted people to know she could afford real fur, but was rich enough not to wear it. The convolution of this deception was absurd.

He recognized that keenly, for he was about to perpetrate one of the most odious deceptions in history. Zoe, at least, was true to her false morals.

"I couldn't very well wear that raggedy wool thing," Zoe said, adjusting her rouge. "It wouldn't do for the wife of the Crown Jeweler."

He felt mocked by the title. If Alba were here, she'd be ashamed. If only she had survived the cancer, she would have carried her royal bearing in her actions, not her dress, in her rare encounters with the royal family. She would have seen his appointment as Crown Jeweler as a humbling honor, not a bragging right. But she wouldn't have wanted it. She was quite content in their flat on Portobello. The disease stole that life from them. When he buried her on that bleak November day, he threw down upon her coffin like so many roses his belief in love, in life, in the God that Alba prayed to futilely each day of her painful illness.

He was plummeting down the deep, dark well of a meaningless existence, when Zoe had grabbed him with both arms. He knew, even then, that their introduction and relationship had been artfully arranged. He wasn't a fool. A woman like Zoe wouldn't have given him a second look if not for Contreras's puppetry. He found he didn't care, like a drunk who could not forgo poison as long as it was served on the rocks.

Zoe floated back into the bedroom. She fished a pair of stockings from the drawer and bunched up the silky legs in her fingers as expertly as Vladimir Horowitz playing Traumerai on the piano. "Will you be seeing Baltasar before the ceremony tonight?" she asked.

Jared wondered if she already knew the answer, but he suspected that Baltasar had severed his strings on her. She had served her purpose. "I'm sure his day is too busy for the likes of me," he said. Another lie. He hardly knew how to tell the truth anymore.

She pointed her toe, slipped it into the foot of the stocking. "You're always selling yourself short," she said. He watched the silk caress her ankle. "You're the one who was commissioned to create the Lux et Veritas sword." The curve of her knee. "Quite an arrow in your quiver." The white of her thigh.

"I'd like to put my arrow in your quiver," he said. He never would have said that to Alba.

Zoe giggled. "Baltasar is a good man," she pressed.

His randiness suddenly rankled. "You don't know him like I do."

"Baltasar believes in you, always has," she said.

He had been even more completely seduced by Contreras than Zoe. The wooing had begun when Alba was still alive. When Baltasar Contreras had contacted him some seven years earlier, Jared thought the man was a bit daft. Yes, Jared's nouveau renaissance jewelry designs had caught the attention of some of the lesser royals at the time, but this plump, arrogant man told him that he would one day become the Queen's personal jeweler and, subsequently, the Crown Jeweler. Of course, Jared maintained a polite decorum with the man. He was the billionaire heir to a pharmaceutical corporation, America's brand of royalty. Most importantly, Alba was starting to get sick. He needed the money.

Shortly after they met, Contreras had custom ordered a set of seven golden rings, each inlaid with a unique gemstone, a ruby, golden topaz, Emerald, Turquoise, sapphire, diamond and jacinth. The inner band of each he wanted engraved with an Abraxas, a mythological being with the head of a lion, the body of a man holding a whip in one hand and a shield in the other and serpents as legs. Jared had told him it really wasn't his specialty, but the pay he offered was too handsome to turn down. Jared should have known then, with the symbol of the Abraxas, which figured in the teachings of the Gnostics, that Baltasar Contreras had more in mind than simple adornments, but the money blinded him. Contreras was paying for client confidentiality, he said, and wanted no one to know of their transactions. Jared agreed.

Zoe poked her naked toes into the other leg of the stocking. "And he's very generous," she said.

"He gets what he pays for," he muttered. Contreras continued to order sets of these rings over the years, paying in person, with cash. More valuable than the cash were Contreras's social connections. It seemed the man knew everyone worth knowing and could manipulate them as expertly as Degas could clay. Under Contreras's tutelage, Jared rose to Her Majesty the Queen's personal jeweler. Jared grew to respect his patron's prophetic judgment and value his friendship. Despite Alba's distrust of the man, Contreras paid for his personal physician to treat her when traditional therapies proved futile.  Contreras, too, had lost a loved one, his mother, many years ago.  He seemed genuinely heartbroken when Alba passed.  After the funeral, Contreras tried to comfort Jared, convince him that he would one day see his beloved Alba again.  Jared wondered how such a brilliant man could be so naive.

Gradually, as if unraveling an ancient sacred scroll, Contreras revealed his true purpose.  His life's goal was to complete his family's mission to find and recreate the Biblical Breastplate of Aaron, a direct link with God.  He assumed that Jared was, as a gemologist, familiar with the Breastplate and its twelve legendary stones, which, like the Ark of the Covenant, had been lost to the ages thousands of years ago.

Jared knew it was coming.  He just hadn't wanted to believe it.  After all, he was one of the Circle of Seven.  It was his sworn obligation to keep this very event from taking place.  That had not helped to save his beloved Alba.  So why not help the one man who had the wherewithal, determination and faith to unearth and recreate the legendary Breastplate?  It would be proof that God did exist, that Alba was basking in a glorious everlasting life.  He found himself lusting after the knowledge, the possibility of seeing his one true love again.  In fact, he owed it to her.

Jared, on occasion, had scoffed at Alba for believing in the grand words of evangelists, but he found himself enthralled with Baltasar's plan.  With the Breastplate, Contreras would build a new empire, succeed where Britain had failed.  He had a multi-national force already in place.  He had lost his mother to terrorists, an evil that was elusive and perpetual, immune to traditional defenses.  The Breastplate would rally the masses.  Some lives would be lost, but humanity saved.  And peace would allow for a higher quality of life, more resources diverted to finding cures to sicknesses like the cancer that stole away his beloved Alba.

From there, it was just one small step into treason.  He had been so beguiled that he hardly considered it a sin.  Part of him felt that he deserved the fortune that Baltasar had promised him.  Indeed, he felt the thrill of victory, the pride of accomplishment when he had actually pulled off what would go down in the history books as the crime of the century.  Not even when he was committing this heinous act did it strike him as wrong.  But now that the thrill of the battle was over, he realized what he had lost.

Zoe was choosing shoes now, rubbing a spot off the toe of the high, strappy ones. "You have to admit, it was nice of him to send up that champagne. Dom Perignon, very classy."

Jared hadn't been sure whether the champagne was for the two of them, or his upcoming meeting with Contreras. He was relieved, and surprised, when Zoe didn't insist on imbibing it. She hadn't wanted to impair her shopping judgment, he supposed, although he could certainly use a drink.

He looked down at his hands. His slender, nimble fingers were his stock and trade, like a surgeon. He could craft the finest detail, one that nobody but he and the bearer of his creation might be privy to, but that's why he stood apart. Now, these fingers were responsible for the care and restoration of Britain's crown jewels, but they tingled with the numbness of a traitor. He stood and walked closer to the fireplace. He forced himself to look into the gilt mirror over the mantel. He tried to command his trembling fingers to tighten the knot in his ascot and straighten the stray, gray hairs that refused to stay orderly. They did not obey.

Jared moved stiffly to the window. He peered down from his seventeenth floor aerie at the people scurrying along Park Avenue. A fight had broken out between two men, one in a suit and the other in tattered jeans. A small group stood and watched. Others barely glanced at the action before moving along, cell phones at their ears.

Zoe came to the sitting room threshold and opened the door wide, posing jauntily. "How do I look?"

Jared smiled, but was overcome with dread. "You're my little vixen," he offered. Their pet phrase rang hollow. He had, indeed, made a deal with the devil, Baltasar Contreras. He wanted to be reassured of the veracity of everlasting life. He grew to realize that reassurance would only mean he would spend eternity in hell for what he had done. And that he'd be meeting that end soon. He had been a fool to think Contreras would simply pay him and let him go. He sat heavily in the Queen Anne wing chair by the hearth.

She padded over to him and alighted on his lap. "What's wrong? You and Baltasar used to be best of friends. He's made you what you are today."

That was precisely why Jared had to betray him. It was his only hope for redemption. At best, it would mean shame. At worst, death. Everlasting damnation loomed on the near horizon. It terrified him more than both of those outcomes. He wrapped his arm around her impossibly small waist, willing his hands to stop trembling. "You'd look just as lovely in a jumper and jeans at a cottage in the Cotswolds."

"But I dress this way for you. I'm the wife of the Crown Jeweler." Her pride was painful. She kissed him on the forehead. "I believe in you, Jared. I believe that you can do anything you put your mind to."

Jared pressed his cheek against her breast. Her heart beat softly. For a moment, he allowed himself to think it would all turn out all right. That the two of them would live a quiet, country life, where people ignored him, if not forgave him. He prayed. For one who had disdained God not long ago, he was praying a lot lately. If he could only turn things back, do the right thing, correct the deadly wrong that he had done, then God might give him a second chance at life. "Am I too late?" he whispered, as if praying for a sign he knew would never come.

She slapped his shoulder teasingly. "Speaking of late," she said, scooching back on his thighs. "I was waiting to tell you this after the ceremony tonight, but," she placed her hand on her tummy and smiled brightly. "We are going to have a baby."

He shook his head in utter surprise. He had long ago given up on the dream of having children. He allowed a sense of hope and joy to warm him like the rising sun. "Are you sure?"

She nodded. "Ten weeks along. I didn't dare tell you until we passed the point, you know, where we lost our last one."

He hugged her tightly. He had been given a sign. This baby, the promise of new life, he was being given a second chance after all. "I am elated, Zoe," he said. "Elated." And terrified. Yet another precious life had been placed in his trembling hands. He knew what he had to do, yet the impending danger reared up like a deadly monster, threatening not only him, but Zoe and his unborn child.

"Let's celebrate," she said. "Forget Neiman Marcus. Order room service. I have an urge for caviar."

"Yes," he answered, reaching for the phone on the desk. Then, "no," eyeing the reproduction Napoleon clock. Contreras would be arriving in a half-hour. He nudged her off his lap. "You've been looking forward to this shopping trip for weeks, getting a new dress for tonight."

She shrugged. "I'm sure I can find something to wear."

Contreras would kill him if he denied the man. He had to get her out of here. "No, darling," he said. He hugged her, then forced himself to release her. "I need to do something, something vitally important. We'll celebrate tonight, like you planned." He quickly crossed the room to the closet and handed her the fake fur coat and Coach purse. "Get the doorman to wave down a cab," he said. "No walking in those heels."

"You shouldn't be afraid," she said. Not afraid, terrified. As soon as the door closed behind her, he latched the deadbolt.

He snatched the cell phone Agent Fox had given him from his pocket. God would not save him from the devil. Maybe Fox could.

Fox answered on the second ring. "This had better be important," he said, by way of a greeting.

"A matter of life or death," replied Jared.

"Same here," he said.

"Baltasar Contreras will be at my door in thirty minutes." That should get the agent's attention. Fox constantly grilled Jared to ferret out his connections to the man who was hosting the banquet tonight. Fox suspected that Contreras had designs on the Lux et Veritas sword. He did not know that Contreras had actually designed it. Jared consistently countered the agent's suspicions with his outward display of annoyingly unflagging patriotism.

Silence, then, "And you know this how?"

Jared swallowed hard. "I've made a deal with the devil, Agent Fox. You've got to help me."

"What did Contreras offer for the sword?"

"He's after something far more valuable," he said. "And if he gets it, the world will never be the same."

Through the phone, Jared heard auto tires squeal to a stop. "No need for superlatives," Fox said. "I'll be there in forty-five minutes."

"Not soon enough," Jared shot back. "I'm afraid for my life."

"And I'm afraid for the life of an innocent girl," he said cryptically.

"If I die, you'll never even know what is lost."

"You're not going to die," he said. "Now tell me what's going on."

Jared paced across the room. "You save me, I'll tell you. Not before."

"Damn it, Jared." He heard the blast of a car horn. "I'm getting on the radio right now to call for backup, an agent from our New York office."

"No!" Jared shouted back. "Contreras has his own men," he searched for the words, "at the highest levels. In your own Homeland Security agency, a man he called Rambo. He will know I am betraying him. Just get here, fast." He pressed end. If his strategy was to succeed, he had to prepare quickly.

CHAPTER **36**

Christa studied the map that Conroy had drawn as a child, in the past. He was right. This all hinged on the past. Alvaro Contreras, a conquistador, developed a scheme to truly conquer the new world, with a poison and its antidote unique to the microcosm of the hidden canyon, completely under his control. The priest, Salvatierra, was sent by the Vatican to recover the Breastplate, but he was commanded by God, so he believed, to destroy it. The Breastplate and their belief in its divine secrets drove these men's destinies. She had to stop it from driving hers, here and now.

"Professor Conroy," she said, snapping him out of some kind of perplexed fugue. She sensed it, too, the subtle lace edging the musty damp of the room, a smell so sweet it was sickly. It was an unnatural smell, enticing and dangerous. She recognized it, from when she saw the phantom at Gabby's house. "You said that Alvaro Contreras told us how the Breastplate of Aaron was connected to this poison, five hundred years ago."

Conroy picked up a small metal globe from the corner of his bookshelf. He held it before him like Hamlet cradling a skull. "Here be dragons," he said.

"That's your reproduction of the Lenox Globe," she said. The original was in the collection of the New York Public Library. Crafted around 1507, the Lenox was one of the first globes created after the discovery of the new world. The now famous phrase, "Here be dragons," was etched in Latin at the threshold of the vast abyss beyond the known world. "Yes, there were dragons," she said, "in the minds of those who lived in the sixteenth century. With the Protestant Reformation and the Age of Discovery in full swing, Europeans were pushing the boundaries of both the physical and spiritual worlds and turning even more to Heaven for guidance. A priest like Salvatierra, he'd see the spiritual influence in everything."

"Whereas a conquistador like Alvaro Contreras was a more practical man," said Conroy.

"Daniel, what was it Alvaro told Salvatierra according to the letter? Something about standing on the platform to reveal the secret?"

Daniel found the passage in the letter. *"Contreras tempted me as Satan tempted Jesus,"* Daniel read. *"Don the Breastplate. Stand upon this platform and call God's light to shine upon you and you will hold the powers of the Heavens in the palm of your hand."* He looked up and frowned. "Clearly, both Contreras and Salvatierra believed in the Breastplate, but I don't see how this connects it to the hidden canyon."

"I am an historian and archaeologist, not a theologian," said Conroy, "but I have come across many clever machinations thought too advanced for primitive civilizations that reveal hidden treasure, not only in material goods, but in the wonder of human ingenuity. If the Breastplate of Aaron can open the gateway to Heaven, then I'd certainly think it could open a portal to a hidden canyon on Earth."

"Which is why Salvatierra destroyed the Breastplate," said Christa, "and scattered the seven stones across the globe. He had seen the bodies of the villagers, the mother who had strangled her baby." Like Salvatierra, that image in particular haunted her. "He thought the power of the Breastplate was divine, but, as in its entire history, the Breastplate has been a means to an end."

Daniel held the letter high. "The Breastplate of Aaron does open a portal," he said, "to an end that is divine, an end that is the beginning."

"If we don't find those seven stones," Christa said, "it's not going to open a portal to anything. And we have less than seven days."

Conroy stroked his chin. "That will be a tad challenging," he said, "not in the very least acquiring Babur's diamond and Saint Edward's sapphire."

"Babur," Christa said. "Muslim, descendent of both Timur and Ghengis Khan. Babur conquered central Asia, including much of India in the early 1500s."

"Babur's diamond is now better known as the Kohinoor," Conroy said.

"The Kohinoor?" She had seen it several times, sitting atop the Queen's crown, on their trips through London as a child. "That can't be. That diamond is in the British crown jewels. Queen Victoria received it from India as part of the Treaty of Lahore in in 1849."

"And you might know Saint Edward as Edward the Confessor," said Conroy. "His Sapphire also resides in the Crown Jewels in the Tower of London."

"Of course, Salvatierra wrote in his letter that the Circle of Seven guardians took the Sapphire east to England and the Diamond west to Asia. But how can Contreras hope to get the Kohinoor Diamond and Edward's Sapphire? They are the most closely guarded gems in the world."

"With inside help," said Daniel. "Contreras commissioned a ceremonial sword, very hush hush. It's going to be unveiled at the G-20 dinner he's hosting in New York tonight. The sword's caretaker is none other than Britain's Crown Jeweler. He's here in New York, arrived today. It can't be coincidence."

"I'd say your odds of success just improved," Conroy said. "If Contreras has the diamond and sapphire, it's easier to steal them from him, a madman, than a Beefeater, although I tossed back a few gins with a Beefeater some years back and I'd say the two are not far apart."

"Even if by some miracle we get the diamond and sapphire," said Christa, "and find the temple, the Breastplate could be destroyed, crushed beneath the collapse that Salvatierra wrote about. The Bible describes the Breastplate as pieces of gold sewn onto a woven tunic. Only the gold on the Breastplate would last all this time. The rest of the tunic would be nothing more than threads."

"Only the gold would endure," Conroy said, "and the human spirit. One must never forget the power of spirit." He smiled. "The spirit is what enlightens." He yanked open the bottom drawer of his desk to the crash and roll of the objects it contained. He scrimmaged around in it, extracting a small archaeologist's hammer and chisel. He slipped them into his jacket pocket and hurried to his office door. "It is not a miracle we need, but a sin. We need to break the seventh commandment. We have little time to save the future."

# CHAPTER 37

A knock rapped on Jared Sadler's hotel room door. He peeked out the peephole. It was Baltasar Contreras, precisely on time. Jared had rang Fox only thirty minutes earlier. It would be fifteen minutes at best before the agent would arrive.

Jared's heart quickened. He clenched his fingers in a vain attempt to stop their trembling. As Contreras pushed him up the ranks to his position of Crown Jeweler, the man had taught him to be a master of deception and Jared had nearly succeeded. He had stolen two of the most revered gemstones in the British Crown Jewels, replacing them with forgeries, and gotten away with it. Nobody even knew a crime had been committed. Now his life, his immortal soul and millions of lives depended on his most challenging deception yet, to deceive the true master of lies.

Jared breathed in deeply and opened the door. "Baltasar," he said, "my friend." He stepped back. He prayed the man wouldn't smell his fear.

Contreras entered and scanned the room like a cougar on the prowl. He was impeccably dressed, as always, in a custom-tailored cashmere suit, blue silk tie that Jared recognized from Harrod's Room of Luxury collection and his trademark linen knit gloves. Contreras did not remove his gloves before the men shook hands. Jared had never seen him without them. Contreras had admitted once that he was germ phobic, not surprising for a head of a pharmaceutical company. His skin must crawl at the thought of the millions of deadly, invisible creatures outflanking him. His firm waged a daily war against them and Baltasar believed in the maxim, know thy enemy, no matter how much that thought terrified him. He wore the original gold ring that Jared had crafted for him over the glove. His featured a stunning pear-cut diamond.

A second man followed Contreras into the hotel room. He was a large, muscular man whose off-the-rack Armani barely contained his beefy physique. He wore a bandage around his left pinky finger and a grim expression despite his brief, forced smile. In his right hand, he carried an aluminum Halliburton briefcase. Jared stepped back again to allow for the man's presence in his room.

Contreras surveyed the furnishings, targeting the paisley Queen Anne wing chair to accommodate his ample girth. He sat and crossed his legs to give the appearance of relaxation, but Jared knew better. The beefy man set the briefcase at his feet and stood, wide-stanced, by the door, his arms like weapons holstered across his chest.

Jared moved towards the writing desk. He tried to keep his eyes from the bottle of Dom Perignon, leaning like a war-weary guard in the silver-plated ice bucket. He noted with alarm that a few drops of condensed water spotted the desk. The atmosphere of dread that Contreras carried into the room made the idea of celebration wildly inappropriate.

"I see you've received the champagne I had sent up," Contreras said.

"Yes, thank you," said Jared. Perhaps he had misread the man, as he often had before. If Contreras desired to toast the conclusion of their deal, Jared was prepared to play along. "I'm afraid they only sent up two flutes."

"That will do nicely," said Contreras. "Won't it Mister Torrino?" He looked towards his man, but this Torrino stayed as stiff and straight-faced as a palace guard. "But first we must conclude our business." He leaned forward. "Today is the day, Jared. Our plan is in forward gear and is gaining speed quickly. Do you have them?"

Jared hesitated. He had been so sure, before. Contreras's very presence reminded him that he had believed in their cause, enough to achieve what others would condemn as treason. How could he deny his conviction that this was not only his duty to Queen and country but his destiny in life?

Baltasar Contreras had shown him how a new empire could rule the world, with a peace and prosperity unequalled in the annals of history. Jared would be instrumental in bringing that about. Yes, some would die, as they had on the fields of Agincourt, in the

African wastelands and in the mountains of India. That was necessary. Jared had understood and accepted that. Only this time their deaths would not be in vain. This new world empire would not fall, as so many of his countrymen had in so many wars to end all wars.

He turned to the window, looked down at the people below. The police who had come to break up the row between the two men had restored the peace and left, quiet and without thanks. No, if Jared advanced Contreras's plan, he would be a traitor, not only to his country but to all of mankind. Much worse than this, in proving that Heaven existed, he would condemn himself to Hell. He would never again see his beloved Alba. His only chance at redemption was to risk betraying Baltasar Contreras and warn Agent Fox about the man's machinations.

Contreras uncrossed his legs. Jared noticed beads of perspiration on the man's pasty brow. "I asked if you had them," Contreras said. "You did replace them with our reproductions."

"Yes, three weeks ago, during the cleaning and restoration of the crown jewels, as planned." Jared recognized the irony that it was the trust he evoked in his staff and the security guards that allowed him the treasonous deception. He had been at once thrilled and repulsed when he committed the act.

"Any problems?"

"Everything went just as you said it would," said Jared. If truth be told, it was Jared's masterful skill, not Contreras's bold plan, which was vital to their success. He had supervised every detail of the clandestine reproduction of the sapphire and diamond. The forgeries were exact replicas, down to their mineral composition, weight, color, cut and clarity. The technology to create these amazing synthetics still amazed him. The forgery was exactly the stone it emulated. The only aspect it lacked was the history. And yet, it was this storied past that gave the authentic stone its undeniable energy. He was beginning to believe in curses.

"Then give the gems to me," Contreras said.

Jared's heart pounded in his chest. He had to keep both his voice and gaze steady. Baltasar had taught him that. And he taught him to start a lie with an indisputable truth. "I was entrusted with the care of the Crown Jewels," he said.

"And you have gone beyond the call of duty."

Followed by a second truth. "The Crown Jewels are the symbol of the continuation of the empire."

"Which is why you did what you did."

And a third. "It is my duty to keep them in my care."

Contreras pursed his lips. "And so you have."

So he would believe the fourth. "I must keep them in my protection until they are placed in the Breastplate. You can trust nobody else," he said, "to have the expertise and skill to mount them properly." There, he said it. Now he would see if Contreras would believe the reason he had hastily cooked up for not simply delivering the gems into his custody. After all, he had been one of the very few that Contreras had entrusted with his entire plan. That's what it had taken to convince him to be part of it.

The gems he had now in his possession were two of the most famous, the most infamous, in history. The world knew that before he had even met Baltasar Contreras. The world, and Baltasar Contreras, did not know that Jared was a guardian of one of these gems. He was one of the Circle of Seven. For five hundred years, the Circle had vowed to keep the seven legendary gemstones ripped from the Biblical Breastplate of Aaron hidden from man. When Contreras finally revealed his plan to restore the Breastplate, Jared became drunk with the idea that his destiny lay not in preventing the Breastplate from being restored, but in using his elite position to once again open this blessed lifeline to God. He could only pray that he had sobered up in time.

Contreras tented his fingers. "I admire your courage, Jared. The way to the Breastplate is perilous."

"Courage I would never have known I possessed, Baltasar, without you. Replacing the diamond and sapphire with our manmade replicas was nerve-wracking, certainly, but actually taking the gems out of England—" Even now, the thought of successfully smuggling two of the world's most important gems into the United States shot Jared through with an unequalled excitement and perverse pride. He had thought of himself as a modern Sir Walter Raleigh, who had emboldened himself with Queen Elizabeth I. Jared had always admired Raleigh's flamboyant story-telling and penchant for ambition and risk. He couldn't help but prefer Raleigh's tall tales that transformed El Dorado into a fabled city of gold over the doom and gloom of Raleigh's contemporary,

Salvatierra, the priest who founded the Circle of Seven to keep man from wielding the power of God. He did not want to remind himself that Raleigh was imprisoned at the Tower of London and beheaded. Jared, as a commoner, would have been hung, drawn and quartered. He swallowed, hard, and wondered if even Raleigh, despite his bravado, had, in the privacy of his cell, dreaded death.

Contreras narrowed his eyes. "It is true that I will need the expertise of a master jeweler as I acquire the other sacred stones and to mount them in the Breastplate," he said. "I would be honored to have you at my side." Contreras held out his gray, gloved hand and opened it wide. "Now, let's see the gems."

Jared could hardly believe it. Contreras had agreed that he still needed him. He would not be killed, not yet. He was prepared to reveal the stones. His deception was playing out perfectly. He loosened his cravat and pulled the neck pouch from beneath his shirt. He had kept the diamond and sapphire next to his heart the whole time they were in his possession, from his workshop in the Tower of London, on the flight across the Atlantic, here in the Waldorf Hotel. He even wore it when making love with Zoe. He told her jokingly that the pouch was given to him by a medicine man for prowess in bed. *It's working!* She would laugh, knowing not to ask more. With the gems in his possession, he'd been as randy as Raleigh.

He opened the drawstrings of the black velvet pouch. He spilled them onto his palm, first the white diamond, then the blue sapphire. Created by violent forces of nature in the dawn of history, rulers throughout the centuries had sought to possess the Kohinoor diamond and Edward's Sapphire. It was said that he who possessed the Kohinoor would rule the world. And the sapphire had been pivotal in the life of a king who would become a saint. Jared found them mesmerizing, a thing created more in the heights of heaven than the depths of the Earth. And though these gems had caused and again threatened the deaths of many, Jared had never felt so alive.

The blue of the sapphire glowed with such intensity it was as if the sky had been sucked into its heart, leaving behind only gray and gloom for the rest of the world. "Saint Edward's Sapphire," he whispered, his breath suddenly short, "named for Edward the Confessor, King of England from 1042 until 1066. It was originally set in his coronation ring."

Contreras stretched his gloved palm, his fingers wriggling in anticipation, towards Jared. "Nearly a millennium ago," he acknowledged, "but as I've told you, its history is far greater and older than that. The sapphire was gestated deep in the Earth a billion years ago. Thrust to the surface in the extreme heat of magma by the power of nature. Found by man in the alluvial deposits of what is now Sri Lanka."

Jared knew well the magnificent sapphires that had been mined in the Ratnapura region of that country since King Solomon's time, ten centuries before Christ walked the Earth. He knew that legendary stones, although often temporarily lost in history, inevitably resurface, heavy with stories of conquest, murder and empires. He could easily accept that Edward's Sapphire was the one mentioned in the Bible as being set in the Breastplate of Aaron. He had felt it. "King Edward once gave away the sapphire."

"And so shall you," Contreras said.

"He was traveling along the road and happened upon a beggar. King Edward had no money, but did not hesitate to take the sapphire ring from his finger and give it to the poor man," recounted Jared. "Many years later, two English pilgrims had journeyed to the Holy Land. In Syria, they were lost in a violent storm. An old man guided them to shelter. He gave them a sapphire ring to deliver to King Edward. The old man said that he was Saint John the Evangelist and that the King had given him the ring when he had come to Earth disguised as a beggar. He told the men that with the sapphire, they should deliver a message. In six months time, the King would be with God in Heaven. The pilgrims delivered the sapphire to King Edward. Six months later, he died of natural causes." Jared turned towards Contreras. "Edward gave away this sapphire and received it back with promise of his heavenly reward."

Contreras frowned and thrust his open palm closer. "And so shall you," he repeated through clenched teeth. He wriggled his fingers again, as if to spirit the sapphire into them through sheer force of will. Torrino, behind him, stepped forward. Jared doubted it was just to get a closer look. Jared could clearly see the butt of a nasty-looking pistol in Torrino's shoulder holster. He plucked the sapphire from his palm and placed it into Contreras's.

Contreras's thin lips curled up into a smile. He did not remove his gaze from the sapphire as he fished a jeweler's loupe from his coat pocket and brought it up to his left eye.    Jared's knees weakened. Contreras was no gem expert, but he was no fool either. As he examined the gem, the man's cheeks flushed. Perspiration beaded on his forehead. Jared half hoped his patron was having a heart attack. He tried to slow his breathing so he wouldn't suffer the same fate.

Contreras scrutinized the stone's every facet, turning it this way and that.   "You say that even an expert could not divine the difference between the real and synthetic sapphire, Mister Sadler," he said, "but I would know.   Edward's Sapphire would emit an energy. I am a Contreras. My ancestor before me held the Sapphire. He would reach for me through the ages."

God help him, he had not fooled Contreras. He couldn't pull off this last masterstroke of deception.   "I, too, felt the Sapphire's energy," he ventured, his voice weak, hoping this truth would hide his lie. No matter what, he couldn't let Contreras have the sacred stones. He'd be responsible for the death of millions, beginning with his own. He had one last, desperate move to make.

CHAPTER **38**

"The seventh commandment," Christa called after Conroy as she hurried to catch up to him. He had already made it out of his basement office and halfway down the dim hallway past the history classrooms to the even gloomier far end. For an old man, he was surprisingly quick and agile. Years of physically demanding field work had paid off. "Thou shall not steal."

"It is not quite thievery," said Conroy. "The object did belong to me, once. I donated it, afraid I'd misplace it, you know. Still, it will probably give the dean the last nail for my retirement coffin. No matter. I remember its connection now, after what you said, Christa."

Daniel tugged at her shoulder. "We've got the map and a copy of Salvatierra's letter," he said. "We don't have time for some wild goose chase."

"If it were wild geese we were chasing," said Conroy, "then you could lead us."

It was Christa's turn to pull Daniel back. He looked as if he might strike the professor. Conroy led them to a utilitarian gray door. A sign on it read, *This door to remain closed at all times.* "You know I absolutely had to open it once I'd read that sign," said Conroy, "if only for the punchline." He turned the chrome knob and heaved it open with a groan, both from him and the door. He flicked on a switch just inside the door. With a series of bangs, three banks of lights turned on. Bulbs caged in metal sconces lined the walls. They illuminated a wide hallway, hemmed with metal bunkbeds that were stripped bare and pitted with rust. Further on, built-in metal shelves were empty but for three stray boxes of Arm and Hammer baking soda, which looked like they'd been left behind decades ago.

"A bomb shelter," Christa said. "Then again, if this was survival, I'd consider death a reasonable option. I could never live underground."

"It's from a time when people feared that our enemy would take us over by destroying our cities and towns," said Conroy. "That would have as much value as a door that must remain closed at all times. The next war will be won by infiltration, not annihilation."

"You're talking about a bio-weapon," Daniel said.

"A poison is much more elegant," said Conroy.

Christa picked up a box of baking soda. It could have dated from the early nineteen-sixties. The label hadn't changed much, like man's lust for world domination. "I wonder what Einstein would think of this fallout shelter. He spent his last years here at Princeton. It was his letter to Roosevelt that inspired the Manhattan Project's race to invent the atomic bomb before the Nazis."

"The world would be very different if we had lost that race," said Conroy. He did not need to add what she knew. They, too, had to win the race with evil.

"Einstein's letter turned into one of his biggest regrets after we dropped the bomb on Hiroshima," she said.

"But we are racing for the cure, not the weapon," Conroy said. "And Einstein would have appreciated the fallout shelter's ultimate use." He pointed to a folding table surrounded by four metal folding chairs. "The custodians sneak down here for their weekly poker game." He opened the door at the far end. "And I use it for my private nighttime excursions into the Hershey Room."

The Hershey Room, one of her favorite escapes. It housed an historian's dream collection of artifacts from around the world, collected initially by Bonnie Hershey, the adventurous, young widow to the railroad tycoon, Harold Hershey, a Princeton grad from the class of 1865.

They climbed a second flight of stairs and stepped through a heavy fire door into a hallway that was as grand as the one that they left behind in the history building was ordinary. It evoked the air of a gentleman's library, with dark, wainscoted paneling and well-lit portraits of important-looking men in gilded frames. She could nearly smell their cigars.

Conroy led them through a heavy, carved oak door marked simply, with a gilt-lettered sign, *The Harold Hershey Memorial*

*Room*. It was dimly lit by the nighttime security sconces, which washed the room in a reddish glow. The mahogany paneling swallowed the scant natural light that slanted through the room's tall, narrow windows from the gloom outside. The Hershey Room had already been closed for the winter break. Their footsteps echoed loudly in the hush. Christa startled when the radiator banged and hissed awake.

"Harold Hershey was a mason, you know," said Conroy, pointing to the painting of the room's benefactor just inside the door. Hershey was seated in a carved wooden chair, dressed in the tuxedo of the era, with a golden pocket watch chain hooked onto his vest button and an expression of barely tolerated patience on his bearded face. Beside him, on a mahogany desk, were glimpses of letters and drawings of the man's fertile and profitable innovations. Behind him, on the wall, hung the familiar square and compass symbol of the freemasons. "Now, there is a connection for you, Christa. The Bible only describes two of the twelve sacred gemstones on the Breastplate of Aaron by name. They are, of course, Urim and Thummim. The masons teach, in their thirteenth, fourteenth and twenty-first degree ceremonies, that the Urim and Thummim were part of the treasury of Solomon's Temple."

Daniel drew alongside Conroy. "Which was destroyed when Jerusalem was sacked by the Babylonians in 586 BC," he said. "When the Ark of the Covenant, which held the original Ten Commandments, vanished."

"Along with the Ark's sister piece, the Breastplate of Aaron," she said, "that held the Urim and Thummim."

Conroy nodded. "The Jewish Kabbalistic traditions concur with the freemasons," he said. "The Urim and Thummim are also significant to the Mormon religion. When the angel Moroni presented Joseph Smith with the golden plates that contained the Book of Mormon, Smith used Urim and Thummim to translate it, thus beginning a new religion." He led them past cases of illuminated manuscripts, Etruscan pottery and Greek friezes taken from a time when travelling aristocrats paying a pittance for a country's ancient artifacts was considered fashionable.

"Islam has its own sacred stone," said Christa, "not of the Breastplate, although their holy stone is connected to the Old Testament. When the faithful make their pilgrimage to Mecca, they go specifically to circle the Black Stone seven times. It is said the God sent the stone from heaven to Adam and Eve, so that it would be the first temple on Earth. And that Mohammad, before he even became a prophet, placed the stone in its spot in Mecca and kissed it."

"That stone, although black, has a colorful history," quipped Conroy. "The Black Stone has been stolen, ransomed, broken into seven pieces, restored and, indeed, is the focus of the Muslim's most holy pilgrimage." He stopped at a case with a small but impressive collection of finely wrought Mesoamerican gold.

"My favorite exhibit," Christa said. It wasn't much. The pieces were small, pendants, ear adornments, but they had survived. The conquistadors, in their hubris and lust for gold, had melted down most of these works of art into gold bars for ease of transport back to Spain. She'd been granted hands-on research of the Mesoamerican collection on several occasions, trying to find evidence that proved that the Spaniards destroyed the pieces not because they did not recognize the mastery of the culture's artisans, but because they did.

"There he is," said Conroy, a hint of affection in his voice. "El Dorado."

Daniel nearly muscled her out of the way. He sighed with disappointment. "That is what you brought us in here for?" he asked.

"That," said Conroy, pointing to the diminutive figurine, "is history."

"It's the piece that you got when you were in Colombia as a boy," said Christa. The piece was simply labeled, *Figurine, Colombia, Muisca, 300-1500 AD*, followed by a catalog number. Only about two inches tall, the golden man's round face was adorned with a feathered headdress and hoop earrings half as big as his face. He wore a necklace, loincloth and sandals. Each hand grasped a golden object, speculated to be his tribe's version of a royal staff and orb. His golden legs were bowed outwards at the knees, as if he was performing a dance. This golden man evoked history clearer than volumes of text.

"This," said Conroy, "is El Dorado."

"El Dorado," she echoed. "Literally translated as the gilded man. The legend began with the Muisca tribe of Colombia. It all started with an eyewitness account of a European, written just one year before Quesada's catastrophic expedition."

"Like the Spanish, the Muisca ritualized their coronations," said Conroy. "Their new ruler was gilded head to foot in gold dust. The ruler and his top aides gathered a bounty of gold and Emeralds. They brought their tribute to Lake Guatavita. There, they built a raft of rushes and floated to the center of the lake. They tossed a wealth of gold and Emeralds into the waters as a tribute to their heathen god. The water, for the Muisca, lives with a spiritual power."

"The gilded man dove into the waters," said Christa, "leaving behind his skin of gold, emerging as the new monarch."

"That one true account transmuted into a legend of the lost mythical city of gold that enthralled the Spaniards and inspired hundreds of miles of exploration," Conroy said. "But they kept their blinders on. They weren't interested in anything except for gold."

"The archives say this figurine once belonged to a medicine man," said Christa. "You never told anyone the story of how you acquired it."

"Jairo's father gave it to me," said Conroy, "in the hospital, in gratitude for saving his son's life from the jaguar. I didn't want to accept it. He said that it had been passed down through generations of shamans. Even then, I knew the figurine had to have great spiritual significance." A blush pinked Conroy's already ruddy cheeks. After all these years, the intensity of the emotion brought on by his memory had not dulled. He cleared his throat. "The El Dorado figurine dangled from a pendant that Jairo's father wore. The pendant," he breathed in deeply, "depicted a giant bird of prey."

"The protector of the Oculto Canyon," said Christa. "Salvatierra described the rock outcropping above the temple hiding the canyon as Demon's Wings."

Conroy nodded. "I was young and heavily sedated," he said, "but it's coming back to me. I wonder now, could Jairo's father have possibly foreseen what has come to pass? Is that why he insisted I accept it even though I knew I wasn't worthy? I do believe that shamans are often endowed with a kind of sixth sense, specifically clairvoyance and precognition. It could be genetic. I conducted a study once, quite fascinating, really."

Daniel groaned. "How is this going to help us get the gems," he asked, "and the Breastplate?"

"Your words, Christa, that gold endures," said Conroy, "jogged my memory. Jairo's father told me. *El Dorado is a guardian, between Earth and Heaven. Only he can show you the way to paradise.* The Oculto Canyon was their Garden of Eden." He bent down to examine the lock holding closed the hinged lid of the glass display case. "You've got to get this figurine to Gabriella," he said. "Perhaps she has to use it with a map, I don't know. But without it, she will never find the entrance to the temple leading to the Oculto Canyon."

"It's gold. The case is locked," said Daniel. His tone was condescending. "I don't suppose you have the key."

"As a matter of fact, I do," said Conroy. He extracted the archaeologist's hammer and chisel from his jacket pocket and, without hesitation, jammed the chisel behind the hasp with a shiver of metal against metal.

"Stop," shouted Daniel. "It's got to be alarmed."

Too late. Conroy pounded on the chisel with his hammer. Alarm claxons blared into the room. Blinding lights flashed on. Christa reflexively cringed at the din and raised an arm to protect her eyes from the sudden glare. Conroy pounded away. The chisel edged its way in behind the hasp, slowly bending the metal.

"They're coming," said Daniel. In between the deafening alarms, heavy footfalls approached rapidly from down the hall. He grabbed Christa's arm. "He's nuts. Let's get out of here."

Christa shook off Daniel's hand. She wasn't about to let Conroy take this risk for nothing. With a snap, the hasp broke open. Conroy lifted the case's hinged lid. He reached in and snatched up El Dorado from its velvet cradle. He thrust the figurine into her hand. "Take El Dorado," he shouted over the alarm. "I'll stall them. Out the window with you. Run!"

They ran all right, in a full out sprint, around the building, back across the courtyard. Christa dove behind a hedge of boxwoods lining the sidewalk near her car. Daniel stumbled in beside her, breathing hard. He pushed his glasses back onto the bridge of his nose. "Great," he said, "we're thieves. I sure didn't predict that part of God's divine plan for us."

Her cell phone chimed. An email coming in. She looked at the screen. "My God," she said. "It's from Ahmed."

"That name Conroy asked you about. Who the hell is Ahmed?"

"My father's friend from Morocco. He's here in New York." She showed Daniel the picture of the stunning cat's eye emerald on her phone. "And he has the Tear of the Moon Emerald."

# CHAPTER 39

Jared knew he had little hope, but he had to try. Contreras brought the duplicate of Edward's sapphire closer to his eye; he had to suspect it was a fake. Jared would grab the champagne bottle, swing at Torrino first, maybe get lucky and clock him in the head. His plan didn't go beyond that. By then, he knew, he'd be dead.

Jared tensed to make his move, but he saw something truly unexpected. Contreras smiled.

Contreras removed the loupe from his eye and closed his gloved fingers around the sapphire. "Well done, Jared," he said. "This is truly the gem of a monarch." Jared hoped the man had not heard his sigh of utter relief. "Mister Torrino, my briefcase."

The beefy man picked up the silver Halliburton case, crossed over to Contreras and presented it to him like a vassal with a treasure chest. Contreras spun the combination locks and released the latches. He opened the top lid, leaving the case balanced on Torrino's formidable forearms. Jared could see that the black velvet lining of the case had been tailored to fit a customized, protective foam. The entire case was built for one purpose. In the velvet, precisely sized hollows awaited seven roughly oval objects, varying in length and width from ten to fifty millimeters. The seven sacred stones.

"And so it begins," Contreras said. He placed the sapphire in the fifth spot from the left. The blue looked proud against the black, terrifying in its brilliance. Contreras drank in a long, slow look. He waved his hand. Torrino stepped back. Contreras set his sights on Jared. "Now for the Kohinoor diamond."

Jared grasped the diamond between his forefinger and thumb with renewed confidence and held it towards the window. Although it was dark and stormy without, the diamond was alive with a brilliance from within. Cut from what was once the largest diamond in the world, he balanced between his fingertips 105.6 carats of purest white. Oval in shape, faceted expertly to fully enhance its inner beauty, Jared felt as if its refractions of light had to be the Earthly version of the tunnel people describe when the "see the light," when they die, are called towards heaven and then are yanked back to life. "The Mountain of Light diamond," he translated from the Persian, *Kohinoor*. "And yet that is a most recent name for the gem. It was first written about 5,000 years ago in the ancient Sanskrit texts. Its first known name was Syamantaka, one of the most powerful gems in Hindu mythology, a gift to Krishna from the Sun God, who wore it round his neck."

Contreras rose from the chair like a specter from the grave. "He who possesses this diamond rules the world."

Jared tightened his grip on the gem. Contreras's desire to hold it was palpable. "And so they have, Baltasar," he said. "But with great power comes great risk. In the 1300s, a mighty Shah possessed the diamond, only to have his army defeated, the stone taken away as war bounty to Delhi. By 1526, it belonged to the sultan, Babur, who claimed the diamond's value could feed the whole world for two days. It was a time of conquest and defeat in the mogul's empires. In 1547, the diamond was temporarily lost in the annals of history."

Contreras stepped ever closer, drawn to the diamond. "Not lost in the history of my family. In the eleventh century, a Moorish invader absconded with the Breastplate from the Holy Land. The Arab brought it in utmost secrecy to Spain in hopes of using its power to retain conquest of the land. But even then, the Breastplate was incomplete, its gems missing, its divine powers diminished. In twelfth-century Spain, as El Cid expanded his conquest, a Contreras captured a Moorish ruler. The coward offered the Breastplate in exchange for his pitiful life. My family's destiny was set in motion. And in the sixteenth century, my ancestor, Alvaro, acquired the last of the missing gemstones, the Kohinoor diamond. He brought the completed Breastplate to the New World, to begin the world anew."

His words intoxicated Jared. Once again, he was dizzy with the thought that he could be a part of a new evolution in the history of mankind. He forcibly drew his gaze from the brilliance of the diamond. "The Kohinoor resurfaced in India," he said, partially to buy time, but mostly for his passion for the gemstone. "Shah Jahan, the builder of the Taj Mahal, placed it in his magnificent Peacock Throne. Yet the Shah was overthrown by his own son, Aurangazeb. Aurangazeb murdered his three brothers and imprisoned his father in the Agra Fort, with only one small window to look over his beloved Taj Mahal, some say only by seeing it reflected in this very diamond. Though the diamond was in Aurangazeb's empire, he, too, was conquered in 1739, his cities sacked, by the Shah who, finally able to obtain this most famous diamond, exclaimed Kohinoor, when he saw it, dubbing it the Mountain of Light."

"And so it is," Contreras said, reaching for the diamond. "And I shall reclaim its true destiny, to create an empire that will finally rule the world."

"Just as the British believed they would," said Jared, "in 1849, when the Kohinoor was handed over to the possession of the Queen Victoria as part of the Treaty of Lahore. At that time, the British empire spanned the globe, including India, large swaths of Africa and, of course, Australia and Canada." Jared was a traitor to all that his country had bled for. Once he handed over this gem, he would either die as that traitor, or live for a chance at redemption. "Now it is said that if these gems were to leave England, the British Empire will fall."

Contreras snatched the diamond from Jared's palm. "Too late for that," he said. He clutched the diamond in his gloved fist and pressed it against his heart. "It is mine." He closed his eyes. When he opened them, they looked even blacker than before. "And I will soon wield its power in its entirety. Alvaro shall be avenged. I will fulfill the destiny that was set forth a millennium ago. I will create the world that God envisioned, where no son will lose his mother to please a false prophet."

Contreras turned away, gestured for Torrino, who approached bearing the open briefcase. He placed the diamond next to the sapphire, into its perfectly matched hollow in the black velvet. He drank in one last look and closed and locked the lid. "I would pay a fortune simply to sit and admire these stones which I've devoted my life to acquiring," he said, "but all my money cannot buy time." He punched his hand from his cuff to look at his watch, a vintage Patek Philippe. "I am very close to acquiring the third of the seven sacred stones. It is a time for action, not accolades."

Jared stole a glance at the clock on the desk. He, too, wished he could buy time. He judged that Fox, at best, would not arrive for several minutes. The realization that he had actually fooled Contreras filled him with elation and self-doubt. It had been far too easy to convince the man to incorporate him into the master plan. Like a poker player who had risked the pot on a bluff, he had to play it out. He thought about Zoe and his unborn child. He no longer cared about the money, nor the heavenly reward. He just wanted to hold his wife in his arms, to feel the breath of their baby on his cheek. "So what is our next step?" he dared to ask. Contreras often indulged in boasting about his intricate plans, no matter how precious the time.

"Your next step is one that cannot be taken lightly," said Contreras. "The sword is in readiness for the dinner tonight."

It was a statement, not a question, but Jared quickly went to the bedroom and retrieved the black walnut box from beneath the bed. As he did so, he saw Contreras hoist the bottle of champagne from its bucket. Without removing his gloves, Contreras removed the foil from the champagne and deftly uncorked it. He shimmied the bottle back into the ice bucket. Jared tried not to look at it too intently.

He brought the box to Contreras, opened it with a flourish. On the plush, maroon velvet lay a bejeweled masterpiece of Jared's own craftsmanship, the Lux et Veritas sword. Its blade was thirty-five inches of finely honed carbonized steel. Its hilt was gold, inlaid with twenty precious and semi-precious stones. But these stones, like the sacred stones, carried with them a certain power in their provenance.

Each of the countries in the G-20 had contributed one of the stones. Each was unique. It was the culmination of months of negotiations to get each nation's representative to agree to which stone their country would contribute. It was only a small prop to the aspirations of the G-20 summit, but almost a miracle that the sword was completed. It surely would not have been if not for Contreras's worldwide network of corporate diplomats and behind the scenes promises of new jobs and affordable medicines. The sword, once presented at tonight's dinner, would reside, in turns, on exhibition in each of the twenty nations, symbolizing cooperation and strength. Looking at the sword with Contreras standing by it, Jared realized that it was this heady commission that had made him arrogant enough to believe in Contreras's mission.

Contreras lifted the sword from the box by its grip. He hefted it upwards, admired the simple yet elegant design that incorporated the twenty stones. He gingerly tested the blade's razor sharp edge. "Just as I envisioned," he said. "You have once again done a masterful job."

"With your inspiration," Jared said.

"There are those who are protesting the meeting of the G-20," Contreras said. "Even those who are determined to derail the world leaders' talk of peace."

Jared laid the sword's box on the desk. "This sword symbolizes everything the terrorists despise," he said. Despite his despicable crime, he was proud of the sword he had designed and crafted. "As one nation passes this sword to another, they pass along a vow of cooperation, an alliance that they will fight together the power of evil."

"It is a threat to the terrorists," Contreras said. "One might even believe that they would kill to defame the symbolism of this sword. It would become a new symbol, of a new ruler who can truly bring about world peace."

Jared stepped back. He could see death in Contreras's black eyes and feel the cold breath of Satan on the back of his neck. Contreras clutched the sword's hilt with both hands. He thrust it forward with the violence of murder. Jared heard a grunt of surprise and realized it came from Torrino. A blow punched Jared in the gut. He doubled over, but was confused. Had Contreras merely struck him with his fist? Then he felt the invasive cold of the steel blade inside him and the warmth of his blood seep into his shirt. He looked down. Contreras released his grip on the handle. It was beautiful, that handle, a masterful design of gold, silver and small but precious gems. It brought a tear to Jared's eye. His knees buckled. He fell backwards, his arms flailing. His hand hit the ice bucket, sending it crashing off the serving cart. Contreras snatched the neck of the champagne bottle, pulling it to safety, as the ice skittered across the carpet.

Jared landed hard on the floor, his arms outstretched. He could not move. He had done good work on the blade, its point so sharp that it had thrust him through and penetrated the wood floor. His sword pinned him there, as his lifeblood pooled around him.

Contreras looked down upon him. He poured champagne into the two flutes, handed one to Torrino. He held his flute towards Jared in a toast. "In death, as in life, you are an admirable gentleman," he said. "You have fallen upon your own sword." He grinned thinly, not without mirth. He drank, then stepped back as a rivulet of blood neared the toe of his Italian made loafer.

"Please, Mister Contreras," Jared croaked. His own voice sounded distant, as though he were already leaving behind his physical self. "Zoe, she's pregnant."

Contreras frowned. He nearly looked regretful. "I will see that she is cared for," he said, "and your child." With that, he turned away. Jared could hear Contreras and Torrino's footsteps as they left the room. He could hear the door shut and latch behind them. And he could hear Alba's voice calling him from heaven, as he fell further and further away from her.

CHAPTER **40**

Christa checked her cell as she hurried along Tenth Avenue, past the lone vender hawking I Love NY t-shirts. She and Daniel had made good time getting into New York, but time was running out. She had to get that Emerald from Ahmed.

Dark storm clouds choked out the daylight above. Buildings pressed in on each side. A biting wind whipped up from the Hudson River. The few people hustling down the sidewalk bent their shoulders to the cold. Christmas stress outgunned holiday cheer these days, but their sense of urgency was frantic, as if the cold gusts were the push before the raging waters of a flash flood that would suddenly thunder down this canyon of a street and wash them away to their deaths. No festive conversations were shouted above the din of honking horns, squealing brakes and the ragged, oppressively festive holiday tunes oozing from the stores. Even the pungent smoke from the street vendor roasting chestnuts wasn't enticing any customers.

"The poison," Christa whispered to Daniel. A vibration trembled through the city, a sense of dread that became more palpable as she neared the Marrakesh restaurant. "It's starting to affect people."

Daniel reached for her hand and held it, tight. His warmth felt out of place. Affection, like fear, had become an indulgence she couldn't afford. She tried Percival's cell again. Still no answer. He would have turned off his cell in the clinic, but the spindly-fingered heebie-geebies were crawling up her spine. Never a good sign.

"Contreras will need a theologian," said Daniel. "Only a high priest can wear the Breastplate of Aaron."

"Daniel, I don't know if I should love your naiveté or fear it. He's not worried about communicating with God. He thinks he is a god."

Daniel clasped his coat in tighter against the north wind. "This Ahmed you're meeting. He's a Muslim. This time in history is not exactly that religion's finest hour. If they get their hands on the Breastplate of Aaron, it could be just the power they need to rid the world of infidels. Converting everyone to Islam is one of their core beliefs."

"The core of Ahmed's belief is to do the right thing."

"As is mine," said Daniel. "Question is, what is the right thing?"

"This is it," she said. "Ahmed's cousins' restaurant." On any other day, she loved this section of the city, the Middle Eastern eateries, from Ethiopian to Turkish. The Marrakesh was one of her regular haunts before her heavy class load this past semester. Its double doors were painted with an intricate Moorish design she remembered from her days in Morocco, an elaborate pattern of geometric shapes painted in rich reds, blues and ambers. They were a work of art and sign of welcome that even the most callous delinquent would not deface with graffiti. Daniel heaved open the heavy door to a room even darker than the gloom outside.

The scents slipped towards her like a magic carpet, gliding her away to a different time, a different place, a different world. Sweet cinnamon, exotic coriander, cool mint. Red, yellow and green lanterns ensconced in pointed arches lighted the interior and somehow didn't look garish. Framed Moroccan travel posters, photographs and small woven rugs with geometric patterns of bold reds, blacks and whites dotted the deep golden walls. Engraved brass trays, four feet across, were balanced on wooden tripods and served as tables. Low settees, slumping ottomans and carved wooden chairs gathered around them. The room was eerily empty. Even the slices of Arabic and busy clank of pots from the kitchen sounded far away, afraid to creep into the gloom. One man sat alone, beneath the poster of camels in a dirt parking lot outside the terra cotta walls of the Marrakesh medina. He rose unsteadily from the low, plush cushions of the settee.

The two of them stood for a long moment, taking each other in. Ahmed had grown more dashing. The slight beard and mustache defined his strong chin. His hair was dark and short, outlining a broad forehead. His eyes were dark, but approachable. Only one thing had changed. He did not smile when he saw Christa. Ahmed had aged not on the outside, but in his soul. She moved towards him. He edged around the round table to meet her. She wrapped her arms around him.

The earthy fragrance of the red sands of Morocco escaped the folds of his shirt. The warmth of the desert sun somehow lingered on his chest when she pressed her cheek against him. It was crazy, worthy of hours of psychoanalysis, but Dad was somehow there, embracing her through Ahmed.

They released each other. Christa gestured towards Daniel. "Ahmed, this is Daniel Dubler." Ahmed offered Daniel his hand. Daniel shook it, brusquely. Ahmed guided her around the round, brass tray table to the settee. Daniel squeezed in next to her.

Ahmed winced as he lowered himself, grabbing at his thigh. Christa reached for his forearm to help ease him down.

"I'm fine," Ahmed said. "It is nothing."

She clasped his hand. "It is good to see you. How are Leila and Ambar?"

"They are with me here, in Brooklyn, at my cousin's home. I have a photograph." He fished it from his shirt pocket and handed it to her.

"They're lovely," Christa said. And they were, true beauties, with midnight black hair, radiant smiles and the unmistakable look of love in their eyes. Ahmed deserved this. She returned the photo. And now for the real question, if she dared. "And my father?" Ahmed had said nothing about him in his brief email.

A small round copper tray with a chrome teapot and set of six small, etched glasses sat on the table. Mint tea, its aroma both comforting and invigorating, in better times. Ahmed poured the steaming tea into three of the glasses. He offered one to Daniel and wrapped Christa's fingers around the other. His expression was grave. "Pirates attacked the treasure hunter ship," he said. "Many good men died, but I was able to save the Emerald. I returned to my village to deliver the Emerald to your father, but his did had been attacked. My mother had already left for the city to deliver Salvatierra's letter and crucifix to you." He clasped her hand. "Your father took the bullet that was meant for my mother. He saved her life."

"How bad is he?"

"I did not want to leave him," he said, "but your father pleaded with me to come. His wish was that I get the Emerald to you as quickly as possible." He couldn't bring his eyes to meet hers. "It will take more than a bullet to bring down your father." In other words, Dad was still alive when he left, but barely. Ahmed leaned in closer. "I do not believe in curses, but when we brought up this Emerald from the depths of the sea, we brought with it the depths of darkness. Friends betraying friends. Good men shot down like beasts."

She reached behind her neck and unclasped the golden chain. She slipped the crucifix from beneath her blouse and laid it in her palm. She held it out towards Ahmed. "Thank you for all you've done. According to Salvatierra's letter, this crucifix belongs to your family." It was the least she could offer, besides giving him back his life.

Ahmed pulled back, raising his palms in defense. "I do not want it," he said. "I want no more part of this." He jammed his hand into his pocket and yanked out a brown velvet sack attached to a long, braided cord. He thrust it towards her, but hesitated. "It is not right, placing this burden on you."

Daniel leaned in suddenly, nearly upsetting the brass tray table from its stand. "We'll decide what's right." He reached for the sack. She pushed him back. "Christa, we are running out of time," he said, his teeth clenched.

"I am well aware of the time," she said. Four o'clock. Two hours before Contreras was going to call, expecting Gabriella's findings, the Emerald and the Turquoise. She laid the crucifix on the table and turned to Ahmed. "And I'm aware of the danger, but I have no choice."

"Nor did I," Ahmed said, "or that is what I tell myself." He drew open the drawstrings of the sack and shook its contents onto her open hand.

The Emerald rolled onto her fingers as if alive with a light from the past. It came to rest in the well of her palm. This was it. The Emerald that once adorned the Breastplate of Aaron. Touched by the high priest in the Holy of Holies. And lost at the bottom of the Atlantic for five hundred years. Contreras predicted that she would be a believer. And, damn him to hell, he was right. The Emerald emitted a tingling, an energy, like the armillary sphere. It couldn't be denied, no matter how deep she'd buried her clairvoyance after her mother was murdered in Peru, deciding it was more of a curse than a gift.

Daniel leaned in closer, his breath on her neck. "That's it?" he said. "I expected something bigger, more extraordinary." He was right. The Emerald, without its provenance, was the deepest of greens, but it was only an inch across. It was a simple cabochon cut, smooth and without facets.

"It is a cat's eye emerald," said Ahmed, "very rare. You can't see it in this light, but it's as if the Tear of the Moon can see inside you, and it does not blink."

"You're sure this is the Emerald that Contreras is after," said Daniel. He grabbed for the gem.

Christa closed her fingers around the Emerald. "I'm sure Contreras is not going to get it, not from me." She pushed the gem into the velvet sack, drew it closed and looped its lanyard around her neck. She tucked the sack beneath her blouse. "Now we have to find the Turquoise."

The street door opened. A shaft of gray daylight stabbed the interior of the restaurant. Two stocky men were silhouetted against the gloom beyond open door. They entered and then stood aside. A third man came in. He stepped forward into the dim light and deftly removed his pistol from the shoulder holster beneath his sport coat. He aimed at Christa. Another, more portly, man stepped in behind him, remaining in the shadows. "Professor Devlin," he said, "how civil of you to invite me to tea."

# CHAPTER 41

Braydon Fox knew it wasn't his rugged good looks that kept catching the eye of the woman at the front desk of the Waldorf. His stern demeanor was out of place in the opulent, gilded age lobby that had tucked the era of the uppercrust New York hotel in a bell jar. The carved Oriental rug, plush upholstery and crystal chandeliers were better suited to an age when women flaunted feathered hats, uniformed men came home on leave from the war in Europe, telegraph boys scampered for tips, and everyone knew the good guys from the bad guys. A covey of excessively cheerful old ladies passed by, all dressed in red with purple hats, but most of the people were dressed in either jeans and sloppy sweaters or business suits.

Fox doffed his trench coat to ensure the receptionist that he was not concealing a bomb, only a wreck of a suit. The entire city was on edge, with the G-20 in town and the feds upping their terrorist alert due to increased chatter. Downtown was a mess. He only had to tune in to the local radio on the drive into the city to learn that the protesters for peace were rapidly re-engineering good intentions into violent threats.

He slung his coat over his arm and sent her a wry smile, then checked his wrist watch for good measure as if waiting to meet someone, and shrugged. She smiled, assured that her guests were not in danger, at least not from him. If only the receptionist knew that the man she should fear had already walked right past her, out of the elevator and onto Park Avenue to a waiting Rolls Royce Phantom.

Fox smothered the urge to follow Baltasar Contreras. He hesitated just long enough to watch the man pull away and make sure Jared didn't duck out after him. Torrino was carrying a metal Halliburton briefcase, not the custom mahogany box that encased the

Lux et Veratis sword. He caught Torrino's worried face in the passenger window as the Rolls muscled its way into a stream of yellow cabs.

He didn't like placing his faith in a man like Torrino. He didn't question Torrino's loyalty, but the man's nerves were all in a knot. Torrino didn't scare easily, but he wasn't stupid enough not to be scared of Contreras. Neither was Braydon. Torrino would have to take care of himself and keep Braydon apprised of Contreras's next move. Braydon was still dealing with Contreras's last move. He didn't like being one step behind. He crossed the lobby to the elevator.

Braydon rapped on the door to Suite 1066, the year of the Norman Conquest, the beginning of a new empire. He and Jared had shared a laugh about the serendipity of it all when they checked in. *The year that King Edward the Confessor died,* Braydon had said. *After almost a thousand years, the sapphire from his coronation ring is still in the Crown Jewels. Tradition. That's where you Brits have it all over us Yanks.* Jared hadn't responded. The man probably thought talking about the Crown Jewels was tantamount to sharing state secrets, even though he understood that Braydon, as a gem expert, probably knew the history as well as he did. Forever harping about his duty to queen and country, Jared didn't seem like the kind of man who could be bought by Contreras, but every man had his price. Contreras was expert at manipulation. Jared didn't know who he was up against.

Braydon pulled out his keycard, sliced it through the lock. With his left hand, he pressed down the brass lever and clicked the door open. His right hand rested on the butt of his nine mil. He kept it in the holster. He didn't want to startle the flirty wife. He hoped all was well, but knew it wasn't.

A sudden, pitiful cry of anguish sounded from within the room. In one move, Braydon drew his pistol, shoved open the door and shouted "FBI." The sharp, metallic scent of blood hit him in the nose. Damn it. Jared lay spread-eagled on the Aubusson carpet, a stain of red seeping across the floral weave. The Lux et Veritas sword was impaled through his gut. This guy was a jeweler. He was no match for Contreras. Braydon should have taken a risk, sent in back-up. Not everyone could be on Contreras's payroll. And he had just let Contreras walk out of here.

Jared flailed his right arm about, grasping for the ice that had scattered across the rug from the silver ice bucket that had fallen to the floor behind him.   He twisted his head towards Braydon, struggled to crane his neck to look up.  He shouted in pain.  It sounded wet with blood. His head lolled back to the floor.

"Jared, don't move," Braydon said in a hushed voice.  None of this made sense.  If Contreras was after the sword, why leave it behind?  Unless Contreras still had a man in the room.  Shit.  The wife.

Braydon swept the room sighting down the barrel of his gun.  On the chrome serving cart were two champagne flutes, one empty, one nearly full, and one bottle of Dom Perignon, nearly full.   The sword's mahogany case, empty, lay open on the writing desk.  The desk lamp was on, the draperies open.  Braydon stepped carefully around Jared.  He moved to the open bedroom door, gun first.  The sheets on the bed lay in a rumpled pile.  Two dresses were flung on top, rejected.  Three pairs of spike heeled shoes were scattered in front of the full length mirror on the bathroom door.  A book lay on one bedside table, a bodice-ripper, had to be the wife's, next to the clock and phone.  Closet doors were open.  The wife's clothes left barely enough room for Jared's two suits.  Three suitcases were stacked neatly in the corner of the room.

Fox eased the bathroom door fully open.  Lipsticks, blush and various lotions and potions cluttered the small vanity.  The bathroom was only occupied by the lingering scent of expensive perfume.  He holstered his weapon, made a perfunctory call to the paramedics, stating only his name, badge number, location and type of emergency.  He snatched a clean white towel from the rack.  He returned to Jared, knelt and wrapped the towel around the blade, pressing down to staunch the bleeding.  The man groaned miserably.  His face paled.

"I've seen worse," Fox said.  He couldn't lie to a dying man and tell him he'd be fine, even a man who had apparently double crossed him. The only reason Contreras would have been in that room, and run through Jared with his own sword, was because Jared had tried to make a deal with Contreras.

"No," he said, his eyes wide with fear.  "You haven't seen worse." Jared lifted his trembling fingers towards Braydon.  "You think I'm a traitor."

Braydon, compassion trumping reluctance, grasped the man's hand. "Doesn't matter what I think," he said. He'd blown it. His charge was bleeding out, fast. Contreras had done worse than stolen the sword. He'd robbed it of its value as a symbol of peace. Fox hadn't pegged the pharmaceutical heir as an anarchist, but that's what this murder would bring to the G-20 banquet tonight. Most of all, he was worried about the little girl. A man who would do this would easily sacrifice Lucia Hunter. She was no more than a pawn in some insane game where Braydon was always one move behind. "Tell me what I need to know."

"Look," he said. "The Kohinoor and Edward's Sapphire." He released Braydon's hand, pointed a shaking forefinger at the scatter of ice from the knocked over bucket.

Fox had been with dying men before. None of them had been delusional. In fact, at death, a man had a better grip on the grim reality of his life than ever before. He scanned the ice, caught a glimpse of blue among the clear cubes. He looked closer. "I don't believe it," he muttered. He held in check the nearly overwhelming urge to reach out and pick up the sapphire. He had to keep the crime scene as intact as possible. His friends on the agency's Jewelry and Gem Team had joked that the only gems in the world that they need not worry about being stolen were British Crown Jewels. They were kept locked away in the Tower of London, under constant surveillance and armed guard. It was high treason to take them out of the country. And they were cursed. Thieves were superstitious. Braydon looked down upon Jared Sadler, Britain's Crown Jeweler. The crown jewels had been taken off public display three weeks ago for restoration. Under Jared's supervision.

"You must believe," Jared croaked, his voice weak. "Or you will never beat him. We have the advantage. Contreras thinks he has the real gems, but he does not. I made two sets of synthetic reproductions. I mounted the reproduction diamond and sapphire into the crown jewels. I gave the second set of synthetics to Contreras." His hand reached upwards. "Contreras has the fakes," he said. "We still have the real stones. Agent Fox, Braydon, it's up to you to make sure that order is restored."

"Edward's sapphire, on display right now in the Tower of London, is a fake," Braydon said, making sure he understood Jared's meaning, doubt heavy in his intonation.

"A perfect reproduction," said Jared, a perverse pride cutting through the pain in his voice, "as well as the Kohinoor."

Braydon turned back to the scatter of ice. He saw it, tossed in amongst the jumble of cubes, a round, multi-faceted diamond more brilliant and purer than arctic ice. He had seen it before, in person and in photos, the most famous diamond on the Queen's crown. "What could Contreras have possibly offered you that would convince you to steal the Kohinoor and Edward's Sapphire?"

"He plans to poison the water and take over the G-20. I believed he could do it," he said. "I still do." Jared's eyes closed.

Braydon shook his shoulder until Jared gasped in a breath. "When, Jared. How is he going to poison the water?" Even though his specialty was jewel theft gangs, he knew very well that the FBI was on the alert for just such an attack. Easy to do. Hard to defend. Could kill millions.

"It's too late for that," he said. "You must find the antidote. You will need the seven stones to restore the Breastplate. Only that will reveal the place where the antidote grows."

Braydon didn't know what to believe. He had to get the information now, sort it out later. The only thing that would give him the upper hand would be to hold the cards that Contreras wanted. By the pallid pate of death crawling across Jared's cheeks, he had little time. "The Kohinoor and Edward's Sapphire are two of the seven stones Contreras wants?" Jared nodded feebly. "Where do I find the others?"

A tear trickled down his cheek. "I was their guardian and I traded it for the words of a false prophet. He was going to restore the Breastplate, to communicate with God. All I wanted was to talk to my Alba, just one last time. She, too, was a guardian. She earned her place in heaven."

A hard knock sounded on the door. A man's voice yelled, "FBI." Braydon had phoned for paramedics. He hadn't called for agency backup.

Jared shot out his hand and grasped Braydon's wrist. His grip was surprisingly strong, like a man who feared being dragged off to hell. "Gather the diamond and sapphire, quickly. As I told you, Contreras has people at the highest levels. You must not let Contreras have the stones."

A heavy boot kicked at the door. "Open up," the man's voice called. Braydon was sure of it this time, the husky, cigar tainted voice, the Slovak Brooklyn accent . It was Rambitskov, AKA Rambo, the man Jared had warned him about, the man in charge of G-20 security. He hated the guy.

Jared passed out. Braydon had to act, not analyze. He swept up the diamond and sapphire. He grabbed a linen napkin, wrapped the gems inside it. He let it drop into his jacket pocket. He stepped over Jared and opened the door.

Rambitskov stepped forward, Glock in hand. He took in the scene with one glance and a scowl. "Damn it, Fox," he said. He did not holster his weapon. "That's the Lux et Veritas sword."

"And that's the man who made it," he said. Compassion was as foreign to Rambitskov as air to a fish. "I've called the paramedics, in case you're interested." His first thought was that Contreras had caught on to Jared's bait and switch and sent Rambitskov back here for the real gems, but he had come too fast. Rambitskov's arrival on the scene must have been part of Contreras's original plan. Braydon was the wild card here. He could see Rambitskov thinking fast.

"All you had to do was babysit this guy, get this sword to the dinner tonight," Rambitskov said. "I'm up to my eyeballs in protesters downtown."

"Anonymous tip that you got a cleanup in Room 1066 pull you away?"

"I don't got to answer to you," he growled. "You know what the press is going to do with this? You let some mealy-mouthed peace protester waltz in here and stab Britain's crown jeweler with his own sword for Chrissakes."

"No evidence points to a protester as the perp," Braydon pointed out, despite the fact Rambitskov was still holding the gun. No doubt the man had that evidence neatly tucked away, waiting to be planted, a letter, maybe, clumsily crafted from a collage of newsprint, a good visual for page one.

"Those diplomats. All they need is a reason like this to slap each other around," Rambitskov pressed. "And stick it to the U.S. of A." He was scrutinizing Braydon, assessing whether he should kill him, or win him over. "I am a patriot," he said. "Are you?"

"I'm for life, liberty and the pursuit of justice," he answered. The ding of the elevator sounded from down the hall. The paramedic's radio chatter and clunk of equipment preceded them to the room's open door. Fox's phone vibrated in his pocket. He looked at the screen. It was a text from Torrino. *Christa Devlin in extreme danger. She got emerald. Prophet wants it. Marrakesh Restaurant, 47 and Tenth. Going down now.* He jammed the phone into his pocket. "Duty calls," he said, taking a step back.

"You can't walk away from this," Rambitskov said. "This is a crime scene. You're a key witness. You leave here, that makes you a suspect."

Two paramedics arrived at the door. They hesitated, stunned by the scene and the palpable tension between Braydon and Rambitskov. Braydon turned to the medics. "The victim is Jared Sadler. He is the guardian of Britain's Crown Jewels," he said. "Save him." He turned and walked down the hall.

Rambitskov shoved his way past the paramedics. If they hadn't been there, Braydon had no doubt that he would have been shot in the back. "You leave here and your career is over," Rambitskov shouted. "You hear me, Fox? You're dead!"

CHAPTER **42**

Christa's hand reached for Ahmed's, not Daniel's, and clasped it.
The carved wooden door of the Marrakesh Restaurant closed with a
thud. Dread fell upon the room like the gloom of night. The four
men approached from the shadows. Although he was the shortest,
Baltasar Contreras was clearly the alpha male of the pack. God help
her, how was she going to get out of this one and save Lucia?

Like in the desert with his pseudo-safari get-up, or at the
playground in his suburban luxe cashmere overcoat, Contreras was
dressed for the occasion, in a custom cashmere suit seamed with a
superior attitude. His gray gloves gave off the air of affectation
paired with his Truman Capote ascot. His stature and bearing made
him a Caesar among the Brutuses of the two thugs from the
playground who flanked him. The fourth guy had the crescent scar
on his cheek. He was the one who had that neck hold on Joseph in
the Arizona desert and attacked Percival's home this morning, the
one who shot her. He had a bandage on his left hand, bracing his
pinky. It did not put him at a disadvantage.

The two thugs bulldozed a path towards the swinging kitchen
doors, knocking aside wooden chairs and upending two round brass
tray table tops, which clashed to the floor. Ahmed stood abruptly.
He rushed towards the thugs with fists clenched, screaming an
Arabic oath. One snapped a pistol from his shoulder holster. He
aimed it at Ahmed's forehead. She reached for him, terrified into
silence. Ahmed stopped short. The second thug kicked open the
kitchen door with excessive force. A startled shout, in Arabic, was
followed by a demand, in English, "Into the storeroom! Now!"

Crescent scar and Contreras drew closer. Despite his injured
hand, he kept a tight grip on the handle of a briefcase. It was sleek
and aluminum, a Halliburton, the type that drug dealers and gun

runners use, the briefcase that contains the launch codes for a nuclear strike and follows the President of the United States. Contreras scraped a chair along the wooden floor, pulling it from beneath the low, round, brass tray table. He unbuttoned his suit jacket with his gray, gloved fingers and sat heavily opposite Christa.

Contreras shifted his chair to an angle where he could keep the dining room and her in his sights. He assessed Ahmed like a cobra gauging his attack. "So considerate of you to bring the Tear of the Moon to New York, Mister Battar," he hissed. "I assume that my man in Morocco and the pirate, Mishad, had a difference of opinion. No honor among thieves and all that. I do hope that your wife and daughter are enjoying their unexpected visit here, although I dare say that 1134 Flatbush Avenue in Brooklyn is hardly the city's finest feature."

"Bastard," Ahmed growled.

"Actually, they call me the Prophet," Contreras said.

The thug near Ahmed coiled his arm. He pistol-whipped Ahmed, striking his right temple with a sickening smack. Ahmed crumpled to the floor. Christa sprang towards him. Daniel grabbed her arm and held her back.

The pistol-whipping brute dragged Ahmed unceremoniously through the swinging doors into the kitchen. Ahmed's slip-on leather loafer was pulled off his heel and abandoned. Christa clasped her fingers into fists. Both thugs came out of the kitchen, neither having broken a sweat. "An apt moniker, don't you agree, Mister Dubler?" A conspiratorial tone laced his voice.

"Among others," said Daniel. He sounded more irritated than afraid. He placed a protective arm around her. "You hurt her and it's over." She should give him more credit. She would have pegged him as an easy surrender. She should have believed her father when he insisted that the crucible tests the true mettle of a person, usually just before they were dropped into a dicey situation.

Contreras cracked his thin lips into the same disturbing grin that he had showed Christa at the playground as she drank his elixir. "You don't trust me," he said. "It all comes down to that, doesn't it? What, and whom, you believe." Christa remained still as Contreras swiveled to target her in his sights. "You're a clairvoyant, Professor Devlin. I'd bet you didn't see this coming." He snickered, then laughed with delight at having the upper hand. "So tell me, which of your trusted friends, the loyal Arab or this mild-mannered high school teacher turned hero, betrayed you and brought me here?"

"Divide and conquer. Is that the best you can come up with, Contreras," she said. With Daniel by her side, she might have a chance against this guy.

Contreras frowned. He extended his gloved open palm towards her, opening it to the faint scent of roses. He still wore that ring, the gold band with a pear cut diamond, over his glove. She'd seen it someplace else and not just at the playground. Her stomach roiled. It was in the NewWorld Pharmaceuticals website photo of Gabriella and Lucia at the company picnic. That disembodied gloved hand, with that ring, was clutching Lucia's shoulder, the rest of him outside the frame of the picture. "Give me the Tear of the Moon Emerald," he prompted.

"I don't have it," she said. Daniel's lip twitched at her lie. Under the table, she pressed her thigh against his. He had to go with her on this, all the way. Ahmed needed a doctor. And she needed to get a step ahead of Contreras if she hoped to get away from him. "Ahmed was afraid to bring the Emerald here, obviously with good reason. You knocked him out before he had a chance to tell us where it is."

He shook his head, disappointed in her. "I could have had him killed," he said, "but I need you to believe, Christa Devlin. I've seen my destiny. I've told you yours. I know you are the one chosen to help me restore the Breastplate."

Restore the Breastplate, maybe, but certainly not for him. "You don't need me," she said. "You need to do the impossible, steal the Kohinoor diamond and Edward's sapphire, and that's just for starters." The Emerald burned in the velvet pouch around her neck. But so did whatever was in that Halliburton. He saw her eyeing it. He licked his lips like a kid who will burst unless he reveals his secret.

He smiled. "You must be thinking, *He can't possibly hope to acquire them. Why, the Kohinoor diamond and Edward's Sapphire are in the British Crown Jewels, the most heavily guarded gems in the world.*"

"It would take a mastermind," she said, egging him on.

"Torrino," Contreras said, gesturing to crescent scar, waving him forward, "the Halliburton." Torrino removed his fingers from the butt of the pistol in his shoulder holster and approached with the metal briefcase. He unlatched and opened it. He lowered it so that those at the table could see its interior. "Blessed are those who believe without seeing," Contreras said, in a mocking tone. His breath reeked of lust. "The Kohinoor Diamond and Edward's Sapphire," he added in a tone so hushed that she nearly asked him to repeat it.

Inside the case, like stars on a moonlit night, sparkled a diamond and a sapphire, brilliant against the jet black velvet. Impossible. Except an aura of energy surrounded the gems. And it wasn't just an aftereffect of the adrenaline still rushing through her system. She'd encountered it before, a shadow of the souls left behind by those who had held an artifact. In the case of these two gems, that meant moguls, monarchs and a saint. "Impossible," she said. "A theft of the Kohinoor and Edward's Sapphire would be all over the headlines."

"You'll hear about it soon enough, when they find the Crown Jeweler's body at the Waldorf," he said. "Synthetic copies of the diamond and sapphire are what the Beefeaters at the Tower of London are guarding right now." He flourished his hand across the case like a trader presenting his wares. "And here are the slots for the Emerald and Turquoise, the two stones that you are destined to give to me."

"I can't give you what I don't have," she said. No, take from him what she didn't have, the diamond and sapphire, that's what she had to do. How, without getting killed?

Contreras nodded to his two thugs. "Professor Devlin, I do not believe you."

The walls pressed in as the two thugs approached. They clamped their beefy hands on Daniel's shoulders and shoved him down onto the settee. They grabbed his wrists and slammed his hands, palm down, onto the engraved brass design. The tray table nearly flipped off its tripod with the force of it. They held him as firmly as if they'd nailed down his hands.

Contreras extracted a small plastic box from his pocket. He dumped its singular contents onto the table. A bright yellow frog tumbled out, kicking its legs to right itself. The thing was tiny, not much bigger than the Tear of the Moon, and twice as bright. Its neon yellow reflected in the brass of the tray table, even in the dull light of the restaurant.

"Observe the Golden Poison Frog, native to Colombia" he said. "Used by the Muisca Indians to tip their darts for hunting. Currently considered the most toxic vertebrate on Earth."

He lifted the small silver spoon from beside Christa's tea cup. The tea's mint aftertaste soured in her mouth as Contreras poked at the frog. The little creature was frozen with fear. She knew exactly how it felt. "Researchers claimed that a dog could die from merely contacting a paper towel that the frog has hopped across. I proved this to be true in my conservatory. Not to worry, it was only a stray, who had trusted the wrong master."

He poked harder. The frog hopped. It moved towards the tea glasses in front of the crucifix and its tumble of gold chain. Contreras's eyes darted from the frog to the crucifix. The frog diverted around it. Not a good idea to read too much into that. Contreras's gaze, too, was diverted, coaxing the frog closer to Daniel's trapped hands. "The poison from one tiny frog can kill two bull elephants," Contreras said, "or a dozen men." Daniel squirmed ineffectively against the thugs' overpowering strength.

"Don't do this," Christa said. The frog hopped. It was now inches from Daniel's fingertips. His fingers were trembling, their heat and sweat fogging an outline on the brass. The thug holding him stretched back as far as he could without loosening his grip.

"One gram holds enough toxin to kill 15,000 humans," Contreras said. "It's a terrible death. Spasms, contractions, heart failure. It is a toxin akin to the poison that will kill your nephew. Unless you give me the Tear of the Moon and I restore the Breastplate."

She saw Daniel's eyeglasses slipping down his nose as his skin grew moist with sweat. "He's bluffing," he said, teeth clenched to minimize even the movement of speaking. "Conroy said frogs raised in captivity aren't poisonous. You can't kill me, Contreras. I'm the one with the degree in theology. You need me as your high priest to wear the restored Breastplate, to interpret God's word."

"He doesn't look like he's bluffing," she said. And she couldn't take the chance. Daniel was in this life or death game because of her. "Contreras, let Daniel go. I'll get the Emerald for you."

"You do and he'll kill Lucia," said Daniel. "And Liam is as good as dead unless we are with Contreras when he gets that antidote."

"Dubler doesn't care about your family," said Contreras. "I know what you're thinking, Mister Dubler. Why settle to be a man of God, when the Breastplate can make you a god of men?" Contreras licked his lips. Bastard. Part of him yearned for her to hold out. He parted his lips with an expression nearing lust. "I will make you my high priest, if she gives me what I need."

The frog hopped again. It poised mere millimeters from Daniel's trembling forefinger. "Stop!" she shouted. "I'll give it to you." She cupped her fingertips beneath the circular rim of the table's tray top. In one sudden, swift motion, she heaved the table top upwards and thrust it away.

CHAPTER **43**

The pop was unmistakable, gunfire, small caliber pistol,
followed by the crash of furniture and a man's scream. Braydon
kicked open the carved wooden door of the Marrakesh Restaurant.
He blasted through, gun drawn. He had to save Christa before it was
too late.

She was with Torrino. No, she was fighting with Torrino, over
the Halliburton. Baltasar Contreras was sprawled on his behind,
arms flailing across the breast of his suit. He looked like a
cockroach stuck on its back, in a panic that its pathetic little life was
about to be squashed. His body guard stood wide-eyed with fear,
and then thrust his gun towards Braydon, taking aim.

"FBI," he shouted. "Lower your weapon." He caught the
twitch in the man's eye before he heard the pop. He ducked and
rolled. A shot splintered the door behind him. He dove behind a
settee. Two more slugs tore into the upholstery.

Braydon thrust his gun around the edge of the settee, ready to
shoot. But the man who fired at him dropped his smoking forty-five
to the floor and doubled over, clutching at his heart. He let out a
choking scream. He fell heavily to the floor, his legs in a spasm.
The body guard to the man's left leapt back, horrified, his eyes on a
small, yellow object on the floor next to his partner's cheek.

Torrino spun Christa away, his hand still clenching the
Halliburton. Jared's fake diamond and sapphire had to be inside.
Another man had his eye on the briefcase. He was that prep school
teacher he had interviewed for any possible leads connecting
Contreras with the Abraxas theft. NewWorld's historian on last
summer's expedition into Colombia. Dubler. Daniel Dubler, as
nervous as he was arrogant. A jerk. Dubler pressed his back against

the wall, his shoulder skewing a framed photo of camels in front of a walled medina.

The second body guard swung up his nine-mil, targeting that yellow object. It was a damn frog. The guy fired and obliterated the creature in one shot. What the hell?

Braydon crouched and aimed. "Federal Agent," he yelled. "Drop your weapon."

The guy pivoted toward him.

Dubler snatched the brass tray top of the nearest table and twisted it towards Braydon, whipping it at him like a giant Frisbee. The guy fired. The bullet zwanged off the brass tray as it flew by.

Braydon ducked and fired and ducked, knocking the pistol from the shooter's hand. He twisted to recover his balance. A second golden object was on the floor at his feet. Not a frog, but a crucifix. It looked familiar. No time to think why. His gut told him to snatch it up. He slipped it into his pocket and stood. He crossed to Christa and yanked her away from Torrino. Contreras shoved himself up with surprising agility, swooping up his body guard's dropped forty-five. Braydon pushed Christa toward the kitchen. "Get out of here, now," he yelled.

She struggled to push him away and scratch her way back to Torrino. "Not without that briefcase," she yelled back. Dubler approached Torrino from his flank. Braydon answered Torrino's undecided look with a quick nod. Torrino yanked his nine-mil from his shoulder holster, blasted a round into the floor just ahead of the teacher's feet. It was like Dubler hit an invisible wall, he stopped so fast.

Behind Braydon, the guy with the shot-up hand snatched up his nine-mil from the floor. He aimed it at Braydon's face. Braydon swiveled and shot him through the heart, killing him close enough to instantly. That seemed to knock some sense into both Devlin and Dubler. Braydon pushed Christa towards the kitchen door with more force than he cared to use. She swept up her daypack, the one she had in Arizona, and rushed ahead of him. The teacher followed on his heels.

Braydon shoved Dubler and Christa down and through the swinging doors. The forty-five blasted. The bullet zinged into the kitchen just over their heads. He shut the doors behind them, grabbed a mop and thrust it through the door handles. It wasn't an effective lock, but it would buy them a few minutes, time enough considering Contreras wasn't the type to lead the charge and Torrino would sooner die than hurt them.

Gas stoves were still turned on, pots boiling, ovens hot. Heady scents of curry and coriander would have been intoxicating under other circumstances. One back door, leading to an alley. That would be their point of egress. One dark-skinned man right out of central casting for Lawrence of Arabia lay on the floor, unconscious, bleeding from his left temple.

Shouts called from behind a heavy wooden door to a storeroom that had been padlocked shut. Christa grabbed a heavy pan with a long handle from its hook. She wedged the handle behind the hasp and yanked the pan down, breaking the hasp off its hinges. Five olive-skinned men in white restaurant kitchen uniforms stumbled into the kitchen. Braydon flashed his badge at them. "FBI," he said. The Arab on the floor moaned, dizzily struggled to push himself up. "Enemy of my enemy?" Braydon asked Christa, nodding towards him.

Christa rushed to the injured man's side, along with two guys from the kitchen staff. "He stood up to Contreras," she said. "Got hit in the head for his trouble." It looked like the Arab had suffered a severe concussion by the way his head wobbled and that he and Christa were close by the way she looked at him.

The Arab struggled to focus on her. "Christa, I feared I would lose you," he said, in accented, slurred English.

"Not me, Ahmed," she said. "And not the Tear of the Moon, either." She pulled a velvet pouch attached to a lanyard from between her breasts beneath her blouse and showed it to her friend. "You need a doctor."

Ahmed clutched at her arm and fought to raise himself. "No," he said. "You need to find the other stones. Or all of this is for nothing."

Christa pressed her hand against his cheek. "I will try," she said.

"The crucifix," he mumbled. "Your father, he said that the crucifix will show you the way." Odd words for a guy who looked Muslim. The guy's friends apparently didn't care for it, either. Their expressions weren't confused anymore, but downright angry.

Braydon kept one eye on Dubler. An adrenaline rush lent the delusion of strength; his behavior would be dangerously unpredictable, like throwing a brass tray and nearly getting him killed.

Dubler contrived a threat by clenching his slender fingers into fists. "Fox, you are an ignoramus," the man seethed, in the kind of nasal voice that matched the elbow patches on his jacket. "You have no clue what you're doing."

"Saving her butt," Braydon answered. "Yours, I don't care about." Braydon pointed his Glock at the guy's feet, to make a point, then stepped between him and Christa.

"Agent Fox," she said, her breaths still short and fast. "Braydon." Her tone was just this side of pleading. She had to be more scared than she wanted to let on. "This is Daniel Dubler. He's a friend."

In his assessment, a friend didn't stand by while she was physically engaged with a potentially deadly opponent twice her weight. And his tray slinging could have been an attack as much as a defense. "Contreras's historian on last summer's Colombia expedition," Braydon said. "I questioned him on Contreras's connection to a robbery in San Francisco." He stepped towards Dubler. "I don't think your boss is here for your employee appreciation lunch."

"He is not my boss," snapped Dubler. "Contreras is my colleague."

"A robbery in San Francisco," Christa interrupted. "Did it involve a stolen gemstone?"

She knew about the stones. Maybe she knew about the poison, too. Braydon had two courses of action. Coerce the information he needed from Contreras, or from Christa Devlin. Easy choice. He had to get her out of here, safely.

A knock rapped on the door. "Agent Fox, you were clever to find us here." Contreras's sickly sweet voice oozed through the cracks. Braydon considered shooting him through the door, just to shut him up. "You fancy yourself Professor Devlin's protector," he said. "But she has something that belongs to me, an Emerald. The only way for you to save her is to return it."

An Emerald. It had to be one of the seven stones Jared was talking about.

Christa stood and crossed to Braydon. She grabbed his arm. "He's lying. I don't have time to explain, but Contreras has poisoned the water here and in Princeton. We need to find seven gemstones to get the antidote."

Twenty minutes ago he would have called her crazy, but her story corroborated Jared's. Braydon nodded to the kitchen staff, who looked even more confused than the guy with the head injury. "Get him out of here," he said. "He needs a paramedic." They half-carried him out the back door to the alley. Braydon started a mental countdown as to how much time he had left before the cops showed.

"Give me that Emerald," Contreras called through the door. "None of you will be hurt. And don't even think about calling for help. You are well aware of my connections."

Right, connections. He had to start making them, quick, separate the good guys from the bad. Rambitskov had the reputation as the Agency's most fanatical flag-waver. But there could be no other explanation for him showing up at Jared's murder scene than he was sent there by Contreras. Rambitskov couldn't have known about Jared's double cross in switching the authentic gems for fakes. Contreras believed he had the real ones in his briefcase. Rambitskov was the expert in crime scene investigation. That had to be his role, maybe to plant some evidence, or make sure Contreras hadn't left any behind.

Dubler grasped Christa's hand. "Give Contreras the Emerald," he said. "I'll stay with Contreras. I'll make sure he restores the Breastplate and gets the antidote to the right people."

"Daniel, you can't believe in Contreras," said Christa, her expression morphing from a strange mix of determination and fear to shock. "He tried to kill you in there."

Daniel swiped his glasses from their perch and pointed them at her. "He would never have gone through with it. It was just his way of convincing you to do the right thing. He needs me, just like he needs you, to find the seven stones."

Braydon was still deciding if he believed Jared's warning about finding these seven sacred stones, but he was sure these two did. Clearly, Dubler had bet his money on Contreras getting them first. The teacher didn't know Fox. Braydon was getting a sharper fix on the teacher, though. "What did Contreras offer you, Dubler?" he asked.

"The life of a little girl," Dubler said, "the niece of the woman I love. I can save her." Damn, the man's cheeks actually blushed red.

Either he was lying outright, or revealing a heartfelt truth. Either way, it reeked of threat. "Christa, you must give Contreras the Emerald," Dubler pressed. The guy was lying, Braydon could smell it now for what it was.

The indecision in Christa's eyes showed that she wanted to believe this guy. "No," she said. "We don't need to give him the Emerald. We've got to get the two gems in that briefcase."

So she, too, thought Contreras's diamond and sapphire were the real deal. Sirens wailed in the distance, drawing closer. A fist pounded on the kitchen door from the dining room side. "Agent Fox." Ill-disguised anger now simmered in Contreras's voice. "The authorities are nearly here. They will arrest you, not me, for your part in the attack of Jared Sadler. You are persona non grata in your Agency now." Rambitskov must have adapted whatever evidence he planted at the crime scene to point to Fox as the attacker. Braydon had been seen leaving the scene, in direct disobedience to orders, by the paramedics. Contreras helped New York's Homeland Security Chief land his job. The Chief wouldn't be inclined to believe unsubstantiated accusations about his benefactor. Even if he could convince him, the delay could cost Lucia Hunter's life. "You have one last chance to hand over that Emerald," Contreras said, with irritating confidence.

"You're the one in the room with the two dead guys," he answered. "And I'd bet you're not carrying the annual report in that briefcase."

"Braydon," Christa said in a hushed tone. He liked the way she said his name, with genuine concern. "I am not going to give him the Emerald, but we absolutely need to get that briefcase before it's too late. If he gets the gems, he won't need Lucia any more. He'll kill her. It's down to Contreras and that one armed thug. Against you, odds are in our favor." Flattering, but he had other plans. She grabbed the mop handle to remove it and open the door. "This may be our only chance at stopping him."

He forcibly moved her away from the door, the mop handle still secure. "Not our only chance, Christa," he said. "Trust me."

The sirens blared, by the sound of it from two blocks away.

"Fox!" Contreras yelled. "This isn't over for me. It's over for you. You hear me. You're dead." Words right out of Rambitskov's playbook. "Devlin, you are chosen to fulfill my destiny. And you will, I promise you that." Two sets of footsteps receded across the floor. The restaurant's heavy wooden front door slammed shut.

Dubler waved his arms wildly. "Damn it," he said. "Contreras is gone. You let him just walk out of here."

Braydon holstered his gun. "That's our cue to leave," he said.

Christa felt around her neck. "The crucifix," she said. "I left it on the table. It's still in the dining room. Ahmed said the crucifix will show us the way. I'm not leaving here without it."

He pulled the crucifix from his pocket, dangled it before her. "I've got it." It wasn't the typical gold-plated cross his mother always wore. This was old, with a strange skull and cross bones at Jesus's feet. An enamel of primary colors decorated the back, along with the words, Lux et Veritas. Like the sword. With a sudden, heavy unease, he realized where he'd seen a crucifix like this before. He was finally one step ahead of Contreras, but this time, his best friend's life was at stake.

CHAPTER **44**

Braydon shoved open the back door into the service alley. Not gun drawn, but ready. Only one way Contreras was going to surrender this fight, and that was toes up. The cold wind whipped the detritus of battered coffee cups, dirty papers and cellophane wrappers into a whirlwind, exacerbating the stench of garbage. Other than that, the alley was clear. If the crucifix was showing the way to the seven stones, then he had better find where it led him, fast.

He signaled for Christa and Daniel to follow him. Christa's face paled as they followed the trail of blood splotches leading from the alley to Forty-seventh Street. He checked around the corner. The Arabs helping their injured friend, Christa's friend, ducked into the Moroccan grocery store across the street. "Ahmed is a good man," he said. "It took guts to stand up to Contreras, only to get pistol-whipped in the head for doing the right thing. A guy like that sticks by his friends and they stick by him. They'll get him the help he needs."

"We're wasting time," Dubler said. "We need to catch Contreras."

"I don't know what you're catching," said Braydon. "But I'm finally one step ahead of Contreras, not chasing after him. My car is this way."

Christa grabbed his arm as they rounded the corner onto Tenth Avenue. They stopped.

"What is it, Christa?" said Daniel. "Do you see Contreras?"

"Phantoms," she said. "I sense shadows, hovering above the people on the street."

Braydon edged Christa behind him. The avenue didn't look that much different from when he had entered the restaurant. Horns honked. Pungent smoke still drifted from the street vendor's cart on the corner as he hunched over his hot chestnuts. Three elderly men with Brooklyn accents still argued and stamped their feet to warm themselves in front of the small market across the street. But everything felt a bit off, like a photo that had been knocked off-kilter on its nail. He took in the well-heeled woman flipping the bird at the taxi passing her by, the parka-clad mother, glancing around in fear as she tugged her dawdling toddler by the hand, the linebacker of the guy chowing down the greasy hot dog from another street vendor, looking like he was fueling up for a fight. Despite the city's tough reputation in movies and books, Braydon knew first-hand that these weren't the typical New York attitudes. "Do you see these phantoms," he asked Christa, "or is just your spidey-sense tingling?"

"I know you think I'm crazy, but I see dark shadows. One is hovering behind that man in the jeans there." She pointed. "Another behind that guy in the suit, there."

Christa hadn't let go of Braydon's arm. Her hand felt right, holding on to him. It could make a man promise to do crazy things, like believe in her and get her to believe in him. He wasn't ready for that, not yet, not by a long shot. "I had a partner who had a bad feeling about a robbery in progress at midnight at a high end jewelry store. She insisted we go by the book and wait for back-up. She wouldn't let me go in for the collar. The place blew up. She saved my life." In more ways than she ever knew. They couldn't wait to get married and spend the rest of their lives together. He thought she'd be safer covering the front of the next store the gang hit. The gang always cleared out the back before they set off the explosion to destroy evidence. He should have stuck with her, protected her, his partner. Instead, he left her in the front while he raced around to cut them off at the back. He'd wanted to get these guys, badly, before they killed someone. He didn't.

Two cruisers careened down Forty-seventh Street. Two more, sirens blaring, were coming fast on Tenth Avenue from downtown. No black Homeland Security SUV, yet. "Only Rambitskov would pull four cruisers off riot containment downtown," he muttered. "The man must have eaten megalomania for breakfast."

Christa kept her eyes on what must be her phantoms. "Rambitskov?"

"New York City's Chief of Homeland Security," Braydon said. "He's working with Contreras. Full disclosure. I hate the guy." He pulled her towards his car.

"Rambitskov," she said. "He'd know how to poison the water supply. And Contreras has a deadly poison. He wants control of the only antidote."

"This poison," he said. "It's a bio-weapon." The poison Jared warned about.

"The poison causes madness, then death, in seven days." She pressed against the pouch between her breasts. "The gems are connected."

He, too, felt for the package in his pocket, the diamond and sapphire tucked into the hotel napkin. Jared had bet his life on the redemption they promised. "I swear on my badge I'm going to kill that guy."

"Which one?"

"Both of them. Rambitskov first."

The argument between the two men with the bad shadows escalated into a clumsy fistfight. Two of the eight cops responding to the restaurant detoured to stop it. That diversion wouldn't last long. He hurried Christa across Tenth, keeping his face turned away from the cruisers as they passed them in the intersection. He had parked in a tow zone on Forty-seventh. He tossed her the Impala keys. "You drive," he said. "I'm riding shotgun." He shoved Dubler into the back. Couldn't risk him running to Contreras, or the cops.

"Turn uptown on Tenth," he said.

"Past the Marrakesh?"

"The cops are too busy storming the place to notice." No sign of Contreras's Rolls Royce Phantom either. He had minutes, at best, before they tracked him down using the GPS on his Impala. He had to use every one of them. "Fill me in on what happened in there."

Her voice was tense, but steady, even when telling about seeing the diamond and sapphire. Then her face paled. "That man poisoned by the frog," she said. "I wouldn't wish that death on anyone."

"Second that," Daniel chimed in from the back seat.

"I know one man I'd wish it on," grumbled Braydon, "maybe two." The traffic crossing Broadway was near a standstill.

Christa handed him a computer print-out from her daypack. "I translated a letter written by a priest named Salvatierra in 1586," she said. "My father had been searching for it for years. It's historical proof that the Breastplate of Aaron not only existed, but was intact and in South America during the conquest of the new world."

He skimmed the letter. It was an amazing story, of shipwreck and survival, of conquest and defeat, an eyewitness account. "Alvaro Contreras," he said. "The conquistador. Could Baltasar Contreras have gotten hold of this letter?"

"No way," said Christa. She jockeyed around a minivan to clear her way across the intersection. "He kept harping about his family destiny. I figure he has his own, independent family history, passed down through the generations."

"Along with the god complex," he said. "That's what these gem thefts are all about? Baltasar Contreras is planning to find and restore the Breastplate of Aaron?"

Daniel guffawed from the back seat. "You're not going to pretend to know what we're talking about."

"I don't pretend," he said. "The Breastplate is described in Exodus, although there is discrepancy in various translations about the placement and type of its twelve gemstones. Famous gems are my expertise. You don't get much more famous than God."

Christa worried the scar on her forehead. "We think that the restored Breastplate is the only way to find the hidden canyon in Colombia where the plant that produces the antidote grows."

"If Contreras doesn't find it, he's got an indefensible weapon in the poison, the perfect blackmail," said Braydon. "If he does, he's got the only cure, worth billions, and an artifact that can be the catalyst for a new world religion." The trips to Colombia, the theft of the Abraxas stones in San Francisco, it was all beginning to make sense. "The crucifix, Christa. Your friend, Ahmed, said it would show you the way. He wasn't the type to proselytize, so I figure the cross must be connected to these seven stones that Contreras is after. Looked old." He grasped the door handle as she swerved around a yellow cab to make the light. "It could be Salvatierra's, the crucifix that the priest offered as payment for the delivery of his letter to the Vatican."

Christa nodded. "Salvatierra gave it to Ahmed's ancestor in 1586 along with the letter," she said. "He was a Muslim, of course.

When he got to the Vatican, the guards didn't want to hear anything he had to say. They threatened to kill him, so he returned to Morocco with the crucifix and the letter, passed it down through the family, until a recipient was proved worthy. My father saved his mother's life. And his mother sent the crucifix and letter to me."

"1586, when armillary spheres were all the rage," said Braydon. "That cliff dwelling in Arizona."

"I went there for Dad," Christa said. "The sphere is a clue to the location of the Turquoise from the Breastplate."

"Turquoise?" Daniel said. "Arizona?"

"This Circle of Seven," Braydon pressed, "that Salvatierra formed to protect the seven stones. Like his letter, the guardianship must pass down through the generations."

Christa pounded the horn in frustration. "That letter is the first I heard about this Circle of Seven," she said. "It turns out my mother was a guardian, of the Tear of the Moon Emerald."

"Families keep secrets better than anyone," he said. "Where's your Mom now?"

"She passed," she said. "Killed in Peru."

"I'm sorry."

"Happened a long time ago."

Time didn't heal all wounds. He knew that from personal experience. "That Navajo shaman who took you to the cliff dwelling, your father's friend."

"I've been thinking about that, too, since I translated the letter," said Christa. "Joseph has got to be in the Circle of Seven. He's the guardian of the Turquoise, but, like much of history, the details eroded away over the centuries. He doesn't know where the Turquoise was hidden, only that the Turquoise is somewhere in the cliff dwelling."

Dubler grabbed the back of Braydon's seat and strained forward against his shoulder belt. "I don't know about this Turquoise and Emerald, but I sure as hell can get the diamond and sapphire. Contreras has them. I need to contact him. He trusts me." Behind those geek glasses, his eyes were round with lust, not fear. Braydon had seen it before and it never ended well.

"That man who died in there," Christa said, "the poison frog barely touched his cheek." She visibly shivered. She reached a hand back and clasped it over Daniel's. "That could have been you."

Braydon grabbed the steering wheel and yanked to avoid hitting a bike messenger, and to throw Daniel back, out of Christa's reach. She gripped the wheel with both hands.

"Contreras wouldn't kill me," Daniel said, righting himself. "He needs me to restore the Breastplate.   To think, we could communicate directly with God."

"It's called praying," said Braydon, "in case they didn't teach that in theology school."

"Christa, we've got to use Contreras the way he used us, to find the seven stones. Restore the Breastplate of Aaron. Save the people not only of the poison in their bodies but the poison in their spirit."

"Sounds like you've been drinking the Prophet's Koolaid," Braydon said.

"I believe him, if that's what you mean," said Daniel. "You're crazy not to.   He stole the Kohinoor Diamond and Edward's Sapphire. He's a mastermind."

"Mass murderer, if we don't stop him," Braydon said.   Christa slammed on the brake for a flock of Japanese tourists crossing the street against the light. The guy in the Mercedes behind them leaned on his horn. "All he's got is a bad attitude in a custom fit suit."

He felt Christa scrutinizing him.   Call it woman's intuition, clairvoyance, or just a good guess, but he was not being completely forthright with them and she knew it.   "Contreras does have the diamond and sapphire," she said. "He showed them to us."

"I'm sure the Prophet told you," said Braydon.   "It all comes down to what you believe.  Pull over."  He pointed out a tow zone space blocking a chained-off driveway across the street from the honor guard of flags from countries around the world that surrounded Rockefeller Plaza.

The tinny music from the ice skating rink filtered through the huddles of tourists eyeing the threatening storm. The usually festive air of the plaza was raw with a palpable tension. The gothic spires of Saint Patrick's Cathedral, just half a block away, looked even more out of place than usual.

He hurried towards the cathedral, Christa by his side, Dubler behind, slowing only to keep from being crushed beneath the torrent of yellow cabs flooding down Fifth Avenue.  Across the avenue, a mob of tourists surged out of the Cathedral's main door.  One heavy-set man was shaking his Sights of New York map and shouting that he would sue.

"Not exactly leaving the church filled with the grace of God," Braydon said. "Stay sharp. The poison could be taking effect." But he couldn't deny the feeling that always hit him when he came to the Cathedral. No matter what a person believed, or felt about the tremendous resources that were channeled into this massive architectural undertaking, the Cathedral was a reminder of the heights that man can attain.

Every detail beckoned his eye to turn heavenward, from the pointed arches over the massive doors, to the twin spires whose delicate decorations and carvings lent a light, airy feel to the crushing weight of the rock. Surely a species that could create this could follow the precepts of the God who inspired it. Yet, here he was again, trying to stop the evil inspired by the lure of growing closer to that very same God.

Dubler's spindly grip hooked his elbow. This guy was getting to be like a tarantula on his back. "Saint Patrick's Cathedral?" the man asked, wrinkling his nose as though he smelled something putrid. Braydon glared at him, hard. Dubler released him and stepped back.

The light changed. As they dashed across Fifth, Christa drew in closer. "You're Catholic?" she asked.

"I've received the usual sacraments," he said. "Baptism, Communion, Confirmation, Disillusionment." He mounted the steps to the double, gilt entrance doors nearest Fiftieth Street. He avoided even looking at massive bronze doors at the center of the Cathedral's Fifth Avenue side. The figures on the doors were American saints, but portraying them in this way was more self-serving than respectful. A man does the right thing because it's the right thing to do, not to be bronzed in perpetuity.

A linebacker of a security guard in an ill-fitting brown jacket shoved out a last determined visitor, a Japanese man who was struggling to keep the three cameras strung around his neck from tangling. The guard turned his focus onto Braydon, Dubler and Christa. "Closing early today," the man growled. "Security reasons."

Braydon grabbed the outer handle, tugging the door open against the strength of the guard. "We're here to see Father O'Malley," he said. With his free hand, he flashed his badge. "FBI Special Agent Fox."

The guard shot them a scowl worthy of a guy eager to break the ribs of anyone who dared threaten his quarterback, then opened wide the door. "He's in the Lady Chapel," the guard said. "Told me if you showed up that I should leave you alone with him and the Rabbi. Expecting trouble?"

Braydon opened his jacket to reveal the gun in his shoulder holster. "Always," he said. The guard nodded. He had to be ex-military, probably a grunt. Braydon and Christa sidled past him and entered the octagonal entrance hall of the Cathedral.

Nothing was an afterthought at Saint Patrick's. The ceiling towered above them reaching into a high dome with dark woodwork stretching the architectural lines of their pointed archways to their natural apex. The ceiling was held aloft by columns tucked into the interior angles of each of the octagonal room's eight sides. Three interior doors led into the cathedral from the entrance hall.

Dubler's hand grabbed the door as the guard pulled it closed behind Braydon and Christa. Dubler was yanked forward, but the guard stopped before closing him off entirely. In answer to the man's questioning look, Braydon said, "He's with her," and nodded towards Christa.

The guard grunted and allowed Dubler to pass, bolted the door behind him and stomped through the door to his right to destroy a village somewhere.

Braydon crossed over the threshold into the far end of the massive nave of the Cathedral, the vast expanse and soaring heights above him, the main altar topped with the gilt monstrance at the end of the long aisle before him. The light filtered through the stained glass windows. The ribbed columns and vaults reached for heaven. The sense of symmetry usually inspired a curious but welcome feeling of being uplifted and grounded at the same time. Except something was way off kilter. No people. It drained the cathedral of its life. Even the flickering votive candles to either side of them could not conjure the spirit of humanity. That's why Mom had loved this place, because it was a gathering place for people, as much as a house of God. Even now, he couldn't pass without lighting a candle for her. He slipped a prayer for her heavenward and a twenty into the collection box. "The Lady Chapel is at the opposite end of the nave," he said, "behind the main altar. Follow me."

"Saint Patrick's Cathedral," Christa said, as they hurried down the aisle on the south side of the cathedral. She craned her neck upwards. "Modeled after the great Gothic cathedrals of 14th century Europe, but only begun in 1858. It always felt lighter, more ethereal to me than most of those that I visited overseas, even those in France. But it always amazed me that those cathedrals were built with the technology and tools of that time. It was a massive undertaking, over a century or more to complete. The bishop who ordered the construction of the cathedral would not live to see its completion."

"The architecture brings one closer to God," said Dubler.

"Stones are not a conduit to God," said Braydon. "Not in the Middle Ages. Not now."

Dubler threw up his hands in exasperation. "You see, Christa. This man doesn't believe in restoring the Breastplate. He doesn't believe in the power of the seven stones."

"I know enough people have killed in the name of God," said Braydon. "If restoring this Breastplate is going to save lives, I will do everything in my power to make it right."

"With the Breastplate, we can speak in the name of God," said Dubler. "If not their lives, we'll save their souls."

"Spoken like a true inquisitor," said Braydon. They had reached the doors to Fiftieth Street. Several rows of wooden pews faced the altar of the Lady of Guadalupe. "Wait here. My friend, Father O'Malley, takes any opportunity to share light and truth with his flock, but Lux et Veritas he keeps close to his heart."

"Lux et Veritas," Christa said. "The inscription on the back of the crucifix, Latin for Light and Truth. This priest, is he a Latin scholar?"

"Not exactly," answered Braydon. "He's an old drinking buddy from Yale. That is, until he went over to the dark side and matriculated to the School of Divinity."

Daniel guffawed. "You went to Yale?"

"Dean's List five," Braydon continued, unperturbed. "I'm surprised you didn't make the connection, Dubler, considering you told me you were an alum. Lux et Veritas is on the Yale logo. That's what got me thinking of my old friend, Tommy O'Malley, and our all night drunken talks about the meaning of life. Stupid college crap. Except for one thing."

Raised voices of two men shot down the side aisle from the Lady Chapel. He couldn't quite make out the words. "Rambitskov shouldn't be able to find us yet," he told Christa, "but if someone comes knocking, you come running."

# CHAPTER 45

Braydon ran past the choir screen between him and the main altar. He rounded the corner by the Pieta to the outer edge of The Lady Chapel. It had been two years since Mom died. She had welcomed death, overwhelmed with gratitude for a life well lived. She had met the love of his life in those last days. She was happy for him. She never knew that his partner's wife had been stolen away.

She'd joke with him that she didn't come here to pray, she could do that anywhere, but simply to drink in the beauty of the delicate stonework highlighting the pointed arches, the tall stained glass windows, the purity of Mary's expression as she stood with outstretched arms above the altar. It was a full cross-town block away from the far end of the cathedral's nave, where they entered from Fifth Avenue, but he cherished the touch of her fragile hand in his, supporting her dwindling weight, as they made that long pilgrimage past the rows of pews to The Lady Chapel, with several rest stops along the way.

Two men stood close by the chapel's altar. They argued in hushed voices, so intent they hadn't noticed his presence. O'Malley was still as tall and thin as a sapling, maybe even shed a few pounds. He gave his black cassock no more shape than a clothes tree would. Braydon kidded him that he joined the priesthood to avoid having to choose a wardrobe. The priest's collar still smacked of sacrilege beneath his ruddy drinker's cheeks and unkempt red hair. The other guy was short, with dark, curly hair and neatly trimmed beard. He wore a felt hat. Despite his round girth, he gave off the impression of being trim beside O'Malley's sloppy demeanor.

"A priest and a rabbi go into a cathedral," Braydon said.

The priest turned to him, quickly strode down the center aisle between the chapel's wooden pews and clenched Braydon's hand in his. For a thin guy, he had a powerful grip. "Braydon, my boy," he said, although the two of them were the same age.

"Tommy," Braydon acknowledged. He wasn't about to call him Father.

The priest's expression turned grave. "You got my phone message."

Braydon shook his head. "Been busy," he said.

O'Malley guided Braydon closer to the altar and the man in the dark suit. "This is Rabbi Ezekial Feinstein. Zeke," he said. "This is my old friend, FBI Agent Braydon Fox, the specialist with the Agency's Jewelry and Gem Team. He's the one I called about our--"

"Unique security situation," Zeke answered, with an Eastern European accent.

"Indeed," O'Malley continued. "A news report just came over the internet. An attempted murder took place in the Waldorf hotel. Britain's Crown Jeweler."

"Jared Sadler," said Zeke. "They have a suspect, an FBI agent who fled the scene."

Braydon felt O'Malley's comforting hand on his shoulder. "They named you as a suspect, Braydon."

The rabbi clutched his gut. "It's sickening. Mister Sadler was run through with the Lux et Veritas sword."

O'Malley raised his hand defensively. "I assured Zeke that you could never commit such a cowardly act."

"They say they have evidence that the attacker is connected to the Protesters for Peace," said Zeke. "That they wanted to disrupt the meeting tonight."

"Doesn't sound like me," said Braydon.

"Exactly as I told Zeke just now," said O'Malley.

Braydon nodded his thanks. "The crime scene unit fed the press a lot of detail for a crime just committed," he said, "not the usual standard operating procedure."

"Apparently they wanted to get the word out," said Zeke. "Homeland security is putting up road blocks downtown. And tonight the G-20 dinner and the UN will be completely cordoned off."

"Of course," said Braydon. "Why use your own manpower to hold the world's leaders captive when you can get the government security forces to do it for you."

Zeke jabbed his finger towards Braydon. "But why would they want to implicate you, of all people, the protector of the Lux et Veritas sword?"

"We've got to talk in private, Tommy."

"Zeke is my closest ally," O'Malley said, "my partner, you could say. The minute he heard about poor Mister Sadler--"

"I came here immediately to tell Thomas," said Zeke. "Jared Sadler and his wife were the caretakers of something."

"Of incalculable value and power," said O'Malley. "Of divine nature."

"Which transcends man's limits and divisions of faith," added Zeke.

"We fear the attack on his life was perpetrated to steal these divine objects," said O'Malley. "That Sadler risked his life to protect them."

Zeke waved his hand as if shooing away a pesky fly. "I tell you, Thomas. That is impossible. Only those in the circle know of their true value. His attack today must be just a coincidence and, as the radio said, committed to send a message to the G-20."

O'Malley glanced over his shoulder and lowered his voice. "You know as well as I do that the attacker was after the diamond and sapphire."

Zeke's cheeks flushed in anger. "The circle has kept the secret for centuries. The danger that could be unleashed."

"Is already here," Braydon said, before O'Malley could jump in. "We have no time for secrets. The water supply in New York and the Princeton suburbs has been poisoned." He filled them in on Baltasar Contreras, his plan to acquire the seven stones and restore the Breastplate of Aaron, that only the restored Breastplate could reveal the way to the hidden canyon and the plant that was the only source of the poison's antidote. It sounded crazy, even to him, but as he reviewed the events of the last two days, it all began to fit together. He held back the contents of Salvatierra's letter. He needed answers, not questions. "The Circle of Seven, it exists, and you two are part of it."

For a moment, both priest and rabbi seemed stunned into silence. Braydon had never before seen O'Malley at a loss for words. His friend finally sucked in a breath. "The Circle of Seven evolved such that one member was only linked to one other member. If one was compromised, then not all would be lost."

Braydon replayed some of those late night discussions in his dorm room with Tommy. He shook his head. "How long, Tommy? How long have you been a member of this secret circle?"

"Long enough to pick my friends carefully," he said, with the old twinkle in his eye. "I am Zeke's second. My second, as you deduced, is Jared Sadler."

"You're telling me that Jared is one of the Circle, along with his wife? I can't imagine entrusting Zoe Jared with a dime store ring."

Zeke pointed an accusatory finger at O'Malley. "I told you years ago that you should never have allowed Jared to stay with Alba. He was your second. It was your responsibility."

"Alba?" Braydon asked. "Jared's late wife?" That made more sense. The jeweler had mentioned her longingly several times, despite his obvious attraction to sexy Zoe.

"Jared is the guardian of Kohinoor Diamond," said O'Malley. "He revealed to me that his second was Alba, the guardian of Edward's Sapphire. The man fell in love with her, deeply, completely in love, and married her. She didn't know that Jared was in the Circle of Seven when they wed. She, of course, only knew the name of her second. But she was a smart woman. It didn't take long for her to figure it out."

"Dangerous," Zeke said. "And we did nothing to stop it."

"As a priest, as a man, I could not divide a bond that was sworn before God. I could not demand that they divorce."

"Alba is dead," said Braydon. "Certainly Zoe didn't take her place in the Circle."

Zeke began sputtering. "Even we are not that."

"Desperate," finished O'Malley. "Jared Sadler became the guardian of both the Diamond and the Sapphire."

"Dangerous," Zeke repeated. "To have one guardian of two of the seven stones. And now, he, too, may be dead."

"I assure you that the Kohinoor Diamond and Edward's Sapphire are safe," Braydon said, "but your Circle of Seven is compromised. This isn't the first time a guardian has died. Who takes his place?"

"They were to have children," said O'Malley. "One questions God's divine plan at times like these."

"I'd rather question who Alba's second in the Circle of Seven was," said Braydon, "but I think I know the answer."

"The guardian of the Emerald," O'Malley said. Braydon remembered why he always lost in chess with this guy. He could see in minutes the strategies that had taken Braydon days to plan. "But we do not know who that is."

"It hardly seemed important," Zeke said. "The Emerald is where no man can attain it."

Right now that Emerald hung between Christa's breasts. "Leave that one to me," he said. "The only name missing is the guardian of the Abraxas." The Abraxas stone that Contreras tried to steal in San Francisco had to be one of the seven. "Since I figure you two guard the Urim and Thummim."

The rabbi staggered, as if about to faint. "Who else knows of the world's most deadly secret? Truly, all is lost."

"Not lost," Braydon said, "but found." He pulled the crucifix from his pocket and dangled it before them. Even in the dull light from the stained glass window, the crucifix seemed to emit a light of its own.

O'Malley made a quick sign of the cross. The rabbi merely gasped.

"Lux et Veritas," said Braydon. "It translates from the Hebrew, Urim and Thummim, two of the sacred stones on the Breastplate."

O'Malley loosened his priest's collar. He pulled an object from beneath his black shirt, a crucifix dangling from a gold chain. It was just how Braydon had remembered it. It matched perfectly the crucifix in his hand.

"This crucifix has been passed down through generations of my family," O'Malley said. "It originally belonged to Pedro Alonso de Salvatierra, a priest at the Vatican in the mid-sixteenth century. He was the twin brother of Juan Jaramillo de Salvatierra, the priest who travelled to the new world jungles to retrieve the Breastplate of Aaron and arrest Alvaro Contreras. Both men owned identical crucifixes. Juan's, the family history contends, was lost with him at sea."

"Juan Salvatierra was the founder of the Circle of Seven," Braydon said. "And you are his descendent. This is putting a serious dent in my ironclad skepticism."

"I shouldn't have questioned God's divine plan," said O'Malley. "Apparently, Our Lord has planned for this endgame for many centuries, before the pieces were even placed on the board."

"It all comes back to Urim and Thummim," said Braydon. "Light and Truth. Guarded by Thomas O'Malley and Ezekial Feinstein. Seems to me you two are breaking your Circle's rules by being in such close contact."

"Urim and Thummim are the most sacred stones of Judaism," O'Malley said.

"Used by Aaron, himself, and the ancient high priest, to speak with God directly," said Zeke. "Truth and Light can never be separated by man."

"The Circle of Seven decided that at its inception," said O'Malley. "The guardians of the Urim and Thummim would work as one force."

"You're making the decisions for the Circle now," said Braydon. "I need those stones, the Urim and Thummim. Contreras must be stopped or millions will die. We have to restore the Breastplate before he can find it. We have to locate the plant for the antidote."

"Never," Zeke shouted. "I made a vow to God to keep the Urim hidden."

"Zeke," said O'Malley, his voice soft but firm. "Our vow is to protect the people from the power of the stones, not to protect the stones from the people. You told me of the violent behavior you witnessed on your short walk over here. It is caused by this poison. The seven stones, replaced in the Breastplate, will lead to the antidote. We must make sure that they do not fall into the hands of the man whose plan may lead to the death of millions. We must put our trust in God, that he has brought the three of us together here and now for a reason."

A bang rumbled down the nave of the cathedral.

"Thunder?" asked Zeke.

Another bang, closer.

"The north entrance doors," said Braydon.

"FBI! Open up!" a deep voice yelled. Another bang, muted by distance, reverberated from the Fifth Avenue doors.

"Rambitskov," Braydon muttered. "Homeland Insecurity. He thinks he's the second coming of Himmler. He shouldn't be here, not yet." Even if he used the GPS tracker to find his parked Impala.

"They wouldn't dare break into a house of the Lord," said O'Malley.

"Homeland Security is not the SS," said Zeke. "They are here to help."

"Rambitskov is here to take the Emerald," said Braydon. "My friend has it hanging round her neck."

"The seventh stone?" said Zeke. "Impossible. The oral history has been passed down for centuries. Everyone in the Circle of Seven knows that the Tear of the Moon is at the bottom of the Atlantic."

"A treasure hunter ship recovered it from the wreck of the San Salvador two days ago," said Braydon. "God's divine plan and all that."

Braydon didn't have to signal Christa and Dubler. They were already rushing down the chapel's center aisle towards him. Daniel was out of breath, more from fear than exertion. "Fox, only a fool would call in Homeland Security," Daniel said.

"I agree," he said, looking pointedly at Daniel. "You make any phone calls back there?" The lure of the world's most important artifact could make a man do all sorts of foolish things. Dubler had made it clear that he felt Contreras had the best chance at retrieving all seven stones and restoring the Breastplate. Braydon had to dump this guy, without losing Christa's trust.

"He checked his email," said Christa. "He was scheduled to tutor a student for finals tonight, had to cancel. I checked my email, too. Helen said Liam is worse. I called Percival. He's mounting a rescue operation to save Lucia."

"He is doing what he thinks is right," said Braydon. "Just as we have to do. Father Thomas O'Malley, Rabbi Ezekial Feinstein, this is Christa Devlin," he said, "and Daniel Dubler." Time to form a tactical strategy, except he had no point of egress on this side of the cathedral. The nearest exits were at the two transepts, one facing Fiftieth Street, the other Fifty-first. Both would be covered. Rambitskov would enter by the main entrance. His team would fan out down the aisles of the nave, trapping them in the box canyon of The Lady chapel.

"It is true," Zeke said to Christa. "You have the Tear of the Moon Emerald. I can feel its energy."

O'Malley ducked behind the altar, the statue of Mary above him looking over them all with an expression of serenity that only comes in stone or with unfettered faith. Braydon moved to the back of the altar. O'Malley was leaning bodily across the altar, reaching around Mary's feet to the ornate, gilt tabernacle. The tabernacle enclosed the Blessed Sacrament, the host that was the body of Christ, the most holy object in any church. And he was fiddling with pieces of its decoration.

"Braydon, this isn't sacrilege," O'Malley said, as usual cued in to his thoughts. "It is a sign of my conviction to keep the power of the stones from those who would use them to do evil." He loosed a hidden latch and pried opened the back of the tabernacle.

"It's never really a game with you," Braydon said. "Is it?" The panel opened to reveal a biometric scanner.

O'Malley smiled. "Model PX-2000, state of the art, just as you recommended."

Christa stepped in for a closer look. "I never would have pegged the Catholic church as early adapters."

"Couple years ago O'Malley asked my advice on a unique security system for a proprietary relic," Braydon said. "As usual, he escalated the whole thing into a game, designing a safe room out of an underground storage area beneath the cathedral." At the time, he pegged it as O'Malley's brand of grief counseling, intriguing him with something beyond loss.

"Braydon always had a little Indiana Jones in him," O'Malley said. "Got to play to people's strengths."

O'Malley placed his palm on the scanner. One red light turned green. Zeke hesitated, then the shorter man nearly hoisted himself bodily onto the altar to reach forward and press his palm on the scanner. The second red light turned green. A latch unlocked with a click. A panel, disguised as solid marble covering half of the back of the altar, slid open. Dubler sucked in a breath. The dim light beyond revealed that the opening led to a steep, narrow stairway.

"I will stop the intruders," Zeke said. He skirted around the altar. He rushed down the center aisle of The Lady Chapel.

Braydon peered into the darkness. O'Malley's wiry, strong fingers gripped his shoulder. "Hurry, Braydon. It's up to you now.

You must protect the Urim and Thummim." He removed the crucifix from around his neck and pressed it into Braydon's hand alongside its original. "This is the key."

"The crucifix is the key?" he said. "You know I was kidding about that." He had placed it in his "imaginary" safe room design as a playful jab at his old friend.

"It was one of your better ideas," said O'Malley. "To me, the crucifix is always the key."

A thud reverberated down the nave, followed by a sudden draft of cold air and the shout, "Homeland Security." It came from the Fifth Avenue entrance. Braydon couldn't see them. The main, raised altar, surrounded by its choir screen, blocked the view. That worked both ways. The assault team couldn't see them. The stairs beneath the main altar descended one floor into the crypt. The narrower stairs at his feet descended even further down, to some sort of sub-basement. "Lead the way," he said, gesturing to Tommy. Christa and Dubler crouched behind Mary's altar.

"Gentlemen!" Zeke shouted at the strike force. "You must not desecrate a house of God!"

O'Malley stepped back. "I must help Ezekial," he said. "I'll stall them as long as I can. You'll recognize what lies below from your design. But realize, my friend, protecting the Urim and Thummim is not a game. The danger is real."

Before Braydon could object, O'Malley hurried down the central aisle of the chapel, swerving left towards the Pieta and the Rabbi, his black cassock flowing behind him. Braydon repressed the urge to follow. Rambitskov wouldn't dare hurt a priest and a rabbi, not in front of the assault team. Tommy and Feinstein were buying him precious time. He couldn't waste it.

He ducked into the opening, his feet quick on the narrow stairs. He leapt off the last riser into a dark narrow hallway. Dubler scrambled down, peeked up Christa's skirt as she followed. Bastard. The panel slid closed behind her, slicing off the shouts of the agents and any fragment of light from above, pitching them into utter darkness. Christa's body pressed against his in the narrow space, her breaths short, a curl of hair soft on his cheek. A current tingled through him, a vibration, like a short circuited wire. Scariest part was, it wasn't coming from the sacred gemstones.

CHAPTER **46**

It kicked in with a vengeance.  Christa had fought it off in the tunnels beneath the cliff dwelling, too distracted by the more immediate and terrifying threat of the beasts that wanted to tear off her limbs.  Now the total darkness intensified her claustrophobia, born when she got trapped in a cave-in at Dad's dig in the Ural Mountains.

Her heart beat so hard that Braydon and Daniel, pressing against her, had to feel it, maybe heard it.  "I've got to get out of here, now," she said.  She shoved Daniel aside, grabbed for the stairway railing. Nothing but black, a heavy, suffocating black.  Sweat pricked at her forehead.

A hand grasped her upper arm.  The grip was strong, confident, a little rough.  It had to be Braydon.  "Not that way," he said.  His whisper sounded like a shout in the confined silence.  Footsteps thumped the floor above.  Determined men, no doubt bristling with weapons and fierce in their black ops uniforms, stomped around the white purity of the Mary statue.

Her heart fluttered.  She couldn't catch her breath.  A burning sensation seared through her cheeks.  "I can't stay here," she stammered out, not about to confess her irrational fear.  She couldn't even talk.  This was ridiculous.  It was dark; they were underground. That's all.  They were safe, as long as she didn't give in to panic.

"No, we can't," Braydon said.  He grasped her hand and coaxed her away from the ladder.  He had to be just inches from her.  His breaths came short and quick.  "We've got to find the Urim and Thummim."

Only one place was more terrifying than the darkness ahead, the threshold she teetered on, the precipice between reality and belief. "But the Urim and Thummim are the two most sacred, powerful and legendary stones in history.    The original Lux et Veritas, the fundamental light and truth."

"I might not bet my life on my faith in divine power," said Braydon, "not yet, anyway.    But I would bet it on my faith in Tommy O'Malley.    He and the rabbi are Urim and Thummim's guardians in the Circle of Seven, passed down to them for generations."

She'd seen the priest's crucifix.    It matched Salvatierra's exactly. "So the Circle of Seven does still exist."    She let him lead her a few feet deeper into the darkness.

"And your mother," he said, "was the guardian of that Emerald hanging around your neck.    Which means you're next."

She yanked her hand from his.    "I'm a history professor, not some mystical guardian.    I don't have Mom's courage, her resolve, her integrity."

"We'll soon find out."    An overhead light tripped on.    She shut her eyes and blinked until they adjusted.    "Motion sensors, just like in my design," Braydon said.    They were in a hall so narrow it couldn't fit two of them side by side.    So much for relieving her claustrophobia.    The light intensified it.    Cinderblock walls, painted white, pressed in on them and led only into the darkness ahead.    No ornamentation, just a low ceiling and two dim fluorescent bulbs behind textured plastic panels.    They hurried on.    At the outer reaches of the light, a second overhead light flicked on; the first one turned off, leaving the staircase up to the chapel in utter darkness, snuffing out any thoughts of retreat.

They reached an intersection.    Three hallways spanned out in front of them.    The light clawed into each hallway only a few feet. Each hallway looked exactly the same, cinderblock, painted white. Except for one thing.    Each hallway had a bronze plaque.    Each plaque was embossed with a different symbol.    The first was a star. The second a cross.    The third, a circle.

"These guardians don't make it easy," she said.    Symbols. Granted they bridged languages, but symbols could be misinterpreted.    Without her gut feeling that she should choose the Pakal over the other three symbols in that cliff dwelling, she'd be crushed right now.    Claustrophobic or not, being crushed was still a distinct possibility.    The massive weight of the cathedral above seemed to bow the ceiling in this part of the hall.

"If Tommy followed my design concept, only one hallway will lead to the safe room," Braydon said. "Go down the wrong one and a motion sensor will trip a door, trapping the intruder and filling the space with a deadly gas."

"Poison gas?" echoed Christa.

"Seems in bad taste now," said Braydon, "but at the time, I thought of it as a game. I had different symbols for the three hallways. Mine had to do with the Trinity."

"Three hallways," said Christa. "Father, Son, Holy Spirit. Which was the right one in your design?"

"Spirit," said Braydon with a shrug. It was the first time she had seen him looking sheepish. "Tommy had a taste for whiskey. The symbol was a tongue of fire."

Daniel pushed by them. "He's a priest," he said, "just like I trained to be. The hallway we should choose is obviously the one marked with a cross."

Braydon yanked Daniel back. "The best security systems are intuitive to the owner," he said, "so they don't have to call in help to remind them how to access the very thing they're trying to keep safe from others. At the same time, the safety system should not be obvious to anyone but the owner. And you are nothing like Tommy O'Malley."

"All right, then," Daniel said, pointing to the second hallway. "That's the Star of David, the symbol of Judaism. Urim and Thummim were the divining stones used in the Breastplate of Aaron by the Jewish high priest during the Temple of Solomon era."

She felt like an idiot, but she held her hand open to each of the three hallways in turn. It was like an electric current laced the air, that metallic, tingly feeling that comes before a lightning strike. "The circle is the right path," she said.

"I'm telling you, it's the star," said Daniel. "The circle isn't a Christian symbol."

"The Circle of Seven," Christa said. "That's what this is all about." But if they chose it, and were trapped, it would be her fault.

"Except it isn't a circle," Braydon said. "You see the two bands? It's a ring. O'Malley drove me crazy with his opera music when we'd meet to play with the design of the safe room. He insisted on listening to Wagner's opera trilogy, The Ring. He said it helped him commit abstract ideas to memory."

"I'm the one with the degree in theology, like your friend, O'Malley," said Daniel. "He'd know that the Star of David is also significant for the number seven. The star's six points and its center are relevant to the seven names of angels and Kabbalistic traditions. Urim and Thummim are two of the seven sacred stones. This has got to be the way." He passed beneath the Star of David and strode quickly down the hallway. A loud click stopped him in his tracks, but no light switched on. He spun around. Before he could retreat, a steel door sliced downward from the ceiling, trapping him behind it. The last thing Christa saw was the terror in his eyes.

"Daniel!" she yelled. "The poison gas!" She lunged for the door, pressed her palms against the cold, hard steel, fighting to push it upwards and free him.

Braydon pulled her back gently. "He's fine," said Braydon. "Even in the game, Tommy objected to the idea of poison gas. I changed it to the trap door setting off an alarm."

As if on cue, an intensely loud siren blared from behind the trap door. Christa clamped her ears with her palms. Braydon was either grimacing at the noise, or smiling at Daniel's bad fortune, maybe both.

"Tommy should have gone with the poison gas," shouted Braydon over the din. "Then Dubler would only be killing himself. That alarm is going to lead Rambitskov right to us."

"We can't leave Daniel," she shouted back. "How do you get that door open?"

"We got five minutes. Then that door opens, but the other trap doors come down, permanently. It was O'Malley's way of allowing the intruder a chance to escape." He raced down the hallway marked with the circle. She ran after him. The alarm faded as they distanced themselves from Daniel, lights turning on then off behind them as they progressed. It had to be a whole crosstown block, the length of the cathedral above, before the hallway dead ended at a bolted steel door. An electronic scanner, like the one that opened the panel to the stairway down here glowed on the wall to her right. "Doesn't make sense," she said, struggling to catch her breath. "O'Malley wouldn't send us down here without a way forward."

"It's not biometric," said Braydon. "In my design, it's a sophisticated metal detector. I figured if I had to listen to Wagner's The Ring when we played around with the safe room design, I'd incorporate a magic ring that gave its wearer special powers. In this case, he'd press his hand on the scanner to gain entry. The scanner will unlock the door when it detects the metal and mineral content of a unique ring."

"Or in this case, a crucifix is the key," said Christa.

"Of course," Braydon said. "When we get through this you, me and O'Malley got a date at McSorley's. Drinks are on me." He placed the crucifix on the scanner. The door slid aside with an ethereal whoosh.

Christa felt her hand clasp Braydon's. It was like a world opened up to them and they were the first to see it. He squeezed her fingers. Together, they stepped across the threshold.

"We are still underground," she said. "Right?" The chamber wasn't even that big, once she got her bearings.

"Seven sides," Braydon said, "appropriate."

"Only ten feet across, but look up there." She pointed towards the high-domed ceiling. It was painted like a cerulean sky blazing with bright halogen lights centered in gold leaf starbursts. "It feels more like a transportation device than a room," she said. And, in a way, it was.

Books and artifacts crowded the walls, beckoning to them to explore other times, other worlds. The "sky" was held aloft by seven classical pillars, one in each interior angle. The door they just entered was flanked by four walls, two to either side of them. Each featured a built-in bookcase, seven shelves high, crammed with books. She drew in closer. They were religious volumes, various versions and translations of the Bible, a complete Jewish Encyclopedia, the Book of Mormon. The third wall to her left featured a collage of framed prints.

Most startling of all was the seventh wall. A life-size depiction of a man dressed in robes, wearing a golden, bejeweled Breastplate, looked like he might step right into the room. The old, bearded man held out his arms in supplication. "Aaron," she said, "brother of Moses. The high priest of ancient Judaism." His expression looked up in pure adoration towards a central, bright light, surrounded by a modernized sun, its seven gilt rays curving outwards to fill the interior of a cupola that formed the hub of the dome. This sun spotlighted a circular pedestal table, about waist-high, in the center of the chamber. The table's top was a map of the world, rendered in a mosaic of lapus lazuli, malachite and marble.

The door slid shut behind them with a hiss and a final thud of a steel bolt sliding back into place.

"That son of a gun finally got me trapped in a library," said Braydon.

"Father O'Malley certainly has an affinity for drama."

"Religion without drama is like a sky without clouds, he always said. I expected to find the Urim and Thummim, not a library teaching about it."

"The stones are here," she said. The electric tingling was so strong it buzzed.

"Lots of clues to their location. Not much time." He looked at his watch. "I figure we got four minutes before Rambitskov finds us." He crossed to the panel with the framed prints, taking particular interest in the one with the old-fashioned mason's square and compass surrounding the letter G, the symbol of the Freemasons. "One of my ex-partners was a mason. Always hated it when cops said they were giving their collars the third degree. The expression started with the challenging questions of the master mason's third degree ceremony. Now it's given to criminals."

"Conroy said the masons, in their 13th, 14th and 21st degree ceremonies, teach that the Urim and Thummim were part of the treasury of Solomon's Temple," she said. "The Jewish Kabbalistic traditions concur."

He pointed to the painting of a man, dressed in nineteenth century clothing, kneeling in a grove of trees, shielding his eyes against a bright light shining from above. "Joseph Smith, founder of the Mormon church, seeing the light from the angel, Moroni. What's he doing here, besides looking holier than thou?"

"Moroni presented Joseph Smith with gold plates that contained the Book of Mormon." She quickly rehashed Conroy's tutorial. "Smith used Urim and Thummim to translate it. I bet O'Malley and Zeke didn't think much of that story, considering the stones were supposed to be under the protection of the Circle of Seven since the sixteenth century."

"Which would make Joseph Smith one of the Circle of Seven," said Braydon. "He used the power of the stones to create a new religion, before they were, once again, lost in history."

"That's all we need," she said. "More fodder for Baltasar's bid at becoming the next Prophet."

"Not if I can stop him. This chamber doesn't follow my safe room design, but I know Tommy. To him and that rabbi, the Urim and Thummim are the center of their world." He rested his palms on the rim of the round map table in the hub of the room. He pointed to the lapus lazuli letter tiles set in the malachite that curved around the outer edges of the world map on its east and west perimeter. "Lux to the west. Veritas to the east." He pointed to six empty squares along the map's northern rim. "So what goes here?"

Christa ran her fingertip over the letters. "It's not smooth. I can feel the edges of the letter tiles. Do you see a pocket knife anywhere in here?"

Braydon slid an object from his suit coat's inner pocket. He handed her a pocket knife. She recognized the scout logo. "Don't tell me," she said. "Eagle scout?"

"On my honor," Braydon said.

Her first love was an Eagle Scout. They had met on the beach in Portugal, where he was vacationing with his family for a week. *Spring break*, he called it. He was so American, so happy to be with her, so accepting of her family's eccentricities. But if he had tried to reach her after returning home, she'd never have known it. She never had a dependable address growing up.

She pried open Braydon's blade. With a little maneuvering that felt like sacrilege, she wedged out the L tile from the "Lux." She quickly pried out the rest of the tiles, placing them across the expanse of the green malachite Asia. "The six spaces must be for an anagram." She scrambled them, sliding them into different combinations. "Travel?"

Braydon shook his head. "Tommy hated to travel, but he loved the Latin language. He always yearned for the pre-Vatican II days, when the mass was celebrated in Latin."

"Good," she said. "I'm fluent in Latin."

"Of course you are," said Braydon.

"My parents made sure of it. Learning Latin was *sine qua non* in the Devlin clan."

"Well, *tempus fugit*."

"We also played a lot of Scrabble," she said. She shuffled the letters, switching her mindset to Latin roots.

He edged around her to scan the bookshelves. "Bibles, every one of them," he said. "Different versions, translations." He moved to the next bookcases. "Translations of the Book of Mormon, the Torah." He crossed to the other bookcases, finally zeroing in on a bright yellow paperback. "Here's one for the rest of us." She nodded at the title as he showed it to her, *Latin for Lay People.*

"Imagine what the translators could do with that title."

"Just remember this quote by Seneca," he said, opening to a center page. *"Fallaces sunt rerum species."*

"The outward appearances of things are deceiving," she translated. "Very appropriate, considering we're in a secret chamber beneath one of the most visited cathedrals in the world." She quickly shuffled the letters into different combinations. The word teased the back of her mind, screaming for her to hear it. It began with a V. She slid the V into the first empty square. The next letter had to be a vowel, most likely I. She slid it in.

"Urim and Thummim were used as divining stones," he said, thumbing through the paperback's pages. "The high priest would use the stones for judgment, to decide if a man was evil or good, guilty or innocent, cowardly or brave. Lux, light. Veritas, truth." He paused. She could feel the word now. She slid in the R, then the T. Braydon slammed closed the volume in his hand. She slipped in the U. Only one empty square remained. She turned to him. They caught each other's gaze and smiled. "Virtus," they said together.

"Meaning virtue," she said, "courage."

"It's listed in this book with other common uses of Lux and Veritas. Lux, Veritas, Virtus is the motto of Northeastern University" said Braydon.

She slid the S into the last spot. In the next instant, a shudder, a loud bang, and the world spun out of control.

CHAPTER 47

Christa raised her hands away from the map table. Its top rotated, spinning the map of the world. The *Lux* side now faced east, *Veritas* west, and the intact letters of *Virtus*, upside down. From deep within the pedestal base of the map table came a series of clicks, then the whir of a motor. "Are you sure your friend, O'Malley, wouldn't use poison gas?"

The spinning stopped. A whoosh of expelled air. She held her breath, just in case, for all the good that would do. The inner circle, containing the mosaic of the world map, lifted upwards.

Seven chrome posts smoothly raised the top of the table. With a whisper, it stopped. She crouched to see into the velvet compartment revealed beneath. Braydon came beside her, his lips parted, eyes wide. "I see wonderful things," she whispered. It was her father's favorite quote when they found a remarkable archaeological artifact in his digs. Harry Burton made the words famous when he first laid eyes on Tutankhamen's tomb brimming with splendid golden treasure. But that find was nothing compared to this.

There, in an unornamented silver box, hardly big enough to hold a pen set, lay a deep red ruby and a golden topaz, brilliant against the black velvet cushion. The gemstones emitted a light from within, a palpable energy. Hardly bigger than a robin's egg, each gem held within it a compacted force, waiting to be unleashed. They captured the brightness of the spotlight shining down from the stylized sun directly above and tripled it, refracting it around the chamber like a sunrise glinting off a pool of rippling water. "Urim and Thummim," she said, her throat dry. She had to have them, to hold them in her hands. A voice, somewhere in the distance, shouted a warning.

*Wait!* The brilliance of the stones blinded and deafened. Nothing existed outside the Urim and Thummim.

She reached in and lifted the box, tilting it between two of the seven posts, drawing it closer to her, freeing the gems from the confines of their little temple.

A sharp pain in her wounded arm. Braydon gripped her. She'd never told him that she'd been shot. He didn't realize he was hurting her. "Didn't you hear me," he said. "This could be booby-trapped."

The silver box weighed heavier in her hands. The ruby and topaz winked in the diffuse light outside the spotlight of the stylized sun. This wasn't the Temple of Solomon, centuries before Christa walked the Earth. They were beneath Saint Patrick's Cathedral, in New York City, with bad guys breathing down their necks. "Your friend wouldn't have sent us down here if he didn't want us to have the Urim and Thummim."

"More like he doesn't want anyone else to have them," he said. "O'Malley would count on me to deactivate any traps before I tripped them."

A loud bang hammered the steel entry door. "Fox!" a man's voice yelled from behind it. "Open up, or I'll blow down this door!"

A sickening thud reverberated throughout the chamber. The floor rumbled and shook. Braydon caught her arm and steadied her as the jolt nearly knocked her off her feet.

"Rambitskov," Braydon muttered. "And he's not just huff and puff."

"Did he really just set off explosives beneath Saint Patrick's?"

"That wasn't him," he said. "Didn't sound like C-4. It came from beneath us."

A deafening grinding noise filled the chamber. Braydon widened his stance and steadied her as the floor shook again, shifting beneath them. Clouds of dust and cement powder billowed from the perimeter of the room. At her feet, the inner circle of the floor rotated 180 degrees. "You know those revolving restaurants on top of skyscrapers," she said. "I went to one once in Tokyo. Got sick." The floor continued to rotate while the seven-sided perimeter remained still. "This is worse."

"I'll keep that in mind on our first date," said Braydon. A lurch knocked them both to their knees. The floor began ascending, just as the hub of the table had risen to reveal Urim and Thummim.

"Set the C-4," Rambitskov's voice called urgently from behind the door. "Now!"

She crouched next to Braydon. The floor rose at an alarming rate. She grabbed his shoulder. "I don't want to get to heaven this way," she shouted over the din of the grinding motors and gears beneath them. The ethereal "sky" of the domed ceiling looked uplifting, but would surely crush them.

"On the table, now!" shouted Braydon. His hands clamped around her. He was stronger than he let on. In one fluid movement, he lifted her on top of the map table. She reached down, grabbed his elbow and helped him as he hoisted himself up. They pressed together and stood, the gun in his hip holster hard against her. Their embrace was essential, with no wriggle room for the two of them, heels on the perimeter of the table top. Essential. Right.

He snaked his arm up, stretched to reach the highest part of the dome, the round section highlighted with gilt rays of the sun. "Looks like this table top is made to just fit inside the dome," he said.

"If it didn't have two, soon to be pulverized, human beings on it."

"Tommy wouldn't let anyone die like this, being crushed by heaven," he said. "Heaven represents life, not death." He grabbed the edge of one of the sun's rays with his fingertips and leaned his weight into it, trying to turn it, like a jar lid. She hugged him tighter to steady him. It didn't budge.

The floor and, with it, the table they were precariously perched on, rose higher. One arm clamped around him, she stretched her free arm into the circular space. Standing on tiptoes, her fingers could just reach the ray of sun. She wrapped her leg around his thigh, her skirt rising up, her bare skin against the smooth wool of his suit pants. It worked. She could reach high enough to line up her fingertips next to his. "Heave," she shouted.

"The sun," Braydon shouted. "We're turning the sun!"

She clamped her arm and leg tighter around him and pressed. With a deafening explosion, it all went black.

CHAPTER **48**

A massive fist slammed into Christa's back. It knocked the air from her lungs. She clamped her hands over her ears. Something wet and sticky oozed from them. Blood? That wasn't the main problem. Her brain spun wildly. She sucked in air. Big mistake. It was thick with dust and concrete powder. The coughing fit hit her like a boxer rapid punches a speed bag. Braydon clamped her shoulders, his eyes searching hers. His face and hair were powdered gray with the fine dust. Amazingly, both of them hadn't been thrown from their precarious, and still rising, table top. He shouted something at her. Looked like a question. Are you okay? She couldn't hear it over the high-pitched ringing.

Through the ringing, muffled shouts, from below. Flashlight beams sliced through the rising dust clouds, strafing the seven sided perimeter. Rambitskov. He must have blown open the door into the chamber below them. It wouldn't take him long to figure out that the two people he was chasing were high above them, on the round platform of a table that was still lifting upwards like a stage elevator.

Braydon shook her, pointed up. He stood, grabbed the rim of the sun's ray, strained to turn it like a giant screw. No, not a screw. A lid. Their table breached the bottom edge of circular cupola. Knees knocked and legs knotted together as they squeezed into a crouch. The ceiling and certain death would crush them in less than a minute. Crushed by heaven. Ironic. While wrapped around a man. Didn't even want to go there. She pressed tighter against Braydon, grabbed his belt to keep his foot from slipping off the table top to be trapped and squeezed flat between it and the cupola wall. The ringing in her ears faded. The gunshots got louder. Bullets slammed into the bottom of the table top. High caliber. Each strike shot a jolt up against the soles of her boots. The map of the world beneath her feet was either going to kill them, or save them.

She pressed her fingertips against the curving ray of sun. A shift of weight. The entire sun twisted beneath her fingers. Braydon grabbed her to save her balance. They pushed again. Something clicked into place.

"Tommy always said a virtuous man could move heaven and earth!" Braydon yelled. He bent over her. She ducked lower. He pressed his back onto the sun and pushed up, struggling to straighten his legs. She reached up on either side or him, flattened her palms against the ceiling, her cheek against his. Together, they pushed upwards. It lifted!

Braydon shifted around, grabbed the circular lid by its rim, heaved it up and pushed it aside. Daylight above! Gloom had never held such promise. Horns honked. Exhaust fumes fingered through the cement powder hanging in the air. The table beneath them continued to rise. Braydon pulled her to standing. She shoved the disc of ceiling away from their small opening. From the top, it looked like an ordinary manhole cover. She scrambled onto the sidewalk. He hoisted himself out behind her. The table top filled the hole, becoming flush with the sidewalk, the blue lapus lazuli and green malachite of the world map scuffed with footprints and dusted in gray.

She nudged Braydon and pointed to Saint Patrick's, across Fifth Avenue. They had traveled an entire crosstown block in the underground tunnel system. Two black SUVs hunkered like guard dogs in front of the cathedral, parked in haste and self-importance, their front tires pawing the sidewalk. A uniformed police officer, hand poised on the butt of his gun, approached the vehicles with slow caution, until his peripheral vision alerted him. He crouched lower, craning his neck to see them through the clutter of yellow cabs speeding down Fifth Avenue in a survival of the fittest race to make the light.

Two grandmotherly tourists stopped just a few feet away to gape at them, these strange, gray creatures creeping up from the underworld. The lady in the red wool coat snapped Braydon's photo with a disposable 35mm camera. "Isn't this exciting, Martha," said the one in the cableknit hat. "They're filming a movie right here. Only in New York," she laughed.

Behind her on the corner, a man wearing a blue windbreaker emblazoned with the yellow, block letters, FBI, had spotted them, too. He was breathing hard, his chest heaving from exertion. One of Rambitskov's men? Who could tell the players anymore? Except for Braydon's gray patina, the guy looked like him. Crew cut brown hair, six-two, all bones and muscle, chiseled movie-star face. He even had Braydon's characteristic slump, as if he didn't want to intimidate anyone unnecessarily. She jammed the silver box containing Urim and Thummim into her daypack. Didn't matter what side this new player believed in, she could run pretty fast, and deal with this on her own, before surrendering the stones to anyone.

Thunder rumbled. The old ladies pouted at the dark sky. "Thunder in December," the one in the cableknit hat remarked. "I never heard of such a thing." They hadn't heard nothing yet.

The FBI man started towards them. The beat cop across the street, with the suspicious way he approached those SUVs, he couldn't possibly be on Rambitskov's payroll. She waved her arms at him. The FBI guy wouldn't dare shoot with a cop watching.

The cop was watching, all right, and drawing his gun and aiming it straight at her. "Demon!" he yelled. "From the underworld! I'll send you back to hell!" He crouched into a shooting stance. Braydon grabbed her, swung her around and flung her behind a large granite pedestal. She fell hard, scraping her palms and knees, then rolled onto her back. The massive bronze sculpture of muscle-bound Atlas towered above her, on top of the granite pedestal. The Art Deco Atlas bent under the weight of the intersecting rings of the cosmos balanced on his shoulders. *My God, an armillary sphere.*

Braydon dove for the old ladies, positioning his body between them and the cop. More shots blasted from Saint Patrick's. The FBI agent on the corner rushed toward them, yanked his gun from a shoulder holster as he ran, and targeted the cop. She glanced around the edge of the pedestal. The cop dove for cover behind the parked SUV. The FBI man shot twice, both rounds punching holes into the SUV next to the one the cop hid behind, most likely, just where he was aiming. The ladies rounded the corner towards Rockefeller Plaza with surprising, if awkward, speed. The FBI man and Braydon raced to Christa's side, diving for the cover of the pedestal. They pressed their backs against the granite, bracing either side of her, handguns up and ready.

"Hello, Fox," the man said.

Braydon acknowledged him with a nod. "Neidemeyer."

Neidemeyer was breathing faster and harder than she was. "Rambitskov's got the entire New York field office looking for you," he said. "Ordered to pick you up for questioning in an attempted murder at The Plaza."

"Attempted?"

"Jared Sadler is alive, barely."

"Talking?"

"Coma," Neidemeyer said. "You feel like turning yourself in, making my life easy?"

"Can't accommodate," said Braydon. "Got to save the world."

"Again?" A bullet thudded into Atlas's massive metal foot of the statue, right above her head. It sliced a shiny, bronze gash through the patina. "I would tell you what Fox did," he said to her, "but then I'd have to shoot you, and it seems like you got enough trouble right now."

"I need her," said Braydon. "Without her, I don't stand a chance." Christa wasn't sure what to think of that.

"Now I know you're in trouble," Neidemeyer said, "Miss?"

"Devlin," she said. That silver box in her pack dug into her spine. "Christa Devlin." They shook hands. His grip was firm; the gesture felt wildly out of place.

Neidemeyer popped up to check the status of the crazed cop, then ducked back down. "Rambitskov authorized deadly force to stop you, Fox. Maybe he's caught that bug that's turning people into raving lunatics," he said. "Maybe you have. That guy in the Plaza was under your protection. He was pinned to the floor by a sword. Evidence at the crime scene implicates you."

A gunshot. The bullet zinged off the granite to Christa's right. "It's a poison," she said, "in the water supply here and in the Princeton suburbs. Not everybody will be affected, but most will. It makes people violent, then kills them, if they haven't already been murdered. Seven days after ingestion, the victim is dead."

Neidemeyer frowned. "I'd say you were the one who is crazy," he said, "but across the street one of NYPD's finest is shooting at you because you're demons."

"You've got to get the word out, Neidemeyer, without inciting panic," said Braydon. "Blame it on a microbe that causes severe stomachaches or something, but warn people not to drink the water. And don't go through Rambitskov. He's with the dark side on this one."

Neidemeyer pursed his lips and narrowed his eyes. "Rambitskov is a nasty piece of work, no doubt about that. The minute I heard he had you trapped in Saint Patrick's, I double-timed it down here. But the man's got red, white and blue running in his veins. He'd never betray his country, kill Americans."

"His plan is to save them," said Braydon. "He wanted to send the G-20 a message, that they better listen because we have a bio-weapon ready to be deployed for which we have the only defense. Problem is, Rambitskov doesn't know his mastermind of a boss doesn't have the antidote yet."

"Got any proof?"

"No time for proof," said Braydon. "Like when we jumped on those neo-Nazis with the dirty bomb in the diamond district. If we waited for proof then, New York City would be a radioactive wasteland. I've got to track down the antidote to the poison and I've got to get it before the bad guys. It's complicated and sounds crazy, but our best shot is to follow the leads to the antidote. As far as we know, it's the only way to save those people."

Neidemeyer's gaze reached down the street to Christa's left. A young couple were going at it, screaming, gesticulating. Their little girl, in a frilly pink dress, cried, kicking and jerking against the safety straps of her stroller. Christa tensed, ready to race over there, scoop up the little girl. At any moment, the crazed policeman could target the child.

The phantoms appeared, as real as the thunder and lightning. Six of them swooped and howled in the wind that whipped down the sidewalks.

Neidemeyer's expression was grim. "We all know something big is happening," he said. "Law enforcement is responding to so many assaults and fights it's like spitting on a wildfire. Even Tough-as-nails Thompson is scared. I've never seen him scared. He called his wife, told her to pack up the kids and head west."

The hairs rose up on the back of her neck. A sudden crash and blinding light ripped through the air. A lightning bolt exploded the top spire of the cathedral.

Static electricity sizzled across Atlas's metal spheres dancing across them in a blinding, blue light. The three of them pressed closer together. The glow fizzled out.

"Okay, something's crazy," said Neidemeyer, "and it's not us."

She pointed at the sphere. Her finger trembled. "The planets," she said, "they're aligned."

Neidemeyer looked at her, narrowed his eyes. "Then again."

"I must have walked by this sculpture a hundred times, but never really noticed. It's an armillary sphere," Braydon said, "like that artifact you found in Arizona."

"A clue to the location of the Turquoise, one of the seven stones." She grabbed his hand. "The spheres are designed to be manipulated. Align the planets. I should have thought of that before. We've got to get to Percival's house, solve the puzzle of the sphere and be on tonight's flight to Phoenix."

He gripped her fingers tightly to hold her down. "Agreed, but let's get there alive." He spun around, quickly stood up, took a shot at the cop. Thwacks zinged the other side of the pedestal as the cop fired back, three times. Braydon crouched back down. "Who is this guy, NYPD's sharpshooter of the year?"

Neidemeyer slipped his wallet out of his back pocket, opened it, and removed all the money he had, pressing it into Braydon's hand. Looked like a couple hundred dollars. He topped the cash with his Mastercard. He hesitated, then unclipped his badge from his wallet. "I would never do this," he said, "for anyone, except you, Fox." He handed Braydon the badge. "You'll need it. Rambitskov put your name on the no-fly list."

"Work it on your end," said Braydon. "There's a retired Colonel, Donohue, has a connection in CDC testing the water. Slim chance, but maybe the only one, if we don't make it back."

Neidemeyer sucked in a deep breath. "Listen, Fox, they're keeping the press in the dark, but kids are dying," he said. "Two in the last hour. Dozens more are already in comas. Old folks, too. You got to make it back." He checked the ammunition in his handgun. "You figure our boy in blue across the street got the standard issue Smith and Wesson 5946?"

"Sounds like," said Braydon. Two more bullets zinged off Atlas's calves, clawing out bronze gashes. "That's it. By my count, he's empty."

"I got this one," said Neidemeyer. "You two get out of here before Rambitskov rises from the underworld behind you."

Neidemeyer leaped up and rushed out from behind the pedestal. Christa stole a look around the edge. Braydon, to her left, trained his gun on the crazed cop, but the cop was just standing there, in the open, staring up at the spires of Saint Patrick's, where the lightning had struck. Neidemeyer dodged through the line of yellow cabs, their horns blaring and brakes squealing. The cop, really, he looked fresh out of college, a rookie. Still looking to the charred remains of the spire, he raised his pistol to his temple. Christa started towards him. Braydon held her back. Neidemeyer tackled the kid.

Neidemeyer held the cop to the ground with his knee and cuffed him. The couple with the stroller still fought each other, oblivious to the danger and their tormented toddler. The poor kid, tears streaming down her flushed cheeks, her dolly dashed in agony to the sidewalk, just out of reach. Christa pulled against Braydon as he hurried her way. "I've got to help that little girl," she said.

"The only way to save her, Christa, is to leave her behind."

# CHAPTER 49

His ears still ringing from the blaring alarm, Daniel could envision the hand of God guiding the speeding SUV, as easily as a boy pushes a matchbox car. Rambitskov was behind the wheel, but Daniel was driving the situation. As the iron gates eased open to let them pass into Contreras's estate, Daniel imagined the gates of heaven opening for him.

Rambitskov was a moron. He had let the priest and rabbi off scot free. The idiot wouldn't believe that those two "holy" men had built that underground chamber to hide the Urim and Thummim. Rambitskov hadn't even heard of Urim and Thummim, the two most sacred stones in history. Worse, he hadn't caught Fox.

To think Braydon Fox was with Christa now. She'd see him for what he was, a brute, a trickster. She'd know that Fox coerced him into the trap in the secret hallway beneath Saint Patrick's, in a vain attempt to make him look like a fool in front of Christa. Worse, Fox ripped his best chance to possess the Urim and Thummim from his grasp. It wasn't the poison that was smoldering inside him, flaming up to thoughts of a justified revenge. He'd smote Fox down.

He'd get Rambitskov, too, for mocking him when he had freed him from the trap. He wasn't scared, even when Rambitskov threatened to deliver him to Contreras, who had almost killed him in a most excruciating manner with that poison dart frog. That's just what Daniel wanted. He could have demanded his right to a lawyer. He could plead for mercy. He would have none of that. He would not trade his destiny so readily. He had a plan.

He leaped down from the SUV as soon as it squealed to a stop. Rambitskov's claw of a hand gripped his upper arm. He refused to wince as Rambitskov dragged him into Baltasar Contreras's mansion, through the ostentatious foyer, to the library. Rambitskov shoved him over the threshold. Baltasar paced by the window, arguing loudly, although he was alone in the room. Beyond the panes of glass, the wind bullied the barren trees, cracking off branches and thrashing them to the ground. What in hell? It looked like one of Christa's dark phantoms, pressed up to the window, glaring, ravenous, but the stormy afternoon was too black for shadows. .

Baltasar crossed the room to the wet bar behind the desk. Everything reeked of wealth. Silver tongs to plink three cubes into his crystal glass. The musical ring of fine crystal as Baltasar lifted the topper off the decanter. "Mister Dubler," he said, pouring himself what looked like Scotch. "You have one minute to convince me not to kill you. Mister Rambitskov, would you be so kind to mind the time?"

The words slapped him in the face. "Kill me?" he said, his voice suddenly hoarse. This wasn't part of the plan. "If the Amazing Hulk, here, hadn't come barging into the cathedral, I'd have the Urim and Thummim in my possession. The Tear of the Moon Emerald, too."

"Fifty-five seconds," said Rambitskov.

"We had an agreement," said Daniel. "You need my expertise in theology and history. Once we restore the Breastplate, I will know best how to use it to communicate with God."

"My ancestor, Alvaro, needed no interpreter."

"Your ancestor failed," said Daniel. "He was wearing the complete Breastplate, but he was defeated by a mongrel crew of sailors and a priest. He did not have my foundation of knowledge."

Baltasar downed his Scotch and poured another. "Rambo, please note that he loses five seconds for each annoying riposte."

"You want to restore the Breastplate to create a new religion," pressed Daniel, "a new world order, ruled by one leader, so that the world will finally be at peace. I've seen the Abraxas website. I know you're the Prophet. You have promised your virtual flock that you would soon communicate to them the true word of God through the restored Breastplate of Aaron. The world needs one leader to attain a global peace. It dovetails with my theory of the ultimate empire. I am part of that vision. You recruited me because I am the only theologian, the only man who can make our vision a reality."

"Your hubris is admirable," said Baltasar, "but I recruited you because I saw you were in the best position to weasel your way into a relationship with the Christa Devlin. Now, Devlin has, how is it said these days, "hooked up" with another man, a far better man, a man against whom you don't stand a chance. Braydon Fox."

Daniel stomped towards Baltasar, but Rambitskov yanked him back. "Braydon Fox," he sputtered. "He doesn't believe in the power of the Breastplate. He can't possibly understand the force of history upon the present. Christa Devlin will never see him the way she sees me."

"Time's up," said Rambitskov.

Daniel crossed to the massive desk and the comparatively small, but so much more powerful, laptop computer. "You are on the verge of starting a new world religion. The catalyst is the restored Breastplate. Your followers are amassed, waiting for the Word, from God, through the Breastplate, through the Internet. You need men, holy men, men schooled in reaching the soul. I stand with you on that threshold."

"Threshold," Baltasar echoed in a whisper. The clink of the ice in his glass splintered through the death-like silence in the room as he set his glass on the corner of the desk. "Best to end with a truth, Mister Dubler," he said. "You will, indeed, realize your dream to talk directly with God."

"I vow to fulfill your destiny," said Daniel, a huge wash of relief and satisfaction flooding over him, "just as I must fulfill mine."

"Your only destiny is a shallow grave," said Baltasar. "I hope you are ready to meet your maker. Mister Rambitskov, have your man take Mister Dubler out back to the hemlock grove and shoot him. I must dress for dinner."

This couldn't be happening, not to him. Rambitskov's claw clamped down again on his arm. He winced with pain. Rambitskov dragged him across the threshold. "Wait," he called out. He had to succeed, save his own life for a greater purpose, even if it might cost the life of an innocent little girl. "Percival Hunter has mounted a rescue operation to free Lucia. He's coming any second with a strike force of retired Special Forces guys. He texted Christa about it."

Baltasar held up his hand, palm out, to stop Rambitskov. For a long moment, nothing moved. Despite the persistent ringing in his ears, Daniel could hear the howl of the wind outside and the wild beat of his heart thumping against his chest. "Put Mister Dubler in the conservatory," said Baltasar. "The girl is there, eating her ice cream sundae for dessert. Then meet me in my dressing room. We must be gone before the strike force arrives."

Rambitskov sneered at Daniel, squeezed tight his grip. "I got no problem mowing down a bunch of old rogues," he growled.

"No doubt these "old rogues" have families, friends in the military," said Baltasar. "They're the heroic type. They'll be missed. Killing them on my estate would compromise my endgame. The little girl has been well-played, but sacrificing my pawn is now my best move. I will both seduce my opponent with false hope and divert attention so I can position my bishop to attack from an unexpected angle." Cunning shone in his eyes, the expression of determined genius that had first earned Daniel's commitment to his enterprise. "Mister Dubler, perhaps I have use for you yet. Remember your Genesis. If you are to play the serpent, then you must be subtle."

# CHAPTER 50

Percival crouched low and pressed his back against the twelve-foot-high stone wall that surrounded the perimeter of the Contreras estate. Lucia, his little princess, he could feel her presence, beyond the wall, inside that fortress of a mansion. Donohue's "recon" man reported her "safe." That guaranteed nothing. Contreras, that madman, he'd kill him if he hurt her. Throttle him with bare hands. But he couldn't. Contreras had poisoned Liam, still in a coma, his skin pale, his eyes shut. Christa had said what Contreras made her drink was probably the antidote, albeit temporary. He needed that antidote. He'd do anything to buy Liam more time. And Gabriella, he couldn't let her down. He had to rescue Lucia and Liam and help her, their next best chance at finding the antidote plant.

He shifted the weight of the Kevlar vest that Donohue had forced him to wear. The waiting was excruciating. The twilight, already darkened by the storm, quickly lowered the boom into the black of a December night. Lucia was scared of the dark. He closed his eyes, pictured the stone wall from the satellite photo. Twelve feet high, three hundred foot perimeter, two feet thick. Do the math. Focus on that. Not on Lucia and Liam's faces and the specter of failure.

Donohue showed no such doubt. This wasn't the first time the man was leading a covert assault. But that wasn't some terrorist hive in there, it was his daughter. He raised the eyepieces of the night vision goggles to talk face to face. "With all due respect, Donohue," he said in a low voice, as the strike force of six men fanned out to either side of the iron gate, "that's my little girl in there. Once your man cuts off the power, I can get in and get her out, no gunfire."

"We stick with the plan," Donohue said. Suddenly, he raised a closed fist. "Don't move," he whispered.

The iron gates to the estate rolled open. A Rolls Royce Phantom cruised through, taking its time, exuding arrogance.

Percival leaned forward. "That's Baltasar Contreras," he said, "in the back seat." Beside him sat a muscular man in a dark suit. "No sign of Lucia." He scanned the interior of the Rolls frantically. "You don't suppose she's in the trunk, do you? She could be in the trunk. We've got to stop him."

"Steady, Percival," Donohue said. "My man reports that Lucia is still in the conservatory. I don't have the manpower to tail Contreras. Mission priority is rescuing Lucia." He angled his head away, pressed on his earpiece and listened, then faced Percival. "We got the cook cleaning up in the kitchen, the butler neatening up the library, the housekeeper turning down a bed upstairs and a new player, a man in the conservatory with Lucia." Donohue flicked on his phone, showed him a photo. "You know him?"

"Daniel Dubler, what is he doing here?"

"That last email from Christa, she said she was in Saint Patrick's with Daniel."

"That's him," he said. "Contreras hired him as historian on Gabriella's Colombia expedition last summer. Wait, this is good news. He and Christa take the kids to the playground. Lucia, she won't be so scared now."

"So he's a friendly?"

"He's a history teacher, for God's sake. Contreras is gone. I'll just go in there and get Lucia out to safety. I'll not risk her life with gunplay, Colonel."

Donohue tapped on the tiny microphone on his earpiece. "Man in conservatory is a friendly. Go, go, go."

The spotlights illuminating the drive and the façade of the mansion flicked out, pitching the grounds into darkness. Percival quickly twisted to look through the bars of the iron gate. The lights in the mansion's windows went dark. The night was black, with heavy clouds obscuring any light from the moon or stars. When he turned back, Donohue had lowered his night vision goggles. Percival did the same, casting the scene in an eerie green. Donohue tapped his radio button twice.

On either side of him, six grappling hooks arced to the top of the wall. Each man scrambled up with surprising agility, considering they were all retired military and at least in their sixties. He followed Donohue, as the man shimmied up effortlessly. The rope was rough. The exertion demanding. Each of the strike force was outfitted with semi-automatics, but he had a taser pistol in the hip holster knocking against his side. The Taser X26, Donohue had explained, was a "stun gun" with a laser sight and reach of thirty-five feet, the first weapon of choice for this unsanctioned operation. The weight of it was both terrifying and reassuring.

He straddled the top of the wall, the wind slapping him with the branches of the thick evergreens. He slipped to the interior of the wall, hung from his fingertips and dropped into the bed of pachysandra below, the impact jarring his feet and knees.

Donohue raised a closed fist, the stop signal, and checked the position of his men. Donohue crouched next to him. "Stay low," he said. "Assume that the internal security cams are on an override and are still operational. And assume armed guards in the interior rooms that my man couldn't see." Armed guards. As marks on the schematic, they had seemed innocuous. Now, sweat beaded on his brow despite the bitter gusts. He recognized Donohue's next signal. Advance. The conservatory was at the rear of the mansion, facing the woods. He followed Donohue as the men split into two groups and flanked the mansion on either side.

They rounded the far corner. Percival let out a whimper. His heart lurched into his throat. In the ghastly green monotone of the night vision goggles, Lucia sat at a table just beyond the glass walls of the conservatory, her back towards him. She was looking around in all directions in the pitch black, frightened, anxious. She clutched a Barbie doll. She reached, unseeing, towards the dark, open laptop in front of her, as if willing it to wake up and say hello. Thunder rumbled in the distance, rattling the greenhouse walls. Lucia twisted round, clutching her knees to her chest. She hated thunder. Percival saw Daniel, too, through his night vision goggles, feeling his way around the table in the dark, the man's arms waving blindly in front of him to guide him.

Percival caught up to Donohue as the man crouched and held up a closed fist. The other two men with them had advanced to the door leading into the kitchen, somehow keeping an eye on Donohue. They stopped, crouched.

Lucia, he couldn't wait another second. She was right there. With only Daniel. No guards in sight. This might be his only chance. He sprinted across the open lawn to the rear door of the conservatory. His legs pounded ahead so fast he nearly tripped over himself. His heart hammered in his chest. His breaths came quick and shallow. Donohue's voice behind him, a muffled shout into the radio. "Rabbit on the loose." What the hell was that supposed to mean? He lunged for the glass door, grabbed the lever handle, yanked it up, down, pushed, pulled. Locked. He rattled the handle furiously.

The strike force was attacking, he was sure of it. They'd be blasting in, guns blazing. Three from the east side of the mansion, two from the west. He and Donohue were to "secure" the conservatory. A shout come from the dining room, then the clash and clatter of pans falling in the kitchen. Two of the men were then to head upstairs, join up with the recon man who had entered through the balcony window and acquire the housekeeper. The men downstairs had to subdue any unforeseen guards.

In the conservatory, Lucia hugged her legs. She was crying, distraught, looking around wildly at the sounds, not able to see the scary things that could have made them. He snatched the taser from its holster. He smashed the butt of the gun into the pane next to the door latch. The glass shattered to the floor. He reached in, turned the lock and kicked the door inward. The goggles obstructed his peripheral vision, but he sensed movement behind him. Donohue pushed by him, rushing across the conservatory for the door that led into the main house. The colonel disappeared into the darkness of the interior.

Daniel, crouching, banged his thigh into the corner of the glass table. The jolt shook the laptop awake. The light from the monitor, amplified by the night vision goggles, hit Percival like a blinding beam. Lucia screamed hysterically. Percival's eyes adjusted enough to see Daniel lunge for her and embrace her as they both stared at him in horror.

"Lucia," he called out. She screamed all the louder, an anguished panic. Dropping her Barbie to the ground, she clung onto Daniel. He must look like a monster. He ripped the night vision goggles from his head and reached out his arms.

"Behind you," Daniel yelled. He swooped Lucia off her chair and curled around her, shielding her with his back.

Percival spun around. A man burst through the conservatory door from the back yard, gun drawn. Percival raised the Taser, aimed, fired. Wires spiraled outward, hitting the man in his chest. A nauseating, electric buzz zapped through the conservatory. The man grimaced, shaking wildly, arms flailing, then collapsed to the floor. A wisp of acrid smoke twisted through the scent of citrus and peat. Percival twisted toward Lucia. She was still beneath Daniel. Thank God she hadn't seen what her daddy had done. He swallowed hard, or, in another moment, she'd see him throwing up. He set the Taser behind a red-berried bush to his side.

Daniel looked up cautiously, his wide, frightened eyes taking in the guard lying, arms and legs splayed, unconscious. Lucia pressed her hands over her eyes.

She was all right. Everything was going to be all right. "Lucia," he said. "I've come to take you home." She slowly pried apart two fingers to peak through. He held out his arms. She pushed off Daniel's chest and rushed into his embrace.

"All clear." It was Donohue's voice, breathing hard, coming from the main house. It seemed very far away, beyond the invisible shield that Percival had mentally lowered around him and Lucia. The lights turned back on. Donohue crossed the threshold into the conservatory. Although he was decked out in black special ops clothing and gear, the man's face softened. He began to resemble his next door neighbor again. The stern colonel blinked the moisture from his eyes as he cleared his throat. "Three armed guards," he said. "My men have them locked away with the staff. They didn't even put up a fight. Shock and awe works, when implemented in the right situation."

"Shock, especially," said Percival, nodding to the guy sprawled on the floor behind him.

Donohue frowned. "Probably alerted by that crash when you busted through the door," he said.

Daniel stood, brushing off his pants. He drew nearer to Donohue. "Baltasar Contreras left here just minutes ago," he said. "We can't let him get away."

"Daniel Dubler," said Percival, "meet retired Colonel Clint Donohue, my next door neighbor."

"Neighbor?" Daniel asked. "Then the authorities haven't been alerted yet?"

Donohue stiffened his stance, crossed his arms over his chest. "We needed Lucia safe before we can go after Contreras," said Donohue. "We did what we had to do, when we had to do it. Hunter tells me you've been in contact with Christa. Where is she?"

"Didn't get caught by Contreras, if that's what you're worried about," answered Daniel. "It's a long story." He looked pointedly at Lucia. "Not G-rated. Suffice it to say you're going to need my help to help her."

"Debrief when we're out of here," said Donohue.

Percival offered his hand to Daniel. He had clearly misjudged the man. Daniel had protected Lucia, helped save her. "Thank you," he said. He couldn't think of anything else to say that came close to being adequate.

"Let's move," Donohue said. He hit his radio button four times.

Percival scooped Lucia up in his arms. She felt heavier than usual, a sure sign that she was exhausted. She was uncharacteristically quiet.

Donohue smoothed back a curl from her forehead. "Kids are tougher than we know," he said.

He nodded. He wasn't so sure. "Come on, Lucia. Let's get you safe."

Daniel picked up the Barbie from the floor and handed it to her, first brushing off the doll's hair and smoothing its dress.

Lucia pouted. "What about Mommy?"

He hugged her tighter. "Mommy will be home soon."

"Can you ask her when, through the computer?" she asked sleepily, letting her head rest on his shoulder. "Mister Profit let me talk to her. She's in the rainforest again, in Colombia."

Percival sucked in a breath. Donohue seemed to understand immediately the implication of what Lucia just told them. Contreras had Gabriella. That's why they hadn't been able to reach her. Donohue grabbed the computer mouse, bent to look at the monitor. It was the blank boot-up screen, asking for the user password. Donohue slammed his fist on the table. He shut the lid of the laptop, pulled out the cords connecting the power and mouse, and tucked it under his arm. "I knew this rescue was too easy," he said. "Fall back and regroup. We need a new plan."

Percival felt stunned. He had his daughter, safe, in his arms, but his wife was in grave danger, deep in the jungle, half a world away.

He felt Daniel's hand on his shoulder. "Percival, we'll get her back," said Daniel. "I have intimate knowledge of that area from our trip last summer. Trust me. Work with me. Tell me what you know. And I swear to you, Gabriella and Liam will be saved."

CHAPTER **51**

Baltasar's Rolls Royce Phantom eased to a stop by the Hudson River pier at the World Financial Center in downtown Manhattan. Little Lucia's innocent smile, her tender curls, teased his mind. Perhaps he should have kept her. A child that age would quickly get over missing her mother and father. It wouldn't be long before she accepted Baltasar as her real Dad. In the next few minutes, he would be well on his way to becoming the most powerful man on the planet. He would need a successor, one whom he could mold from a young age. And it was about time that a woman ruled the world. "Have you ever thought about having children, Rambo?"

"Yeah, that's why I don't have any," Rambo answered, without a hint of mirth. The man was inscrutable.

Baltasar's driver opened his door. The biting, howling wind sprang at him like a hungry beast from the water's edge. He stepped out of the car, shrugged into his tuxedo jacket and straightened his bow tie. He scrutinized the mega-yacht at the far pier. It dwarfed the other yachts and pitiful sailboats in front of it. One hundred and eighty feet long and three, tapering stories high, its sleek lines looked more ominous than pretentious, something Captain Nemo might design if he wanted to terrorize the seas from the surface rather than below it. Mohammad El-qazar owned it, the shadow who controlled the finances of Saudi Arabia. He had named his ship *The Flying Carpet*.

"There they are, Rambo," Baltasar said, "twenty of the most powerful people on Earth, in control of the most profitable corporations and, by rote, the twenty largest national economies around the globe. They call themselves the Alliance, but not since the gods of Mount Olympus has such a league of self-styled deities held so much hatred for their peers." They moved like shadows in the backlight of the windows that encircled the massive lounge on the yacht's main deck, and so they were. "They are the shadow G-20, the masters who pull the strings of the public G-20 finance ministers at the banquet tonight. They work to control the world through their huge conglomerates, from media monopolies to oil cartels, causing booms and busts, poverty and prosperity, war and peace."

Rambo skirted around the rear of the Phantom and came to his side. "If I were them," he said, nodding to *The Flying Carpet*, "I'd shoot you the minute you walked in."

"That is why you, my dear Rambo, are not them," he said. "They could have killed me with a single phone call, but their greed stopped them. They are trained not to leave money on the table, as they put it, at any deal. They thought I might still be useful to them."

"They kicked you out," said Rambo.

"They were afraid of my power," he said. "I love power. But it is as an artist that I love it. I love it as a musician loves his violin, to draw out its sounds and chords and harmonies."

"Nero?"

At least the man had recognized that what he just said was a quote. "Napoleon Bonaparte," Baltasar corrected.

"Before or after he was exiled to Elba?"

"Rambo, they are not gods," he said. "They only think they are. Indeed, they are quite vulnerable, as I shall show them."

"So are you. One bullet to your brain, then dump your body right over the side wrapped in a spare anchor chain," said Rambo. "No witnesses. Even the rats have gone into hiding."

"Eerie, isn't it?" He breathed in deeply. Despite the chill, a warmth tingled through his extremities. The streets were under a virtual martial law, emptied of all but the crazies and the cops. "It feels apocalyptic. I like it."

Rambo dug his phone from his pocket, read the text. "Homeland Security," Rambo said. "Christa Devlin is booked on the overnight flight to Phoenix. An FBI special agent is escorting her, badge said Neidemeyer. It's got to be Fox."

"For once my outrageous tax bill has gone to something useful," he said. "Homeland Security should be granted extraordinary powers. It comes in very handy."

"I got your private jet fueled and ready at Newark. I'll catch Fox and Devlin, after I make sure you live through this."

"Why, Rambo, I'm touched that you are concerned about my welfare."

"I'm concerned about my wealth," he said. "They kill you and our scheme is dead in the water."

Baltasar grinned at the play of words. Perhaps his friend had a sense of humor after all. "They will not kill their savior," he said. "No, my dear Rambo, you need to go after the gemstones. I'm counting on you for that."

"I'd feel better if I rode shotgun on this one. Nobody the wiser. Anyone with a uniform and a gun is tamping down the riots and fights. They're conveniently overwhelmed, with all the NYPD, FBI and Homeland Security guys we got manning the perimeter around the United Nations and Trump World Tower in response to the threat against the G-20 banquet."

"Pity the Lux et Veritas sword won't be presented. It was a masterful piece."

"It made its point," said Rambo, straight-faced, but pausing for effect. "You wanted quiet down here tonight. You got it."

"If only they knew the true threat was gathering aboard that yacht just there." The silhouettes moved in a kind of shadow play across the yacht's windows.

"There's more wealth in that yacht than in the Federal Reserve down the street."

"And so much more ready for a substantial withdrawal," said Baltasar.

"I still don't see the need to get those damn stones."

"Trust me, Rambo. Victory depends on it. You get the stones for me, you'll get your riches, enough to start three of your mercenary armies, wage your own war against terror," he snugged the cuff of his glove, "and win it. So do refrain from killing Devlin and Fox until you've acquired the stones in their possession."

Baltasar started down the pier, alone, carrying only his laptop under his arm. He sensed the reptilian eyes of snipers who had trained their sights on him. The armed guards lurking in the glow of the instruments of the control room crowning the topmost deck had no doubt alerted the shadow G-20 below to his presence. They could very well be scanning him for bombs and weapons with prototype gadgetry. But something else was targeting him, even more sinister.

He adjusted his bow tie. He had been preparing for this moment for years, but he hadn't anticipated the specter of dread that hissed at him from above. It was though a dark menace had swooped down from the storm and attached its claws to his shoulders, its cold, stinking breath blowing away glory and replacing it with fear. He had to use that fear to strengthen his resolve. He had to be ready to cross the threshold to his new empire. No more would these industry barons toss him away like an easily discarded knight. Tonight, he would teach them that he was the chess master.

CHAPTER **52**

Baltasar stepped aboard the *The Flying Carpet* yacht, at the stern, the luxurious expanse of the rear deck in front of him, leading to the aft doors of the main lounge. The 20-person Jacuzzi had been covered, the teak chairs cleared away. The gusts whipped around the half-moon mahogany wet bar with its gold-plated rail, a nod to the sheik's guests who imbibed alcohol.

As Baltasar neared the lounge, he could more clearly hear the argument from within. One of the sheik's infamous Black Guard manned the lounge door. An ignorant visitor might think of the Black Guard as a piece of theater, his dark skin clothed in flowing black headdress and robe, a scimitar sheathed at his hip. Baltasar knew the men could kill him instantly with a mere two fingers if commanded to do so. The sheik, like his Moroccan predecessors, flaunted his power over these descendants of slaves from sub-Sahara Africa, relying on their fierce loyalty and lack of tribal bonds.

The guard uncrossed his massive arms from his chest. He checked Baltasar's laptop, turned it on to make sure it wasn't a bomb. For a moment, he narrowed his eyes, as if sizing up Baltasar's head to be sliced off by his scimitar. Instead, he returned the computer and opened the door, his hand huge on the gold-plated handle.

Baltasar smiled. The shadow G-20 had received his email and believed it. He crossed the threshold into a masterwork of Moorish design. Traditional teak paneling had been redesigned into intricately carved arches. On the far wall, a fountain, tiled with geometric patterns of blue and white, spouted water from the mouth of a bronze lion's head. The ceiling was festooned with golden and red striped silk draperies, that billowed to the corners, then fell voluminously to the floor. They lent the air of a sheik's palatial tent.

A man in a white kaftan sat cross-legged in the corner playing the tear-dropped shaped guitar known as an oud. Baltasar thought the evocative music beautiful, strumming into the room the history of a powerful people, a power and beauty that would soon be his to wield.

Baltasar met head-on the glares of the usual suspects, nineteen men and one woman, gathered around in conspiratorial groups of three or four, standing with Scotches in hand or sitting stiffly on the overstuffed divans. Every detail in their clothing, from silk shirt to diamond cufflink, was custom-made with intimidation, not fashion, in mind.

The Arab stepped forward, his white robes flowing around his sandaled feet. "Welcome to my humble accommodations," said the sheik, as always bowing to his tradition of hospitality. He gestured to the young man balancing four flutes of effervescing Veuve Clicquot on a silver tray. Baltasar watched the servant, eyes downcast, approach. Admiring the man's bronze complexion through the golden champagne, he lifted a flute. The Arab shooed the servant away. Without a sound, the bartender, waiters and musician left the lounge. "Now, Baltasar Contreras, you have one minute to convince me not to have your head sliced off." He slashed his finger dramatically across his throat. Really, the man should have been a movie actor. Baltasar almost laughed at the irony of the situation.

Baltasar raised his flute in a toast. "All we need is the right major crisis and the nations will accept the New World Order." He paused for effect. "These are not my words. They are the words that David Rockefeller spoke here in New York before the United Nations business council in 2004. The world is on the threshold of that major crisis. My international network is poised to deploy a new weapon of mass destruction, a poison that can easily contaminate a water system. It has a kill rate of ninety percent." He sipped the champagne, savoring the liquid crafted to be dry.

"You lying son of a bitch," drawled the Texan, his nemesis, who had led the charge to exile him from their mighty Alliance. "Kill Contreras now. He's all hat, bluffing, that is. If he uses this bio-weapon, he's as dead financially as we are."

"Unless I had the only antidote," said Baltasar. Implied pretext was so much more effective than outright lies. "You rallied the group to kick me out and take my place. You made them fear that my ambitions would usurp their goals. Congratulations, you were right, Tex." He savored saying the nickname. Everyone in the room knew that it enraged the Texan. "Two years ago, when you so foolishly forced me out, I convinced the United States government, under the auspices of the Homeland Security Department, to contract with NewWorld Pharmaceuticals to develop a doomsday scenario incorporating a drug or poison that could infect a water supply." He sipped the champagne. "Paranoia, I discovered, is immensely profitable. The irony is that it was the Treasury department head whom you, Tex, allegedly control, who arranged funding for the contract."

The other men were eyeing the Texan with ill-concealed rage. "Your threat about this poison cannot be true, Baltasar," said the Frenchman, the one titan who had argued against expelling him from the group. "It will ruin all of us."

"You know it is true, mon ami" said Baltasar. "You all have read the information that I emailed to you earlier today. You have seen the streets of New York this afternoon. My man released the poison into the water system here in the New York City and in Princeton, New Jersey, as an example, so you would believe. Within hours, the poison incites extreme paranoia, in its early stages, followed by aggression and a violent madness. The fights, riots and murders will escalate. Those who are not killed by others will fall into comas and die within seven days."

He paused for effect, let that sink in. By the blanching of their faces and downing of their drinks, it had.

"It is late," Baltasar pressed on. "The markets are closed for the weekend. What would happen if this crisis hit New York on a weekday? What if hundreds of thousands of New Yorkers suddenly fell ill, with an incurable ailment with a high fatality rate? What if traders and financial industries in Manhattan had to close their doors?"

"Financial catastrophe," muttered the German.

"Markets around the world would collapse," added the Dutchman.

"Even the threat of such a disaster would send the developed world into a financial decline that would spiral out of control," said the woman from Moscow.

The German downed his Scotch. "How much," he snarled, "to stop this insanity before the markets open?"

Baltasar watched in satisfaction as they all turned to him. That's what he loved about this group. They made decisions quickly and conclusively. "I have another obligation to attend to," he said. "The instructions and amounts are in this computer. You will see the sums are quite reasonable, no more than the budget of a developing nation. I'll expect the money wired into my Swiss bank accounts by midnight tonight."

"I, for one, will not pay into this protection racket," the Texan drawled. He made a move to leave, but didn't.

"But you are getting far more than protection," said Baltasar, to the group.

"We want the antidote," said the Arab, "as part of the deal."

Baltasar smiled. He was expecting this. "I will sell to you not only the antidote, but the poison, a weapon of mass destruction for which you will own the only defense. Fear not, my friends, you will continue to be a master of the new world order, but only if you play your next move wisely. If not, then I will rebuild my empire the Biblical way, from what little is left of the world in ruins."

# CHAPTER 53

When Christa rang the doorbell of the Donohue home, she expected the Colonel, decked out in black ops uniform and armed with some macho machine gun, to thrust open the door. Instead, Daniel, all eyeglasses and corduroy blazer, greeted her. The world had been truly turned on its end. So what the hell, she hugged him, tight. He kissed her. She let him. "Percival told me what you did for Lucia," she said, without releasing her embrace.

"I made sure Lucia is safe," he said, "with Helen. Donohue has got a man guarding them and one at the clinic with Liam."

Braydon advanced over the threshold. "Brilliant move of yours, Dubler," he said. "Tripping that booby trap beneath Saint Patrick's, getting yourself kidnapped so you could save Lucia."

Daniel tensed and pursed his lips, searching for a response and coming up empty.

"Thank you, Daniel," Christa said. She wasn't sure why, but she kissed him, again, even though her thoughts were on Braydon. She released him and followed the sound of voices to Donohue's library. Braydon, following behind her, shoulder bumped Daniel out of his way, on purpose.

Donohue's library was about the same size as Percival's, with the same dark paneling, but that's where the similarity ended. A big screen television commanded the far wall, next to a wet bar braced with a platoon of liquor bottles. A billiards table took up most of the floor space, fronted by a phalanx of manly sized recliners and couches. The air smelled of stale cigar smoke and whiskey.

She crossed the room, embraced Percival and, much to his chagrin, Donohue. He was wearing a soft flannel shirt, not a flak jacket. The colonel patted her back awkwardly. "Grab a sandwich," he said. "Percival and I are just reviewing the last details on Colombia. The veggie one is on whole wheat."

A plate of Dagwood sandwiches, a second dish of home-baked cookies and a carafe of coffee showed that the elusive Eleanor Donohue's instincts as a military wife had kicked in, but the thought of providing for her vegetarianism went beyond the call of duty. She picked it up, gratefully. Grilled eggplant had never tasted so good. It felt great to be alive, still.

She half listened to the men's plans of Blackhawk helicopters and strike forces, Braydon asking questions while refueling with roast beef, Daniel pretending to understand. From the laptop they'd confiscated from Contreras's orangery, they knew that Contreras's men had kidnapped Gabriella. Percival was determined to leave as soon as possible to rescue her, which, Donohue insisted, they could only accomplish using brute force. Braydon argued against it, too many potential civilian casualties. Their voices raised, she hoped the two men wouldn't resort to using brute force against each other. The thought kept knocking in her brain. Daniel could be right, to work with Contreras, not try to battle a man with generations of planning and a worldwide network.

She had nothing to add to the talk of P-90 machine guns and C-4 explosives. Instead she honed in on the bookcase by the fireplace. It was filled with photos of a boy, as a cub scout, dressed as a pilgrim for a Thanksgiving play, receiving his high school diploma, in full dress uniform in front of the chapel at West Point. It was Clive, Donohue's only son, who had been killed in Iraq. Trophies, from the Pinewood Derby, MVP football player, the Chess Club, filled another shelf. On an upper shelf, an American flag, folded into a perfect triangle, was encased in its own glass case. The shelf above that was empty, as if saved for a future that never came, no wedding photo, no grandson in his arms.

She blinked, her cheeks suddenly hot. The sandwich turned pasty in her mouth. Tears filled her eyes. What an idiot. She didn't even know the boy.

"My wife heard us talking about the Breastplate." It was Donohue. She jumped, nearly dropped her sandwich plate. He had come up so silently behind her. "She's got it in her head that if we can restore it, we can make sure Clive is okay, maybe even talk to him again." He sighed heavily. "Only one thing on this Earth doesn't die, and that's a mother's love."

She quickly wiped her cheeks with the back of her napkin. Nobody could see her in this state. She didn't have the right. She swallowed hard. "And a child's love for their mother," was all she could manage to say.

"Christa." It was Percival, calling her back. "I've got the armillary sphere."

Donohue straightened his shoulders and marched back to the bar.

She drew in a deep breath, turned around and joined them. "I told you about the shooting, across from Saint Patrick's," she said. "We took cover behind the Atlas statue. That's when it hit me. Atlas is carrying an armillary sphere on his shoulders."

"Armillary sphere?" Daniel asked. "As in a renaissance model of the known universe?" She knew he said that just to prove that he could add value to this conversation, but she found that oddly endearing. Could he love her, like the Colonel loved his wife?

"It could be a weird coincidence," she said. She lifted the sphere from the bar. It felt heavier than she remembered. She ran her fingers over the cool, brass interlocking rings, then the smooth marble base. She could be wrong. It could be too much of a coincidence.

"Or divine providence," said Daniel. She was glad she hadn't been the one to point that out. "That's what you two were talking about. The Turquoise, one of the seven stones, you think it's in Arizona."

"The Yikaisidahi Turquoise," she said. She twisted the outer brass ring. It was stiff with age. The cool metal warmed in her hand as she manipulated it into place. "On Atlas's sphere, the symbols of the planets are aligned. Of course, planetary alignment is scientifically impossible, depending on your definition of alignment, but it doesn't stop people from believing that the Mayans predicted it will happen in 2012 and end the world in a massive cataclysm." She felt the click more than heard it, like the tumblers of a safe aligning. "The guardian who hid this sphere in that cliff dwelling had traveled through Mayan lands." Another ring twisted. Another click. "And he was an astronomer." She pulled.

Nothing. "Apparently it's going to take more than a planetary alignment to show me that I'm on the right path," she said. Damn, she'd been so sure. And that was always her downfall.

Braydon tugged it from her grasp. "Never give up on yourself," he said. He double checked the position of the rings. That was annoying. Then he grabbed the pedestal of the sphere in one hand, the marble base in the other, and twisted. It moved, unscrewing like a jar lid. He lifted off the top of the base, sphere and all. Along the inner rim of the base was a finely crafted locking mechanism that had held the lid in place. He handed her the open base. "Or you'll never know what you can accomplish."

A secret compartment had been carved out of the interior of the base. She peered in, tilting it towards the bar light to cast away the shadow. "Paper," she said. "It's old, centuries old." She carefully removed the sepia-toned parchment. Paper this old could disintegrate in her fingers. She placed the open marble base on the bar and, carefully, unfolded the parchment. It opened to a ten-inch square. On one side was an ink rendering like she had never seen before. She swallowed, hard. "It's a map."

Braydon edged in closer. They all did, hovering around, straining for a better look. "Does it show the location of the Turquoise?" Daniel asked.

She tilted it towards the light. "It's faded, but I can make it out. The drawing is signed by Tristan de Luna."

"Presumably, Luna is the first guardian of the Turquoise," said Braydon. "The man who brought it to Arizona from Colombia."

Daniel reached to grab the map. Braydon knocked away his hand. "But the Turquoise," Daniel said. "Does it show us where to find it?"

"No," Christa said. She looked up. "This is a map to the location of the Demon's Wings, marking the temple at Oculto Canyon. This is a map to the lost Breastplate of Aaron."

For a moment, the silence was heavy in the room, the gales whistling outside. "That's no help," Daniel said. "We already have a copy of Conroy's map showing the location of Demon's Wings."

"Except," she said, "both maps are not the same." She snatched up her daypack with her free hand, unzipped the outer pocket, pulled out Conroy's map and unfolded it. She placed both maps on the bar, side by side. "A lot changes over five centuries. Empires rise and fall. New lands are discovered. Rivers change course." She stepped back so the others could get a closer look at the two maps.

"The bend in the river," Braydon said, not surprisingly, the first to spot the anomaly. "It's further south, relative to Demon's Wings."

"I'd judge about ten miles," said Donohue. "And Conroy's map has no tributary leading into the Tequendama River."

Christa had to smile at the irony. "Alvaro Contreras damned the tributary from the Oculto Canyon back in 1586," she said. "That action eventually changed the course of the Tequendama River. That's why Baltasar Contreras can't find Demon's Wings and the Oculto Canyon."

Braydon smiled, too. "They're looking in the wrong place."

"Alvaro Contreras, by trying to dominate nature, set up generations of his descendants for failure," she said.

"Let's not get cocky," Braydon said. "Luna's map will get us to the canyon, but we still need to find the Turquoise."

She picked up the marble base of the sphere. Its black interior swallowed the light. She tilted it, heard a metallic clank. She turned it upside down. A key dropped into her open palm. It was wrought iron, spotted with rust, but looked completely intact, despite its obvious age. "It looks like a strongbox key," she said. "The handle of it, I recognize it, the circle with the equator and meridian, like a cross, inside. It's the symbol for Earth."

"Like on the brass ring of planets on the sphere," Daniel said. He licked his lips and reached for the key. "That priest friend of Fox's had something to do with this, positioning that Atlas statue above the only escape to his damnable underground trap."

"Only one problem," Braydon said. "O'Malley came to Saint Patrick's ten years ago. That Atlas statue is art deco. It was erected in the nineteen-thirties."

"And," said Christa, "O'Malley didn't even know Joseph was one of the Circle of Seven. He didn't know about this sphere. Nobody did." She held up the key, the Earth symbol between her fingers. Divine providence? Maybe. But God wasn't going to find those gemstones for them. "This is the key to finding the Yikaisidahi Turquoise. And the only way to find where it's locked away, is to track down the man who hid it five hundred years ago."

CHAPTER **54**

Baltasar Contreras felt like shooting someone, in the face. He had planned for Percival Hunter making a move to rescue his daughter, but for them to make such a mess of things. It felt like a violation. Doors were busted in. Chairs were overturned. His maid claimed she needed the night off to recover. And, in a strange way, he missed little Lucia. She had left behind a void that he hadn't known before.

As a consequence, Daniel Dubler's arrival was extraordinarily bad timing. Nonetheless, Contreras allowed him into his library and poured him a brandy. He had to be civil to the man. It was only sporting. He had to find out what the wimp knew.

Dubler swirled his brandy in his snifter, but in an unpracticed, jerky movement. "This armillary sphere, Mister Contreras," he repeated, drinking his Courvoisier XO too quickly, "that she found in the cliff dwelling in Arizona." He paced back and forth, his fingers pulling through his disheveled mop of hair in agitation. Perhaps the poison was taking effect. "I'm telling you, the map hidden in its base will give you the exact location of the hidden temple, and that strongbox key Christa found has got to lead to the Turquoise. Christa and Fox are on the next flight out to Phoenix. You wouldn't have known that, without me."

Baltasar had to admit, only to himself, the armillary sphere had been a bit of a mystery. He didn't like mysteries. "You will be justly rewarded, Mister Dubler, for your loyalty to me and your betrayal of your friends."

Dubler raised a fist at him. It shook. "I am not here to betray Christa," he shouted. "I came here to save her." He snatched up the decanter, splashed the brandy into his snifter, swigged it. "Fox is trying to convince her that I would just get in the way in Arizona.

You and I, Mister Contreras, we're the only ones who can restore the Breastplate and find the antidote. Christa will soon see me for what I am."

"For both our sakes, I hope she doesn't."

Dubler tensed up so tightly that it was a wonder he could breathe. "Not yet," he muttered through clenched teeth. "I am going to the airport, right after I leave here. I'm going to be on that flight to Arizona. I will get that Turquoise from Fox."

"For that, you will have to kill him."

Fine brandy had a calming effect on Baltasar. Not so with Daniel Dubler. The man's pasty face flushed with rage. "I will not kill Fox," he said. "I will show him mercy. I am a man of God. That will be my proof to Christa, when she sees me wearing the restored Breastplate, like my predecessor, Aaron, brother of Moses, before me."

"Go to hell," he said, not expecting Dubler to be sharp enough to catch the subtle warning.

"You need me, Contreras." He pointed his trembling finger as if firing off a curse. "You need to bring me with you when you go to restore the Breastplate."

"You have served your purpose, Mister Dubler."

"I told you about Donohue's plans," he said. "He only needs forty-eight hours to organize his strike force for Gabriella Hunter's rescue attempt. And knowing Percival, that nut is already boarding a plane to Colombia." Baltasar merely sipped his brandy as the man approached him with clear menace. "I am not going to sit around here doing nothing while the greatest Biblical artifact in history is found, restored and put to the test."

"On that," he said, "we agree."

It was as if Dubler hadn't heard him. "I am trained in the priesthood," he pressed. "The Bible clearly states that the Breastplate is only to be worn by the high priest."

"In the beginning, priests were chosen by God through the people," said Baltasar, "not by a controlling, power-hungry hierarchy. I am The Prophet. The people have chosen me." He found himself hoping that Dubler would convince him not to kill him, again. Something about the man, his ambition, his faith, intrigued him. "I can see that you will not be eradicated easily, Mister Dubler, like an exotic weed with tendrils deep underground."

"You and I," he said, "we can start your new religion, together."

Baltasar swirled his brandy. It looked like blood. "Sacrifice," he said. "It is the lifeblood of any true religion. You always focus on what you want, Dubler, not what you must give. I have sacrificed much." He gestured around the room, to the shelves bereft of family photos, to the plush trappings which meant nothing to him, to his father's vacant wheelchair by the window. "That is why you were rejected for the priesthood," he said. "You do not understand the need for sacrifice. You are not willing to make the ultimate sacrifice."

Dubler smiled. It was pitiful. "I would die for this cause," he said. "I know now. It is my destiny."

Baltasar nodded. He pushed the red button beneath the lip of his desk. His two bodyguards appeared instantly. "Mister Dubler," he said. "I envy you. You have fulfilled your destiny. Mine, I fear, will be a battle of faith that the world has not seen before." Dubler sputtered and screamed as the guards dragged him away. Baltasar drew closed the heavy drapes. He did not care to give witness to another's sacrifice with his own looming ahead.

# DAY 3

## CHAPTER 55

"So much for mastering Beethoven's Pathetique sonata on the piano," Christa said, hoisting herself up the barely distinguishable toe and finger holds carved out of the cliff face.

"You're some kind of historian savant," said Braydon, huffing with exertion, "can speak fluent Latin and now you're telling me you can play Beethoven's Pathetique."

"Never tried," she said. "And I won't be able to now. My fingertips are so raw I could become a jewel thief and not leave behind a print."

"Most just wear gloves."

Last time she was here, was it less than forty-eight hours earlier, she had followed Joseph up the cliff by moonlight. With the old man's confidence ahead and everything in shadow below, the ascent was perilous enough. Now, she led the way as the late afternoon desert heat beat upon her and Braydon's shoulders. The low angle of the December sun targeted them like a laser sight. The promise of cool from the shadow cast by the opposite wall of the canyon crept up below them, but it only made the sun seem more powerful.

Three vultures circled lazily overhead. Braydon had named them, Huey, Dewey and Louie, a trick of his, naming dangerous animals to make them less scary. *Works with sharks, too.* She didn't ask. Her throat was too parched.

The raptors eyed the two of them, their canteens dangling from their belts, and their daypacks, with bad intent. The surplus canteens were one of the few essentials that Braydon had picked up at the general store, using the last of Neidemeyer's cash. Rambitskov was sure to find out about their flight to Phoenix, but a credit card trail to the general store in the nearby one-horse town of Dry Gulch would give him exact time and location. Braydon quickly outfitted them with some high energy snacks, sunscreen and an extra army green daypack, a duplicate of the one she had bought here two days ago. Her new "lucky" pack.

She had changed into her khaki hiking clothes and broken-in boots. He wore an old t-shirt from a climb up Kilimanjaro, jeans faded in all the right spots and boots that looked like they had traveled as much as she had. He looked good, really good. Part of her was glad that Daniel had never showed at the airport. Part of her worried. People were getting crazier. Traffic had been backed up for miles. Accidents caused by the winds blowing down branches were coming to blows between drivers.

"It's no mystery to me why these cliff dwellings were abandoned," Braydon called up to her. She had briefed him on the history of the area as they had searched for the hidden entrance to the tunnel leading up to the cliff dwelling that she had used to escape to the valley floor--right into Contreras's hands, as it had turned out. They found it, but someone had caused an avalanche of rocks and scrub brush to bury the entrance. That left climbing the cliff face the only way from the valley floor to the dwelling, just as in Anasazi times. "I'd take my chances with ferocious enemies and animals over climbing this cliff just to sleep easy at night."

"Only because you haven't come up against the ferocious animals in these parts," she said. It came out more ornery than she meant, but she was lousy with exhaustion. She had gotten a little, restless sleep on the overnight flight to Phoenix and couldn't keep her eyes open on the dusty, six-hour drive to get to this spot that was beyond remote in the vastly empty Navajo reservation. The stress of constant danger was taking its toll.

"My brothers and I fought," he continued, "a lot." She wasn't daft enough not to realize he was keeping up this repartee to make sure she was alert. "My mom use to yell at us to go play outside. All we had to worry about was the train track, not a hundred-foot drop.  As an Anasazi, I wouldn't have made it to puberty.  No wonder their villages died out."

"It's a cycle of history."  She pictured Braydon as a young boy and liked what she saw.  "Civilizations rise and civilizations fall."

"Don't buy into Contreras's *raison d'être*," he said.  He coughed. His throat must be as dry and dusty as hers.  "And don't use the word "fall" right now."

"Safety is an illusion," she said.  "We think we've protected our children by anticipating a terrorist act like poisoning the water, when all we've done is helped create a situation that places them in more danger."

"Not an illusion," said Braydon, "just elusive.  Sometimes the line between good and evil is as hard to hold onto as the toeholds on this cliff.  But we've got to try.  Christa, we will save Liam and the others."

Christa's foot slipped.  She flattened her chest against the cliff. Braydon gripped her around the ankle to steady her.  She glanced downward to see a cluster of small rocks tumble into his face.  He turned away.  The rocks clattered down the cliff face, smashing apart as they fell down, down to the valley floor.  She'd have thrown up, but her throat had glued itself together.

"Or die trying," Braydon quipped.

"Not this way," said Christa.  She stretched upward, hooking her fingers over the lip of the plateau.  She pressed her toes into the cliff and pushed enough to sling her forearms over the lip.  The interior of the arched cave and the ruins of the cliff dwelling were just ahead of her.  She was almost there.  Her biceps trembled with the strain, as she heaved her body onto the plateau.  She flopped onto her back, arms outspread.  Her strength was zapped, except for one more motion.  She thumbed her nose at Huey, Dewey and Louie, black against the cloudless cerulean sky.

Braydon scrambled over the edge and snatched his gun out of his daypack.  He scanned the area in a wide arc.

She went for her canteen.  "Nobody here but us ghosts," she said.

"Is that sarcasm, or precognition?"

"I'm not sure anymore."  She unscrewed the cap of her canteen and swallowed a long draught of water.  It had lost its chill, but nothing had ever tasted so good.  It was like aloe on a sunburn, that wonderful sensation of wet on her desiccated throat.

Braydon, apparently satisfied they weren't under immediate threat, took a swig from his canteen and pressed the comparatively cool green plastic against his flushed forehead. He took in the view of the river below. In the distance, the spotless blue sky merged into an ominous black thunderhead, which was bullying its way across the plateau like an angry buffalo.

"I'm glad we're not in a slot canyon right now," Christa said. "That thunderstorm in the distance can create a flash flood in a canyon miles away, even one with a blue sky overhead, send a ten-foot wall of water down it. Just last week two hikers were crushed and drowned in a slot canyon near here while a group of tourists watched in horror from above."

"I was just going to say nice view," he said. He stood, brushing off his khaki shirt and pants, turned towards the dwelling. He planted his fists on his hips, his expression intent. She could see he was surveying the rooms and open windows not as an archaeologist, nor an historian, but as an FBI agent. "We stick to the plan. We get as many of the seven stones as we can and call Donohue. He'll have his task force and Colombian contacts ready to deploy. We go with him to Colombia, free Gabriella, find the temple, get the antidote, save the world and take the rest of the day off."

"Let's get started," she said, stepping forward.

He pulled her back. "You told me that this cliff dwelling was buried under five centuries of sand until that windstorm a few days ago."

"Joseph and I were the first people to set foot on it since it was abandoned in the sixteenth century."

"Set foot being the key words." He crouched and pointed to a footprint in the sand. "Here's your Trek hiking boot, ladies size 8." He edged forward. "And this has got to be the smooth sole of Joseph's moccasin." He pointed to a third trail of footprints leading into the ruins, which had merged with and obliterated Joseph's and hers. "Standard issue army boots. Look like they dropped down from the top of the cliff, probably rappelled with ropes, either the night you were here, or yesterday."

She swallowed, her throat dry again. "They still here?"

"If they were, we'd be looking down their gun sights, not at their footprints." He moved to the far side of the plateau and crouched again. From the expression on his face, she knew it was bad. And it was.   A cluster of large, clawed prints converged on a circular pattern in the sand. "The beasts," he said, "who chased you."

"Wolves," she said, with as much confidence as she could muster. In the light of day, the idea of evil shapeshifters that she had told him about on the plane last night sounded absurd. "They must have got here through the tunnels."

"Weird.   Whatever they are, they arrived after the soldiers left. Their prints are on top of the boot prints." He stood and followed the trail of prints with his eye.   "And the trail ends abruptly," he pointed, "before reaching the cliff dwelling."

"It looks like they doubled back," she said.

"And didn't come as crows from the sky," he crouched again, "but from beneath the ground." He bent closer and blew away the silt.  A brush of his fingers revealed a straight edge leading to a right angle.  She knelt beside him as he ran his forefinger clockwise along the edge.  She ran her finger counterclockwise.  Their fingers met, revealing a square, perhaps three-feet wide. He extracted his Eagle Scout pocket knife, opened the main blade and wedged it into the crack. "Help me lift it," he said.

"Why do I feel like we're opening Pandora's box?"

"As long as we find hope at the bottom, I'm game."

She wedged her fingertips into the crack beside Braydon's. She could barely get a purchase on it.  Slowly, they angled the heavy stone upwards.  As it rose higher, she gripped it with two hands, pressing her palms against its surprising weight.  It was a stone, rough on its underside, which had been chiseled at an angle to fit into place. Braydon kept his left hand on the stone, grabbed his gun with his right. "Guess I should have loaded in silver bullets."

"Skinwalkers aren't werewolves," she said. "You got to dip the bullets in white ash to shoot them."

"Now you tell me."

The top of the stone reached its apex. One last heave flipped it heavily away from them, sending plumes of silt up like smoke. The boom of its fall echoed ominously from below.

Braydon targeted his gun into the opening, but all they could see was darkness beyond the pine logs that framed the square opening. Sunlight beamed on the top of a crude wooden ladder, its hand-hewn pine rungs attached to the two posts with a rough twine.  She could just make out a segment of a circular wall in the beam of sun, built with rough stone bricks. "I think it's a kiva," she said. "Like the ceremonial rooms I told you about."

"But they didn't use it for black magic," he prompted, "like turning people into Skinwalkers."

"Can't say for sure," she said. "Historians only speculate that the kiva in ancient times was used for rituals. This Yikaisidahi cult was an anomaly, even in its day, influenced as it was by a completely alien culture, Tristan de Luna's, the young apprentice to the conquistadors, the first guardian of the Turquoise."

"An alien culture, the conquistadors, with a proclivity for ruthless violence," he said, "and a religious fanaticism that had already been perverted through its inquisition. Sounds ripe for training evil killers to me."

"Fanaticism doesn't always end in fatalism," said Christa. "From what we know about the first guardian, he was an intellectual, a gentle soul, whose father sent him with the conquistadors so he would man up, as they would say today."

"These grave-robbing, curse-spewing, evil-doing Skinwalkers, you know, the ones who appear to be protecting what your gentle soul brought here," he said. "Are they active during the day?"

Christa shrugged. "Most say Skinwalkers conduct their black magic only at night."

"You sense any phantoms or other evil things set to skin us alive down there?"

"No more than up here."

"I don't find that reassuring," he said. He handed her a flashlight from his pack, then zipped the pack closed and shrugged it over his shoulders. He hiked his leg into the opening, his foot finding a rung, while keeping his handgun trained on the room below.

She followed. The handhewn rungs bowed under her weight. The ancient twine whined and fretted against the posts, but the ladder proved sturdy, protected all these years from the elements.

As her foot hit the earth floor, that old scent of earthy silt filtered into the air, irritated at being disturbed after so many years in silence. Dust mites floated around her in the shaft of sunlight, lending a sense of being underwater, if it weren't so utterly dry. The sudden coolness of the interior wasn't refreshing, but chilling. She flicked on her flashlight. She needed to see something, anything, besides the beasts that lurked in her imagination, ready to spring from the shadows and rip out her throat.

The underground room was circular, about twelve feet in diameter, with walls of stone bricks and a ceiling of thick pine logs. "Open doorways," she said, surveying the interior walls with her flashlight. "I count seven, each one about five feet apart." Each was barely wide enough for a man to squeeze through, into a tunnel that swallowed her light like the mouth of a hungry snake.

To their left, about six feet away from the far wall, her beam hit a stone structure that looked like it had been used as a fire pit, with a back wall several feet high and two side walls tapering down to the floor. It was open to the center of the chamber. The charred logs of an ancient fire remained, still lingering, remarkably, with the scent of ash.

"No footprints," said Braydon, "of Skinwalkers, or evil guys in army boots. This floor hasn't been walked on for centuries."

Her flashlight beam snagged on something behind the fireplace. She leaned in closer. It looked like, it was, the toe of a boot. "So we don't have to worry about him," she said.

Braydon approached the fireplace like a cop smoking out a shooter. She let him go first. They circled around to the back of the stone structure. She stopped herself from retching, again.

A mummified corpse sat propped up against the stones. His eyeless head gaped at her, his gray, leathery skin stretched taut over cheek and nose bones. Hair sprouted from his scalp like a weed, turned red by some freak of nature, the tendrils curling down past his shoulders. His desiccated skin had shrunk around his mouth into a toothy, anguished grimace. His jacket and pantaloons, once plush, burgundy velvet, were now his shroud, faded, torn, rejected even by the insects.

"First guardian, Tristan de Luna, I presume," said Braydon.

"So he just sat here and died?"

"Or they closed him in," said Braydon. "It would have been nearly impossible for one person to lift that stone blocking the opening."

"Or he had the people lock him in, to protect the Turquoise before they abandoned the cliff dwelling."

Braydon sucked in a deep breath and patted down the corpse. Patches of velvet disintegrated in his fingers. Luna's head crept over to a pitiful angle. "Either way," he said, "he doesn't have the Turquoise on him and he's not going to be telling us where to find it. That key we found in the base of Luna's armillary sphere isn't any good without the strongbox it unlocks."

"Maybe he has told us," she said. "These openings in the wall have got to lead somewhere." She walked over to the nearest opening and beamed her flashlight inside. "After a few feet, the passageway splits into two."

"Seven openings from this chamber," said Braydon. "Assuming one of the passages leads to the Turquoise, we got fourteen possibilities."

She poked her head into the tunnel, probed her light deeper. "Then into two again."

"I'm not much of a gambler," he said, "but I don't like these odds."

"So how do you solve a puzzle?"

"I find out all I can about the guy behind it." He scrutinized the skeleton. "Our guardian here had a passion. Astronomy. He not only brought the Turquoise here, but carried his armillary sphere across the Atlantic to the new world. Then he brought it here and hid it."

"And he named the Turquoise after a Navajo constellation, Yikaisidahi, It Waits for Dawn."

"How many planets would your average sixteenth century astronomer know about?"

"Six," she answered. "Saturn was the furthest planet they could see."

"Seven passages," Braydon pointed out.

"Of course," she said. She shown her light and felt her fingers along the inside of the first opening. "Your friend, O'Malley, wasn't the first person to use symbols to guide people along the right path. Symbols have been used since the dawn of recorded history. Symbols *were* the first recorded history." She felt something with her fingertips, blew away the dust only to have the fine silt cloud around her face. She coughed and blinked it out of her eyes. "The symbol of a circle atop a cross," she said. "Venus's hand mirror." She hurried to the next passage and found a globe with an equator and a meridian. "Earth." She fished the key out of her pocket and held it up. "The same symbol as on the handle of the key."

Braydon checked out the next passage. "I'm pretty sure this is Mars," he said, "a circle with an arrow slanting upwards."

"Mars's shield and spear," she said, already finding the next symbol. "Jupiter's thunderbolt," then, "Saturn." She was rushing now, out of breath. "A circle with a point in its center, the sun," she called from the next passage, then, at the final opening, "Mercury's winged helmet."

"If you start at the Sun, the order of the planet symbols on the seven doorways go around the perimeter of this chamber in order of distance from the Sun, starting with Mercury, ending at Saturn," said Braydon.

"The guardian's armillary sphere was state of the art for the mid-1500s. Copernicus had just come out with his model of the Sun being the center of the universe, rather than the Earth. Very radical at the time. " She shone her flashlight around to all seven entryways. "But where do we start?"

A thudding sound rumbled from above them. They both looked up, but could see nothing through the small opening to the plateau in front of the ruins. Christa listened as the distant sound grew louder. "Thunder?"

"Chopper," said Braydon. "No doubt commandeered by Homeland Security. Your tax dollars at work. With a chopper at their disposal, they won't take the time to climb up from the valley floor. They'll just rope down from above like they did before." He grabbed the timber and twine ladder, yanked it down and tossed it aside.

"What are you doing?" she said. "These tunnels could be dead ends. That could be our only way out."

"We go up there, that's a dead end, if you catch my drift, and the bad guys get the sacred stones we already have," he said. "We can't let that happen."

"The key has the Earth symbol," she said. "We could start there, but then what."

"Luna's sphere was Copernican," he said, "with the Sun as the center of the universe. The center of Luna's universe was that Turquoise. We start with Saturn, follow it to the Sun, the center. That's where we'll find the Yikaisidahi." Without waiting, he ducked into the opening.

CHAPTER 56

Christa wedged into the tunnel marked with the symbol for Saturn. She swallowed back her fear. Those beasts had to come from somewhere and a dark, dank tunnel fit the bill. She found herself pressing against Braydon, only partially because of the confined space. "Your decisiveness is both enviable and exasperating," she said.

"It had better be the right decision," he said. "We won't get a second chance."

At the split of the passageways, she shone her light on the symbols carved into the rock just inside. "Jupiter to the right, Earth to the left."

Braydon crouched and crabwalked down the right-handed passage. The tunnel looked as if it had been hewn out of the solid sandstone. Good thing the floor was rock, not sand. Their footsteps left no prints. Even if Rambitskov's men deduced what tunnel they had entered out of the confusion of footprints they left behind in the main kiva, they could only follow them so far before having to divvy up their hunting party. "I think we're headed downhill," she said, "a good sign," but the darkness before and behind them was complete. They had gone at least fifty yards before they reached the next split. "Mercury to the right. Mars to the left," she whispered. Shouts channeled through the tunnel from the plateau in front of the ruins above them.

"To boldly go where few men have gone before," said Braydon, heading to the left.

"Going," she said, "but not boldly. In fact, my knees are shaking."

"That's just strain from the climb up the cliff face," he said.

"No, it's the weight of the mountain pressing down on top of us."
She sniffed. "Does the air smell stale to you?" It was growing
difficult to breathe. Rather than the baking heat of the sun, a damp
chill permeated the tunnels, as if it emanated from another, darker
world.

"Smells like the catacombs under Paris," Braydon said.

"You mean where they buried their dead." Lovely thought.

"I chased a jewel thief down there," he said. "Beneath Paris are
two hundred miles of passageways brimming with skeletons. The
guy got lost. Started leaving a trail of diamonds, like bread crumbs.
He never was seen again. I figured he died down there. I got the
diamonds, though."

"If you're trying to take my mind off those beasts that might be
stalking ahead of us, waiting to make sure we don't come out alive,
it isn't working."

"Actually, I was trying to take your mind off those beasts behind
us" he said. "There are worse places to be."

"I'm sure there are," she said. "I just can't think of one."

Despite the confined space, Braydon quickened his pace and she
hurried to keep up, her heart beating faster as they delved deeper into
the tunnel system. Each footfall sounded like thunder in the
complete silence. Every few yards, a patch of pebbles would break
loose from the vibrations of their steps, pelting her head. If any
section of the tunnel collapsed, they'd be trapped.

They followed the Earth, Venus and Mercury tunnels in rapid
succession. Whispers of splashing water gurgled towards them. As
they descended, it grew louder, more distinctive. Braydon stopped.
She plowed into him. He flicked off his flashlight.

By the single light of her flashlight, she could see that Braydon
was looking heavenward, his lips parted in wonder. She followed
his gaze. Above her was a night sky filled with stars, too many stars.
It was like no night sky she had seen before, even on a moonless
night in the desert, away from any glare of civilization. "I may be
clairvoyant, but I didn't see this coming," she said. "How can we
have found our way to the outside of the cliff? And how can it be
the middle of the night?"

"They aren't stars," said Braydon. "They're glow worms. We're
in an underground cave."

"If we're still underground," said Christa, "why does the air smell fresh and cool, like the desert night?"

"I've seen these bioluminescent bugs before," he said.

"Tracking another jewel thief?"

"In Alabama," he said. "I found him hiding out in Dismals Canyon, same place Aaron Burr hid for a couple days after killing Alexander Hamilton in a duel. Jesse James hid out there, too, so they say. At night, these glowing bugs they call Dismalites line the canyon walls like stars. And where there's bugs," he began. He flicked his flashlight back on and shone it at the ground in front of them, only it wasn't ground. The flashlight beam reflected a vast pool of water so still it looked like a solid mirror, but for a tiny ripple expanding from below them. Their tunnel ended about twelve feet above the surface of the pool, as if they stood on the lip of a waterfall that had gone bone dry. Just above them and to their left, her flashlight beam illuminated another tunnel like theirs, but with a slender waterfall trickling down from it into the pool. "There's water. We've reached the end of the trail."

She scanned the cave with her flashlight beam. It barely penetrated the dark. "How long must it have taken a little waterfall like that to carve out an underground lake this size?" she wondered aloud.

"Longer than five hundred years, I hope," said Braydon, "or the Turquoise could be underwater."

She traced the shore of the lake with her light. When Braydon merged his beam with hers, she could just make out the opposite shore. A large, natural opening in the rock waited like a gaping mouth, at least twenty feet wide and high, its lower lip just sipping at the water's surface. A small stream flowed out of the underground lake down the cavernous passageway. "Turn off your light," she said. Although she had spoken in hardly more than a whisper, her voice seemed to boom across the cavern.

With both their lights off, the sparkling universe of glow worms above was even more magnificent. She blinked to coax her eyes to adjust faster to the near darkness. "Do you see it?" she asked, pointing, although she was sure Braydon couldn't even see her hand in the dark. "Look across the lake, towards the cavern opening on the opposite shore." She could make it out for sure now, a distinct golden glow penetrating the darkness.

"The sun," said Braydon. "That opening across the lake must lead to the outside and to the Turquoise, if our luck holds. That young cop outside Saint Patrick's accused us of being creatures from the underworld. I'm beginning to feel like one."

"Well, I don't see Charon pulling up in his boat to give us a ride," said Christa. She could see just enough by the glow of the worms to see Braydon's raised eyebrows. "The guy in Greek mythology who carted dead people across the river Styx to Hades," she explained. By his smirk, she gathered he had already known that.

"Then I guess we're getting wet," he said. He jammed the flashlight into his pack, put it on and lowered himself out the end of the tunnel. "I found a couple toeholds," he called up. She leaned over to see him and heard a splash. She flicked on her light. He shielded his eyes against its sudden brightness. "Refreshingly brisk," he said, "and only a couple feet deep."

He pulled out his flashlight and shone it on her as she followed him down. When her foot plunged into the water, the cold snapped her breath away. "We'd better move fast before our feet numb up," she said.

Braydon pushed ahead of her through the water. The splashing noises seemed like a corruption to the pure silence of the cave. Her sodden hiking boot sucked her foot downwards and the water seemed more viscous than normal. The bottom of the lake was slick, with the occasional drop or rise that fooled her in the dark and almost tripped her. At any moment, an unexpected drop-off could plunge her into a frigid, life-sapping black. She found herself reaching for Braydon's hand. He held hers, tightly, until they reached the opposite shore.

He didn't let go of her hand as they followed the trickling outflow from the underground lake down the passageway, their flashlight beams searching the walls as the passageway narrowed. Before long, she had to fall in behind him because the space was too constricted to walk two abreast. He squeezed her fingers. The tunnel continued to brighten. Then, as they curved around a smooth, undulating bend, the rock walls glowed with a stunning golden red. Above her, a circular tube led up from the stone ceiling through twenty feet of solid rock to reveal a circle of indigo blue sky above. A shaft of light from the setting sun beamed down upon them. "I didn't think I'd be so glad to feel the heat of that desert sun again," she said as the beam fell upon her shoulders.

"That's not the heat that worries me," said Braydon. He nodded towards the direction they were heading. Their passage dead ended about hundred yards ahead. It was blocked by a tumble of rocks and downed tree trunks interlaced with thorny scrub brush.

"We can't get out that way," she said.

"And we can't go back the way we came. Rambitskov's men might have night vision goggles, heat sensors. It won't take them long to find us."

"We'll have to find the Turquoise, double back, find another tunnel that leads outside to the valley."

"Then where the hell is the Turquoise?" He opened his arms and turned slowly. "This is it, the place of the sun. We've got to be standing right on top of it."

"Or right below it," she said. She pointed up the shaft. About twelve feet up, just where the shaft narrowed into a smooth tube of a chimney, a niche had been chiseled out of the rock. In the niche, the sun glinted on a wrought iron strongbox.

# CHAPTER 57

Christa stepped back from the sunbeam that shone down into the narrow tunnel like a spotlight. She craned her neck for a better look at the strongbox in the niche carved out of the smooth tube to the sky above. "The strongbox looks sixteenth century," she said. "Wrought iron, not much rust. And," she fingered the key in her pocket, "it has a keyhole."

"Good thing Luna is dead," said Braydon, "or I'd punch the guy. Why did he have to place it so high up."

"It probably wasn't so high five hundred years ago," she said, splashing the stream at their feet with the toe of her boot. "Water erosion."

"I'll hoist you up," said Braydon. He stooped down. "Get on my shoulders."

She hooked her legs around his shoulders, intimately aware of his hands clasping her bare thighs. She wasn't cold anymore. In fact, heat flushed her cheeks. She steadied herself by walking her palms up the cool, stone wall as Braydon balanced himself beneath her, straightening his legs and raising her up. "I can almost reach it," she said, stretching one arm. "Get closer."

"Happy to oblige," he said, clasping his hands tighter on her legs. "It's real smooth down here," he said, "the wall, I mean." He edged in even closer to the wall. "Makes me wonder."

"How a tunnel through a solid mountain could erode so quickly, even given five hundred years." She fished the key out of her pocket and shifted her weight forward. "That stream at your feet isn't very strong."

"You said a thunderstorm in the distance can send a flash flood down a slot canyon," he said, "wipe out everything in its path."

"More powerful than dynamite," she said, straining to reach higher, clenching the key between her forefinger and thumb. "I'm almost there."

"Just how long will that run-off from the storm across the valley take to reach here?"

"Any time now."

"For the run-off to reach here, or for you to reach the strongbox?"

"I don't want to drop the key."

"I don't want to drop you," he said.

A sudden, cool breeze swooshed by them from the direction of the underground lake. It was followed by an ominous bellow, the sickening warning of an unstoppable force.

She hoisted herself another inch, tried to jam the key into the keyhole. "I can't get the key in."

"Just grab the box, Christa. Pull it down."

She clasped the carry handle on the front of the strongbox and yanked. It didn't budge. "These strongboxes had holes in the bottom," she said, "so that they could be bolted down."

"Just like people do today, with gem safes in their homes. They're not much good if the thief can walk out with the entire safe and its contents." Her weight shifted on his shoulders as he twisted beneath her towards the direction of the underground lake. He quickly turned back, edged in closer, got her another half-inch higher. "Keep trying the key."

She jammed it again. "I'm in!" She twisted the key. The lock disengaged with a thunk. She hoisted up the lid, pushing it with all her strength to break apart the rusty seam. Braydon couldn't get her any higher. She curled her fingers around the top edge of the strongbox. She hoisted herself up with her arms, balancing the bottom of her hiking boots on his shoulders. His hands grabbed her ankles as she wobbled. She reached her hand blindly into the inside of the strongbox, hooking the inside of her elbow over its sharp ironclad rim. She pawed around frantically, her fingers feeling nothing but smooth, cold metal. She stopped. Her fingers landed on a protuberance, round, about the diameter of a golf ball. She scooped it out and, hanging on to the strongbox with one hand to steady herself, she opened her palm. In the glimmer of the sunset captured by the shaft, a piece of the sky glowed in the palm of her hand. The stone was the purest Turquoise she had ever seen. More than that, it emitted a now familiar energy. "It's the Turquoise," she said. "I've got it."

Suddenly, Braydon was yanked out from under her. Closing her fingers around the Turquoise, she fell backwards, arms flailing, but she didn't hit the ground. Her backside plunged into a rush of freezing water.

She clamped her hand around the Turquoise. She'd be damned if she dropped it now. The rush of water was like a furious serpent and she the bronco rider on its back. It pushed her beneath the surface. She bobbed up, coughing, sputtering. She fought to breathe as frigid water splashed into her mouth and nose.

"Keep your feet downstream!" she shouted, swallowing a mouthful of water for her effort. The walls of the tunnel flashed by as the flood rocketed her down the passage. She caught glimpses of Braydon ahead of her, struggling to stay afloat. It got worse. Ahead. The dead end. The barricade of rocks, scrub brush and tangled tree trunks blocked their exit. They were rushing headlong into it.

She searched frantically for something to grab onto, to slow her down. The head of the flash flood steamed ahead, like a train engine out of control. In seconds, Braydon would be crushed against the barricade.

A deafening boom blasted down the passageway. Light poured in as water blasted out. The head of the flood blasted through the barricade. Braydon shot out of the passage, Christa right behind him. The force sent them tumbling, head over foot. Braydon grabbed her in his arms and yanked her aside. They rolled, tumbled and crashed to a stop in a heap in the desert sand, the water coursing beside them, gushing as it merged into the once tepid waters of the valley's river.

She laid on top of Braydon, their wet bodies like one, breathing hard. He didn't want to let go any more than she did. Reluctantly, she rolled off of him and swiped her bedraggled, dripping hair from her face.

Braydon sat up, coughing, visibly slowing his breathing. He twisted to look back at her. The sky behind him had turned a dark blue, the sun kissing the top of the canyon opposite them before it winked out behind it, leaving them in twilight. She propped herself up on one elbow. She held her fist up to him and opened her fingers. The Turquoise seemed to almost hover, reaching for the blue of the sky. His mouth stretched into a smile. He laughed, really laughed. And she found herself laughing with him. Crazy laughing. She knew it was the incredible stress playing games with her emotions. She didn't care. She threw her arms around Braydon, pressed her wet body to his.

Suddenly, he hugged her tight and rolled her over, thrusting her against the face of the cliff. A bang echoed down the valley. Braydon jerked against her. Something warm and sticky was on her hand, blood.

# CHAPTER 58

Christa could barely react before Braydon hoisted her up and pressed her back against the rough rock of the cliff. His gun appeared in his hand. He was craning to look up while not moving out into the open.

"Shooter is at the ruins, above us," he said. "He can't get a bead on us if we stick close to the face of the cliff, but he won't wait long to reposition. The jeep is our only chance."

She yanked the pouch from beneath her wet-t-shirt, opened it and pushed the Turquoise inside, tugging the drawstring closed. A red splotch was staining Braydon's wet shirt sleeve, up by his shoulder. "You've been shot," she said. "You need a doctor."

"I'm going to need a coroner if we don't stay out of range."

She looked up, quickly taking in the silhouette of a man aiming a scoped rifle. He stood on the precipice of the plateau in front of the cliff dwelling. "If we move, he'll kill us."

"Not if we move fast and plaster ourselves against this cliff."

A bullet zinged into the sand ten feet in front of them.

Christa pressed her back against the sandstone, still warm from the sun. Braydon edged along the base of the cliff. She followed. A bullet hit the ground, closer to her toes, only six feet in front. A second bullet stung the ground beyond where they started. "The shooter can't see us," she said. "He doesn't know what direction we're heading."

"He will soon enough." He stopped. The pinon grove and their jeep waited just across the river. She could barely make out the jeep in the darkening light. They had camouflaged it, covering it with scrub brush. It would be hard to spot, especially from above. The shooter could have lost them, think they doubled back.

"No shots in the past five minutes," she said. "They must have given up and gone home."

Braydon smiled, then grimaced in pain as his injured shoulder scraped the rock, leaving behind a bloody splotch. He snapped forward for a quick peek up. "They're rappelling down from the cliff dwelling," he said.

"They can't hit us while they're descending."

"Unless they left behind that sniper to keep us pinned down." He checked his gun. "I'll cover you. When I start shooting, you start running and don't stop until you get in that jeep."

He dashed forward. His feet splashed into the river. She heard the sharp report of a rifle from above. He spun around, aimed up towards the plateau and fired.

She ran into the river with all her strength. The water, once tepid, was wild, forceful. It roiled thigh-deep down the valley, churning with the detritus of branches and tumbleweeds. A tree trunk smashed into Braydon's shins, hurling him into the water.

She rushed towards him, struggling to keep herself upright. She grabbed Braydon, heaved him up. He was sputtering, fighting to breathe.

"Get out of here." He tried to push her off. "Get to the jeep."

"I'm not leaving you," she screamed above the roar of the water. She wrapped his good arm over her shoulder. He stumbled along beside her. She glanced behind. Three men, dressed in special ops black, were nearly boots on the ground. A fourth hung from his rope, taking aim with his free hand. She forced Braydon down and ducked. The bullet hit the gnarled trunk of a pine just ahead of them.

As soon as they cleared the river, Braydon pushed her forward. "Start it up," he said. He clutched his injured arm to his chest, the pistol in that hand, and rushed to yank the scrub from the top of the jeep.

She tossed her pack in the rear, threw off a tumbleweed and climbed behind the wheel. "I hear something," she yelled. She twisted to look behind her, blindly turning the key in the ignition. Her fingers were shaking and it wasn't from the frigid water. "Two Land Rovers, black, coming up fast." Dust billowed behind the SUVs. They were speeding down the dirt track into the valley. "They're coming in our only way out."

Braydon grabbed his pistol with his good hand. He aimed at the incoming SUVs, pulled the trigger. Missed. She turned the key. The engine roared to life. Braydon aimed again. This time the lead Land Rover swerved and skidded, its front tire blown. It stopped a hundred yards away, the second Land Rover swerving to a stop behind it. Braydon hoisted himself into the passenger's seat.

She threw the jeep into drive and jammed her foot onto the accelerator. It started forward like a slingshot. She yanked the wheel around. The men who had rappelled down the cliff raced across the river. One detoured down river, flanking them from behind. Three of them positioned themselves between the jeep and the dirt track in an arrow formation, two in front, one in the center further back, their rifles aimed straight for the jeep. The only way through them was to run over them. She stepped on the gas. "Move!" she screamed at them, honking the horn wildly. Braydon targeted them with his pistol. She closed in on them. They remained still, didn't even blink. She saw no way around. The pinons were too close to allow a detour. "I can't do it," she screamed at Braydon. "I can't run them over."

"Don't slow down," he yelled back. He targeted the man in the center with his pistol as they bumped and rattled toward them, his hand bouncing wildly. "I can't get a bead on him."

She could see their faces now, their set expressions. Without warning, the man on the left lowered his rifle. A look of sheer terror crossed his face. He was looking at something behind the jeep. Christa stole a look back. The fourth man, the one who had circled in behind them, was no longer there. She dared to twist around. A black, wolf-like beast had flattened the man. It was holding him down, howling and growling, as the man twisted and fought to free himself. Three more black beasts were tearing up behind them at breakneck speed. "Skinwalkers," she whispered. She could barely speak the name, barely believe the shadows of terror materialized in these vicious animals.

She turned front, gulping in breaths. Her heart beat fast and hard. The three men who had positioned themselves in front of their jeep were running ahead of them now. They were fast, but she quickly caught up to them in the jeep. She could see a beast on her left side, leaping through the air. It pounced on the man. He screamed, terrified, as the beast's jagged teeth closed on his throat.

The second beast pounced on the man on Braydon's side, shoving him to the ground. As the man screamed, the beast stretched wide a black, toothy jaw and clamped it over the man's face, crunching down. The last man on Braydon's side stopped and faced the third beast. He fired, stepped back, fired. The beast slowed, stalking him. The bullets pelted its haunches, but had no effect. The man stumbled back, firing again and again. The beast crouched. It pounced, flinging the man away bodily, right in front of the jeep as she sped forward.

Christa yanked the wheel to the side to avoid running him over. The jeep swerved and spun. They mowed down a sapling, barreled through a thorn bush and slammed into an old pinon. Braydon was forced forward, his forehead smacking the rim of the windshield.

The black Land Rover skidded to a stop twenty-five yards away, its wheels shooting up a plume of dirt and pebbles. Two men stepped out, both wearing button down shirts, open at the collar, dress pants and spit polished shoes. The man with the crescent scar. He was the one who shot her at Percival's house, who was with Contreras at the Marrakesh restaurant. She had to get Braydon out of here. He was conscious, but woozy.

Two beasts paced the edge of the dirt track, waiting, stalking. They were jet black, with matted fur, like wolves, but larger, with oversize forequarters and glowing, golden eyes. The larger of the two bared its teeth, snarling. They looked even more terrifying in the twilight than in the dark.

The man that had been flung in front of the jeep reached his hand towards the driver of the Land Rover. A beast stood over the downed man, its paws on his chest. The beast's mouth gaped open hungrily. Drool dripped from the beast's sharp canine tooth onto the man's cheek. "Rambitskov," the man pleaded. "Get me out of here."

"Torrino," Rambitskov said in a voice that was preternaturally calm. "Go get Devlin and Fox and bring them to the Land Rover. Professor Devlin," he added in the same, steady tone. "You'd better bring the stones with you, or I will throw you right back to the beasts."

Torrino moved cautiously toward them, his eyes not leaving the beasts, his hand on the butt of his gun in his shoulder holster.

Torrino, that was his name. She couldn't possibly overpower him and Rambitskov. She couldn't make a run for the Land Rover and leave Braydon behind. And she couldn't let Rambitskov get the stones. He was keeping them alive for a reason. She had to use that to her advantage. She had only one priority now. Get away from the beasts.

She eased down from the jeep. She and Torrino helped Braydon down beside her. She reached into the jeep and slowly looped her arm through the straps of their packs, easing them over her shoulder. Torrino stretched Braydon's good arm over his shoulder and half-carried him to the Land Rover.

They reached the far side of the Land Rover. She opened the back door. Torrino slid Braydon in, flopping him across the back seat. Torrino slowly opened the front passenger door. "Get in," he said, then, in a whisper, "Get behind the wheel." She didn't question. She did as she was told, too terrified to hope.

The beast on top of the man on the ground craned his neck upwards towards the rising moon. It howled, that same sickening primeval sound that had pierced the desert night when she was first here with Joseph. The man beneath the beast began weeping, his chest in his black ops uniform shaking up and down with his ragged breaths. "Rambitskov, please," he cried.

Rambitskov eased his handgun from his holster. He aimed. He fired, once. The man's face was stricken with wide-eyed shock. A hole appeared in his temple, then a trickle of blood. The beast atop the man clamped his teeth on to the man's throat and tore at it, shaking his snout violently back and forth, nearly severing the man's head.

The other two beasts crouched and loped towards Rambitskov. Torrino quickly climbed into the Land Rover and shut the door. "Drive!" he shouted. She threw the gear into reverse. She twisted to look behind her. Trees, everywhere. A crash now would disable their last working vehicle. Rambitskov shouted at them, cursing, shooting at the beasts, then shooting at them. A bullet shattered the window at the rear.

Rambitskov sprinted in a new direction, going for the shelter of the disabled SUV, with the tire Braydon had shot out. Its door was open. Rambitskov dove into it. His foot kicked out at the beast as it lunged after him. The beast stumbled back. Rambitskov slammed shut the door. Christa yanked the wheel around, sending her Land Rover into a spin. She threw it into Drive and pressed the accelerator to the floorboard. The car fishtailed, stuttered and shot forward. As she sped into the darkening desert, Rambitskov's Land Rover came into view in the rear view mirror. Three beasts flung themselves against the windows to attack the prey inside.

"I wouldn't wish that death on anyone," she yelled over the engine noise and the ghastly howls of both beast and man.

Braydon groaned. He pushed himself up to look woozily out the shattered rear window. "Be careful what you wish for."

# DAY 4

## CHAPTER 59

Braydon's shoulder knocked against the padded panel door of the Homeland Security SUV they'd seized in the desert. He awoke from a dream that on any other day would have scared him more than the real world. He was sweating, breathing fast. Remnants of sharp teeth dripping drool bit through his brain. Scariest part was, in the dream, he was the beast, poised to kill Rambitskov.

They had just driven onto the Bay Bridge. He could see that much and not much else. The notorious San Francisco fog cocooned them in white. Steel girders smacked into view and vanished behind them. Ahead, the peaks of the city skyline, punctuated by the distinctive pinnacle of the TransAmerica pyramid, pierced the fog. A time traveler from long ago might think it was a cloud city, a wonder of the future, if not for the intrepid, or foolish, sailor who plied the waters of the Bay close by the docks below.

No more foolish nor intrepid than they were. Torrino, behind the wheel, had to be punch drunk tired. They had driven through the night and most of the day from Arizona. He was driving like a New York cabbie, careening around a Camry piloted by an elderly gentleman who clearly feared plunging off the edge of the bridge in the fog more than the impending apocalypse.

"I'm as curious about life after death as the next guy," Braydon said, "but I'd rather not find the answer at the bottom of San Francisco Bay."

Torrino's eyes darted to see him in the rear view mirror. "Tell that to the guy chasing us," he said.

He twisted back, couldn't see more than twenty-five yards. "You know, the first symptom of that poison is delusions." He faced front to see Christa looking at him. God, she was beautiful. Her brown hair curled from beneath the brim of her funky plaid cap. A hand-painted winged, tattoo-like design blazed across the back of her black sweatshirt. She grabbed the papers on the lap of her sustainably harvested cotton skinny jeans to keep them from being flung to the floor with the momentum of Torrino's evasive maneuvers. And she was no delusion.

With her free hand, she grabbed onto the handle above the door to steady herself. "Glad to see you're still among the living."

"She was worried about you," he said. "I told her you were harder to keep down than my mother-in-law's Arrabbiata sauce."

"Thanks, I think," he said. In fact, the bullet graze in his shoulder throbbed like Ali was punching him from the inside and he couldn't shake off the devil pressing hot fingers against his forehead where he'd smashed into the Jeep's dashboard. "You sure we got a tail?"

"Picked us up at the entrance to the bridge," Torrino said, craning over the steering column to distinguish vehicles, girders and other deadly obstacles through the almost solid white. "Black Hummer, not exactly inconspicuous."

"I disabled our GPS tracker," he said, "which means they were waiting to hunt us down because we're hunting down the Abraxas stone."

"Which means," Torrino said, "the Prophet didn't get the real deal in that museum theft in this fair city nine months ago."

"And he knows we don't have it yet," Christa said, "since we're heading into San Francisco. But, if he thinks we have a lead on the Abraxas, why chase us down? Why not follow us without letting us know?"

"Contreras must already have boots on the ground here," Braydon said. "He's one step ahead, again. He didn't send this tail to follow us. He sent them to stop us."

"I'd bet Stonington is in on this," Torrino said.

"Who's Stonington?" Christa asked.

"High-end fence," Torrino said. "Braydon saw Contreras meet him at his Nob Hill penthouse just after the Abraxas theft."

"Stonington is way out of his league with this one," he said. "I'd be worried about him if he wasn't such a slug." He checked the bandage on his arm, no blood seepage. After their near escape in the desert, they made a quick detour to the hospital. While he got stitched up, Christa checked in on Joseph and told him they'd found the Turquoise. Joseph gave them his file on everything he knew about the Circle of Seven. "Contreras needs that Abraxas stone as desperately as we do. We've got to get it first. Torrino, lose that tail. Christa, fill me in."

"This is amazing information." She flipped back to the first page in the file. "We knew Joseph was in the Circle of Seven, the guardian of the Yikaisidahi Turquoise," she said. "The one person he knew in the Circle of Seven was the guardian of the Abraxas. The Circle worked that way. Each guardian knew only one other guardian. If one was compromised, the others would be safe."

"That chain is only as strong as its weakest link," he said.

"And it broke," she said. "The Abraxas guardian pegged his nephew, Adam, to inherit the guardianship, but this was back in the 'sixties. Adam was drafted to Vietnam."

"So no time to train him."

Torrino slammed on the brake and swerved to the outer edge of the bridge. Out of the fog, an exit appeared, Treasure Island, smack in the middle of the Bay. He yanked the SUV onto the exit ramp.

Braydon twisted around. The Hummer swerved across two lanes, sending that old man's Camry into a squealing stop against the girders. The Hummer thread the needle of the exit ramp. "Didn't shake them taking the exit," he said.

"I'll lose him down below," Torrino said. "I visited this place when we were here last spring, read about it in a guidebook, *San Francisco and Beyond, 101 Affordable Excursions*. Pays to be on a budget."

Christa pressed her hand against the dashboard as they spiraled down to sea level. The narrow road hugged the shore of the sparsely wooded island. "The uncle was ready to train his next choice as guardian if Adam was killed," she said, "but he didn't dare pass the secret to another until he was sure it was necessary." They passed an impressive half-moon shaped building accented with tall, vertical windows and post-art deco details. She pointed at it. "Isn't that—"

"The setting for the exterior of the Berlin Airport where Indiana Jones took off in the blimp in the Last Crusade flick, without all the swastikas," Torrino said. "Living the dream, baby." He floored the accelerator, bulleting through the fog along the shoreline.

"The key word being living," she said. "I can't see twenty yards ahead of us."

"Neither can the guys chasing us," Torrino said.

She turned back to the notes. "Adam finishes his tour, comes home to San Francisco, but the uncle collapses from a massive coronary. He barely lived long enough to tell Adam about the Abraxas, how important it was. He had no time to educate the kid. Joseph came to San Francisco to fill in the gaps, but Adam disappeared."

"Don't tell me," Braydon said. "Adam was eaten by a vicious, mythical beast that lives in an underground chamber that hides the Abraxas stone." One thing he had learned about these Seven Stones. They were pried from beneath the Earth and, whether it was divine providence or the laws of inevitability, a powerful force was determined to return them from whence they came.

"Worse," said Christa. "He started a secret religious cult centered on the stone. It goes back to the Abraxas stone's origins."

"It always comes down to that," Braydon said, "the fight between good and evil."

"Hang on!" Torrino yanked the steering wheel to the right. The SUV listed to the left, its massive weight shifting onto the outer tires. Then it straightened as it made the curve. Behind them, the Hummer careened forward, brakes screaming. It bolted up as it bucked over the curb, leaned sideways and crashed onto its side, sliding through the fog, until it vanished with a loud splash. "Score one for good," Torrino said. "I knew that beast wouldn't make the curve."

"Don't get cocky," Braydon said. "Contreras wouldn't send just one Hummer after us, unless he had a contingency. And the Abraxas was both good and evil."

"That's right," Christa said. "It's a mythical creature to the early Gnostics of the second century, a name for the supreme being that encompassed both good and evil."

"With the head of a lion, the body of a man holding a whip in one hand and a shield in the other and serpents as legs," Braydon said.

She raised the page to show the drawing in Joseph's notes.

Torrino glanced over. "It doesn't look like no supreme being to me."

Braydon wasn't about to admit that this "supreme being" had haunted his nightmares, more than once, since researching it after the San Francisco museum theft. "Back then," he said, "supernatural beings didn't teach the followers to follow their rules. They terrified them into following their rules."

"The Abraxas creature was engraved on ancient gemstones," Christa said, "along with the name Abraxas, to be used as charms. This note from the Jewish encyclopedia points out that some Abraxas stones had Hebrew names carved into them along with Abraxas, showing the influence of Judaism in ancient societies."

"So the guardian didn't as much start a religious cult," Braydon said, "as revive one."

"We are so close," she said. "Think about it, Braydon. We've got the Urim and Thummim stones in my pack, along with the Tear of the Moon Emerald and Yikaisidahi Turquoise. And now we're going after the original Abraxas Stone that the Gnostics revered in the second century."

Torrino followed the road back up into the fog cloud and blended into the Bay Bridge traffic. If they had a second tail, Braydon couldn't see it. "It's dangerous," he said. "The FBI has dealt with religious cults before. It never ends well."

"You got to admit, Adam was ingenious," Christa said. "He comes home from the Vietnam War, where everything is a deadly threat and suddenly faces the responsibility of guarding a powerful gemstone, used by Aaron in Biblical times. San Francisco in the late 'sixties would have been ripe for a cult like this. What better way to protect the stone than build up a cult of fanatics devoted to keeping it secret and safe?"

"Only problem is," he said, "these cults tend to get out of control, like Charles Manson's group of crazy murderers who brutally slaughtered the Hollywood star, Sharon Tate, when she was eight months pregnant and wrote the word, *Pig*, on the door in her blood."

"Manson," she said, scanning the page. She stabbed a paragraph with her finger. "Manson referred to himself as Abraxas, both God and the Devil, in a parole letter. You don't suppose?"

"No," he said. "I don't. I rely on facts. Manson has been behind bars for decades. The real Abraxas stone is still out there, or Contreras wouldn't have hired Stonington to find it."

"Manson was like a Skinwalker, a guy turned evil, only he didn't shift shapes," said Torrino. He took one hand off the steering wheel to finger the simple, silver cross he always wore around his neck.

"But I can see the connection," she said. "The Abraxas cult learned from the Manson murders in 1969 to keep their cult underground, literally and figuratively."

"The question is, do they know about the connection to the other seven stones."

"Not sure," she said, "but it says here that some believe the seven letters of Abraxas represent the seven classic planets."

"The sun through Saturn, like in the tunnels that led to the Turquoise," said Braydon.

"Not this time," said Christa. "The classic planets are those objects in the sky that were visible from Earth without a telescope. Sun, Moon, Mercury, Mars, Venus, Jupiter and Saturn, the same heavenly bodies that inspired the names of the seven days of the week. And for you mathematicians out there, the numerical values of the original Greek letters spelling out Abraxas add up to 365."

"As in 365 days of the year," offered Torrino.

"Or, if you were a second century Gnostic," said Christa, "the 365 spheres or heavens."

"I'm having enough trouble following the rules of getting into one heaven," said Torrino. He slowed to merge into the exit for the city.

"Did these cult members know that this particular Abraxas stone was pried out of the Breastplate of Aaron?" asked Braydon. "That was supposed to be the Circle's best kept secret."

"And it was," she said. "Better kept than most. Until the early 1970s, the stone was buried in the hull of a ship beneath the streets of San Francisco."

"An underground ship?" From the 1500's?"

"No," said Christa, "although the original guardian did arrive by ship. He came aboard a British ship exploring what is now the

California coast. It was very hush-hush at the time. I studied about this when I worked on my thesis on the conquistadors. Sir Francis Drake had explored the coast, named it New Albion and claimed it for England. He sailed north searching for a Northwest Passage, information so valuable that Drake's brother was tortured by the Spanish to reveal their discoveries. Queen Elizabeth the First ordered subsequent, secret explorations up the coast. Some say Drake had started a colony right here, on this bay. In any case, according to the oral history Joseph learned from the Abraxas guardian years ago, the original guardian of the Abraxas came north on a British ship, came ashore. He intermarried with the indigenous people. Fast forward almost three centuries to the gold rush. Hundreds of ships were cramming into San Francisco harbor. One of those ships is the Niantic, a whaler out of New England. Its crew deserted, fleeing to find their fortune in the gold country."

"And how did a ship end up underground?"

"A whole section of San Francisco is built on top of ships abandoned during the gold rush," she said. "Like most of the 500 or so ships that brought gold seekers to San Francisco, the Niantic's crew deserted to seek their fortune. Without a crew, the Niantic was floated in and left aground when the tide receded to serve as a hotel and baggage storage. The city kept burning down. The Niantic kept getting rebuilt. Eventually, dirt was filled in around the hull to create land on which to build a new Niantic hotel. The Niantic became the fanciest hostelry in the city, under the direction of the man whom we now know was the guardian of the Abraxas stone. He made a fortune."

"The real riches of the gold rush weren't found in the mountains," he said, "but the pockets of the treasure-seekers' Levis."

"Joseph printed out a photo."

She showed it to him. It was a scale model of the Niantic as converted to a hotel, a diorama from the Maritime Museum. Piers encircled the dry-docked ship. The entire hull had been roofed over. Its main cabin had been built up into a two-story wooden structure, presumably the tavern.

"He hid the Abraxas stone in a safe in the bow of the hull just before it was buried," she said, "figured its hiding place was foolproof. Problem was, the Niantic wouldn't stay buried. It was rediscovered during excavations in 1872, and in 1907 after the devastating San Francisco earthquake and fire. Excavators found cases of champagne, but the stone remained hidden. Then, in 1969 came the plans to build the Transamerica Pyramid, practically on top of the buried hull of the Niantic."

"I've been down that way, when I first went undercover as Contreras's bodyguard," said Torrino. "It's not on the waterfront."

"Six blocks away," said Christa. "That shows how much of the city is built on landfill around abandoned ships."

"Pyramid," said Braydon. "I bet the prospective cult members ate that up."

"Especially since one of the earliest references to Abraxas is an ancient Egyptian demon," said Christa. "The current guardian's uncle told him he was going to inherit the guardianship. A weighty responsibility, but he figured he had it made, guarding a stone that was buried. His uncle left the substantial family fortune and political influence, along with guardianship of the Abraxas to his nephew. But he didn't get a chance to tell him who his second was."

"It had to be the rabbi," Braydon said, "O'Malley's friend, Ezekial, in New York."

"Makes sense," said Christa. "Joseph's oral history from the Circle of Seven is sketchy after that. Two months later, in 1969, he knew they started surveying the TransAmerica pyramid. He figured that's what prompted Adam to start the Abraxas cult. The stone was in the bow of the ship, only accessed by the cult's secret passageways."

"Great," muttered Braydon, "underground again."

"I don't like the idea any better than you do," she said, "but it worked. The bow of the ship remained hidden, even when another section of the Niantic was excavated in 1978 for a building on Sansome Street. Excavations were hurried and the bow remains intact, under the parking lot."

"So where does this black magic woman come in?" asked Torrino. "The one Joseph told you about."

"Apparently, according to Joseph's notes, she was instrumental in recruiting the founding members for the Abraxas cult," said Christa.

"Someone named her the Black Magic Woman," said Braydon, "probably for a reason."

"Adam must be in his sixties by now. He was probably part of the counter culture of San Francisco back in the 1960s," said Christa. "After his tour in Viet Nam, the sudden death of his uncle pushed him over the edge. Before he disappeared, he told Joseph he had to seek out peace and redemption."

Torrino guffawed. "And he thinks he found that in a woman?"

"It was either that or black magic," said Braydon.

"Same difference," said Torrino.

"Save your punches for the bad guys," said Christa. "She was his psychoanalyst when he got back from Nam, treating him for what we now call Post Traumatic Stress Syndrome. Before long, she advised him to cut off all communication with Joseph."

"Adam was vulnerable," said Braydon. "She used him.'

"This black magic woman must have been a master at twisting minds around her finger," she said. She adjusted the map on the SUV's GPS screen. "Joseph thinks that the connection still exists. It may be the only way to find Adam and the Abraxas. The nav system has five listings for Black Magic Woman."

"We must be in San Francisco," griped Torrino.

"A clothing boutique, magic shop, record store, psychic and get this," said Christa, "a medicinal marijuana distributor."

"Could try the psychic first," said Braydon. "If it's not the right place, she could look in her crystal ball and tell us which one is."

"Could go for the weed shop," said Torrino. "Then we wouldn't care if it's the right place."

"The record store," said Christa. "Black Magic Woman is best known as a song title by Santana."

"Agreed," said Braydon. "Carlos Santana is from San Francisco."

Torrino snapped his fingers and grinned. "Abraxas," he said. "It's the name of one of Santana's albums."

Braydon leaned forward. "I'm not going to ask how you know that," he said. "Or why you didn't mention it earlier."

"I've been distracted," said Torrino, "saving your asses."

"The record store is just a few blocks away," said Christa. "Turn right."

Within minutes, the SUV was "arriving at destination, on left." The Black Magic Woman Record Store didn't have much of a storefront, just a tired, sun-faded display of a few record albums in the window. The Open sign hung gamely on the front door, but the street was nearly devoid of traffic. This was the city's financial district and it was Sunday afternoon.

Braydon glanced at the GPS map. "Torrino, you can walk to a BART subway stop a few blocks up Clay Street," said Braydon. "It will take you to the airport."

Torrino parked the SUV, twisted around and snarled, "Forget about it, Braydon. I'm covering your back on this one."

"Go home to your family," he said. Torrino had called home as soon as they got out of the dead zone in the desert. His wife and kids were already tucked away in the pre-planned safe house, but Braydon knew his friend was worried about them, for good reason. The madness in New York was escalating and though the poison might be confined to Manhattan and Princeton water systems, the crazies were not. The news reporters were giddy with the stories of increased violence spreading out from the city like rats with the plague.

"I'm telling you," said Torrino. "There is no way Rambitskov could make it out of that desert on foot, even if he did survive the beasts."

"Doesn't matter," said Braydon. "Your cover is blown."

As if to seal the deal, Christa leaned across and embraced Torrino. "Thanks," she said, then, after a moment, sat back. "And let me know if you find out anything about my nephew, Liam. I still can't get through on the phone."

Braydon held out his open palm. Torrino reluctantly handed him the car key. Braydon didn't tell him what he saw parked down the street. Stonington's vintage Alfa Romeo, a bloody handprint smearing the inside of the driver side window.

CHAPTER **60**

Braydon stepped out of the car. Christa followed. They crossed Sansome Street to the Black Magic Woman record store. The thick fog had rolled in from the bay, casting a surreal gloom over San Francisco. Although only mid-afternoon, the streets were dark with storm clouds, but the air was preternaturally still. It had the feel of Gotham at midnight. The Transamerica Pyramid pierced through the fog and clouds like a beacon for malevolent aliens.

"Closing early, man," the aging hippie called from behind the counter as Braydon led Christa through the door, "due to the end of the world." Decked out in tie-dye shirt, granny glasses and long, gray hair in a Willie Nelson braid, the hippie had a weirded-out look in his eyes like he'd gotten hold of the brown acid. The Doors song, The End, played loudly on the speakers. Braydon half expected to hear Huey blades thumping above them and the odor of napalm in the air.

The record store was as surreal as the street, as if they had crossed a threshold to 1969. There wasn't a CD in sight. Bins of albums crammed into the small space. Psychedelic posters on the walls promoted the "upcoming concerts" of the Grateful Dead, King Crimson and Jimi Hendrix. Behind the counter, an old black and white television was tuned to a news channel broadcasting the riots in New York. Like primeval predators stoking up for battle, a mob danced around a car engulfed in flames and black smoke in front of the Public Library.

The hippie's movements were frenetic as he selected and rejected albums to place in the old whiskey box on the glass display counter in front of him. "Apocalypse now, man," the hippie shouted over Jim Morrison crooning that, "all the children are insane." Braydon appreciated the hippie's sense of drama, but he wasn't about to surrender to the lyrics, especially given that Morrison's next line was "ride the snake to the lake."

If angels could fall, then so could guardians, he figured. War could do that to a man. But he couldn't see this hippie as the Charles Manson type who could command a legion of cultish barbarians.

Christa elbowed Braydon and nodded towards the one album cover framed on the wall behind the counter. It was a frenetic, psychedelic collage of a jumble of boldly colored images, most distinctively, a winged female figure in red hovering over its shadow creature in black and two words, barely distinguishable from the chaotic background, *Santana* and *Abraxas*. The poster next to it featured a quote, red letters on black. *I watched as the Lamb opened the first of the seven seals. Then I heard one of the seven living creatures say in a voice like thunder, "Come!" I looked, and there before me was a white horse! Its rider held a bow, and he was given a crown, and he rode out as a conqueror bent on Conquest.* The quote was labeled, *King James Bible, Revelations 6:1-2.*

"I'm looking for the Black Magic Woman," Braydon shouted over the guitar riff.

The hippie straightened up, his eyes suddenly clear and focused on them. He depressed a button on the 'sixties vintage, manual cash register. The cash drawer opened with a ringing clang. The hippie pulled something out. He thrust it towards them. Braydon reflexively yanked Christa behind him. The hippie clenched a handgun, looked like a M1911 Remington single action, semi-automatic, standard issue handgun in Viet Nam. "I don't want to do this, man," the hippie said.

"Then don't," said Braydon, adrenaline zinging into his system. He was nearly one hundred percent sure that he could get the drop on this older, drug-addled threat, but killing him wouldn't get them any closer to the Abraxas stone, and winging him would put Christa in more danger.

"She said you would come. She told me if anyone else came looking for her, I should kill them," the hippie said, visibly disturbed, his voice as shaky as the hand holding the gun.

Christa stepped out from behind him, her arms outstretched. "Joseph of the Circle of Seven sent us," she said. "He told me to tell you this. A brave man dies but once, a coward many times."

The hippie narrowed his eyes. He was either drawing a bead on Braydon's forehead, or struggling to wrap his mind around Joseph's message. He relaxed his stance just enough that Braydon could make out the peace sign tattooed on the inside of his elbow, where he might have shot up heroin in the day. "You're too late," he said. "The black magic woman took him to the Abraxas. He thinks he will find the stone, but he will only find his end."

"She took whom?" asked Christa, worry honing her voice.

The hippie shook his head, lowered the gun to his waist. "The man with blood in his eyes. He boasted that he had battled the hounds of hell and lived. He said he would snap every bone in my body, from small to large, until I told him where to find the Abraxas. He was a giant of a man. He could do it, and he would, he told me, to save our country."

"Rambitskov," Braydon seethed. "He beat us here. And he's probably got Stonington." Which explains the bloody hand on the Stonington's car window.

"The little guy," Adam said, "in the fine suit."

"Sounds like Stonington," said Braydon.

The hippie's grip on the pistol loosened even more. With his free hand, he toyed with the love beads around his neck. "The first horse of the Apocalypse rides a white horse, the horse of Conquest. It can be the conquest of good, or of evil."

Braydon lunged forward. He snatched the pistol from the hippie's hand. "I'm putting my chips on good," he said. He checked the gun's magazine. Empty. He looked at the hippie. "No bullets. I guess you are, too." He set the gun down on top of the glass display case.

Christa stepped forward. "You've got to take us to the Abraxas, now."

"The man before you fell under the spell of Basillades," said Adam. "He failed in getting the Abraxas from her. What makes you think you will succeed?"

"Because we have to," said Braydon.

The hippie's face was ashen. "I can't see any more death, whole villages wiped out," he said. "I can't."

"Whole villages wiped out," said Christa. "That's the same words Salvatierra wrote in his letter about Alvaro Contreras ravaging the Muisca Indians."

"This guy isn't reliving the times of the conquistadors," said Braydon. Then again, in a sense, he was, just on a global scale, but Braydon didn't want to completely blow the old hippie's mind. "This time, you can stop it, Adam," he said. He pointed to the television. "This isn't Nam. It's New York. Children are dying. You can save them if you help us."

"You have not seen the Abraxas," he said. He hugged his arms across his chest. His eyes were darting back and forth. "You don't know its power, man."

"You're a guardian," said Braydon. "One of the Circle of Seven. Your uncle chose you because he knew you could protect the Abraxas stone."

"My uncle didn't choose me as guardian," said Adam. "It was supposed to be my cousin. He died in Nam. He was killed because I didn't cover his back. They were coming in to napalm that village. He went to save this kid. I tried to stop him. I was scared, man. Then the jets come. No more village. No more cousin." Adam grew more agitated. His hands shook. He paced back and forth behind the confines of the display counter. His hand dove back into the cash register drawer. Braydon tensed, but Adam was only getting a joint. He stuck it between his lips, snatched a lighter from beside the cash register, and lit it with trembling fingers. He breathed the smoke in deeply, closed his eyes. When he spoke, smoke came out in puffs with the words. "This isn't my destiny," he said. "I didn't ask for this."

Braydon lunged across the glass case and grabbed Adam by the scruff of his t-shirt. "I didn't ask for this, either," he said, "but some crazy guy poisoned *our* city and *our* villages this time. And the only way to save them is for you to lead us to the Abraxas. Your cousin's death, all your buddies in Viet Nam, they fought for nothing if you don't help us now. This is the only way to save your country."

"That's what the other guy told me," he said. "You know what I did."

Christa sidled around to the back of the display case. She lifted the needle off The Doors record on the phonograph. The silence brought relief. Jim Morrison had gotten to the part where the minor chords could mesmerize even a sober listener into wanting to escape into a drug-induced unreality. Christa laid her hand gently on the hippie's arm. "Knowledge isn't persecution," she said.    "It is redemption. Take us to the Abraxas."

The hippie looked up at her, then out the window towards the street. His gaze focused on the stepped base of the Transamerica pyramid. From this angle, he could only see the angled girders of the ground floor anchoring the forty-nine floors tapering to a point above. "Beneath the pyramid is a tomb," he said. "All who enter it are cursed."

"It wouldn't be the first time," said Braydon. "And I'm going to make damn sure it's not the last. In the past two days, I've been shot at, chased by phantoms, nearly crushed beneath a cathedral, half drowned in a flash flood, and attacked by Skinwalkers. I'm not giving up now."

Adam worried his love beads. "And you survived all that," he said. "Far out, man."

"Sort of like a miracle," said Braydon, "if you want to think of it that way."

"So you believe this is part of God's plan," said Adam.

"I believe this is part of God's nap," said Braydon. "And I wish He'd wake up."

"But He saved you," said Adam. "So He could save me."

Braydon hadn't thought about their calamities being a godsend, but, he had to admit, the phantoms, the flood, the Skinwalkers, all of it actually did save them, brought them here, to this place. "Listen, we're not here for a rap session, Adam," he said. "If we don't get that Abraxas, a lot of good people will die."

Adam gestured for them to follow him. He led them to a storeroom in the back, then to a steel door. Adam shifted a pile of beat up boxes. Behind them, on the wall, was a keypad. Braydon watched as Adam punched in the code, 666, the sign of the beast. Easy to remember, at least. The door opened to a set of metal stairs descending a good twenty feet, one landing halfway down. Braydon couldn't shake an ominous feeling of dread, and it wasn't only that he was building up to a severe case of claustrophobia.

Adam led the way down the stairs from the back of his record store. Braydon followed his trail of marijuana smoke, trying not to breathe in too hard. This situation was whack enough without being stoned.

At the bottom of the stairs, the passageway reminded him of an underground bunker, a fall-out shelter of gray cement walls dimly lit with caged bulbs every fifteen feet. It bent at a right angle ahead, then another. The cement floor was slick with moisture. A damp chill pervaded. He and Christa followed as Adam's Birkenstocks scuffed around the corner ahead.

A howl, followed by a scream, reverberated down the passageway. Christa slid to a stop. So did Braydon. He strained his ears, but could hear only the patter of Adam's footsteps getting further away. Then, something else, at first low, hard to hear, a chanting. Although they hadn't moved, the chanting grew louder.

Braydon slipped his gun quietly from his holster. He stepped in front of Christa, moved forward cautiously, gun first. Over the chanting, he heard Christa breathing hard and fast behind him. No, it wasn't her. It was him. A terror like none he had ever experienced gripped his gut. A giant fist was squeezing the air from his lungs. He wanted nothing more than to turn back. The chanting grew louder, faster. It was a rhythm of harsh, unfamiliar syllables, repeated, over and over.

The passageway turned another corner. He came around the edge of it to find Adam, standing stock still in the passageway. Not ten feet ahead, it opened to a low-ceilinged room. The faint scent of old ash, from fires of long ago, wafted towards him, along with another, more acrid, more disturbing odor of something smoldering. The chamber was lit with torches, the light dancing on the walls, playing with the shadows. One thing was distinctive, the charred, curved timbers forming the periphery of the chamber. It was the skeleton of the hull of the Niantic.

Adam was trembling. "I can take you no further," the hippie said. "It's up to you to get the Abraxas now."

Braydon edged by Adam to get a better look inside the chamber. He wished he hadn't.

Stonington, or what was left of him, hung from an old iron loading hook in the middle of the chamber. His face was grimaced in agony and stiff with death. His chest had been stripped bare. Red marks covered his torso. The burning odor had come from Stonington's seared flesh. A group of seven monk-like figures in white robes circled around him, hooded heads pointed down, their chanting fading now. A large man in a red robe stood by

Stonington's body.  His right fist clenched a cattle prod.  It was Rambitskov.    A   sickening   nausea   roiled   in   Braydon's   gut. Rambitskov hadn't reacted to their presence, although he was staring right at them.   The man's eyes were bloodshot and unblinking. Rambitskov had been drugged, or hypnotized, or traumatized, perhaps beyond repair.

Braydon retreated a step.   "Fall back," he whispered to Christa. He couldn't let her in there.  He couldn't even let her see in there. "We're not going in without backup."

An eighth monk in white stepped towards them from the far wall. He aimed a gun at them, a Sig Sauer P 229, probably Rambitskov's. "I'm sorry," Adam said from behind him.  Braydon turned back to see that Adam, too, held a gun, a .45.  "But unlike that relic in my cash register, this gun is most definitely loaded."  Adam backed up three steps, out of range of Braydon's fist, which he most definitely wanted to punch through the hippie's face.  "Do not anger her by attempting escape," Adam added.

A black-robed woman came beside the monk with the gun.  She lifted her hood and let it fall upon her shoulders.  Her face was wrinkled with age, but her hair was jet black, bangs cut straight and sharp at her brow line.   Her eyes were outlined in kohl, like an Egyptian.  Her lips were flaming red.  A woman like that refused to accept her mortality, a dangerous attitude, especially if she believed, like some ancient cannibal, that killing others would imbue her with renewed vigor.

She held a small, black box in her hand.  It had four buttons.  She pushed the top one.  A steel panel started sliding shut, slicing off the passageway between Christa and their escape route.  Christa twisted around, and lunged towards the closing panel.  She grabbed the edge of it with her fingers.   She yanked them away as the door slid shut with a metallic clash.

"I am Bassillades," the woman in black said.   "You seek Abraxas, the all powerful one, the ruler of life and death.  You cannot run from what you seek."

# CHAPTER 61

Braydon had confronted crazies before, put his share of them
behind bars, but this woman calling herself Bassillades wasn't crazy.
She was, simply, evil. The intent to kill, just for the pleasure of it,
glimmered in her eyes, along with raw intelligence. He half
expected her to tell him that resistance is futile. He half expected
she'd be right.

He could shoot the monk with the Sig Sauer, kill him instantly
with a bullet to the forehead. But that might prompt Adam to pull
his trigger. Adam didn't seem the type to shoot him in the back, but
he couldn't count on that. Even if Adam shot him, he'd have a good
chance of spinning around and dropping Adam with a quick shot to
the heart. That would leave Christa to wrestle the remote away from
black magic woman, press the button, and open the steel panel
blocking their escape route. Rambitskov would be slowed down
stumbling over his and Adam's bodies to chase Christa. It might
give her enough time to escape. More likely, Rambitskov or black
magic woman would overpower her. Worse case scenario, Christa
would be taken alive, without him to help protect her. The reek of
Stonington's seared, dead flesh intensified in the confined
passageway. Braydon could not gamble with that possibility. He
stepped forward into the chamber.

Braydon let Adam take away his gun. Rambitskov advanced
menacingly, wielding the cattle prod like a knife, his eyes unseeing,
yet seeing all. The black magic woman, Bassillades, raised her hand.
Rambitskov stopped. The seven monks in the white robes stepped
back in unison, their faces still hidden, downcast. They expanded
their circle until they had reached the periphery of the chamber, and
stood like statues with their backs against the charred timbers.

Bassilades nodded towards Stonington's body. "Remove him," she said to Rambitskov. Rambitskov slipped the cattle prod into the baggy pocket at the side of his red robe. He moved stiffly to the body, circled his arms around it and hoisted it up. Stonington's cuffed hands, the skin on his bloodied wrists rubbed down to the bone, jerked off the iron loading hook. Rambitskov hefted the body over his shoulder like a sack of grain. He dumped it unceremoniously on the right side of the chamber.

Flickering torches had been jammed into holders between the charred timbers of what was once the bow of the Niantic whaling ship. Other than that, the chamber was without features, crudely dug out of the landfill, except for one old, cage-like jail cell, about five foot square, to Braydon's left and a closed steel door on the opposite wall. In a neon-hued painting upon that door, a depiction of what had to be Abraxas, dominated the chamber. The creature had the head of a lion, the body of a man wielding a shield in one hand, a whip in the other. Its legs were two serpents coiled around each other. The serpents' heads bared their fangs, ready to strike. Still, that door could be a second exit, a possible means of escape. The door had no knob, nor keypad like the door that Adam had unlocked to enter this underground hell. This steel door had to be mechanical, opened by that remote control which Basillades just slipped into her robe pocket. It fit the pattern.

Braydon nodded towards Stonington's body. "Why the torture?" he asked Basillades. If he was next on the hook, he needed a reason.

"The shock brings nothingness to the mind," she said. "Nothing is the same as fullness. In the endless state fullness is the same as emptiness."

"She quotes Carl Jung," said Adam. "The Seven Sermons of the Dead."

Christa drew in closer to Braydon. "Jung was a contemporary of Freud," she said. "He delved into the dark recesses of human psyche and its relationship with God and the afterlife. And Basillades was the second century founder of Gnosticism."

"That's great fodder for your unification theory of history," Braydon said. "Not so good for us."

Adam moved closer to Stonington's body. To Braydon's utter surprise, Adam lowered himself to one knee, and made the sign of the cross. "This man was not supposed to die," Adam said. "His heart failed him."

"Like your uncle's heart, Adam," said Christa. "He trained you to be guardian of the Abraxas. You must protect the stone, but not from us." She pointed at Basillades. "You must protect the stone from them."

Adam buried his face in his hands. "I saw too much death," he said. "Whole villages destroyed. I knew the power of evil. I needed help. My uncle had warned me that the Abraxas was a key to the power of God, but I had seen the power of the Devil. All I wanted was peace. All I want is for the killing to stop."

Braydon kept his eye on Basillades. She circled the room at a slow, steady pace. She spread her arms wide, and said, "During the night the dead stood along the walls and shouted."

The white robed monks looked up. "We want to know about God!" they shouted. "Where is God? Is God dead?"

"There is a God about whom you know nothing," Basillades said, "because men have forgotten him. We call him by his name." She raised her arms heavenward. "Abraxas!"

"More Jung, I presume," Braydon said. He scoped out the white robes. They were men, all eight of them. Hard to tell if they were armed, but their eyes were weirded out, like Rambitskov's. That made their intent deadly, and a drug, like PCP, could lend them extraordinary strength. The monk with Rambitskov's Sig Sauer had positioned himself next to the steel door at the far end of the chamber. He opened his robe and tucked the gun into the belt of his army surplus khakis, and then raised his pointed hood over his head. He looked down, like the other monks. This black magic woman had been Adam's psychoanalyst when he returned, damaged, from Nam. She clearly had mastered mind control. "You chose the wrong shrink, Adam," he said.

"Evil is out there, Adam," said Christa. She moved closer to the hippie, trying her own hand at mind manipulation, to Adam's core values, not a perversion of them. "An evil man poisoned the water system in New York. He poisoned my nephew, a little boy. That poison is what is causing the madness in the streets. We need to stop him. The only way we can do that is with the Abraxas stone. We need your help, Adam."

An increased agitation jerked Basillades's movement. She began rotating as she spoke, her face heavenward. "The dead approached like mist out of the swamps and they shouted."

The white robes advanced in a step. "Speak to us further about the highest god!"

Bassilades seemed pleased to oblige. Braydon didn't like the look of her arrogant smirk. "Abraxas is the god whom it is difficult to know," she said, as if lecturing to a class. "His power is the very greatest, because man does not perceive it at all. Man sees the summum bonum, the supreme good, of the sun, and also the infinum malum, the endless evil, of the devil, but Abraxas, he does not see, for he is undefinable life itself, which is the mother of good and evil alike."

Adam stood. Braydon wasn't sure if his expression signified despair, or fear. "She speaks the third sermon of the dead," Adam stammered. "She summons Abraxas."

A howl screeched from behind the steel door. He had to get Christa out of here. He could cut off the head of the snake, attack Basillades, grab the remote control for the door and freedom, fight off Rambitskov and the white robes as long as he could while Christa escaped. But when Hercules cut off Hydra's head, the serpent grew two in its place. He wasn't beyond learning from myths at this point.

Basillades waved her hand. Rambitskov grabbed Christa from behind and shoved her into the jail cell, crashing her against the far wall. He clanged the door shut behind her. Christa grabbed at the bars, rattled the door. Locked.

The white robes bowed their heads deeper. They started chanting, in barely more than a slow whisper, "Summum bonum, infinum falum. Summum bonum, infinum falum."

Braydon advanced towards Rambitskov. Every cell in his body was determined to hurt him for hurting Christa. "Rambitskov, I should have made sure those beasts tore you apart," he growled. Rambitskov pulled the cattle prod from his pocket, thrust it against the jail cell. Christa's hands sprang away as the electricity jolted across the metal bars.

"You can save her," said Adam, "but not like that. You must beat the monster and she will be set free."

Basillades clenched her outstretched hands into fists. "He is the monster of the underworld, the octopus with a thousand tentacles, he is the twistings of winged serpents and of madness," she said. "He is the lord of toads and frogs, who live in the water and come out unto the land, and who sing together at high noon and at midnight."

"Listen to Jung's third sermon," said Adam. "She is preparing you to face Abraxas."

"Jung, again," said Braydon. He was listening, all right, madness, frogs. He didn't need Christa's unification theory to show him that connection. A poison dart frog was what started all this. "Jung was a nut, but he was a prophetic nut." He scanned the chamber to find anything that could be used as a weapon. "I prefer the Navajo philosophy. Remember Joseph's message to you, Adam. A brave man dies once, a coward many times."

The white robes chanted louder. "Summum bonum, infinum falum."

"Remember Viet Nam, Adam" said Christa, urgency edging her voice. "Your cousin didn't want to see defenseless people hurt. Honor his legacy. Give Braydon his gun, at least."

Braydon approached Adam, his eye on his gun, tucked into Adam's belt. Adam still held the .45, aimed at him and cocked. "I am not the enemy," he said.

In his peripheral vision, Braydon saw Basillades plunge her hand into her robe pocket. She brandished the remote control like a knife. She pointed it at the steel door depicting the Abraxas. She pushed the red button.

The steel door slid aside with a reverberating clang. A cold, dank draft slunk in from the darkness beyond. The torches flickered, died down, then brightened. The monk nearest the door shifted his weight nervously, almost imperceptibly, bending his neck closer to the dirt floor. Fog rolled in from the doorway, like smoke from a wildfire. Then a putrid smell wafted into the chamber, mixed with the unmistakable scent of brine. Braydon's thoughts raced. The passageway beyond might tunnel through the buried ship hulls to the outside, perhaps a hidden exit to the waterfront. He just had to secure the way for Christa to escape the jail cell.

He peered deeper into the black of the passageway. Something shiny and golden approached, the torch light refracting back at him. "Something wicked this way comes," he muttered. A giant lion's head loomed suddenly in the opening. It was a mask, no, a helmet, its facepiece a fierce rendering of a lion pounded out of metal, with a wide, grimacing frown. A fierce scowl outlined the openings for the eyes. The lion's mane was a nest of stylized serpents.

The doorway was large, but it could not accommodate the bulk of the beast. It stooped to pass through it. The monks chanting grew louder and quicker. "Summum bonum, infinum falum. Summum bonum, infinum falum." The beast stomped fully into the chamber. It straightened to its full height. It was a giant of a man, lionhead helmet from his shoulders up, dressed like a gladiator from his shoulders down, in a layered leather skirt. His feet were shod in knee-high, studded leather boots, rather than sandals. One meaty hand wielded a large bronze shield, the other a long, serpentine whip.

"Abraxas is truly the terrible one," Bassillades shouted over the chanting. Her voice hungered for terror. "The sun and also the eternally gaping abyss of emptiness, magnificent even as the lion at the very moment when he strikes his prey down. He is the monster of the underworld... He is the bright light of day and the deepest night of madness. He is the mightiest manifest being, and in him creation becomes frightened of itself."

"The Abraxas!" Christa shouted from behind Braydon.

"This isn't a supreme being," Braydon shouted back over the chanting. "Superior, maybe," he added. The guy was built like Arnold Schwartzeneger on steroids.

"No," Christa shouted. "The Abraxas stone! It's hanging around his neck."

The beast raised its shield and rent the air with a mighty roar. Hanging from a thick, metal link chain around the behemoth's neck, dangling over the guy's heart, an alabaster-colored, engraved stone was mounted on brass metal that looked like an oversized skeleton key. Like the key of an old jail cell.

"The Abraxas is the key," said Adam. "To your liberation."

From the fog creeping in around the monster's feet, three snakes, rattlers, slithered over the beast's boot clad toes. Each snake was fatter and longer than the last, four-plus footers, each of them.

Braydon remained stock still as the snakes slithered frantically towards him, skirting his feet in a desperate attempt to find dark shelter. The monster leaned back. He recoiled his whip. Braydon turned away. Not quick enough. The whip slashed across his back like red hot fire. The searing pain brought him to his knees.

Christa cried out. By her pained expression, his wound must look as bad as it felt. Rambitskov lowered the cattle prod, and, if only for a moment, confusion, maybe even fear, focused Rambitskov's eyes. Whatever they drugged him with was wearing off. Could be good, or bad.

Braydon turned to see Adam fleeing through the tunnel that the Abraxas had emerged from. The steel door slammed shut behind him. The rat fleeing the sinking ship.

Braydon remained crouched. The Abraxas towered over him. This first hit had better be good. He sprang upwards, thrusting all his weight against the giant. He forced the Abraxas back, about two steps. The monster pushed Braydon off, drew back his shield and slung it forward. The full force of the monster's shield rounded into Braydon's chest, propelling him backwards. He crashed against the wall where they had first entered the chamber.

Braydon didn't take his eyes fully off his opponent, but he could see the biggest rattlesnake racing across the floor towards Christa and the darkest corner of the chamber. Christa pressed herself against the wall as the snake slithered through the bars. It saw her, a threat, blocking its way to survival. It coiled, rattling its tail furiously, ready to strike. Rambitskov moved towards the snake. He thrust the cattle prod through the bars, aiming for the snake. In an instant, the snake sprang at him, slicing through the bars. Its teeth clamped down on Rambitskov's calf. The snake slithered completely through the bars and quickly crossed the chamber.

Braydon had his own snake to worry about. The Abraxas recoiled his whip. He sprang it at Braydon. Braydon grabbed the whip with his left hand, and clamped down on it in sheer agony. He twisted the whip around the back of his wrist and yanked back, tearing it from the monster's grasp.

Basillades waved her arms about as she screamed over the thunderous chants of the monks. "There is nothing that can separate man from his own God, if man can only turn his gaze away from the fiery spectacle of Abraxas."

Braydon pushed himself up. He sprinted forward, leaping for the loading hook. He grasped onto the hook, but his hands were slick with blood and sweat. With every bit of determination, he swung forward, using his momentum as his weapon. He pounded his feet into the beast's lion helmet. His opponent's head jerked back. Braydon landed on all fours. The beast howled. In retaliation, it swung his boot-clad foot at Braydon with all his might. Braydon twisted, but the glancing blow to his chin brought stars to his eyes. The warmth of his blood spurted over his face.

Braydon clutched at the ground to steady himself. It was gritty, hard. The chanting hammered into his brain as dizziness threatened to blind him. "Summum bonum, infinum falum. Summum bonum, infinum falum." He grabbed two fistfuls of pebbles and thrust them at the face of the beast. Some met their mark, penetrating the mask's eye holes. The beast instinctively clamped his hand to his eyes. He flailed outwards with his shield, knocking Braydon across the chamber into the bars of the jail cell.

"He is the brightest light of the day and the deepest night of madness," Basillades screamed, her voice like a Banshee. "To see him means blindness; To know him is sickness; To worship him is death; To hear him is wisdom; Not to resist him means liberation."

The chanting suddenly stopped. Braydon tensed at the sudden silence. The monks must sense that he was close to being killed. Braydon grabbed onto the bars of the jail cell. His heart pounded in his chest, but his strength was spent. His bloody hands slipped on the steel as he struggled to heave himself back into the fight. Christa thrust her hand through the bars, grabbed onto his shoulder. "Stay down," she said.

Braydon shook his head. "I've got to beat him to save you."

"No," said Christa. "Bassilades said it. Not to resist him means liberation."

Braydon locked his gaze with Christa's. It went against every fiber of his moral being to crouch weakly while this monster prepared to deal him the final, deadly blow. Then he felt Christa press something into his palm. The cattle prod. He grabbed it, hid it against his chest as he stooped over it. The beast's deep, irregular breaths behind him grew louder, closer. The crunch of the leather boots put him within arm's reach, maybe. The putrid odor sharpened. From the beast's shadow cast by the torchlight, the giant stood above him, shield raised high. It would crush Braydon's skull in an instant.

In one sudden, swift movement, Braydon spun around.  He thrust the cattle prod up, jamming it into the man's ribs.  The electricity bolted up the giant's  torso, jagging up to his metal helmet.  The man went into violent spasms, uttering guttural, inhuman grunts.  Coils of smoke and the acrid stink of singed flesh escaped his wound.  He dropped his shield, clanging, to Braydon's side, and clawed at his lion helmet.  The electric current danced around the mane of serpents.  The man's eyes through the slits in the mask rolled back into his brain.

Braydon pulled away the cattle prod.  He lunged upward.  He clamped his free hand around the Abraxas stone and tore it from the man's neck.  The Abraxas teetered, then dropped backwards like a felled oak, landing with a thud.

Braydon's fingers were raw, trembling from the strain of the battle.  He fumbled the Abraxas key into the lock, his vision blurred, his brain misfiring.  He sensed movement behind him.  He hurriedly turned the key.  Christa yanked open the door.  He spun aside as she burst through it.  She swooped up the Abraxas shield.  She swung it with all her might, striking Basillades from the side.  The black robed woman fell, unconscious, to the floor, her robe fluttering around her like a shroud.

Beyond her, to Braydon's left, Rambitskov bulldozed his way through three of the monks, knocking them down like bowling pins.  The one with the Sig Sauer flung apart his robe and yanked the weapon from his belt.  Rambitskov fell upon it like a hungry animal.  Rambitskov tore the gun from the monk's hand, then shot him between the eyes.  The gunshot boomed in the confined space.  Blood and bone splattered the monk's white robe.  Black dust and pebbles peppered down from the dirt ceiling.

Christa frantically searched through Basillades's black robe.  "I found the remote," she yelled.  She pointed it at the trap door blocking the passage back to the record store.  The door clanged open.  "We got the Abraxas stone," she yelled.  "Let's go."

The chamber thundered with gunfire.  Rambitskov shot the monks, three as they attacked him, four of them in the back as they fled for the passageway back to the record store and escape.  The entire chamber began to shake.  Dirt from above rained down.

Braydon jiggled the Abraxas key out of the lock of the jail cell door.  He'd been around Christa too much.  He could now feel the power of the stone in his hand. It infused him with a second energy. He'd need it. He had a gun aimed at his forehead, Rambitskov's Sig Sauer.

Rambitskov's face was pallid, his expression a grimace. The snake venom had to be getting to him, but not fast enough. Rambitskov grabbed Christa by the elbow, yanked her to her feet. The remote flew out of her hand, dashing against a charred timber. The remote's cover popped off. The circuitry inside dropped to the ground. "Hand me the Abraxas stone, Fox," he growled. "It's the only way to save our country, and her."

Braydon had counted twelve shots, a full mag for the Sig Sauer. But Rambitskov could have loaded one in the chamber. Braydon asked himself if he was feeling lucky. He wasn't. But he couldn't hand over the Abraxas. Rambitskov could lock them in here and let them be buried alive.

Christa jammed her elbow into Rambitskov's gut and spun away from his grip. Braydon was beginning to love this woman. With his injured hand, he swept up the shield, screaming through the pain, and attacked. A gunshot boomed. The shield bucked back in Braydon's grip. The bullet punched right through the metal, but it was deflected to the right of Braydon's shoulder.

Braydon crashed into Rambitskov like a bull into a brick wall. The force of the hit wrenched his wounds with pain. A rumbling sound filled the chamber as more dirt, chunks now, dropped from the ceiling. The timbers on the far end creeked and cracked. With a sudden displacement of air, an avalanche of dirt crashed down in front of the escape route to the record store. It pounded down on the bodies of the monks, blocking the portal entirely.

Braydon coughed. The air was choked with dust. The torches sputtered and dimmed. Rambitskov lay unconscious. Braydon opened his fingers. The Abraxas stone was red with blood, but intact. "Okay," he said, "we're trapped, underground, with a bunch of dead people and unconscious maniacs, the ceiling about to collapse and bury us alive, but, hey, we got it, the last of these seven sacred stones." Maybe it was the energy of the stone, maybe just the surprised joy of still being alive, but Braydon couldn't help but smile at Christa. "Guess that means we're destined to live through this," he said.

Christa gathered the pieces of the broken remote. "Did I tell you I don't watch much television? It's because I can't work the damn remote." She tried to match the cover with the buttons onto the circuit board.

"I have complete confidence in you," said Braydon. "I'm not even going to point out that we have limited oxygen in here." He snatched up Christa's daypack, and fished out the silver box that held the Urim and Thummim. He opened the lid, and blinked. It was true, the stones, themselves, emitted some kind of energy, almost radiating light. He wiped as much of his blood as he could from the Abraxas stone, noting the monster with the lion head and snake legs carved into its back. He held out his hand to Christa. "I hope you're a Mark Twain fan," he said.

"You're either an amazing judge of character," she said, frantically piecing together remote's cover, "or really, really bad at last requests."

"Twain said to put all your eggs in one basket, then watch that basket," he said. "Hand me the neckpouch with the Emerald and Turquoise."

She hesitated, then slipped the lanyard from around her neck and tossed the pouch to him. "You might not know what the hell you're doing," she said, "but I trust Twain."

"I know that Turquoise has a hardness of 5.6 to 6.6 on Mohs scale, which means it will crack if struck forcibly," he said. He pulled apart the pouches drawstrings, and tumbled the Emerald and Turquoise onto the velvet lining of the silver box. The five stones winked and flashed, even in the dimming light of the oxygen-hungry torches. "Jacinth, the Abraxas stone, can be brittle, too. Shame if they shattered at this point." The box didn't have enough space for the diamond and sapphire wrapped in the hotel's linen napkin in his pocket. He placed the napkin, and the silver box, into Christa's pack and zipped it shut.

With a whoosh, the rear steel door, the one with the portrait of the Abraxas, slid open. The cool, dank, brine air that had cast fear into Braydon earlier now brought in hope. He nodded at Christa. "I knew you could do it."

Christa stood, her expression confused. "It wasn't me," she said.

Adam appeared, brandishing a Vietnam-issue Army rifle. His eyes scanned the chamber. "I heard the gunshots," he said. "I had to come back to help. I realized that this was the only way for me to find peace. I will not die again as a coward."

"Happy for you," said Braydon. "Now let's get out of here."

Braydon handed Christa her pack, shouldered his, and followed Christa and Adam into a passageway much like the one they had used to get to the chamber from the record store. Cement walls lit by caged, bare light bulbs, except there were no corners and the passage seemed to lead them up a gradual incline. On the left, they passed a ten by fifteen foot barred room, spartanly outfitted with a bunk, sink, toilet and a crude wooden desk and chair. The only items on the desk were a used syringe and rubber tourniquet. Gray overalls hung from the single hook on the wall. Workmen's boots had been placed neatly below. It must have been where Bassillades had the man transform into the Abraxas. Braydon found himself feeling sorry for the man who had just tried to fight him to the death, and nearly succeeded.

The air grew cooler, moister. A dim gray seeped in from the gloomy outdoors ahead. The tang of brine air enveloped him. They emerged beneath a pier on the Embarcadero. The fog was thick. He could barely make out the massive structure of the Oakland Bay Bridge towering above them. On another day, it would look surreal. Today, nothing was more surreal than reality.

"This way," Adam said. "Up here. I know a safe place where you can get cleaned up." He led them to a metal staircase zigzagging up to the pier. As he reached the top, Braydon scanned the wide, long, and empty cement pier, probably only active when the big cruise ships docked here. The only boat tied to the pier was a moderate-size motor yacht, which would look like a behemoth against the J24 sailboat now tacking beneath the Bay Bridge but was dwarfed by the immensity of the commercial pier.

They hurried down the pier. "A friend of mine is that yacht's main cook and bottle washer," he said. "The owners are only here in summer. You can stay as long as you like."

The yacht was docked fifty yards down the pier. Braydon figured he could make it just that far before collapsing. He was worried about Christa. She was uncharacteristically quiet, a bit shell-shocked. A hot shower, and food, would do them both good, but they couldn't linger. Donohue was waiting for their call. The retired colonel would have mustered the strike force and arranged transport to Colombia by now. "You've redeemed yourself, Adam," said Braydon. "And thanks, but we need to get cleaned up, make a phone call and clear out."

A gangplank led onto the foredeck of the motor yacht. Its name was scripted in nautical blue on its hull, *Flying Carpet II*. Adam held open the door to the main cabin. It was luxuriously decked out in rich, mahogany paneling, velvet lounge chairs, with richly framed antique maps lining the walls. Braydon hesitated. A familiar aluminum briefcase sat on the glass coffee table. Someone was sitting in the lounge chair at the far end of the cabin. The chair swiveled around to face him. It was Baltasar Contreras.

# CHAPTER 62

Braydon's first reaction was to kill Contreras with his bare, bloody hands. He advanced across the yacht's cabin to do just that. Two men sidled through the aft door of the cabin, both armed and no doubt dangerous. One had an Uzi, a bit overkill. The other, a Glock handgun. Braydon stopped his advance by the mahogany bar. A sudden dizzy spell threatened to topple him. He shook it off. "Baltasar Contreras," he said. "You're under arrest for the attempted murder of Jared Sadler."

Baltasar grinned, and then laughed outright. "Agent Braydon Fox," he said. "I knew you would be a worthy opponent, but look at you. Adam, do get a fresh towel from behind the bar, there. I do believe Agent Fox is dripping blood on my Aubusson carpet. Adam told me about your battle with that marvelous Abraxas beast in the gladiator outfit. I do wish I could have seen you in action."

Adam, unbelievably, edged past Braydon to get behind the bar. "Busted," Braydon seethed at him. "From guardian of one of the world's most precious objects to gofer."

Christa must have sensed that Braydon was going to do something stupid, like strangle the hippie with his own love beads. She came beside him and grasped his arm. She turned to Adam as the hippie offered Braydon a white terry bar towel. "Why did you do                          it,                          Adam," she asked. "What did Contreras offer you?"

Adam's face was no longer ashen, but flushed. He shakily laid the towel on the bar in response to Braydon's sneer. "Peace, man," he said. "Baltasar Contreras will use the sacred stones as they were meant to be used, to restore the Breastplate of Aaron, to bring peace to the world."

"He kidnapped my niece," she said. "He poisoned the water supply which will kill thousands of people in New York. He has brought madness, not peace."

Baltasar Contreras stood. His bodyguards tensed. "I did not poison the water to kill people," he said, "but to save them."

"Gabriella knew about your plans to manufacture the poison," said Christa. "She was desperate to find an antidote. She knew that was the only way to stop you."

"And yet Gabriella was the one who set this catastrophe in motion," said Contreras, "simply by trying to stop it. Then, in Arizona, your finding that artifact prompted me to have to try to take it from you. Agent Fox, here, told his superior about my involvement. Of course, Mister Rambitskov was kind enough to provide a fake alibi, but the risk of exposure became too great. We had to act. Rambitskov wanted the poison proven as the perfect weapon of mass destruction, so that he could fund his precious Homeland Security department, protect the nation from the fanatics."

"Takes one to know one," Braydon grumbled.

"You cannot deny the divine signs," Contreras pressed. "The cliff dwelling revealed, the Emerald salvaged, the Kohinoor diamond and Edward's sapphire successfully purloined, the G-20 meeting, even as we speak, in New York,." He raised his arms upward. "I am the Prophet. My followers around the world await my missive upon restoring the Breastplate. I know now, more than ever, that God is calling me to reveal His wisdom, to bring peace to His world."

"World peace?" said Christa. "You want world domination."

"That I have nearly obtained," said Contreras, grabbing the air with his fists. "Within an hour of the New York stock exchange opening bell tomorrow morning I will become one of the richest men in the world. I came into a large amount of capital this weekend. In fact, I had my investor from Abu Dhabi throw in this Flying Carpet II yacht as a bonus. I was prescient enough to short the market. As the market plunges, my fortune will skyrocket. Before the feds can place a stop on trading, I will have transferred it all, under my shadow corporation, of course, into an account that is untouchable. With that wealth and the power of the Breastplate, I will, in fact, dominate the world."

"What's left of it," said Braydon. A plan was forming in his head, but his brain was so exhausted, he wasn't sure if it made sense.

"All I am giving to the people is what they are yearning for," Contreras said. "Something to believe in."

Braydon turned to Adam, still behind the bar. He scanned the bottles lined neatly up on the shelf behind the hippie. All top shelf liquor, all topped with a silver pourer, their pointy spouts like royal guard helmets. "Scotch, rocks," he said.

Adam looked to Contreras, who nodded. "Agent Fox," said Contreras, as Adam dropped cubes with silver tongs into the crystal glass on the bar. "Speaking of rocks, thank you so much for taking the trouble to acquire them for me. I knew you would succeed."

"Which is why you sent your dog, Rambo, after them," said Braydon. He grabbed the bottle from Adam's hand, poured his own Scotch. It trickled like liquid gold from the silver spout.

"A wise man must have contingencies," said Contreras.

So true. "I suppose you'll kill us if we don't give them to you."

"I may kill you even if you do," said Contreras, "but both of you have proven yourselves worthy of a place in my new empire. Just as I promised, Professor Devlin, your niece is home. I allowed her to be rescued. Cooperate with me and she will be truly safe, along with all the others. I do prefer to avoid bloodshed unless it is necessary. I am a peaceful man." Contreras sat back down in the plush lounge chair, shifting his weight, leaning back. "You both know as well as I do that I am in the best position to restore the Breastplate and find the antidote," he said. "It is my destiny. I am the chosen one."

"Chosen by whom is the question," said Braydon.

"The question you should be asking yourselves," said Contreras. "You have been haunted by phantoms, nearly crushed beneath a cathedral, half drowned in the desert, and attacked by mythical Skinwalkers. Don't you see that a higher being is trying to stop you?"

"Good point," said Braydon, eyeing the silver spout on the Scotch bottle, judging if it was strong enough.

"Braydon," said Christa, "you can't possibly believe him."

"Christa, you expect me to believe that these stones have a supernatural power," he said, "an energy, and when replaced in this Biblical Breastplate, they will create a direct connection to God. Solve the mystery of life after death. All Contreras is saying is that you're right. Something else, something extraterrestrial, is at work here."

"As in divine?" she said. "Consider this. The phantoms in New York seemed to be shoving the two men into a fight. It distracted the police so we could get away. We weren't crushed beneath Saint Patrick's Cathedral, but shown an escape route. The flash flood saved us from the men who were chasing us. The Skinwalkers killed those who would kill us."

"All I care about is getting the antidote," he said, the Scotch hot on his dry throat. "Saving those people. Saving your nephew."

"Agent Fox, you and I seek the same goal," said Contreras. "You've done enough. You're injured, exhausted. Even if you did find the Breastplate before me, it would do you no good without all seven of the missing sacred stones." He leaned forward, reaching for the silver Halliburton briefcase on the coffee table. He opened the case, and rotated it so that Braydon and Christa could see its contents. "The Kohinoor Diamond and Edward's Sapphire. Two of the most famous and stunningly beautiful gems in the world."

Contreras's diamond and sapphire were stunning. Braydon couldn't tell the difference between the fakes in the briefcase and the authentic diamond and sapphire that he had taken from Jared's hotel room, the gems that were wrapped in a linen napkin in Christa's daypack. Jared had been a master, and Braydon had to control his rage at Contreras's brutal attack on the jeweler. "But even the Kohinoor and Edward's Sapphire find their true glory only with their peers." He poured himself another Scotch. "The Breastplate can only be restored if one man has all seven sacred stones."

Contreras snapped his briefcase shut. "You are experienced enough, Agent Fox, to know you don't have a chance of taking the diamond and sapphire from me. You are unarmed. You have no possible weapon at your disposal nor means of escape. My men would shoot you down before you get twenty yards down that pier."

"There is that," he said, "and the fact that you have the means to quickly distribute the antidote. You have made me persona non grata in the Bureau. It will take me days just to convince them that this crazy story is true."

"My international network is ready to unleash the poison, or distribute the antidote, at my command," said Contreras. "Those two envelopes on the bar." He leaned forward, smiling. He looked smug. "One is for each of you. Each contains a number to a one million dollar Swiss bank account. All you need is the proprietary access code, which I shall give to you when you give me the gems."

Braydon downed the Scotch. It didn't even begin to dull the pain. The slash from the whip throbbed across the back of his shoulders. He set his glass on the bar, his blood smearing the cut crystal. He took the towel Adam had placed on the bar. He wrapped it around his right hand and grasped the shoulder strap of Christa's backpack. She gripped onto the strap, stepping back, trying to yank it from his grasp. He looked at her. "Give me the pack, Christa," he said.

Her expression of betrayal hurt him more than any of his wounds. "You can't give him the stones," she said. "You can't trust him."

"I'm asking you to trust me," he said. "Remember. We learned, together, from Seneca. We survived the trap in Saint Patrick's. We'll survive this." He didn't dare say aloud the Seneca quote in Latin. Contreras might recognize it. He had to trust in Christa's brilliant mind, and in their experiences together. After the events of the past two days, she knew better than anyone. *The outward appearances of things are deceiving.*

He pulled the pack forcefully off her shoulder. He unzipped the main compartment, and extracted the silver box. He faced Contreras. "I wondered," he said, "what one of the richest men in the world would pay for these." He opened the box, swiveled it around, and showed Contreras the contents. The five sacred stones shimmered in the black velvet. "Make it two million for each of us," he said. "And throw in this yacht as a bonus. We could live pretty well on this Flying Carpet until this all blows over."

Contreras leaned forward, his mouth agape. He licked his lips hungrily. A man like him, he'd want to make this moment last, prove that he was in control of his lust, and everyone else. "You are hardly in a position to negotiate, Agent Fox," he said. "Now that I know for sure that you have all five stones here, I can simply kill you."

"You still need to find the Breastplate," said Braydon. "We know how to find the temple. You're looking in the wrong place."

"A foolish consistency is the hobgoblin of little minds, Fox," said Contreras. "I know about the armillary sphere, and Tristan de Luna's map."

Braydon snapped the silver box shut, jammed it back into the pack, and zipped the compartment closed. "Dubler," he muttered. He expected as much when Dubler didn't meet them at the airport. He would like to believe that Contreras took Dubler under duress, forced him to talk, but he knew better.

"Mister Dubler came to me to save you, Professor Devlin." Contreras sipped his Scotch like a cat swallowing the canary. "Now you have the chance to save him. Bring me the gems, Fox."

"Don't do it, Braydon. Daniel wouldn't have betrayed us unless he was near death."

Contreras grinned. "That statement I cannot refute."

Christa stepped closer to the bar, fists clenched. "He'll kill Daniel once we give him the gems," she said.

"Mister Dubler will most certainly be dead," Contreras said. Contreras tensed his shoulders. The two guards stiffened, their hands moving to their guns, their eyes on Christa.

Braydon swung Christa's pack over his left shoulder, on top of his pack. "Looks like you've got us in checkmate," he said. She was drawing attention to herself, and off him, too well. He picked up the bottle of Scotch with his good hand, and clutched his glass with his hand wrapped in the towel. He made his way towards Contreras, casually pouring himself another Scotch as he skirted to the back of the teak dining table by the window, more importantly, on the opposite side of the cabin from Christa.

From the corner of his eye, he saw Christa lunge across the bar, reaching for Adam's gun. In one, swift movement, he jammed the pointy silver spout of the bottle into the window. With a crash, the safety glass shattered. A torrent of small crystals rained to the floor. Braydon dropped his glass. He thrust himself forward, leading with his towel-wrapped hand. He dove through the broken window to the starboard deck. He rolled and tucked onto the fiberglass deck, staying low, behind the cabin wall. The meathead bodyguard with the Uzi let loose, accomplishing nothing more than shattering the remaining shards of glass and everyone's eardrums.

Braydon could barely hear Contreras shouting at the guy to cease and desist. Braydon was in position by the time the bad guys scrambled onto the deck to flank him. The thug with the Uzi was to the stern. The guy with the Glock to the bow. Contreras was behind the man with the Glock, holding Christa in a chokehold. Adam decided not to join the party, probably hiding behind the bar thinking it's all a bad trip.

The side decking was narrow, just enough for one person to walk comfortably the length of the boat. Braydon stood, holding Christa's pack over the railing, dangling it above the water. "One step closer and the pack goes overboard," said Braydon.

Contreras tightened his hold on Christa's neck. For a pudgy guy, he was strong. "Then I would be forced to break Professor Devlin's neck," he said. "And cancel my offer of employment."

"Release her, and I'll toss you the pack. The five stones are in it."

"You can forget about your signing bonus," said Contreras.

"I figured if I traded this pack for those two envelopes, all I'd be signing is our death warrants," he said. "But I do trust you to do one thing, get that antidote. A guy like you won't stop at being one of the richest men in the world. You need to be on top. Once your pharmaceutical company is the only one manufacturing that antidote, you'll have unmatched power and influence on a global scale."

Contreras grinned. "It is a shame that you don't trust me," he said. "You would make such a companionable number two in my budding empire." He released his chokehold on Christa. She sucked in air, rubbed her neck, stepped away.

"Jump over the side, Christa" Braydon said. "And swim for the staircase under the pier."

"I'm not leaving you," she croaked out.

Contreras forcefully shoved her over. She screamed in surprise, and splashed into the water. Braydon recoiled his arm to toss the pack to Contreras. Then, he twisted, flinging the pack into the water as far from the pier as he could throw it. He dove into the water, the cold stabbing him with a thousand needles. He clawed to the surface, sputtered for air, and pierced through the water in a racer's freestyle after Christa, his pack scraping excruciatingly against his wound. The bang of weapon fire came from the thug with the Glock. Bullets slit and zinged into the water to either side of him. "Forget them!" shouted Contreras. "Get that pack before it sinks."

Braydon twisted around as he swam.   The thugs dropped their
firearms and dove into the water, fully clothed.  They raced for the
pack, surface diving to grab it as it sunk beneath the waves.

Christa had reached the staircase.  She helped him out of the
water.  They were both shivering, just this side of hypothermic.

She yanked him up.  "Come on.   The thugs are in the water.
Let's go back for those stones."

He was bent over, heaving in breaths.  "I got them," he said.

"The diamond and sapphire," she said, "in Contreras's briefcase.
Not the five stones we had.  I figured you must have switched packs
and still have those."

That made him catch his breath.   "That obvious?   I'm glad
Contreras isn't as smart as you."

"He just doesn't know you like I do."

He pointed at her.  "I knew I'd get you to like me."

"I'll like you even better when we have the diamond and
sapphire."

"Promise?"

"Sure, I promise."   She tugged on his arm.  "Let's get to the
yacht before those thugs."

He sloughed the pack off his shoulder, unzipped the main
compartment.   The linen napkin was moist, but little water had
seeped into the pack.  He placed the napkin on his palm, and opened
it, showing her the Kohinoor Diamond and Edward's Sapphire.
"What we got," he said, "is real.   And I will never give that up
without a fight."

# DAY 5

CHAPTER **63**

Christa clenched onto the armrests and the remnants of breakfast roiling her stomach as she peered out the Blackhawk helicopter window. Gusts buffeted the chopper like a cat with a toy. It skimmed above a rainforest canopy so dense it formed a second layer of Earth. No wonder some of the tribes of western Colombia still lived in isolation. To penetrate that canopy was to cross into a different world. The treetops shook with anger, raising fists of green that threatened to swat down and swallow up any human invaders. It was a good thing that, like Braydon, she caught a few hours of dead sleep on the overnight flight from San Francisco to Bogota. The adrenaline that shot through her system with each downdraft wasn't about to let her rest here. She had just hours to find the temple, restore the Breastplate and return with the antidote plant from the hidden canyon.

From the pilot seat in front of her, Donohue's voice crackled over her headset. "Radar shows squalls coming in fast," he said. "Once our skids hit the ground, we got a ten-minute countdown before we head out. Make it count."

"We can't see them," Braydon said. He sat next to her, his eyes focused intently on the rainforest below. "But they sure as hell can see us."

He was right, if the guerillas were down there. Typical military thinking, outfitting everyone and everything in camouflage, for all the good it would do. Even the chopper was painted in camouflage greens and browns, a Blackhawk in service in the war on drugs, now commandeered by Donohue from a local contact in the CIA. It was big and powerful enough to hold a dozen men and their weapons. But even with the intermittent thunder and howls of wind, anybody on the ground would see and hear it coming.

In addition to the camouflage fatigues from the cap to the heavy tread army boot, Braydon carried a hefty sidearm on his right hip, a knife that Rambo would envy on his left. She had been coerced into carrying a more manageable .22 pistol in a hip holster, and what Donohue had termed a pilot's survival knife, a five-inch non-glare blade with a sawtooth edge on one side for cutting branches. The weapons, like the camouflage, only gave the illusion of self protection.

Donohue's spotty transmission crackled through her headset. "The storm is screwing with the radio, but we're still picking up Hunter's homing beacon."

Christa pressed her hand against Donohue's seat back to balance against a nasty knock of wind. Braydon winced as his back scraped across his seat. He had refused to spend the time to go to a hospital after the fight with the Abraxas. He insisted he needed a quick fix, just enough to get through the next twenty-four hours. After that, it would be too late anyway. Donohue's medic had patched him up, and thrust a handful of painkillers at him.

Christa's headset sizzled with a fizz of the lightning that flashed behind them, then Braydon's voice. "We're flying into a trap," he said. "Contreras let us get away from that yacht way too easy."

"Almost getting killed was easy. Surviving it," she said, "not so much."

"He's played us against ourselves before," he said. "We're overlooking something."

"Don't overlook what we're looking over," she said. She gestured out the window. Endless variations of green. "The nearest village is miles downriver, and that was no more than a half dozen round buildings with thatch roofs. The only way in or out of here is by air or dugout canoe." She pointed at the serpentine waterway snaking through the dense jungle. "They can't beat us without a helicopter."

"Thar she blows," said Donohue. He nodded towards Christa's side of the chopper. "The Demon's Wings rock formation. Given Luna's map, that's got to be it at our ten o'clock."

From the air, it did look like the backs of a pair of whales arching above the ocean of green. Donohue maneuvered the chopper downwards. A different perspective emerged, the curved shoulders of a hunched bird of prey so large that it towered above the tree canopy.

Braydon scoured the jungle with field glasses. "Contreras's guerillas could have a platoon staking out the temple and we wouldn't see them in that vegetation," he said. "Gabriella said they were close to finding it when Percival rescued her."

"I don't see anyone," she said. "And they don't have Luna's map."

"They had Dubler," he said. "He had seen Luna's map."

Christa grabbed her armrest as Donohue corrected against a downdraft. The colonel's expression was grave. "At least they didn't get the original from your brother-in-law. He is damn lucky he wasn't killed and Luna's map wasn't compromised," Donohue growled, his anger clear even through the headset. "He should have waited for my strike force before engaging the enemy."

Donohue's zeal for military parlance put her on edge. "He had the Muisca Indians fighting with him," she said. "The shaman had convinced the tribe to attack. Their families' safety was at risk. They were ready, pumped up. In military terms, he had an overwhelming force to scare off Contreras's guerillas." The news in the last radio transmission to reach them was better than they could have hoped for. Percival, alongside the Muisca fighters, had rescued Gabriella. Then the other boot dropped. Percival had been shot in the gut. He needed medical attention. And Gabriella had twisted, maybe broken, her ankle in the skirmish.

"Doubtful," said Braydon, "Hardline mercenaries would not retreat before a math professor, a botanist, and a handful of brave but primitively armed Indians. His wife's life was in danger. That kind of thing can make a man act, not think."

"For once I agree with Fox," Donohue grumbled. "But we got to stay on target."

A bang of distant thunder rattled the sides of the chopper. The concussion shoved the chopper sideways.

Donohue, intense but calm, corrected. "Crap," he said. "That felt like anti-aircraft fire."

"No such luck," said Braydon. He pointed out his window. Christa leaned forward to look beyond Braydon. An immense plume of smoke billowed into the sky from the mountains on the horizon.

"What happened to God being on our side," she said, her throat dry. "The volcano. It's erupting."

Donohue banked the chopper for a better view. "Who in hell did you piss off this time, Fox?" Lightning fizzed through her headset. Thunder rumbled, shaking the chopper. "My men's clearing is up ahead," said Donohue. "ETA two minutes. We land, get the intel, take off. We are out of time, people. As soon as we take off with my strike force, Hunter, Gabriella, my medic and the shaman will head downriver in the dugout canoe for the Doctors without Borders clinic. We swing by and help with evacuation when the mission is complete."

"Isn't that volcano in the direction of the temple?" she said.

"I figure about twenty klicks west of our target," said Braydon. "How does a Blackhawk handle in an ash cloud?"

"I've flown in worse," said Donohue, "but let's not stop for tea."

The clearing was ahead, at a bend in the river. It looked like a scar, a bullet hole punched through the green. In less than three hours, the strike force had arrived, secured the area, and cleared away the nearly impenetrable jungle with two chainsaws, machetes and muscle. Their three motorized dugout canoes nosed the shore like curious fish. A small wood fire fought bravely against the wind, sending out its plume of smoke, a scaled down version of the deadly cloud growing on the horizon.

The chopper circled before landing. Christa counted eight of Donohue's men, all dressed in full combat fatigues, each with a camouflage helmet with goggles. Each clutched a machine gun clipped to his vest like a mother with her baby. The chopper wash flattened the scrappy vegetation at their feet. The men were poised, ready for action. They were all retired military, but not one of them had to suck in a beer belly. Each looked like they could take out three guys half their age and better armed.

She twisted in her seat to find Percival. He was lying on the ground at the edge of the clearing nearest the fire. That had to be the shaman bending over Percy's prone body. The man, dressed in what looked like red Bermuda shorts and a feathered headband, was blowing smoke over Percy, taking a puff off a long-stemmed pipe, then blowing again. Gabriella sat on Percival's other side. She let go of his hand and waved both arms at the chopper, her expression both fearful and relieved. Christa swallowed down a flood of emotion at seeing her sister.

As the skids set down, one of Donohue's men ran to them in a crouched position and slid open the door on Christa's side of the helicopter. Donohue toggled a series of switches, and turned to face her. "This is Leader," he shouted. "Retired Navy seal. He'll be in command of the ground force at the temple."

Christa nodded. She removed her headset and scrambled out, staying low to avoid the wash of the blades, holding on to the brim of the camouflage hat that held back her hair. Braydon stayed behind with Donohue in the chopper, shouting a conversation with him and Leader, something about another helicopter in the vicinity thirty minutes earlier. She crossed the clearing and hurried straight for Percival.

She crouched when she reached Gabriella. They shared a tight but abbreviated embrace. Percy didn't look good. His face was pale, clammy. He was either asleep or unconscious. An IV bag hung on a makeshift pole whittled from a sapling. The steam from the tea in a metal cup by his head carried a sharp, woodsy aroma. The medicine man no doubt had concocted the potion. One or the other of the liquid elixirs, maybe both, might be the only thing keeping him alive. She lifted the coarse blanket covering him. His wound had been bandaged, but blood was seeping through.

Gabriella's ankle was expertly bound with a stretchy, flesh-colored bandage, but her foot was bare and dirty, too swollen for her boot. She still wore her "field uniform," as she called it, khaki shirt, shorts and a tan old-style photographer's vest with multiple patch pockets, but it was torn, streaked with mud and smelled of sweat. She looked like she hadn't showered, or slept more than a few hours, in days.

Gabriella grasped her hand and squeezed, but it felt weak, depleted. "Any news on Liam?"

"Nothing since the last radio transmission."

"I'm going to kill Contreras for what he did to my son."

"Get in line, behind me."

The shaman muted his chanting. He no longer blew smoke over Percy. The small, old man sat back on his haunches. His eyes were black and sharp as obsidian. He understood every word she had said. The shaman, against his bare, brown chest, wore a pendant of gold. It was beautifully crafted, a bird of prey, with hunched wings, its pounded gold beak sharp, its talons outstretched, curved and hooked. Gold, as Conroy said, endures. And so did certain friendships.

Gabriella gestured towards the shaman. "This is Jairo Salaman." She spoke a few words in the local dialect. Salaman nodded.

Conroy's golden El Dorado figurine was in the velvet pouch that once held the Emerald and Turquoise. She unbuttoned her camouflage shirt, opened the pouch's drawstrings, and let El Dorado dance onto her open palm. She held it towards the shaman.

A glitter sparkled in his black eye. A smile formed from his wrinkle of a mouth. "Conroy," the shaman said.

"Your old friend told me to bring this figurine to you," she said. "Conroy remembered your father's words, that El Dorado is a guardian, between Earth and Heaven. Only he can show you the way to paradise. Only El Dorado can show us the entrance to the Oculto Canyon."

Salaman untied the leather string that held his golden eagle pendant. He took the El Dorado figurine from Christa's open palm, and hooked it onto the eagle's talons. El Dorado dangled below the eagle. Salaman spoke. Gabriella translated. "Jairo says that the words passed down to him are, when the eagle of the Earth meets the eagle of Heaven, El Dorado will be the guide."

"That's it?" asked Christa. "What does it mean?"

"It's been five hundred years," said Gabriella, "but less is lost in translation than you might think."

"Thanks, Gabby. Very helpful."

Salaman held the leather string out towards her. Christa bowed so he could tie it around her neck. The beautiful golden pendant looked incongruously fragile and beautiful against her camouflage shirt. It was a reminder that it wasn't the pendant's creators who had caused this pending catastrophe. "I will do all I can to follow El Dorado's guidance and return this pendant to you," she said directly to Salaman.

The old man nodded.

"As I told you over the radio," Gabriella said. "I showed Luna's map from the armillary sphere to Jairo. Now that we know where to look, he recognized the landmark. What Tristan de Luna called Demon's Wings the locals call the Rock of the Black Eagle."

"Donohue eyeballed it from the air. He says that it's three miles northwest of here, up in the foothills," said Christa.

"In the forbidden territory," Gabriella added. "Head towards the Rock of the Black Eagle, which rises above the jungle. He says that legend claims that the eagle clawed away a clearing with its talons. The clearing is long grown over, but that is where you'll find the entrance to the temple and, from there, the Oculto Canyon." She fished a folded paper from her breast pocket and opened it.

"We?" It was a detailed botanical drawing of a plant, rendered in colored pencil. It had coarsely serrated, triangular leaves, a hairy stem, and a large flower with four broad, ruffled petals in yellow with a semi-circle of purple where the petal joined the bristly yellow center of the bloom. A cutaway drawing showed a green, bulbous pod, its pinched top crowned with a multi-spoked wheel of lime green.

Gabriella pointed to the sketch. "Jairo described this plant for me. When he was very young, he was too eager to try the ways of the shaman. In gleaning the poison from the dart frog, his finger slipped. The poison entered his system. He was dying. His father was desperate. His father ventured into the forbidden territory to search for the plant that legend says could heal his son," she said. "His father would not speak of what he had seen there, but he returned with a plant which he and his fathers before him had never seen before. He dared only to bring a few leaves and seed pods from the forbidden territory, but he was able to extract the cure. Jairo lived. The leaves died and the seedlings would not flourish."

"The antidote plant," Christa said. "The plant that started all of this."

Gabriella nodded. "This is the plant we seek. Jairo has seen it nowhere else in the jungle. It must be unique to the hidden canyon's cloud forest microcosm. His father told him the legend says this plant grows alongside the stream that is the canyon's blood, that whoever drinks the water in the stream will have life."

"The Quesada expedition," said Christa, "Alvaro Contreras gave his poisoned men the water to drink. It saved them."

"The results should be immediate," said Gabriella.

Christa took the sketch from Gabriella. "Got it," she said. As if. She studied the sketch with a sick feeling in her stomach. The sketch was expertly drawn, no doubt about that, but within ten feet radius grew at least thirty different species of plant. The subtle shades of green were dizzying.

Gabriella slid her injured ankle in closer. She tried not to grimace. Percy groaned, as if sensing his wife's pain. "I'm coming with you, Christa."

"We don't have time for this."

"I'm the expert botanist. It's my son whose life depends on finding the antidote plant."

"I will find it, Gabby." *I don't know how, but I will.* If only she could truly believe that.

"There are things that you," she hesitated, "don't understand. It's the Breastplate of Aaron. There are forces here, deadly forces."

"You don't think I can handle it."

"You can't," she said. "You abandoned Dad. You don't believe anymore. Not since Mom."

"Abandoned him? I only stayed with Dad for as long as I did to take the pressure off you," she said, "so you could be with Percy, start a family. Leave Mom out of this."

"Haven't you figured it out by now? Mom is why we are in this. My family might die because we didn't find the Breastplate first."

"Yet." Christa pointed at her. "Didn't find it first, yet."

"I can't give up, not when my husband and son could be dying." She struggled to stand. Her ankle buckled.

"You aren't giving up. You're going to that clinic. You're getting ready." *And you're on drugs if you think I'm going to let you slow us down.* "Believe in me, Gabriella. One last time." Wanting to believe, it's what got her into this mess in the first place. Now it might be the only thing that saves her.

Braydon jogged up to her side and crouched. He quickly surveyed Percival's condition, and nodded to the shaman by way of

greeting.    Salaman nodded back.    "Gabriella Devlin Hunter,"
Braydon said.  "Remember me? Special Agent Fox."  He shook her
hand.

Gabriella narrowed her eyes.  His good looks weren't lost on her.
Nor the determination in his eyes.  "Fox," she said.  "My daughter's
favorite animal."

"I was hoping for your sister's."

"I should go with you on this," Gabriella said.

"We will get that antidote, Dr. Hunter.  We will save your son in
time.  We may be at the doorway to Hell, but nothing is going to
stop me from getting back."  He gestured to the four men nearby.
They double-timed it over.   Three of them surrounded Percival,
lifted him bodily, one of them grabbing the IV bag.  "We'll complete
the mission, double back to the clinic and medevac you two out of
the clinic downstream."  They carried Percival towards the canoe.
"Donohue's medic was on the front line in Iraq," he said.  "Percival
is in good hands, and that clinic has the equipment and supplies he
needs.  Christa, you get the intel?"

Christa showed him the sketch.  Braydon eyed it intently, as if
taking a mental photo.  "This is Jairo Salaman," she said.  "He's
confirmed that the plant we need grows along the stream in the
Oculto Canyon."

Gabriella grabbed the canvas drawstring bag from the ground
next to her and thrust it at Christa.  "Fill this sack with the plant's
leaves, stems, and roots, but, most importantly, the seedpods.
They'll be the round balls on top of the stems of plants not in flower.
If this papaver works like the opium poppy, we can extract the latex
from the seedpod to make the antidote.  Take a live specimen with
the dirt intact if you can.  It's unlikely I can propagate it outside the
Oculto Canyon microcosm, but it's worth a try."

"The entire water system of New York and Princeton is
poisoned," said Christa, holding up the empty sack.  "Will this be
enough?"

"Contreras only needed a minute amount of the belladonna toxin
to poison the water supply.  My research shows that the antidote
plant will work in the same way.  Jairo agrees, and his expertise is
unmatched."

The fourth soldier helped Gabriella to stand and hooked her arm
over his shoulder.  "Agent Fox," said Gabriella, "I've got a field lab

set up back at the village. Jairo and I are ready to quickly process the plant specimen into an extract that can be used as the antidote."

Braydon nodded. "Donohue and I have got Washington gearing up for mass distribution." He eyed the distant volcano plume rising into the storm clouds above the jungle canopy. "He's already got the jet fueled and ready for the trip to the States."

Gabriella reached for his hand, squeezed it. Christa was aching to do the same. Salaman rose silently and stood next to her.

Braydon turned to go. The shaman grabbed his arm with his wiry fingers. The old man's words sounded like jibberish, but his urgency was clear. "Jairo Salaman warns you," Gabriella translated. "The temple is protected by a tribe of spirits. No, the word is more ominous than that. By a tribe of phantoms, of ghosts. This ghost tribe are fierce warriors. They are the descendants of the men that the conquistador, Alvaro Contreras, enslaved to defend the temple. The men had no families to return to. Their wives and children had been killed. They made a pact to become warriors, to protect the temple from any outsiders, so that the magic could not kill again. They may be legend. Or they may be real."

Like the phantoms she had been seeing, the shadows she had thought were malevolent, but, in talking with Adam, realized might have been helping their cause. This time, the phantoms would not be on their side.

"If these men do exist," said Braydon, "they are fighting for what they believe will save others. They are protecting their home. Fighters like that don't surrender, but intruders like us have no right to kill them."

The shaman spoke. Gabriella translated. "The ghost tribe will never allow the Breastplate to leave the temple."

Braydon turned to the shaman. "Tell him that we'll do our best not to engage them, but we have to complete this mission or a Contreras will kill many families again."

Salaman was a good foot shorter than Braydon. He was shorter, even, than Christa, but his presence was commanding. As he spoke, he gestured toward the El Dorado pendant around her neck.

"Jairo says that El Dorado will serve as a talisman. Perhaps if the ghost tribe sees it, they will know you are not their enemy," said Gabriella. "But the ghost tribe is not of this village, or, in our way of thinking, of this world. The ghost tribe has its own laws."

Braydon eyed the pendant. "Thank you," he said to the shaman. "We will return it to you when our mission is complete."

Christa took one last look at Percival in the dugout canoe, and hugged Gabriella goodbye. She hurried to catch up to Braydon's long strides as he crossed the clearing towards the chopper, the stink of volcanic sulfur leading the way to hell.

CHAPTER **64**

*Please allow me to introduce myself. I'm a man of wealth and taste.* The driving beat and ominous words of the Rolling Stones' *Sympathy for the Devil* blasted through Christa's headset. The tension in the chopper ratcheted up. The men sat stony-faced and silent. The one they called Buck bobbed his head to the Stones' rhythm. They had been in jungle combat before, bad stuff, special ops. Even they knew they had faced nothing like this. *I was around when Jesus Christ, had his moment of doubt and pain.*

She tugged at the harness that Braydon had strapped over her camouflage fatigues. Don't think about it. Stick to the plan. Focus on that. Trust in the men in your unit. Live. *I rode a tank. Held a general's rank. When the blitzkrieg raged. And the bodies stank.*

Below, the impenetrable canopy of browns and greens blurred into a single hue as the helicopter skimmed over the rainforest. Inside the chopper, an alien force in camouflage came to invade an unknown planet. Like the conquistadors. *But what's puzzling you is the nature of my game.* No wonder the conquistadors thrived on arrogance, ruthlessness and determination. Humility and hesitation were as deadly as mustard gas in this new world. But what about the next?

Her backpack felt heavy on her lap, her hand numb from the energy emitted by the seven stones inside it. The Breastplate of Aaron, it was real, not just a historical reference in the Bible. More than three millennium ago, God had chosen the brother of Moses, the high priest of Judaism, to wear the Breastplate, to hear directly His word. It was a time when the power of God was a given, beyond questioning, a time of heaven-wrought plagues and parting of the sea. *So if you meet me, have some courtesy, have some sympathy and some taste. Use all your well-learned politesse. Or I'll lay your soul to waste.*

"Holy crap," Braydon's voice crackled over the headset as the song faded out. "Any chance of that interfering with our mission, Donohue?"

Christa snapped up her head. The volcano on the horizon had morphed into a terrifying display of pyrotechnics. Although the sky was a cloudless blue, lightning flashed across the black plume of smoke rising miles into the air creating the effect of a living, ominous being. It was the embodiment of an angry, Old Testament God, who would spew out death and destruction to an ungrateful race. Either Him, or the Devil.

"Might knock out radio communication," said Donohue. "I never like relying on technology anyway."

Braydon held up Tristan de Luna's map. It was like looking at a black and white photo, the details were so exact. "Demon's Wings dead ahead," Braydon said. "My CCD teacher taught that God had cast Satan into hell. Guess we found him."

"Or he found us," said Christa. The chopper slowed. If anything, the jungle directly below looked even more impenetrable and ripe with danger. The only breaks in the canopy were the two curved precipices of granite towering above the trees. At this angle, they indeed resembled the crests of wings, rounded on the top, rivulets or erosion running down the sides forming patterns like feathers. God had cast his fallen angel, Lucifer, here, turning him to stone while the planet was in its infancy. Lucifer, furious but immobile, watched in humiliation as the jungle grew around him, encompassing him through the eons. He waited, excruciatingly hungry, to witness the bloody folly of the men who would follow his evil call. Plenty were greedy to oblige.

Braydon peered at the rocky outcropping. "According to Salvatierra's letter, this demon has got plenty of dead people in its belly, from the last Contreras who was here five hundred years ago. Baltasar Contreras's guerillas want us to end up as carrion, too. Any sign of them, Donohue?"

"With this cover, they could be mounting an army down there and we wouldn't see it," said Donohue, scanning the jungle below.

"On the positive side," said Braydon, "Contreras's modus operandi is to wait and let us figure out how to find the entrance to the temple, then move in for the kill."

"We got your backs," said Donohue, "but make it fast. Those guerillas might already be in position. And that volcano could blow any minute." As he banked the chopper, a gust shifted the metal bird sideways. The wash of the rotors fought against the wind that bullied the treetops. The chopper hovered above the dropsite, one hundred meters downhill and due west from the bottom of the Demon's Wings.

Donohue raised his left hand, pointed his finger, and circled it. Without a word, each man grasped the carabineer attached to the cable that ran above their heads, and checked the rope from the carabineer to their harness, giving it a tug to make sure it was secure. They straightened goggles, clasped helmet chin straps, patted their weapons. As if in one motion, the spine of a creature preparing to strike, they unbuckled their seatbelts and surged towards the sliding door.

"Go, go, go," Donohue said, signaling the same command with a pointed wave of his hand. The man nearest the door slid it open. Christa threw up her hand against the blast of searing sunlight. The chopper gasped in hot, sticky air like a drowning man breaching the surface. Without hesitation, the men tossed their ropes out the door, and slid down them backwards, sucked into the belly of the jungle.

No way. She couldn't even look down there, never mind rappel down. "I can't do this," she yelled over the powerful thwump of the chopper blades. Her harness must be caught on something. She couldn't breathe.

Braydon grasped the sides of her helmet, put his face close to hers. "Look at me, Christa."

His face was a blur. Gray dots danced in front of her. Damn, she was going to faint. She forced herself to focus, her eyes on his.

"Christa, we are in this together, all the way," he said. "You have got to believe that." He grasped her hands, placed her left one above her harness, the right one below. "Lower yourself down, like I showed you. I'm right beside you."

She felt other hands on her, strong, confident hands. Leader was guiding her backwards. Out the door. Her butt was hanging in the air. The blue sky was so vivid, it could swallow her whole. She wanted to reach out and grab the sides of the helicopter, hoist herself back into it. And she would have, except she kept a vise grip on the rope that dangled down into the forest below. "Just sit back," he said.

A hand pressed on her shoulder. Braydon's. "Keep right beside me," he said. "This is the fun part."

For a moment, just a moment, his eyes looked just like Dad's. Leader, or someone, wrenched her feet off the skids. "Crap!" she screamed into the headset. Falling fast. Grab onto the rope. Slow down. Sky above, then green tree tops. Then bam. Her feet jammed onto the ground. Her knees buckled. Her butt slammed onto a pile of leaves and soft peat.

Braydon rushed to her side. He unhooked the rope from her harness, signaled the helicopter. Donohue banked and ascended towards the crest of the Demon's Wings as the rappelling ropes were gathered into its belly like recoiling guts.

Her feet and butt hurt, but the surrounding rainforest assaulted her other senses. The greens and browns gave off a primeval odor of life that hadn't quite sorted itself out. Ferns towered above her head. Leafy bromeliads clung to every branch, flourishing on the humid fecundity of the air alone. The canopy sheltered them from the blow and bluster of the winds that battled in the treetops. Down on the forest floor, the symphony of hundreds of different bird songs, the occasional startled screech of a monkey, the cacophony of millions of insects surrounded her. The air was stiflingly hot, heavy with humidity. It took on the substance of a living being, it was so thick with moisture.

The strike force had scoped out the perimeter and regrouped into their planned formation. Leader checked an electronic GPS, frowned. He exchanged it for an old-fashioned compass. "Colonel Donohue's mission in the air is to find a viable point of egress out of the canyon," he said. "Ours is to find that temple and the passage into the Oculto Canyon. This way."

If he said so. She had lost all sense of direction in the thick jungle. But the adrenaline zinging through her screamed at her to move, now. Leader was happy to oblige. For men weighed down with packs and automatic weapons, they started out at a fast clip. The point man hacked a path with his machete through the tangle of vines and undergrowth.

Braydon came to her side. "You landed pretty hard back there," he said.

She couldn't keep her eyes off his. She was falling fast, that was for sure. Nothing like a few near-death experiences to bond two people. "My father has been right all along," she said. "We're close, Braydon, to restoring the Breastplate of Aaron, to opening the portal to a life beyond death." Maybe to Mom. So why did it scare her? Why did it prick like a thorn at the surface of her thoughts, that this was wrong?

"As long as it's a portal to the hidden canyon," said Braydon, "and that antidote. As far as the rest of it, I'm more concerned about life before death." He looked at her pointedly.

They double-timed it up a sloping hill. She sucked in breaths. Sweat dripped into her eyes. These guys had to be feeling the heat and humidity. Leader held up a closed fist. The men stopped. It was a clearing, more like a domed room, about twenty feet in diameter, with a pounded earth floor. The tree canopy created a ceiling so thick it had been impossible to see the clearing from the air. Across the clearing, the side of the cliff was carpeted in moss, ferns and epiphytes.

Braydon's hand went to his side, poised by his sidearm like a lawman trying to stare a horse thief out of a shootout. "This clearing isn't natural. The tribe who made it, and maintains it," he said, "are not ghosts."

Leader cocked his gun. "More likely men armed with blowguns and poison darts," he said. "I don't like it."

"No time for mistakes," Braydon said. "And no visible sign that a temple exists underneath centuries of dirt and overgrowth. The entrance could be buried anywhere, assuming the whole temple didn't collapse five hundred years ago."

Christa fingered the gold pendant around her neck. Like the conquistadors, they weren't about to give up, thinking, ironically alike, their mission should surmount the natural order. Unlike the conquistadors, she valued the worth of learning from the past. "Like the shaman said, El Dorado will be our guide," she said. She untied the leather thong that held the pendant. She craned her neck, squinting to see the shoulders of the Demon's Wings through wrinkles in the leaf canopy. She held up the pendant, shifted it, raised it higher. "Time may change all things," she said, "but some slower than others. There!" The gold eagle's wings on the pendant aligned with the curve of the Demon's Wings rock formation. El Dorado danced below.

Braydon brought his cheek against hers. Squinted. Smiled. "El Dorado marks the spot," he said.

She refocused her eye on the steep hillside directly beyond the golden man. "That moss," she said, "exactly where El Dorado's feet are, it's a darker green."

"Leader, cover us," Braydon said. He sprinted across the clearing. Leader's arm held her back. Not that he needed to. She was literally paralyzed with fear. Braydon bounded twelve feet up the steep slope to the green patch of moss.

"This ghost tribe," she said. "If they want us dead, we won't even know it until we are. I've seen the poison work. Seizures, pain, convulsions. Kills almost instantly. And they are expert hunters. They won't miss just because we're on the edge of the clearing, not in it." She was saying this more to convince herself than Leader, but he released her.

Leap of faith time. If some divine destiny had brought her this far, and she was almost willing to believe it had, then it wouldn't end here. Not this close. History and fate didn't work that way. She tied the pendant back around her neck, sucked in a deep breath of wet air, and bolted across the clearing.

She scrambled up the slippery slope of the canyon wall to Braydon's side. He tore away at the patchy mosses. She joined in, the soil cool, moist, heavy with the stuff of life. About eight inches down, her fingertips scraped against something hard, a rough surface. "Granite," she said.

Braydon jabbed his knife into the moss, prying away a clump of it, and tossed it to the bottom of the hill. "I think I see an edge." They clawed away the soil around the edge, revealing more of it, reaching a corner, then another. "Manmade," he said. "No doubt about it." It was a chiseled block of stone, five feet long, nearly one foot tall. "Looks like the lintel."

"Which means the open portal to the temple could be right below it." She cleared away the last layer of soil off the lintel's far end. An eye, carved into the granite, glared at her. Snap! It was clear, unmistakable, the sound of a branch breaking beneath a footfall. She twisted towards the forest. Braydon pivoted in front of her, shoved her to the ground and drew his pistol. Leader, across the clearing, crouched, aimed. Ready.

A shadow, no, movement trembled the bushy ferns beyond the perimeter. Braydon's finger hooked the trigger. Louder crashes, crushing leaves. It was big, heading this way, fast.

A tapir bolted into the clearing. It was rotund, squat, like a dark-skinned, pre-evolved pig. Its round eyes were wide with terror, its nostrils flared. It trumbled across the clearing, its belly scraping against the creeping groundcover, then scampered back into the jungle.

Braydon turned and helped her back to her feet. "Sorry," he said. "Didn't mean to scare you."

"Question is," she peered deeper into the dark forest, "what scared it?"

"Ten to one it's not a phantom. We're running out of time." He crouched by the eye she'd uncovered and peeled off a layer of lichen. "Salvatierra talked about geometric carvings, eyes above and on either side of the mouth, the portal, which once poured forth life-giving water."

They shifted downhill. She grabbed the pilot's survival knife from its scabbard; thrust it into the soft peat. Braydon did the same. They tore at the soil enmeshed with a multi-layered weave of roots and tendrils. "I've been thinking," she said. "This isn't a free-standing temple,"

"More like a dam," he said. He tossed away a chunk of soil, sending it tumbling down the slope. "Built to block the pass through the canyon."

"The Demon's Wings are the crests of the opposing canyon walls." She pried out a stubborn rock. "The clearing is the barbicon."

"Like a fortified entrance to a medieval castle."

She paused a moment, looked at him. "FBI training kicking in?" she asked. "Infiltrating medieval fortifications 101, in case it ever came in handy?"

"It is coming in handy." He yanked away a thorny bush. "Personal interest of mine, infiltrating places that are impregnable." He looked at her pointedly to press home his double entendre. "Problem is, you've got to keep tweaking your approach."

"Glad you realize brute force isn't the answer to everything." She thrust her hand into the spongy peat, down to the rough texture of the granite below. "I found the right edge of the open portal."

"In fact," Braydon cleared away more dirt from his side, "barbicans were becoming obsolete in Alvaro Contreras's time because attacking armies had improved their siege strategies and artillery, but it would be an ideal defense in the new world."

"It's brilliant, from a historical standpoint," she said. "Alvaro Contreras was able to restore the Breastplate of Aaron in Spain and bring it to the new world to call upon its almighty powers. This temple was far removed and easily defended from monarchs and cardinals who would slaughter anyone usurping their rule. Once he was sure of the power of the Breastplate and the poison, he was ready to conquer the world."

"I figure from the dimensions of Demon's Wings and the height and width of this hillside, the temple has got to be a good forty feet deep," he said. "The chamber must be at the far end, nearest to the hidden canyon. Salvatierra wrote that Contreras had strangled the river that once flowed through here. I'm guessing that's where we'll find the retaining wall of Contreras's dam."

"And beyond the dam, the canyon and the antidote plant."

"I need you," he said. His digging revealed a massive boulder blocking the entrance. Christa hooked her arms around it, next to his. Together, they yanked and rocked the boulder. Braydon groaned with the exertion. "When this thing lets loose, stand back."

They ripped the boulder from the spot it had held for five hundred years. It bashed down the hill like an indignant giant, smashing ferns and mosses, leaving a trail of black soil in its wake. Before them, a dark tunnel gaped open. It exhaled a fetid, ancient breath.

"Stinks to high heaven," Braydon said, turning away with a grimace. "Must be the way in." He stepped forward.

She grabbed his arm. A phantom hand reached out and clutched her throat. "You go in there, and you're going to die," she said. "I sense extreme danger."

"Anything specific? I mean, other than armed guerillas honing in on us, a ghost tribe with poison blow darts and the erupting volcano?"

"Something worse," she said.

He switched on the flashlight. The temple's passage swallowed the beam of light like a starving animal. "It's just another underground passageway into the shadowy depths of spirituality," he said. "More to tell my therapist."

"You have a therapist?"

"Planning on getting one," he said. "Or you and I could get together for weekly sessions after this is over. I'm a good listener. We could save each other a bundle."

"We're about to communicate with God," she said. "I think you're covered."

"This is the Old Testament God," he said. "I confess to Him and He'll smite me down with that lightning from the volcano."

As if on cue, thunder cracked the sky above them. Then, another sound, the sharp report of gunfire. Leader's men crouched and fanned out along the perimeter of the clearing, laying down cover fire. The clearing exploded with noise. Braydon grabbed his Glock. Gunfire flashed from behind tree trunks and vines. Donohue's men fired back furiously. Two of them lay on the ground, writhing in pain. One grabbed his calf, the other, his shoulder. Their buddies dragged them closer to the perimeter and cover. The one who had given Christa the fresh orange back in Bogota, nicknamed No Bull, fought hand to hand with a scrappy but huge guerilla dressed in muddied black pants and t-shirt and wielding a machete.

Leader gestured forcefully at Braydon. "Fall back into that tunnel," he yelled. Braydon shoved her over the threshold of the tunnel, firing rapidly, the noise blasting.

The acrid smoke of gunfire mixed with the tunnel's stench. "No way could they have hacked their way through the jungle that quickly," she said, "even if they saw our drop zone." The energy from the seven stones tingled through her spine. "You're were right. Daniel must have tipped them off."

"Dubler wouldn't be the first man to sell his soul to the devil for a chance to talk to God." Braydon took aim, targeting the guerilla fighting No Bull. "Under the right circumstances even good men make the wrong decision."

"Including you?"

"All the time," he said. "Leader wanted to send you down the river with your sister, keep you out of the line of fire. I told him I didn't stand a chance without you."

Same here, not that she'd admit it. "I guarantee you had no chance of leaving me behind."

"Glad to hear it." The guerilla threw a right cross at No Bull's chin with the handle of the machete. No Bull stumbled back. Braydon's finger squeezed the trigger. A deafening bang. The guerilla grabbed his chest and flung backwards, his machete arcing through the air.

Leader gave a sharp wave of his hand. "Go, Fox! Now!" From either side, Leader's men ran in front of them, laying down covering fire. No Bull swooped up his gun and led the left flank.

Braydon spun, grabbed her hand. Together, they ran towards the cold, dark stench of death.

# CHAPTER 65

Christa ran deeper into the tunnel. She crouched. It grew narrow, darker. Braydon's footsteps scruffed the gravel behind her. Those guys back there, they could be outmanned, outgunned. Two of them already wounded, in pain. Sacrificing for her, for this one and only one chance to do the impossible. To restore the Breastplate of Aaron, to open a passage to a hidden canyon, to a life-giving antidote. To the life beyond death. And, God help her, she believed she could do it. Because she had to do it.

A diffused light brushed the tunnel ahead. She glanced back at Braydon. "The end of the tunnel, Braydon. This sounds crazy. But I can feel it. I can feel the energy in the Breastplate."

"Not bright enough to be much of an opening," he said.

"It's got to be the inner chamber of the temple." She quickened her pace.

"Could be a trap."

"Could be salvation." She skidded to a stop and clenched her stomach. A headless skeleton lay sprawled at her feet, just inside the chamber. What had been jaunty red pantaloons was now a faded rag of a shroud, eaten away, disturbingly, at the corpse's privates. Ribs poked out of what had been a linen tunic. A remnant of a sole was all that was left of his boots.

He didn't die alone. Headless skeletons lay scattered around the packed earth floor, each shrouded in faded, torn clothing, bristling with ancient blow darts. Their bones were picked clean by insects long dead. Their skulls, arranged in a ghastly pyramid, gaped at her from the far corner, hollow eyes filled with rage and pity. A ray of daylight speared through a circular opening in the stone ceiling directly on sun-bleached craniums. Its glow illuminated the circular walls in an eerie red. It looked more like a large cistern or well than a place of worship.

"If these poor bastards were Alvaro Contreras's conquistadors, then where are their metal Breastplates, not to use the term lightly?"

"Braydon, we don't have time for a history lesson."

"That shaman said the ghost tribe would never let anyone else abuse the power of the Breastplate. Maybe they beat us to it, by five hundred years."

"Only the nobles and rich could afford body armor," she said. "And Spain wasn't about to subsidize fortune seekers who were likely to wind up dead. These guys were required to pony up their own clothing and weapon, or they wouldn't get paid. And a knife didn't count. That was considered a tool. Usually their "armor" was a thick leather tunic at best. The term conquistador wasn't even coined until 1830."

"This guy had chain mail," Braydon said, pointing to the skeleton nearest him. The linked metal pieces forming his tunic were stiff and brown with rust.

"One of the lucky ones," she said, "so to speak."

The muted raps of gunfire echoed around the chamber. Leader's team wouldn't be able to hold their attackers off much longer.

She grabbed Braydon's hand. "Salvatierra wrote that he buried the Breastplate of Aaron under the pile of heads," she said. They leaped over the corpse, and crossed to the pyramid of skulls. They crouched by it.

"History is not going to repeat itself," she said. "Not here, not now." She reached for a skull. This guy was dead, long dead. It was bone, that's all. "Not under my watch. Contreras's men were mad to think they'd draft the tribesmen into their new army by poisoning their families." She set it aside. Next one would be easier, maybe.

Braydon picked up a skull with massively decayed teeth. "Poor sap," he said. "You should see the cavities. I'd feel sorry for him," he tossed away the skull, "if he hadn't committed genocide. Hold on."

Christa leaned in closer. "Gold." It glinted in the sunlight, a wink through a hollow eye.

He tossed away the cranium and hastily pushed aside two skulls.

She grasped his arm. This was no dream. The Breastplate of Aaron. It was real. It was there. Within reach. "It's magnificent," she whispered, her throat dry. The Breastplate was square, hammered out of gold, attached by golden filaments to a tunic finely woven of threads that were ghosts of their former bright blues and reds. On the gold square, the mounts for the gems were equally spaced in four rows of three. It was intoxicating. She struggled to stay focused. She had to remember every detail. For Dad. "Five of the gems are still intact."

"The agate, amethyst, beryl, onyx and jasper. The first seven mounts are empty. Simple bezel setting," he said. "Bent from Salvatierra's rushed extraction of the gems, but the gold should be pliable enough to reset the stones." The boom of an explosion blasted through the tunnel from the valley. The concussion rocked the chamber.

"Time for a leap of faith," she said.

"Wait. This fabric will disintegrate the minute we pick it up."

"No, Braydon, it won't."

She grabbed the tunic by the shoulders and lifted it. A jawbone clattered off one corner. A whistle of wind spiraled around the chamber. Just wind, that's all. The tunic stayed completely intact. It looked like it had been preserved in a climate-controlled museum case.

The earth rumbled. Braydon flinched as a chink of rock popped out of the far wall and crashed at his feet. "God's telling us to either get the hell out or to hurry the hell up," he said. "You get those seven stones back in the Breastplate. I'll work on getting us out of here."

Right. Stay focused. She crossed to the platform. The tunic was heavy, awkward with the weight of the golden Breastplate. She laid it on the platform.

Braydon moved to the perimeter of the room. "Something's wrong," he said.

"You mean besides being surrounded by headless bodies and being chased by guys who want to kill us." She shrugged off her pack.

"The way their bodies are placed. It's not natural."

She looked around her as she unzipped her pack. He was right. The bodies formed a crude ring, the pyramid of skulls forming the ring's "stone." And she was in the center. "This is the platform Contreras was standing on when Salvatierra found him," she said. "Where he wore the Breastplate. They were defending him."

"Two swords, rusty, two pikes, only three knives in what must have been leather sheaths before being eaten away," Braydon said. "All by their sides. Hard to believe that the poison darts killed them so quickly that not a single one of these trained killers had a chance to swing a pike."

"Not pikes," she said, "halberds, those long shafts with the nasty-looking metal ax. Very deadly, still used by the Vatican guard today. But I'm not letting live guys scare me off restoring the Breastplate, and certainly not dead ones." First out, the linen napkin from the Waldorf Hotel. She opened it, revealing the diamond and sapphire. Magnificent. Mesmerizing. Her hands trembled. It wasn't just the extraordinary history compressed into their facets, the fact that these two gems had altered the fates of sultans, kings, killers and saints. They actually glowed. And that humming in her ear, it wasn't an aftereffect of the deafening gunshots. She laid flat the napkin, from the room where Jared Sadler had been left to bleed to death. She placed the Kohinoor Diamond and Edward's Sapphire on it. These gems altered fates. She had to respect that, fight not to fear it.

"One thing I learned mountain climbing," he said, "the summit is only halfway there. Getting down is what kills a lot of people. Or, in this situation, getting out of this temple. The Breastplate is a means to an end. Our primary mission is to retrieve the antidote." He pivoted towards the skylight. Thick, furry roots twisted down from the overgrowth above, like fingers reaching into a coffin. The ceiling was a good twenty feet up. He jumped up, just catching the end of the longest root dangling down. He yanked on it. Soil tumbled down. The vine snapped. He ducked as it coiled onto the floor.

She fished out the silver box, opened the lid. The five sacred stones glimmered and winked. It was a miracle, yet a feeling of dread nudged at her consciousness. These stones had caused thousands of deaths. What made her think they could save lives, too? Open a portal to her mother? Bring her father home?

Braydon stepped over the corpses to check out the far wall. It looked Incan, finely carved granite blocks, fitted perfectly together. Solid, apparently impenetrable. He flicked on his flashlight.

As her eyes adjusted, the details became distinct. Three words were painted, actually smeared by hand, in red, on the far wall. Ipse venena bibas.

"A local dialect?"

Christa swallowed hard. "Latin," she said. "Salvatierra's language of choice, but the locals must have written it later. According to his letter, Salvatierra barely escaped with the seven stones when the temple started collapsing."

Braydon sniffed it. "Much later," he said. "Smells and looks like some kind of berry juice." He turned towards her. "It's still fresh."

"It's a line from a Catholic exorcism in the middle ages, addressing Satan" she said. "Ipse venena bibas. May you drink the poisons yourself."

"I was hoping for This Way Out," he said. "I smell sulfur, and this wall is granite."

"Brimstone," she said. "In Biblical times, sulfur was called brimstone."

"As in fire and brimstone?" He extracted his Eagle Scout knife from his pocket, opened the blade, and jimmied it between two of the tightly fitted stones in the wall. He showed her the blade. A yellow powder tipped it.

"The kind of sermon that reminds sinners that hell awaits those who don't repent."

He dipped his finger in the yellow powder, placed it on the tip of his tongue. "The kind of sulfur that's mixed with gunpowder to make an explosive," he said.

"You remember Contreras's last words?"

"Something about breaking your neck."

"No, I mean Alvaro Contreras, to Salvatierra," she said. "*The gems of the Breastplate reveal the secret to my domination. Don the Breastplate. Stand upon this platform. Call God's light to shine upon you. You will hold the powers of the Heavens in the palm of your hand.* I'm no Eagle Scout, but I know how to start a campfire with a magnifying glass focusing sunlight on dry tinder."

"I'd rather use C-4, but if it's brimstone we got, then we'd better remember the Bible." He came to her side.

*"You shall make the Breastplate of judgment,"* she said. *"And you shall put settings of stones in it, four rows of stones: The first row shall be a sardius, a topaz, and an Emerald."*

"The sardius is the ruby, the Urim," said Braydon, "from the Hebrew, to see light, flame." She snugged the Urim into the first empty setting. It fit perfectly. Braydon helped her bend the gold bezel around the stone, locking it into place. Her fingers tingled again, as if electrified. "The golden topaz is the Thummim, for completion, integrity." As she set the Thummim into the next setting, the ethereal voices grew louder, more realistic. It wasn't wind through a crack in the wall. It sounded like a cross between a human's wail and an animal's howl. The sound was wafting into the chamber like the beam of light from the opening above them. Monkeys? The spat of gunfire echoed through the passageway from the clearing. She quickly placed the Tear of the Moon Emerald.

Braydon handed her the Yikaisidahi Turquoise. *"The second row shall be a Turquoise, a sapphire, and a diamond,"* he said.

She placed the Turquoise. As he fitted the gold setting around it, she drank in one last look at the Kohinoor Diamond sparkling in her palm. She didn't want to let it go. She fit it into its mount, and quickly did the same with the Sapphire.

He handed her the Abraxas. *"The third row, a jacinth, an agate, and an amethyst; and the fourth row, a beryl, an onyx, and a jasper. They shall be set in gold settings.* The Abraxas has got to be the jacinth. The rest of the stones are still intact."

The voices grew louder, an edge of terror and might to the glory. "Braydon, do you hear them?"

"I'm more concerned about what I don't hear." He was shouting, over the voices. He had to hear them, too. "The shooting has stopped. Might not be a good sign," he said. "The Breastplate had better work the way I think it will.

"Stand on the platform wearing the Breastplate," she pointed up, "and the gemstones will focus the sunlight coming through that skylight to the far wall."

"The beam will ignite the sulfur, and, with any luck, blow a hole through to the hidden canyon."

"State of the art technology, for the sixteenth century," she said. She fit the Abraxas into its setting, wrapped the gold around its perimeter to hold it in place.  She grasped his hand, pulled him close. "We've done it, Braydon.  We've restored the Breastplate of Aaron."

He embraced her, tight.  Before she realized it, they kissed.  She was infused with love and joy, drunk, giddy.  From Heaven?  From more earthly desires?  She didn't give a damn.  The room grew brighter, the air clearer.  The golden Breastplate, alive with the twelve precious stones, emitted a light and energy that blocked out the world outside the two of them.

He leaned back, unbuttoned the top button on her camouflage shirt.  His fingers touched her neck, emitting a tingle like she felt from the gems.  He lifted the El Dorado pendant, made sure it was visible.  "I'm not one to believe in ghost tribes," he said, "but a man in my position, restoring a lost Biblical artifact with legendary, mystical gems, shouldn't question matters of faith and history."

"El Dorado changed the fate of the world before," she said.

A gunshot blasted through the chamber, gashing the wall behind them. Braydon drew his his Glock from his hip holster. Rambitskov spun Braydon away from her, shoving him across the chamber. Contreras grabbed her by the collar, yanked her up against him. He pressed a knife to her throat, the pilot survival knife Donohue had given her.  Somehow, her twenty-two pistol was gone, too. Rambitskov backed away to the entrance, his pistol smoking.

# CHAPTER 66

Braydon stopped himself from drilling Rambitskov through the forehead with his Glock. Contreras could retaliate by piercing Christa's carotid artery with the knife he held against her throat. She was still alive. He had to work with that. The ethereal voices had vanished, sucked out of the chamber like light into a black hole. He'd been a fool, mesmerized by the Breastplate while Contreras infiltrated the chamber without resistance. Braydon didn't need God's choir to tell him that Rambitskov wanted nothing more than to do unto Braydon what Braydon wanted to do unto him, except the man's overkill M16 semi-automatic assault rifle would obliterate his brain in seconds. Same result, just messier.

Rambitskov was outfitted in U.S. military issue jungle fatigues. It was a disgrace to Donohue's strike force, each one a proven war hero, who, by the sound of the spattering gunfire, still engaged in a fierce fight in the clearing against Contreras's guerillas. Contreras was head to toe in some crazy Old Testament getup, a long white gown beneath a multi-hued, brocade, short sleeve tunic. Sandals on his feet. The man was clearly insane, but that didn't make him any less deadly.

Christa looked small against Contreras's bulk, but she didn't look scared. If anything, she looked angry, on the verge of trying something very brave, and probably fatal. Contreras tightened his grip on her. "Agent Fox," he said. "Let's not start off with a cliché. You know what to do."

"Kill them," Christa said, her hands clawing at Contreras's arm crushing her chest. "Get the antidote."

Contreras grinned. "This is your chance at redemption, Fox," he said. "Or will you be responsible for this partner's death as well?"

He pressed the tip of his knife against Christa's skin. She grimaced. A drop of blood trickled down her neck.

Braydon crouched, laid his Glock on the ground, raised his hands. He mentally placed the weapons in the room. The swords and halberds were his best bet, but only if he could get the jump on Rambitskov's M16. Even then, the bastard had a good fifty pounds and four inches on him and the cold blood of a gang fighter.

Rambitskov kept his weapon trained on Braydon's chest. "Kick over the Glock," he said. Braydon complied. It skidded across the gravel on the pounded earth floor. "And the Ka-Bar." Braydon expected that, too. He unsheathed the survival knife and, denying the impulse to throw it into the fleshy part of the bastard's throat, he tossed it just in front of his army boots.

Rambitskov shifted the M16 to his left hand, crouched and picked up the Glock with his right. He stood, licked his lips, and smiled. They had nicknamed him Rambo. He certainly looked the part. He stuck the Glock in his belt, pulled a device from his shirt pocket. A C4 remote detonator.

"We would not want any interruptions," said Contreras, "and your little strike force is putting up more of a fight than expected. We lost four of our bodyguard detail just getting us to the entrance of the passageway. The only way out of here," he grunted as Christa squirmed, "will be through the Oculto Canyon." Without taking his eyes off Braydon, he nodded.

Rambitskov flipped open the yellow safety at the top of the black box. He placed his thumb over the red button, and pressed down.

The explosion blasted into the inner chamber with a deafening roar. The concussion knocked Contreras off balance. Christa gouged her elbow into his middle. Braydon lunged forward, tackling Rambitskov with all his might. The man's M16 fired wildly as he flailed back. Braydon snatched the weapon from his grasp. He barely had purchase on it as Rambitskov swung around, slamming into his side with doubled fists. The M16 clattered into the tunnel as a cloud of smoke and dust billowed out of it into the chamber. Braydon quickly closed his mouth and narrowed his eyes against the onslaught of debris.

Rambitskov, gasping for breath, convulsed in a fit of choking coughs. He cried out as one hand flew up, too late, to shield his eyes from the stinging smoke.  He reached blindly for Braydon's Glock. As he pulled the pistol from his belt, Braydon kicked it away.

The dust cloud billowed through the chamber, snuffing out the daylight coming from the hole in the ceiling.  The M16 was unreachable, buried in the black smoke of the tunnel.  His Glock had clattered a few feet to his right.  Contreras pushed Christa aside to grab for it.  Braydon dove for the Glock.  A force bowled him backwards, pounding him against the wall.  Rambitskov.  Braydon tumbled away as Rambitskov's fist pounded into the air where his face had been.   With the survival reflexes of a streetfighter, Rambitskov pulled back before slamming his knuckles into rock. Braydon tucked and rolled towards the nearest skeleton.  He grabbed the hilt of the conquistador's sword.  Its leather scabbard disintegrated as he snatched it away from the skeleton.  The weapon was heavy, its blade dulled and jagged with rust.

Rambitskov was quick to respond, grabbing a halberd and swinging it around, slicing through the air.  Braydon ducked and rolled.  Only his agility and training would save him.  Christa was in trouble.  Contreras shoved her mightily into the far wall.  She banged her head on the granite, staggered.

Contreras swept up a sword from the nearest skeleton.  He advanced towards Christa.  "Live by the sword!  Die by the sword!" he screamed.

"Christa!" Braydon yelled.  He tossed her the sword.  She caught it by the hilt, parried Contreras's thrust.

Rambitskov's halberd came at his ribs from the side.  He leaped back.  The point of the halberd slashed across his torso.  It tore through the fatigues, and sliced his skin.  It hurt like hell, but he blanked out the pain.  Christa had taken the advantage, slashing, thrusting, their sword clangs echoing against the granite walls. Contreras, surprised, was on the retreat.  But it wouldn't be long before his strength outmatched her agility.

The smoke was dissipating.  The sunbeam, thick with dust, penetrated the chamber.  Its light glinted on the golden Breastplate, flat on the stone platform. The sun was moving past its zenith.  Soon, the beam would not be focused on the platform.  Salvatierra wrote that the sun had to be shining on the Breastplate for it to reveal its power, including the secret to finding the canyon.

Braydon doubled over. He clutched at his wound, grimacing in pain. A man like Rambitskov would relish the chance to take advantage of an opponent's weakness. Rambitskov raised the halberd above his head, building up energy for the final, decapitating blow.

Braydon grabbed the knife from the skeleton at his feet. He propelled himself forward, lunging blade first, straight for Rambitskov's gut. Rambitskov twisted away. Braydon pushed off the halberd's fierce metal ax. Rambitskov slammed its wooden shaft down on his shoulder, the crippling force of it dashing him to his knees. Braydon angled the knife upwards and sliced into Rambitskov's soft belly with a sickening slurp. He could barely keep his grip on the hilt as the man's massive weight collapsed onto the rusty blade.

Braydon crouched and staggered out from under Rambitskov as the giant thumped to the ground. The fight, the slash across his torso, the agony of his shoulder, he had to shake off their dizzying effect. He was breathing too hard and fast. The loud clang of a sword clattering to the ground gripped his attention. Christa had knocked away Contreras's sword! "Finish Contreras off!" he yelled. He pointed towards the skylight. "The sun! We're out of time."

But her eyes weren't on Contreras. She was focused on the Breastplate. As if it was going to judge her. This was no time to get religion. Contreras pulled something from the pocket beneath his tunic. Not a gun. A cylindrical object. Some kind of weapon? Contreras brought the cylinder to his lips, aimed it at Christa. A blow gun! She twisted her grip on the sword, held it over her shoulder like a spear, recoiled her arm, aiming straight for Contreras. Contreras puffed out his cheeks, and blew into the gun.

Braydon dove in front of Christa. She let loose her sword. A sharp needle stung him in the side of his throat. He grabbed at it and yanked it out of his skin. A blow dart, bright yellow, two inches long. Animal tranquilizer? No. Poison. A searing pain burned into his brain like knives in his eyes. His knees buckled. The musky, primeval odor of the chamber intensified with the sinister smoke of modern day explosives. The sounds of a scream and spat of gunfire grew muted, distant. He heard a shout. Christa? He hit the ground, hard, vaguely aware that his shoulder was twisted in agony. He felt a force roll him onto his back, and a soft caress of Christa's fingertips on his cheek as everything in his vision turned a crimson, bloody red.

CHAPTER **67**

"Braydon!" Christa screamed at him. *He couldn't be dead, not here, not now, not like this.* She shook his good shoulder. His chest was gashed, oozing blood. The point on the side of his neck where the dart had hit was turning a viral red. He fought for each breath. "Get the antidote," he said, his voice slurred. "Forget about me."

"Not a chance," she said. "That blow dart, Contreras must have tipped it with the poison." She pressed her cheek to his. It was hot, feverish. "The antidote is just beyond that wall. I know it is. Hang on." He grabbed her closer. He gasped, trembled violently. His hand dropped to the ground. She leaned back. His eyes were open, but unseeing. She pressed her fingers to neck. No pulse. She shifted her fingers, pressed deeper. Nothing. This couldn't be happening. "It's not supposed to end this way, Braydon." Hot tears burned her eyes. She swiped them away. "I will not let it end this way."

Contreras was sprawled against the far wall, bloodied and unconscious. The point of the sword she had thrown had penetrated his thigh, but not deep. He had tripped backwards, hit his head. It lolled over his left shoulder, blood dripping from his temple.

The sun beamed directly down on the Breastplate and its gems, alighting it in a shimmering brilliance. But not for long. Sixty seconds, maybe, before the sun passed beyond the skylight. She rushed over, grabbed the Breastplate, and lifted it. Electricity zapped through her hands. A spasm shook her to her knees. Her heart beat furiously. A weight crushed her throat. She hefted the Breastplate and punched her arms through the tunic sleeves. The Breastplate fell onto her chest. This thing was heavy, and it wasn't just the weight of the gold.

The sun grew blindingly bright. The gemstones glowed and sparked, filling the chamber with a kaleidoscope of colors, spinning, twisting. The spectral voices returned with a fury. Not just voices. Beings. Phantoms. They spiraled around the room, terrifying in their beauty.

"I'm not afraid of you!" she screamed above the cacophony of whistling songs. Lying to God. Great. She fought to stand. Her knees trembled, threatened to buckle. She opened her arms in supplication. "Is this what You want? For a good man to die? For an innocent boy, Liam, to die? Help me, for God's sake!"

The gemstones came alive with light. The sun beam struck her chest with the force of a fist. It clutched at her, drawing the light from the twelve gemstones. Lasers of color refracted to a point inches from her heart, twisted together and speared at the granite wall. The laser beam burned into the center of the Latin epitaph.

The ground trembled. She struggled to stay standing. This couldn't be real. It was crazy to think this would work. It had to be a hallucinogenic gas emitted by the volcanic shifts in the chamber. A nervous breakdown wasn't beyond reason. Colors became sounds. Sweet fragrances brushed through her hair. Pure emotion burned through reason like the sun through a cloud. Love and joy lifted her physically from the ground.

It couldn't be. But it was. Nothing had ever been more vibrantly indisputable. "Mom?" She was here. In this room. More than a presence. Pure emotion. Tears streamed down her cheeks. A hand wiped them dry, then whisked away from her. "Don't go!"

A blast—gunfire, from behind. The bullet drilled into the ceiling above her. Her feet descended, dropping onto the ground. Chunks of rock pelted down. The phantoms swirled around her, a white wind. She reached out, but dared not move. No matter what, that beam had to stay on target. "Mom!" she screamed. "I love you! I miss you!" She was still here. She had to be.

"Blasphemer!" Baltasar shouted over the voices. She craned her neck, keeping the Breastplate in the sunbeam, its laser targeted on the wall. Baltasar was struggling to stand. The tunic covering his leg was red with blood. He gripped Braydon's gun, aimed at her. "I am the one who must wield the power of the Breastplate. I am the Prophet."

"You'll be a mass murderer if you stop me now." The concentrated beam from the gemstones washed the granite wall in a red glow. A wisp of smoke escaped from the seam between two boulders.

"And who is God, but a killer of non-believers? The core of every era in history, of every masterpiece, of every individual is our need to believe."

"The need to believe is a question," she said, "not an answer." Of course, a slow match. It had to be. Used in the early 1500s. Once lit, it smoldered, set off gunpowder in weapons. "Isn't that why you said the Vatican executed Alvaro? If Alvaro used the Breastplate to find all the answers, then we wouldn't need any prophets."

"I am the answer," he said. "I will give the people that which their souls desire. I will teach them the rewards of piety and the catastrophic consequence of evil. I am the one who must open the portal to the Garden of Eden. I must bring about the genesis of a new world. I will find the fruit of salvation. I will return not only with the sacred Breastplate, but with the antidote. I will be the savior not only of souls, but of lives."

"Not if you shoot me in the back," she said.

"You are not worthy!"

"No, I'm not." She pressed her feet into the stone platform to keep the quaking ground from tossing her down. "But I'm here. And this is our only chance. Your ancestor hid a fuse between the granite blocks. And an explosive. The refracted beams from the gems is lighting the fuse, like using a magnifying glass to start a fire. But only if I don't move."

"When I saw him, I fell at his feet as though dead," Baltasar shouted above the din of the earthquake. "Then he placed his right hand on me and said: "Do not be afraid. I am the First and the Last. I am the Living One; I was dead, and behold I am alive for ever and ever! And I hold the keys of death and Hades." He was quoting the Bible, Daniel in Revelations when he dreamed of the coming apocalypse. As long as it kept him from pulling the trigger. "Write, therefore, what you have seen, what is now and what will take place later. The mystery of the seven stars that you saw in my right hand and of the seven golden lampstands is this: The seven stars are the angels of the seven churches, and the seven lampstands are the seven churches."

The sun passed by the skylight. The refracted light left the Breastplate and flew across the chamber like an arrow from a bow, piercing through the granite wall. It disappeared. The light. The voices. The colors. Gone.

A gloom settled over the chamber. The roars of the distant volcano rumbled through the temple. The sound of defeat.

Then, a spark. A wisp of smoke. A flare. The fuse was lit. Time to take cover, to protect Braydon.

Contreras pointed the gun at her, his hand shaking. "The Breastplate. Now! Or I will shoot you."

The only way the Breastplate would save her now was if she let it go. She tore it over her shoulders, flung it towards him. "Go to hell!" She ran to Braydon, grabbed his arms. His hands felt cold. He was still, without life. She heaved with all her might, dragged him away from the granite wall.

The blast exploded through the chamber.

CHAPTER **68**

Christa huddled over Braydon's body, her cheek against his. He was cold. A rock smashed onto her back, knocking the breath from her. And it hurt like hell. She couldn't hear over the ringing in her ears. Worse, it was too dark to see anything. That meant it hadn't worked. The explosion hadn't blown a portal to some legendary Garden of Eden, never mind to the afterlife. She twisted around onto her back, got stabbed with pain for her trouble. Above, the skylight no longer welcomed in sunlight. A massive tree trunk had crashed on top of it, allowing only wrinkles of blue sky to penetrate, and even less hope.

"Damn it!" She kicked away the skeleton, the "lucky one" with the chainmail that lay near her feet. Its bones flung away in a mocking dance. "Damn it to Hell!" She turned her head to look at Braydon, lying beside her. His eyes were closed. Other than that, he hadn't moved. She laid her hand on his. "We could have been something," she said. Oh, what the hell. "I could have loved you, Braydon. Maybe," it shouldn't be so hard to say it, "maybe I already do." As far as the rest of that overwhelming love and joy that she felt had filled the chamber when she wore the Breastplate, it had been shattered into more bits of rubble than the granite wall.

She got onto her knees, looked up. One last chance. And she was no longer too proud to risk it. "God, in Heaven, I swear," she said. "Save him, and I will believe. You can keep your Breastplate. And I'll still believe."

Nothing. No, worse than nothing. That bastard, Contreras, was still alive. His face was a mess, sliced by flying shards of granite, blood smeared around his eyes. He pawed his way towards the Breastplate. It had somehow survived intact, like some spiritual force field protected it, if you believed in that sort of thing. And she didn't believe, not anymore. She didn't even want to believe anymore. He had nearly reached it. She couldn't let him win, not after what he'd done to Braydon, to anyone she had ever loved. "No way," she said. "Not now. No way in hell are you going to get it." All she had to do was pry Rambitskov's dead fingers off that halberd. A worthy weapon for her last act on Earth, or maybe her first one in Hell.

She pushed herself up, and stopped. Braydon's fingers clasped hers, squeezed, and let go. She twisted towards him, brought her cheek to his. His skin was no longer cold, but hot, feverish. His breath puffed weak and rapid on her neck.

He groaned, barely audibly through the insistent ringing in her ears. One word. "Water."

She felt for his pulse. It was ragged, but beating. Thank God. He was alive. Yes, thank God. There wasn't a doubt in her mind that he had been dead. And yet he lived. She shook her head. "Welcome back," she whispered. She didn't understand. She didn't need to. The portal to life beyond death had opened. It worked both ways. He was moving his other hand, out to his side, reaching out, scrabbling his fingers. In the mud.

She leapt over him, dug her own fingers into the cool, damp soil. "I see it, Braydon." It wasn't more than a trickle, bubbling through the jumble of stones that was the granite wall and seeping across the packed earth floor. She rushed over to its source, tore away a layer of stones. A whiff of river-cooled fresh air puffed through the lingering sulfuric stink of gunpowder.

A huge boulder blocked the way. It had to weigh three hundred pounds. On top of it balanced a massive pile of smaller rocks. "Hold on, Braydon. Don't give up." And more to herself. "Never give up."

She ran over to Rambitskov. Swallowing hard, she wrenched his meaty, and now pasty white, fingers off the halberd. The halberd's shaft was strong, probably seasoned ash. Even the insects hadn't eaten it away. The top half of the shaft was reinforced with iron, probably carbonized, but still pitted with rust. It would have to do.

She set the rock that would have to serve as her fulcrum into place and jammed the halberd's point beneath the boulder. If Archimedes could move the Earth with a lever, then she could at least try to save it with one. She pressed down. Nothing. Except laughing. It was Contreras. He had reached the Breastplate. He was fondling it, in his own world, his new world, where he was the savior. But he wasn't looking at it. His eyes, red with blood, stared off. The flash from the blast must have blinded him, at least temporarily.

She laid all her weight on the end of the shaft. It shifted. A loaf-sized stone on top of the huge boulder wobbled and clattered to the ground. Then another. The boulder was balanced precariously on a scrabble of stones. One more good press could topple it. The shaft snapped. She tumbled to the ground, her knuckles bashing onto the rocks. The boulder tilted forward. She reached for it, pushed her shoulder against it. It rolled away, crashing to the floor, a small avalanche of rocks tumbling after it.

A cool, fresh breeze blew into the chamber. A jagged, five foot hole opened a window to a jungle tangled with every hue of green in every natural shape and texture. It may not be a Garden of Eden, but it was a cradle of life, its living essence compacted, ready to burst forth and multiply. Ready to save lives. A narrow river unfurled beyond the exterior of the demolished temple wall. It wound through the dense vegetation, carving a tunnel through the green, a passage into a deeper unknown. Intrepid arrows of sunlight pierced through from sky to ground, but it was easy to see why the Oculto Canyon was hidden from above. It wouldn't be more than an undulating dip on the ocean of green that was the rainforest canopy.

Contreras was keening back and forth, clutching the Breastplate to his breast. He still gripped the pistol in his hand. He was crazy-eyed, dazed, maybe still blinded. Tears made tracks though the blood on his cheeks. She could take the Breastplate from him, bring it home, to Dad, the most powerful artifact ever lost to man. She shouldn't have been so quick to promise God He could keep it, if He saved Braydon. But God had been mighty quick to keep his end of the deal. If you believed in that sort of thing.

She grabbed Braydon's arm, tugged him into a half-sitting position, his weight heavy, unresponsive. She wrapped his arm around her shoulders, grappled him around his waist.

He found his footing, but clenched on to her for support. "Glock," he said, pointing. His pistol was within arm's reach. This time, she didn't hesitate to get a gun in her hand. She swooped it up, jammed its cool, hard steel into her belt, and then shouldered her pack. Her pilot survival knife was near it. She slid it into its sheath on her left hip. They stumbled towards the jagged hole. She high-kicked her leg over to straddle the thick wall, heaved him up and steadied him against the broken stones.

She slid down the exterior of the temple wall, her boots splashing into a shallow pool, catching Braydon as he hoisted himself over the wall and tumbled beside her, faltering into the water.

"Dam," he said. "Alvaro Contreras made the temple into a dam." His voice was slurred.

The river formed a reservoir as its downward spill hit the temple. The shallow pool was about thirty feet wide. "Most of the river water must seep into a subterranean channel, beneath the temple," she said. The canopy above it was so thick it formed a green dome. It had the feel of a natural chapel, almost inspired her to pray again, but only to get the hell out of there.

The water permeated her boots and socks. It was warm, viscous, maybe affected by the volcanic activity. The air was cool, dry, nothing like the humidity they had left behind. It carried the scent not of oppressive fecundity but a delicate fragrance of a floral bouquet. The ringing in her ears gave way to the yelping of startled monkeys, the screech of a hawk and the rush of a distant waterfall.

"We're being watched," Braydon said. "Stalked."

"I sense it, too," said Christa. She scanned the shadows. Nothing. "Maybe it's the volcano. I can't see it beyond the forest, but it's like the ground and air are electric. You saw the plume of smoke. The volcano was creating its own lightning."

She helped Braydon to his feet, half carrying him as they pushed their way through the shallows of the pool to its far bank. She lowered him onto a bed of a sage colored groundcover with velvety leaves. They didn't look deadly, like the pitcher plants big enough to feed on small monkeys that hung from the branches above them. She half expected a pterodactyl to swoop down from above.

Braydon fought to focus on it all. "Garden of Eden," he muttered. "More like Jurassic Park."

"That's good," she said, as long as some dinosaur snake doesn't find them. "It means it hasn't changed much in the past five hundred years. The antidote plant, it's got to still be growing here." Somewhere. She pulled out Gabriella's sketch. "One foot tall, hairy stem, low-lying serrated lobe leaves, and a large flower." The chaos of the jungle was like a damn kaleidoscope, with every color a hue of green. "Yellow petals, look for that, four of them on each flower, around a half-circle of purple. The green, bulbous pods, they'd be distinctive." And they were nowhere in sight.

She laid her hand on Braydon's forehead. Despite the air-cooled water saturating his clothes, he was burning up. He struggled to sit up. She tried to hold him down, but his strength was surprising.

He gripped her arm, but weakly. "Ghost tribe," he said, forcing his lips to form the words. "Behind those trees."

She spun around, saw only trees, menacing looking trees, heavy with vines, but rooted to the ground. Braydon could be hallucinating, like Liam had, or he had a better grip on reality than she did. The poison was moving fast through his system. Maybe that promise God had made wasn't God promising anything after all. The high fever could kill quickly. She pried his hand away. "The shaman said the antidote plant grew along the river bank," she said. "I'm heading upstream." She grabbed her canteen out of her pack and splashed against the tepid current. The fleeting feeling of overwhelming joy in the presence of the Breastplate was darkened by an equal sense of dread, like a dark cloud blocking out the sun. Phantoms, she could feel them, watched her, and these were no heavenly apparitions.

She had faith, all right, in history, but the dam had changed the river's course. Man's mucking about with nature could have destroyed the delicate microcosm of the antidote plant. It wouldn't be the first time that man playing god had ended badly. She ducked beneath an overhanging vine, mossy fingers grabbing for the water's surface. An arrow of sun pierced the bank ahead. Around the bend, a yellow bloom, nearly hidden in the green. She rushed to it, a bed of poppies, piercing up out of the mossy groundcover.

Quickly, she unscrewed the cap of her canteen, dumped its contents, and plunged it into the warm stream waters. Air bubbled up as the clear water displaced it. She hurried back to Braydon and held the canteen to his trembling lips. He took a swallow, coughed. She steadied him, searching his eyes for the focus of regained lucidity. Gabriella said the results should be immediate. It had to work. They hadn't come this far to lose now. Braydon grabbed for the canteen. He drank more. He pushed it away, the water sloshing out the top. His eyes were wide, as if evil flanked them from every dark shadow. "Leave me," he said. "Get the antidote plant. Get out of here. Climb up to the Demon's Wings. Donohue will see you there, airlift you out. It's your only chance. I'll hold them off as long as I can."

"We're leaving together," she said.

"They're surrounding us, positioning to attack."

She peered into the dense vegetation and shadows. She could see no human, no movement beyond the wind rustling the leaves. But, after the past three days, if Braydon said they were out there, she believed him, poison or no poison. She pressed the Glock into his hand.

She raced upriver, slipping on the slick vegetation hidden by the water as she rounded the bend. She fell upon the poppies, grabbed a stalk, but it was thick, fibrous, impossible to snap off. She grabbed the pilot's survival knife from its sheath. With the serrated blade, she quickly sawed off six bulbous seed pods and shoved them into the sack. She snatched a handful of leaves, packed them in around the pods. Then she dug into the ground around a mature, flowering poppy. The soil was moist and loose but the roots reached deep into the ground. Too much time was passing. She pried away a stone, its sharp edges scraping her fingers. The earth emitted a primeval odor as she violated the pristine ground. She yanked the last tendrils of the roots clinging desperately to the soil and stuffed the plant into her sack, tugging the drawstring closed.

A deathly quiet had fallen around her. The only sound was her splashing and the hammering of her heart as she rushed back to Braydon. She stopped, the water coursing around her ankles. He was gone. Only the impression he had left behind in the crushed vegetation remained. The ghost tribe could have attacked, dragged him away. Impossible. Braydon at least would have got off a shot.

She crept out of the river. Keeping low, she hurried to the shallow pool against the temple wall. Braydon was standing there, at its bank, to her right. His face was flushed, but his legs were steady. The antidote was working. But he wasn't alone. Contreras dropped down from the hole in the temple wall, splashing into the shallow pool. He wore the Breastplate.

Contreras stood unsteadily. The water rippled around his legs. His white robe, bloody and tattered, undulated like snakes slithering from his knees. He raised his hands aloft, the Breastplate magnificent and gleaming golden even in the gloom of the dense forest. The gemstones sparkled and flared. He breathed in deeply. A grimace of ecstasy contorted his face. "And he shewed me a pure river of water of life," he shouted, "clear as crystal, proceeding out of the throne of God and of the Lamb."

"You got the antidote plant?" Braydon asked her.

"In the bag," she said.

Braydon staggered. The antidote's cure was immediate, but certainly not able to help his other wounds and pure exhaustion. "Then we got what we came here for," he said. His eyes scanned the perimeter of the shallow pool. From the shadows, they materialized. The ghost tribe. Men, naked except for loin cloths and streaks of body paint, like skeleton bones, white against their dark skin. Half of them raised their blowguns to their mouths. The others stretched arrows back, taut in their bows.

Blood pounded in Christa's ears. She reached for the pilot survival knife at her hip. Braydon laid his hand over hers, stopping her. "Only way out of this one, is diversion and retreat," he said. "Priority one is getting that antidote out."

Contreras squinted. He swiped the blood from his eyes. He closed one eye, opened the other wide. "You are my people," he shouted. "My Adams. This is the genesis of our new world."

The Indians swiveled toward him, targeting him with their blowguns and arrows. As the first circle of the ghost tribe closed in, more emerged from the shadows. But the ghost tribe was closing their circle in front of her and Braydon, as if they were just another tree on the edge of the pool. "They're not after us," she whispered. Her fingers flew to the El Dorado pendant around her neck. "I'm wearing the El Dorado talisman."

"More likely what you're not wearing. They'll never let that Breastplate go beyond the temple walls."

"I bring you peace, my people," said Contreras. "I bring you the cure for your village. I fulfill my ancestor's promise." He raised his arms, lolling his head from side to side. "Mother!" he wailed. "I did this for you! I am here, Baltasar. Mother, tell me I have earned your forgiveness."

"I almost feel sorry for the man," Braydon said.

"No matter what he's done, we can't just stand by and watch," said Christa. "They'll kill Contreras."

"Brutally," said Braydon, "and I don't intend to stand by.  I intend to get us out of here."

"Contreras," she called out.  "Take off the Breastplate.  It's the only thing that might save you."

He looked around wildly.  He couldn't see them.  "Save me," he shouted.  "From my moment of triumph?  Never."

A guttural wail rose from the inner circle of the ghost tribe.  They moved as one, a mighty predator pouncing for the kill.  The intensity of their anger, the force of their determination blew across the pool like a hot gust.

"Now!" Braydon yelled.  He grabbed her hand, pulled her towards the steep slope that was once the temple wall.  He pushed her ahead of him.  "Climb up to the Demon's Wings.  When they're done with him, they'll come after us!"

She struggled and stumbled upwards, slipping on the slick moss, grasping at rough vines and roots.  Contreras's screams of agony and the murderous howls of ghost tribe filled the forest.  The sounds of murder drove the animals, insects and birds into a frenzy.  The ground, the air, everything was alive, moving, panicking.

Braydon stumbled behind her.  He strove to gain ground, his energy flagging.  "Keep moving," he yelled to her.  Below, the shallow pool was a mass of naked backs and arms and fists, rising and pounding down.  Tendrils of red blood crept through the clear, blue water.  The motion paused, then, as one, the ghost tribe looked up.  They let out a horrifying howl, and surged towards the slope.

The ground shuddered violently beneath her.  She flung herself down and grabbed onto a vine with all her strength to keep from being thrown down the hill and into the hands of the angry tribe.  The very earth was disintegrating.  Braydon's hand pressed on her back.  "Hurry," he said.  "The temple's collapsing."

The slope to their left exploded into an avalanche of dirt and stone.  A huge tree heeled, groaned and toppled with a thunderous crash.  She glanced down.  The ghost tribe scrambled closer, dodging granite blocks that crashed downwards.  On the eastern horizon, the crest of the volcano appeared above the tree line.  Its black smoke plume was alive with lightning.  It roared, a primitive beast clamoring to destroy the world.

Another sound filtered through the percussive bursts of destruction, an unnatural rhythm, a thumping.  The Blackhawk!  It rose above the Demon's Wings from the west side of the pass. Donohue was perched at the open door, signaling to them, beckoning them, shouting something she couldn't hear over the din.

She and Braydon fought their way up the hill, the wash from the rotors gusting down on them. The detritus swirled around her stinging her eyes. Soil gave way to the curved sheer granite of the rock outcropping. She clung on desperately as the earth jolted beneath her. Her palms scraped against the rough rock. The chopper's skid touched down. She lunged for it. The ground lurched violently. Braydon's arms embraced her from behind. Donohue's hands grasped her wrists, his grip firm, crushing. She planted her feet on the rock and pushed as Donohue hoisted her into the chopper bay. Her knees slammed with a clang onto the hard steel. She quickly twisted around, grabbed Braydon's hand. Donohue grabbed the other. They yanked together. Braydon dove into the chopper.

"Go!" Donohue yelled. The chopper bolted up. Blowdarts and arrows pinged off its metal skin.

As the chopper banked, she clung onto a handhold. Below was total destruction. The entire temple was collapsing beneath the hillside that had buried and hid it centuries ago. Men, dirt, rocks and trees tumbled into the shallow pool, burying it in a mountain of rubble, Contreras and the Breastplate obliterated beneath it.

"The Breastplate," Donohue yelled above the roar of the chopper. "Where is it?"

"Gone," she yelled back, pointing to the rocks still piling onto Contreras's tomb. "Buried." She held up the canvas sack. "I've got the antidote plant."

Donohue nodded, but, even as the chopper rose higher, his eyes stayed focused on the hell below.

# DAY 6

## CHAPTER 69

"Baltasar Contreras is dead," Christa said, more a question than a statement of fact. Braydon swerved around another smoldering taxi as he sped the Humvee down a vacant, deserted Fifth Avenue. She repeated that in her head. They were driving a Humvee down Fifth Avenue. "This is real. Isn't it?"

"He is dead," Braydon confirmed. "This is real." He eyed the bare-chested maniac in torn jeans howling at the twilight. "The National Guard is policing the curfew, distributing the antidote. They'll track down the last stragglers."

She had never liked the unnaturalness of the city, the scraggly trees sprouting from squares of earth cut out of the pavement, the sky only seen as a backdrop to synthetic canyons of steel, glass, and stone. For her, the people that coursed through the city's automaton body like blood through its veins gave it life and meaning. Without them, the city was a dead hulk, not a testament to what man could build, but to what he could destroy.

She lowered the window, despite the raw chill, but heard only sirens, an occasional wailing, and the wind whining though the streets, whipping the detritus of the riots with the acrid stench of burning tires. "How many dead?"

"Too many."

"But Daniel is alive," she said. "That text Daniel sent me, telling me to meet him here. It's not some Machiavellian move from the grave by Contreras."

"You said it, not me," he said. "But Contreras didn't plan for this one, not this time. I would have liked some back-up, and a fully loaded P-90, but at least we got use of the Humvee."

"You don't need an automatic weapon." She had earned a degree in weapons talk in the past few days. "We're meeting Daniel."

"That is a non sequitur."

Braydon was as stubborn as he was spent. She could tell by the glaze in his eyes that he was barely lucid through the constant pain of his wounds. They had both collapsed with sheer exhaustion on the military jet back to New York from Colombia, but it was like a drop of water to a man dying of thirst. It only gave them enough to survive through the next ordeal, maybe. She wasn't thinking straight, and he wasn't either. Except he was armed with a pistol. "When we get to Saint Patrick's, I should go in alone," she said. "If he is affected by the poison, you might spook him."

One steady look from Braydon told her it wasn't even worth pursuing that argument. "You mean I might shoot him," he said. "I told you I won't unless he gives me no choice. You are not going in alone. End of argument."

The Humvee blasted aside a big screen television that looters had abandoned in the street. She braced her hand against the dashboard as Braydon ran the Humvee up over the curb onto the wide sidewalk in front of the cathedral and threw it into park. Across Fifth, the statue of Atlas relentlessly shouldered the burden of the armillary sphere. Graffiti had been spraypainted on his magnificent marble base. It read, "REPENT OR DIE!"

Braydon slipped his handgun from its holster, checked the bullets in the clip, and chambered one. He nodded his chin towards the graffiti. "We're not going to," he said.

"Repent?" she asked. "Or die?"

"Neither," he said. "Not here, not now, and not at the hands of Daniel Dubler." He thrust open the door and leaped down.

She followed, rushing to catch him as he bound up the steps to Saint Patrick's massive bronze doors. "Daniel didn't betray us," she said. "If he went to Contreras, he risked his life to help us. Now we have to help him." She grabbed his shoulder. "Daniel won't hurt me," she pressed. She didn't want to say these next words, for a lot of reasons. "He loves me."

Braydon hesitated. He, too, had trouble forcing the words. "Another non sequitur," he said finally. He heaved open the door and entered the cathedral, gun first.

She heard a distant voice lofting through the stone cathedral walls as they crept from the vestibule into the massive nave. "Latin," she whispered to Braydon. They crouched behind the bank of red votive lights, all of them lit, all still flickering, prayers being sent to God on wisps of smoke and hope. The overwhelming love and joy she had felt in the temple chamber in the presence of the restored Breastplate felt much further than half a world away.

They approached the Lady Chapel. Daniel had texted her to meet him there. At first, she was thrilled that he was alive. Now it scared her. In a crouching run, Braydon made his way quickly down the length of the nave, stopping at the Pieta, the last bend before the Lady Chapel at the far end of the cathedral.

She could only make out the language, the intonations, not all the words, but enough. "It's Daniel. I think he's saying a mass," she said, crouching next to Braydon, "a requiem." She squeezed her eyes shut. "A mass for the dead."

"Come!" the voice called out in English, shouting from the altar of the Lady Chapel, the word echoing down the rows of empty pews.

"Don't do it, Braydon!" A second male voice. "Get out of here!" Followed by a scream of agony.

Braydon hunched his shoulders. His face turned ashen. "Damn it. That's O'Malley. Dubler's got him."

One look at Braydon's eyes was all it took. He wouldn't hesitate to kill Daniel. She pushed away from him. He grabbed for her, called her name in an urgent whisper. She sprinted the distance to the Lady Chapel. She stopped at the far end of the pews. Father O'Malley lay unconscious on the floor in front of the altar, his cassock torn from one shoulder. His bloody handprint streaked across the mosaic on the front of the altar, smearing the angel announcing to Mary that she would bear the son of God.

She didn't know what that creature was standing behind the altar of the Lady Chapel, but it was not Daniel Dubler. He was wearing Daniel's jeans and tweed sport coat, but he was covered in dark, loamy soil and smelled of decaying leaves. She had to take the chance that his inner core, his soul, could still be in there, buried, not yet dead. "I'm glad you're alive, Daniel," she tried lamely. O'Malley groaned, tried to lift himself, and collapsed. She rushed to the fallen priest. She crouched by his side.

A sudden force yanked her back and upwards. The press of an arm against her neck choked out a scream. She elbowed the fleshy part of Daniel's gut and kicked the unyielding marble of the altar. Daniel was preternaturally strong, with poison, with madness. "Daniel, stop!" she yelled. Daniel swatted her, hard, on the side of her head. She felt her arms being pulled upwards, then cold steel around her wrists, and an ominous clicking sound.

Daniel's dirt and sweat-streaked face closed in on hers. "You won't leave me again," he said.

Her arms were cruelly stretched, wrists handcuffed to a chain. The chain was coiled like a snake around the feet of the ivory Mary statue. "Daniel, what have they done to you?"

"God willed it," he said, his voice powerful. His eyes focused on hers, softened a moment. "Contreras's men were burying me alive. I called out to Our Lord. They laughed. Like demons they laughed as the storm raged through the forest around us."

"I got the antidote, Daniel," she said. "I've got a vial here, for you, in my pocket." She pointed with her chin.

"God smote them, Christa. Even as they flung the earth on me, God flung a lightning bolt from heaven. It castrated the oak that was to be my tombstone, crashing it to the ground. One of the men was crushed. The other fled. God saved me, Christa. For this." He spread his hands outward, looking down upon the altar. A laptop computer, not a silver chalice, sat on it. He opened it. The screen glowed blue on his face as it hummed to life.

He was too far gone. She had to try another tack. Braydon, in her peripheral vision, was flanking the altar. "God saved you," she said, "and me. We need to work together on this, Daniel." Whatever this was. "Let me go. I won't leave you."

He bent down to the right to reach something from the shelf below the top of the altar. He pulled it out, pointed it at her forehead. It was a frigging P-90, that automatic machine gun that Braydon had tried to coerce from that National Guardsman with the Humvee. Daniel smiled wryly. "It belonged to that killer crushed by the oak," he said. "Fox!" he yelled now. "I know you're out there. Show yourself. Hands up. Or Christa will help me save mankind from Heaven." He kept the gun pointed at her, but turned bodily towards the altar. With his right hand, he typed frantically on the keyboard.

God help her. Those words took on new meaning. The barrel of the machine gun loomed in her vision. She could see the damn bullet, poised to kill. "Daniel, Baltasar Contreras is dead," she said. "It's over."

"Contreras is dead," he said, "but the Prophet lives, in me. You think I'm insane, but I've never seen anything more clearly. Contreras set up a worldwide network of followers, but they've never seen him. They are waiting, praying for the Prophet to speak to them. I will be that voice. You and me, Christa. We can bring world peace. We can use our power to create the ultimate empire, one that saves the people, one that will not fall."

"The Breastplate of Aaron is destroyed, buried." She tugged at the chain, tried to move away from the gun. He was focused on the computer screen, not her.

"You must believe, Christa." He tapped awkwardly, covering the whole keyboard with one hand. "This computer is my Breastplate. After God saved me, he led me to it, bade me to take it from Contreras's library. God showed me the password. In one keystroke, my followers will release their poison in the water supplies of the major cities of the world. All will know God's power, manifested through me. I only need to press Send to cross the threshold into the genesis of a new world."

"Give it up, Dubler," Braydon said. He had circled back to the nave end of the Lady Chapel. Just as she first saw him in the Arizona desert, he emerged from the shadows, the dim light glinting on his gun. Rather than a cottonwood tree, he braced himself against a marble column, across a river of pews. He stood pistol first, right arm straight out in front of him, his forearm steadied with his left hand. He was positioning himself to get Daniel to shift his target from her, to him. "Donohue's spooks hacked into Contreras's network," he said. "They've already launched a covert operation to neutralize his followers."

"You're lying," Daniel yelled. He swung the machine gun toward Braydon. With a bloody scream, he pulled the trigger. Bullets spat out of the barrel in a fury of noise and smoke.

Christa kicked at Daniel's legs as the deafening bangs exploded around her. Spent shells rained down, hot and hard. Braydon didn't stand a chance. And he could have been bluffing. Donohue might not have succeeded in hacking into the Prophet's network. If Daniel pressed Send, thousands more would die. They'd never be able to create and distribute the antidote in time to save them all. She yanked at the chains. The Mary statue shifted. She yanked again, bullet casings gouging Mary's marble feet with metallic clangs. Her wrists hurt like hell. Warm trickles of blood seeped down her forearms. She twisted her hands to wrap the chain around them and gripped the links in her fists. In one mighty pull, she heaved with every bit of strength from within, and without.

As if in slow motion, Mary toppled forward, her expression placid, accepting. Daniel turned, raising his arm to shield himself. She ducked towards the side. The statue fell upon Daniel, smashing onto his forearm and temple. He dropped the machine gun at her feet. Now free from the statue, she snatched up the gun, pointed it at him. He staggered, one hand to his head, blood flowing down his cheek. He poised the other hand above the keyboard, his finger above the Send key. Christa pulled the trigger.

# DAY 7

## CHAPTER 70

Christa awoke to the muted, staccato voice of Braydon's boss in the FBI, a petite Korean woman who made up in spunk what she lacked in physical stature. The woman's heels clicked down the length of the nave, fading into the dark. Christa raised her head from the wooden pew. O'Malley had given her a velveteen kneeler as a pillow, and did a bang-up job bandaging her wrists. The both of them had refused to call the paramedics. Plenty of people were hurt worse than they were.

Her back stiffened as she pushed upwards. She had aged years in these past few days. Braydon sat next to O'Malley on the steps leading up to the main altar. The Bureau had spirited away Daniel's body in the night. A crime scene investigation was deemed unfeasible and unnecessary in this state of emergency. Like her own guilt and self-psychoanalysis of her part in Daniel's death.

She pushed up her aching body, walked stiffly towards Braydon and sat next to him. "Gabriella called me," she said, "before I conked out on the pew last night. They took Liam home. He's going to be okay. Percival, too."

Braydon nodded. The first light of dawn filtered into the nave through the stained glass windows. "They've lifted the curfew in the city. Got a lot of mopping up to do."

The door from the Fifth Avenue side of the nave opened. The three of them stiffened. Hesitantly, they stood to see beyond the rows of pews. Braydon's hand went to the butt of his gun. An old lady tottered in, feathered hat, hunched shoulders, leading a flock dressed like her, in dark, wool coats, warm hats, and the occasional cane.

O'Malley placed his hand on Braydon's arm. "It's Mrs. Pennington," he said. "She comes to morning mass every day."

"Sunrise is a tad early for mass," he said, "even for old ladies."

"Braydon," O'Malley adjusted his cassock to hide the rip and smoothed back his mop of red hair, "it's Christmas."

The three of them watched as the old birds tottered down the center aisle to their perches in the front pews. Then something more remarkable. Others followed them into the nave. A group of teens decked out in black leather. Three women, in platform heels and hot pants, who were decidedly not nuns. Parents with young children, their eyes full of wonder and latent fear.

A ringtone chirped Beethoven's Ode to Joy. O'Malley fished his phone from his pocket. "It's my rabbi friend, Ezekial Feinstein," he said.

Christa and Braydon watched as the people poured in, silent, shell-shocked, filling the pews, helping those who needed help, the injured, the infirm.

"Ezekial says he has opened his temple doors. The crowds are jamming in, people he has never seen before," said O'Malley. "He says it's happening all over the city."

O'Malley started down the center aisle, greeting the people, welcoming them, quietly, with understanding, not celebration.

"I wish Dad was here to see this," she said. She could tell him that the Breastplate had connected her with Mom. That she knew Mom was loved, happy, and in a place where to forgive was a given. If you believed in that sort of thing. But that was a prayer that wouldn't be answered. She had called, texted, emailed, and received no reply. Helen had told her to accept his death.

"Makes you want to believe," Braydon said, "one last time."

"O'Malley is with his family," she said. "All I want is to be with mine." She clasped his hand in hers. "Come with me."

He smiled. "I believe I will."

They walked down the side aisle towards the exit.  A man ambled toward them, relying heavily on a cane.  He was dressed in worn, baggy pants, a scruffy leather jacket, and a wide-brimmed fedora, a man who'd been through hell.  The man raised his face to hers.  It was Dad.

CHAPTER 71

"Merry Christmas," Donohue said, raising his stainless steel cup filled with aguardiente, the local sugarcane alcohol.

The strike force, except for the two perimeter guards, welcomed the break, sweating and puffing as they rested their old bones on the jumble of boulders. "Merry Christmas," they toasted.

One swig downed the drink, and they were back at it. Picks and shovels, they didn't dare use dynamite and risk destroying the Breastplate of Aaron.

"Got another one," Leader called out. He stepped back and grimaced at the stench. He had seen his share of corpses as a Navy Seal, but it was worse here, in the heat and humidity. He made a sign of the cross and dragged the crushed body of the savage to the others awaiting burial.

The volcano rumbled and spewed out more of its sulfuric stink. They were running out of time. The Joint Chiefs had been alerted to the situation. Donohue's orders were clear. He had completed the first part of his mission. He had collected every last leaf the antidote plant they could find. He was to return to Washington immediately with the plants, before the spreading ash of the volcano completely closed the airspace and any hope of air travel out of the region. The Joint Chiefs were taking a page from the Prophet's playbook. Soon, they hoped to wield the power of a bio-weapon for which they had the only defense. They placed their faith in the hands of scientists working to synthesize an antidote that God had hidden away in this unique microcosm since the birth of creation. Arrogant fools.

As far as the Breastplate of Aaron, the Joint Chiefs were determined to keep it the best guarded secret in history. They were marshaling an elite team from a nearby base to extract it, no doubt to squirrel it away in some ultra-secret research facility. They believed in its power, not to open a portal to Heaven, but to explode into an international incident.

Like Salvatierra defying the Vatican, Donohue had to defy the order of his commander. He had to achieve his own mission to right a wrong, even if it risked his life, even if it risked his immortal soul.

He fingered the dog tags hanging around his neck, Clive's dog tags, not his. *You have to find the Breastplate,* Eleanor had begged before he left for Colombia, *for Clive. The Breastplate will prove that life exists beyond death. If I know that our son can live beyond his death, then I can live again beyond his death. He needs to know our love for him has no end.*

Soon, they would unearth the Breastplate of Aaron. This wasn't the end of his mission, but the beginning.

## ABOUT THE AUTHOR

Pamela Hegarty has adventured in more than thirty-five countries on six continents. She has summited Mount Kilimanjaro, backpacked the Inca Trail to Machu Picchu and camped with lions in the Serengeti. She is the author of *San Francisco & Beyond: 101 Affordable Excursions*, *Best Places to Kiss in New England* and *Best Places to Kiss in Northern California (Second Edition)* and a contributor to seven *Fodor's* guidebooks. She has published more than three hundred articles in *Woman's Day*, *Good Housekeeping*, *McCall's*, *Diversion*, *Country Inns*, *San Francisco Focus*, *The Peak* (Hong Kong), *Explore* (Canada) and other magazines and newspapers. She welcomes readers to contact her through her website at pamelahegarty.com or at skycastlepublishing@verizon.net. Follow her on twitter at @pamelahegarty.

Made in the USA
Lexington, KY
05 August 2012